FAKE CHESS:
A Superhero Comedy Adventure
Book 3 of Fake Superhero
Lucas Flint

An Annulus Publishing Book

Annulus Publishing, Oklahoma City, Oklahoma,

2023

Published by Secret Identity Books. An imprint of Annulus Publishing.
Copyright © Lucas Flint 2023. All rights reserved.
Contact: luke@lucasflint.com
Cover design by Miblart (http://www.miblart.com)
No part of this publication may be reproduced, distributed, or transmitted in any form or by any means, including photocopying, recording, or other electronic or mechanical methods, without the prior written permission of the publisher, except in the case of brief quotations embodied in critical reviews and certain other noncommercial uses permitted by copyright law. For permission requests, send an email to the above contact.

CHAPTER ONE

Dreaming about chess is a sign of two possible issues in a person:

1) They play way too much chess and should probably devote at least a portion of their time to something less obsession-inducing, such as croquet or marbles, or;

2) You're suffering from some kind of post-traumatic stress disorder from having to play a game of chess against a guy LARPing as a chess piece, with your friends' lives at stake

As a doctor—although not a 'real' one because I'd never actually gone to med school—it was tough to diagnose myself sometimes, especially when I was asleep. But the second diagnosis did seem a bit more believable to me right now, mostly because I had a recurring nightmare of that exact scenario.

I found myself standing in the middle of a massive chessboard, black and white squares laid out in alternating color patterns. Behind me, the White pieces stood together like an army waiting to battle, but the pieces were ridiculously huge. The pawns alone towered over me, their marble-like surface shining under a light that seemed to come from nowhere and everywhere. The main pieces towered even over them, making me feel very, very small, and very, very powerless.

On the opposite side of the board, the Black pieces were lined up similarly and were just as tall as their White counterparts.

They somehow looked even more intimidating than the White pieces behind me, their dark surfaces reflecting the bright light overhead rather sinisterly.

And for some reason it was *really* cold, cold enough that I could see my breath. Chills ran up and down my spine, while the dusty smell of freezing stone entered my nostrils. Even my tightly-fitted cloth gloves did little to fight off the cold or keep me warm, and I might as well have been naked for all the good my stupid superhero costume did. It didn't help that I was missing my Mind-Bender Crown, either, leaving me feeling very vulnerable.

I looked around the chessboard in confusion, whipping my head this way and that as I tried to make sense of my environment. "Hello? Is anybody there? Hello?"

The utter silence was deafening. It was as if I was stuck in the cold void of space, shouting into utter emptiness that had no beginning or end. Maybe that's overly dramatic, but dreams are pretty dramatic in my experience.

That was when the familiar young, male voice of my nephew, Joaquin 'Goggles' Manuel, said, "Uncle ... help ..."

I whirled around on the spot, desperately searching for my nephew, only to stop when I spotted him. Or what I *thought* was him, because what I saw couldn't possibly have been Goggles, even if it did have his young, bronze-skinned face.

The White pawn directly in front of me had Goggles' face on it. His eyes were even covered by his trademark goggles. But from the neck down, he was a literal pawn. An expression of absolute fear and pain was written across his young face, making him look as if he was suffering.

"Joaquin?" I said with a soft gasp. "What happened to—"

"Brother," came a deeper male voice to Goggles' left. "Brother, please help ..."

I looked to Goggles' left and felt my heart crack at the sight of my older brother, Bryan 'Brave Storm' Manuel, who looked like an older version of his son except with shorter hair and more lines

FAKE CHESS

in his skin. His face, like Goggles', was seemingly attached to the face of another White pawn that was on the board. And like Goggles, he wore an expression of pure pain and agony on his face, as if the very state of his being was nothing but pure torture.

In fact, when I looked up and down the line of White pawns, I saw that all of my teammates' faces were represented. Lumberjack, Cavewoman, Shining Armor, Paranoyd, Holiday Man ... the faces of every person on the team were represented. Even Penny Parker, the reporter on my payroll, had her face set upon one of the pawns.

"What the hell?" I said, stepping backward. "What happened to everyone? Why is everyone cosplaying as pawns?"

"You did this, Doctor," said Lumberjack, his Canadian-accented voice thick with pain. "Because you failed us ... because you failed *everyone* ... we are all going to die ..."

"Doctor Mind's fault," Cavewoman chimed in an equally lifeless but still painful voice. "Doctor Mind's fault. His fault."

"Doctor Mind's fault," everyone suddenly started chanting in unison. "We are all dead because of Doctor Mind. It is Doctor Mind's fault. Doctor Mind's fault. Doctor Mind's fault."

As the chanting continued, I put my hands on my head and said, "Please! I didn't mean to fail you guys. It was an accident. Please forgive me. I don't even know what you're talking about."

But it was no use. None of my words seemed to get through to my friends, who continued to chant *Doctor Mind's fault* like it was some kind of terrible ad slogan for a new line of shoes or something.

Then a new, yet familiar Eastern European voice behind me said, "You hear the voices of your friends, Doctor. They all blame *you* for their predicament."

I whirled around again but didn't see the source of the voice at first. That is, until I looked up and found myself staring directly into the 'face' of a gigantic White pawn.

No. It wasn't actually a pawn. It was a giant human being *dressed* as a pawn, the E2 pawn specifically, which was reflected by the massive 'E2' painted on his face in red paint. His actual face was completely obscured by his mask, but that did not stop me from sensing the malicious cruelty hidden behind it.

"E2?" I said, my voice sounding a lot more echo-y in here for some reason. "What are you doing here? This is my dream, not yours."

E2 chuckled. "Your dream? Or your nightmare?"

The droning chants of my friends behind me suddenly picked up in volume and pace. I now felt like I was being bombarded on all sides by the loudest rock music played from the biggest speakers:

"Doctor Mind's fault ... Doctor Mind's fault ... Doctor Mind's fault ... your fault, Doctor ... you failed us, Uncle ... brother, you didn't save us ..."

Grunting, I tried to ignore the chants, but I couldn't. Even slamming my hands over my ears did nothing to protect my hearing. Actually, when I covered my ears, it was like I could hear them in my *mind*, which was far creepier and weirder than hearing them with my ears. Their words bounced around inside my head, making me feel like my skull was about to burst from the sound.

"I'm sorry," I said, my voice barely audible above the mindless chants. "I'm sorry. I don't know what I did wrong, but I'm sorry."

E2's maniacal laughter could be heard overhead suddenly. " 'Sorry' isn't good enough, Doctor. If it was, your friends would not currently be blaming you for all their woes."

I looked up at E2 again. He somehow seemed even bigger than before, the Black pieces before him looking more proportionally correct. He raised one massive hand and picked up the King's Pawn on his side of the board.

FAKE CHESS

"But I am a merciful opponent," said E2. "Unlike certain individuals I know, I do not believe in prolonging the suffering of my opponents. I do not enjoy cruelty or torture ... much."

Another wave of "Doctor Mind's fault" knocked me to my knees on the solid stone chessboard, but I managed to keep my gaze fixed on E2 above. "Please ... make it all end. It's too much ... too much ... too—"

"If you wish," said E2. "Checkmate, Doctor."

With that, E2 brought his Black pawn down on me.

I didn't even try to move. I was so overwhelmed with sadness and guilt that all I could do was watch as the bottom of the pawn came down on my head.

But the very instant the oversized chess piece crashed down on top of me, I felt two small, but strong hands shake me awake and then heard Goggles' familiar excited voice to my side shout, "Uncle, wake up! You gotta see this."

Waking up with a start, I looked around wildly. For a moment, I wondered where the giant E2 was or what happened to the oversized chessboard that I'd been unfortunate enough to find myself on.

I was sitting in the seat of a rather cramped airplane, the air dry and stale. The leather seat I sat upon was kind of lumpy and rough, though infinitely more comfortable and better on my knees than the stone chessboard had been. The hum of the airplane's engines could be faintly heard, while the warm temperature of the plane's interior was a sharp contrast to the utter cold of the void in my dream. The scent of coffee and crackers filled the air, which came from the table in front of me, which had a barely-touched coffee cup in front of it along with some crackers that looked just as untouched.

Rubbing the sleep out of my eyes, I said, "Uh, what? What's going on? What happened?"

"You fell asleep, Uncle," said Goggles, his voice slightly concerned. "During the flight."

LUCAS FLINT

I looked to my left. Goggles, my sidekick, sat in the seat to my left. He wasn't wearing his sidekick costume this time, however. Instead, he wore a black hoodie over a red t-shirt and jeans, his dark, messy hair looking even messier than usual. His green eyes looked up at me with a mixture of worry and concern. "Are you okay, Uncle?"

"Uncle Roger is probably fine," said my brother's voice to my right. "He's just tired after a twelve-hour flight."

Again startled, I looked to my right. Brave Storm, my brother and fellow Fakers teammate, sat in the seat beside me, his tablet set up in front of him, having paused a movie he was watching. He looked just like he did in the dream, if in significantly less pain and misery. He wore a tan button-down shirt and blue slacks, which made him look rather different from his son.

Rubbing my face, I said, "Has it really been twelve hours? No wonder I'm exhausted. I've never flown that long before."

"Me neither," said Goggles. He jerked a thumb over his shoulder. "Maybe that's why everyone *else* is asleep."

I looked to my right across the aisle. My other teammates were all also asleep. Shining Armor leaned against the window on the opposite side, snoring softly, while Paranoyd and Holiday Man slumped in their seats, with Holiday Man resting his head on a soft stuffed Easter bunny that he'd taken with him. Cavewoman and Lumberjack sat in the row directly behind those three, with Cavewoman snoring like a backfiring truck and Lumberjack muttering in his sleep about destroying all trees.

And they all looked as safe and secure as they usually did. None of their faces were surgically attached to oversized chess pieces.

And I definitely did not see any giant E2s trying to crush me with Black pawns.

Although I'd known that it had been a dream, seeing my friends safe and sound took a huge weight off my shoulders. Looking at everyone else also reminded me of why we were on

FAKE CHESS

this plane in the first place.

Last month, I'd gotten invited to the first-ever International Superhero Chess Tournament in Cheskia, a teeny tiny Eastern European country between Russia and the Ukraine. Cheskia was not known for much beyond producing more chess Grandmasters in the last century than the next ten countries on the list combined. My invitation had come from the Chess King himself, while the Cheskian government was paying for all the expenses associated with the trip. That included the plane tickets for my team, food, hotel ... literally everything.

Being a proud money-grubbing miser, you can see why an all-expenses-paid trip to a foreign country appealed to me. Foreign travel was expensive, especially if you wanted to bring seven other people with you.

Maybe it would have been smarter to leave some of my teammates behind in Freedom City, Oklahoma to keep the peace while I was away, but I didn't like letting my teammates out of my sight for even a second. I was worried that one of them might accidentally burn the whole city down while I was away or something worse. Besides, supervillain activity in the city had dropped through the floor recently, so I figured the FCPD could handle the normal criminal scum that they usually dealt with.

Of course, there was no direct flight from Freedom City, Oklahoma, to Chess City, Cheskia, so our flight had taken us through several layovers and flight changes, especially once we got to Europe. That had been stressful enough, especially when we stopped in Germany and Lumberjack nearly incited an all-out brawl with a bunch of environmentalist activists protesting some kind of new factory getting built. Although Germany might not be fascist anymore, I found that their government and police were still pretty good about threatening to crush you if you didn't pay fines.

In any case, Germany had been our last stop in Europe before we boarded a plane to Cheskia. Supposedly, the last leg of the trip was just two hours, but I must have fallen asleep at some point without realizing it and therefore did not know what time it was.

"How long have I been out?" I said, rubbing my eyes again.

"An hour and a half," said Goggles. He pointed out the window again. "But there's something I really want you to see. It's cool and weird."

Sitting back in my seat, I said, "Thanks, Goggles, but I've looked out many plane windows in my time. The sight is impressive the first few times, but then it gets kind of stale."

"But Uncle, I doubt you've ever seen *this* thing before," said Goggles. He pointed out the window again. "I can't really describe it. You should look for yourself."

Feeling a bit annoyed at Goggles' insistence, I nonetheless leaned across his lap to look out his window, sure that I would see nothing other than the steep, craggy steppes that I wouldn't be able to make out any details from thousands of feet up in the air.

That was why I was shocked when I saw what could only be described as the world's largest chessboard stretched out on the ground below us for miles and miles in every direction for as far as the eye could see.

CHAPTER TWO

THE CHESSBOARD below made the oversized chessboard in my dream look positively tiny. Vast tracts of perfect black and white squares covered the countryside everywhere. Yet I could still see trees, bushes, roads, and buildings and cars below, though they just barely stood out against the blackness and whiteness of their environment. It almost looked like someone had covered half the country in snow and the other half in soot before carefully cutting it into neat squares and rearranging it to resemble the world's biggest chessboard.

"What ... am ... I looking at?" I said.

"The great country of Cheskia, of course," said a smooth feminine Eastern-European-accented voice behind me.

Startled, I looked over my shoulder to see a pretty young woman standing in the aisles between our seats. She was probably in her early twenties, with short, curly blonde hair done in a very professional style. Based on the blue-and-white Arid Airlines uniform she wore, I could tell that the woman—whose name tag read 'OLGA'—was one of our flight attendants. She was smiling in a friendly way, but there was a hint of distance underneath the expression, as if she was trying not to be *too* friendly toward us. A whiff of vanilla perfume wafted off her form.

"*That* is Cheskia?" said Goggles, pointing out his window at the chessboard below.

Olga nodded, her hands clasped in front of her skirt. "Yes."

"But it looks like a giant chessboard," I said. "Scratch that. It looks like *God's* chessboard."

Olga giggled. "Funny. That is actually one of the country's old names. God's Chessboard. Very fitting, too, because when Cheskia was first founded, it was designed to resemble a chessboard by the very first Chess King."

Brave Storm stared at Olga in disbelief. "Are you telling me, miss, that your government *deliberately* designed the entire country to look like a huge chessboard?"

"Indeed," said Olga, looking at Brave Storm as if he was a bit daft. "Isn't it beautiful?"

"Most countries are not designed to look like giant chessboards, ma'am," said Brave Storm. "Or like any particular shape."

Olga furrowed her brows. "Huh. How strange. You foreigners certainly come from odd countries."

That seemed a bit rich coming from a Cheskian, but then Goggles said, "But how did they color everything white and black? Did they just dump a lot of paint on everything or what?"

Olga giggled again. "You are a funny American! No, that's not paint. Due to the unusual environmental pressures that have been put on Cheskia, the plants in this country are all either white or black. The dirt also is white or black, depending on where you go, and each region in the country is named after a different square on the chessboard. For example, we are en route to E1, which is the location of Chess City, the capital of the country."

My head hurt as I tried to wrap my mind around her explanation. "So the *shape* of the country is deliberate, but the *colors* are natural."

"Quite so," Olga said cheerfully. "Admittedly, the government does put a lot of resources into making sure that

FAKE CHESS

black plants only grow on Black squares and vice versa, but that's merely a matter of science, not nature."

"You sure do know a lot about Cheskia for being a flight attendant," Brave Storm observed. "If you asked me why America looks the way it does, I wouldn't even be able to tell you that."

Olga drew herself up proudly and, brushing a stray strand of hair out of her face, said, "Cheskia's education system is the envy of the whole world. It is also the only country in the world to make chess education mandatory, which is part of the reason why Cheskia has produced so many Grandmasters."

"I knew that, at least," I said with a nod. I jerked a thumb over my shoulder at the country below. "It was the literal shape of the country that I knew nothing about."

"You didn't?" said Goggles, giving me a puzzled look. "But Uncle, I thought you were a chess player who knew everything about Cheskia."

I raised my hands defensively. "I didn't say I knew *everything* about Cheskia. I just happen to be a fan of several Grandmasters from there. Learned a bit about the country by listening to their interviews, although none of them ever mentioned the country's literal shape."

Interest appeared in Olga's eyes and she leaned forward, practically across Brave Storm's lap, to look at me closer. "Wait, you play chess, sir? Are you a Grandmaster yourself?"

Leaning away from the woman's slightly manic gaze, I said, "Er, no. I'm not even an International Master, honestly. I'm decent, but not the best."

"Oh," said Olga, disappointment leaking into her eyes. "Are you coming to Cheskia to participate in a tournament or something?"

I nodded. "Yeah. I was invited to the International Superhero Chess Tournament by the Chess King himself."

11

The light in Olga's eyes changed again, this time to something that looked ... suspicious?

No. Not suspicion.

Realization.

Olga pulled away suddenly and brushed her hair back. "Ah, so you must be the famous Doctor Mind who I've heard so much about."

I looked at Olga in surprise. "You've heard of me?"

"Of course." Olga's smile seemed cooler for some reason. "There aren't very many chess-playing superheroes in the world, so you have always stood out to the people of Cheskia. At least, to those of us who are interested in that kind of thing. The video of your defeat of the infamous Death Skull did go viral in Cheskia, though, at least among those of us who care."

I raised an eyebrow. "That's an odd way of putting it."

Olga shook her head and smiled at me again. "Never mind. I am simply excited to get to meet a real-life superhero for the first time, especially an American superhero like you."

It was my turn to get suspicious of Olga, but her statement prompted another question from me. "You've never met a superhero before?"

Olga shook her head. "No, never. We have only one superhero, which is more than enough for our country. We are mostly protected by the Four Arms of Cheskia instead."

"The Four Arms of Cheskia?" Goggles repeated. "What are those?"

"The Chess King, the Chess Queen, the Bishops, and the Knights," Olga recited immediately, like an old nursery rhyme she'd memorized a long time ago. "Along with the might of the Cheskian military, the Four Arms have traditionally protected Cheskia since its founding. They're a bit like superheroes themselves, although their methods tend to be a little different from how you American superheroes operate."

FAKE CHESS

I rested my chin in my hand. "The Four Arms ... sounds like a superhero team name to me, although I'm still partial to 'Fakers,' of course."

"And you even brought your team with you?" said Olga, looking around at the seats nearest mine. She clapped her hands together excitedly. "I had heard rumors that the Chess King had invited you to the tournament, but didn't realize that included the entire team as well. How exciting."

"Only I'm participating, I'm afraid," I said. I gestured at my sleeping teammates. "They're just along for the ride."

"I see," said Olga. "Well, it will be interesting to watch you play against the superheroes from the other countries. It will certainly be a unique tournament, at any rate."

"Exactly how many other superheroes are going to be in this tournament, if you don't mind me asking?" I said. "I tried to look up the numbers online, but couldn't find anything definitive. Lots of speculation, though."

Olga clasped her hands together apologetically. "I am sorry, but I do not know any more than you do about the tournament. I am a simple pawn in the grand scheme of things, so I am never told important things like that."

Goggles frowned. "No need to be so tough on yourself, lady. You're a real person, too. You're nobody's pawn."

Olga giggled again. "Thank you for the kind words, but 'pawns' is simply what we call the citizens of Cheskia. We are all pawns of the Chess King and his Queen. That is all."

I rubbed my chin. "Pawn with a capital 'P' or a lowercase?"

Olga looked at me in confusion. "Lowercase, typically. Why do you ask?"

I shrugged. "No reason, other than I met a guy who called himself a 'Pawn' back in America. Went by E2. Ever heard of him?"

Olga's expression changed so quickly that I would have dismissed it as my imagination going crazy if I didn't see it with

13

my own eyes. For a very brief moment, she looked as if I'd accused her of being a terrorist plotting to kill hundreds of people.

But then her kind, polite, and perhaps *too* professional smile returned. "I am sorry, but I have never heard of anyone who has named themselves after a position on the chessboard. Sounds like you superheroes run into some very strange people."

I frowned slightly, but said, "We do. Lots of weird people in the world, including ourselves."

Olga once more giggled. "Very true. Well, unless you need anything else, I must get going. It was nice getting to chat with a famous American superhero. Hopefully we will get another chance to speak soon. Good luck with the tournament!"

With that, Olga walked down the aisle, stopping a few rows down to speak with another passenger, an elderly man wearing a top hat and monocle. I watched her for a moment, but Olga did not do anything suspicious, so I turned my attention to my lap in thought.

"That Olga lady was kind of cute," said Goggles. He sighed. "Wish she was a little younger, though."

"Definitely pretty," said Brave Storm. He elbowed me. "I saw the way you were looking at her, Roger. Bet if you'd asked her out she would have said yes."

Startled, I looked at Brave Storm in astonishment. "Asked her out? What are you talking about? I'm not interested in her *that* way."

"Then why were you looking at her so intently, Uncle?" said Goggles. His eyes became wide and strangely focused. "Like this. It was kind of creepy, actually."

I grimaced. "Er, it was ... nothing. I just was interested to learn more about Cheskia. It's definitely a weird place, isn't it?"

Brave Storm nodded. "Definitely, and we haven't even stepped foot there yet. Wonder what it will be like once we're actually on the ground."

I also nodded, but felt my attention starting to wander. My

FAKE CHESS

eyes drifted back to Olga, but she'd already retreated further down the aisle, near the cockpit, where she stood with a couple of her fellow flight attendants, chatting animatedly with them in a language that I assumed was Cheskian.

I will admit, I lied to my brother and nephew. Not about my feelings for Olga, but why I had paid her such special attention. It had less to do with her looks or personality and more to do with the fact that I suspected she knew more than she let on.

Maybe I was paranoid, but I didn't think so. It was suspicious enough that the Chess King would send one of his servants to play me in a life-or-death game of chess, only to invite me to a tournament not even a week later, and pay for all my travel expenses, too.

But it was even more suspicious how Olga apparently knew nothing about E2 or his involvement in getting me to come to Cheskia in the first place.

No, I strongly suspected that Olga knew something about E2 and the Chess King. Seemed odd that a simple flight attendant and 'pawn' would know anything about whatever was going on in the highest echelons of the Cheskian government, but I couldn't rule out anything at this point.

In any case, I sincerely doubted I would learn more about the Chess King's real motives for inviting me to Cheskia on this flight. Now that we were actually in Cheskian airspace, it wouldn't be much longer before we landed in Chess City.

And after my interaction with Olga, I was starting to look forward to our arrival even less.

CHAPTER THREE

OUR PLANE landed at the Cheskian International Airport about half an hour after my conversation with Olga. The pilot repeated the warning twice, once in English, the second time in Cheskian, which was when I realized that a large number of our fellow passengers were apparently Cheskians returning home from America. Most of them looked like normal people to me, though, aside from the distinctive blond hair and sharp features that appeared to be common to people from that country.

Stepping into the Cheskian International Airport terminal, however, was when it *really* struck me that we were no longer in America.

The airport floor had the same black-and-white design as the country, making the terminal look like a big (but smaller than the country itself) chessboard. Paintings of different chess pieces were hung along the walls in between screens that listed the times of departing and arriving flights. The airport itself smelled strongly of some kind of savory bread, I think, though I couldn't tell where the scent was coming from. It was also kind of cold, even though the airport seemed to have some sort of central heating. I caught a glimpse of snow outside, which seemed odd for April, but maybe Cheskian winters lasted longer than American ones.

Terminal A—which was our airport terminal—was also rather

FAKE CHESS

empty. Aside from us and the other passengers aboard our plane, there weren't very many people in the airport. It looked almost deserted, which made me think that they must not get a lot of travelers.

Lumberjack stood next to me, stretching his large, muscular arms and legs. "Ahh! Nice to be on solid ground again. I felt trapped like a rat in that teeny tiny little plane. Fresh air is always good on these old bones. Gives me more energy to fight the trees."

"We're not causing another international incident, Lumberjack," I said. My eyes scanned the terminal while other passengers filed out behind us. "No tree-chopping."

"For a whole *week*?" said Lumberjack in disbelief. He lifted up his huge duffel bag and shook it. "Then why did I bother bringing my favorite tree-chopping ax at all?"

"How did you get your ax past—" I shook my head. "Never mind. We're here to play chess. Not chop down trees."

Lumberjack pouted. "All right. I suppose I can restrain myself, although if I happen to see a particularly big tree that looks like it really needs cutting—"

"Where are we supposed to go now, anyway?" asked Paranoyd, hefting the straps of his backpack over his shoulders. He looked at me questioningly. "Didn't you say that the Cheskian government is supposed to meet us here?"

"That's what the email I got from our travel agent said," I said. I pulled out my phone and, tapping my email app, opened it up and started scrolling. "Let's see … yeah. Says here that a 'representative from the Cheskian government' is supposed to meet us at Terminal A with a shuttle to take us to our hotel."

"I don't see any government representatives," said Holiday Man, whipping his head this way and that. "As a matter of fact, I don't see anyone else at all other than ourselves."

"Was this all some kind of big joke, then?" said Paranoyd with a gulp. "Did we just get pranked into traveling all the way to

17

Cheskia just to get stranded in a shitty little airport?"

"There's probably just been some kind of misunderstanding," said Shining Armor with a smile. "Doc, can you contact our representative and let him know we're here?"

I looked at my phone again and sighed in frustration. "No. Our agent didn't give us a name or even a description. Just said to wait by—"

A loud rumbling sound interrupted me, a sound I felt more in my bones than heard with my ears. The other Fakers also must have heard it, because they started looking around uneasily for a moment. Even the other passengers had stopped to look and listen, expressions of confusion spreading across their faces.

"Did anyone else feel that?" I said, slowly lowering my phone to my side.

"Cavewoman did," said Cavewoman, clutching her suitcases tightly. "Feel it in her feminine intuition."

"An earthquake?" said Brave Storm. "Cheskia *does* get earthquakes, right?"

"Earthquake season is over," said the same top hat and monocle-wearing passenger I'd noticed before. He spoke with a crisp British accent, leaning on his cane, scanning the room with the look of a seasoned soldier or police officer. "It must be something—"

An explosion suddenly ripped through a nearby terminal, followed by a series of shrieks and screams, which were punctuated by gunfire that struck the glass ceiling overhead and sent shards of glass falling down. The other passengers around us suddenly dropped to the ground or started screaming, but my teammates and I just looked over in the direction of the explosion. A large smoke cloud obscured one of the entrances, making it impossible to tell who was inside it.

"An explosion?" said Goggles, dropping his bag in surprise. "A bomb?"

Before I could answer Goggles' question, half a dozen

FAKE CHESS

silhouettes suddenly appeared in the smoke cloud before emerging from within. Six men, armed to the teeth with what appeared to be machine guns, entered the terminal with the practiced ease of trained soldiers, sweeping their guns back and forth across the room with stunning fluidity.

Even more concerning than the guns they held, however, were their costumes. They were dressed like Black pawns, with some modern military gear tossed over their costumes for good measure. They looked a bit like E2, except even more dangerous and lacking any sort of identifying number on their masks.

"Who are they?" said Brave Storm. "They look like pawns."

"No idea," I said, "but maybe if we move fast—"

"Do not move, airline passengers!" one of the Black pawns suddenly cried out. "If anyone moves, everyone dies."

I froze when I saw the six Black pawns pointing their guns at us. They were close enough that they could easily follow through on that threat if they wanted to. It helped that their appearance was quite intimidating, especially the guns.

Now, normally, I wouldn't be so scared by a bunch of cosplayers with guns, even real guns. My Mind-Bender Crown was strong enough to deflect, stop, or even redirect bullets. If I wanted to, I could probably disarm all six of them before they even realized they were about to get their asses kicked, and my teammates could handle the rest.

Unfortunately, I'd packed my Mind-Bender Crown along with all of my other superhero gear into one of my bags when we departed. I honestly didn't think I'd need to wear it until we got to Cheskia, and even then, I certainly didn't expect to find myself being held hostage with the other airline passengers. And I didn't dare try to unpack my Mind-Bender Crown because I suspected those Black pawns would correctly interpret that as a threat and riddle me with more bullets than I wanted inside my body. The rest of my team was also unarmed and in no position to arm themselves, either. That effectively left us as defenseless as the

19

other plane passengers, even if you took into account our fighting skills (which weren't terribly useful from a distance, unfortunately).

"W-Who are you guys?" said Goggles with a gulp.

The Black pawn who had spoken before shifted his gun toward Goggles, causing Goggles to flinch and a streak of fear to strike my heart. But he did not shoot, fortunately. "We are the Black Pawns of Cheskia. Our goal is simple: The complete overthrow of the King Magnus Laskar II, also known as the Chess King of Cheskia, to free the people from his unjust rule."

"You are not freedom fighters," snapped one of the other passengers, a thirty-something businessman with a distinctly Cheskian accent. "You are terrorists who have murdered many people, including my brother."

The Black Pawn turned his gun and fired on the businessman. The businessman collapsed onto the ground, groaning in pain as he clutched his stomach, where he'd been shot. Blood rapidly leaked out of his stomach onto the floor, adding the scent of fresh blood to the air, which did not make the situation any better, let me tell you.

"Anyone who tries to help that man will suffer the same fate," said the Black Pawn, turning his attention back onto the crowd. He hefted his gun, its black barrel shiny and smoky under the light from the ceiling above. "Unless there is anyone else who would like to die for a king who cares only about himself."

"Why are you doing this?" asked an elderly woman who stood with a small girl who couldn't have been older than six, likely her granddaughter based on the way she clutched the girl. "We have done you no harm. None of us have anything to do with the Chess King."

"It's nothing personal, I assure you," the Black Pawn said. "Our intel suggests that one of the Chess King's superhero guests is supposed to be on this flight. Specifically, Doctor Mind, from the United States of America."

FAKE CHESS

I might have shrunk back just a little when the scary guy with the scary-looking gun singled me out, but fortunately I don't think my teammates or anyone else noticed. Nor was the Black Pawn looking directly at me yet, either, which perhaps meant he hadn't spotted me. Hey, I might have been a superhero, but I was still kind of getting used to the whole 'bravery' thing.

"Why do you want him?" asked the elderly man I had noticed on the plane before, the one wearing a monocle and top hat. "Did he wrong you in some way?"

"No," said the Black Pawn with a shake of his head. "In truth, Doctor Mind has done nothing to us. He would simply make a very good hostage for us to ransom against Laskar. Our intel suggests that Laskar personally invited Doctor Mind to his ridiculous superhero chess tournament, including paying his travel and hotel expenses. Therefore, it is obvious that Laskar has a vested interest in making sure that Doctor Mind arrives safe and unharmed ... and is likely willing to pay a fair sum of money to do it."

"What about the rest of us?" said the grandmother. She pushed her granddaughter back behind her a little. "What will you do to us?"

The Black Pawn tilted his head to the side. "It depends. If you let us take Doctor Mind, then we will spare the rest of you. If, on the other hand, you attempt to prevent us from acquiring Doctor Mind or try to escape or resist us in any way ... well, you can ask the mouthy businessman what happens to those who cross the Black Pawns."

I gulped. I'd never even met the Chess King and yet the Black Pawn's analysis of the Chess King's opinion of me did not seem entirely incorrect. Granted, the Chess King and I were hardly buddies, but I had wondered why the Chess King went to such lengths to bring me all the way out here in the first place. Now whether the Chess King would care enough to actually pay whatever ransom the Black Pawns would demand in exchange for my freedom, I didn't know.

"What're we gonna do, Uncle?" Goggles whispered to me, nudging me in the side with his elbow. "Attack?"

I shook my head ever-so-slightly to avoid drawing the terrorists' attention to us. "No. Without our equipment, we're sitting ducks. Even if we were costumed up, we'd still be at a disadvantage. Those Black Pawns could probably gun us all down before we took even one step forward."

"Personally, I'm more offended by the fact that they didn't mention the rest of us," said Paranoyd, folding his arms in front of his chest. "No offense, Doc, but I'd like to think that the Chess King would be willing to pay a ransom for us, too."

"Let's focus more on defeating these terrorists than the fact that we're not all equally desirable here," I whispered. I glanced around the terminal briefly. "Okay, I think I've got a plan. Listen up and—"

"Doctor Mind!" the commanding voice of the first Black Pawn echoed through the empty terminal. "Come here now!"

Startled, I looked up to see the first Black Pawn pointing his gun in my general direction.

"Come over here," said the first Black Pawn in a deadly serious voice. "Now."

I gulped again and took a step forward, but then the first Black Pawn pulled on the trigger of his gun and a bullet whizzed by my face, just barely missing my left ear. I came to an abrupt stop, my heart pounding and my hands getting sweaty. The people surrounding me, including my own teammates, had ducked or jumped to the side when the Black Pawn shot at me, but none of them had been hurt, fortunately.

"Not you," the first Black Pawn said. He shifted his gun to the right slightly. "I am referring to *him*. The *real* Doctor Mind."

Puzzled, I looked to my right, wondering who he could possibly be referring to …

FAKE CHESS

And saw my brother, Bryan 'Brave Storm' Manuel, shock and confusion on his face.

CHAPTER FOUR

"ME?" SAID Brave Storm, putting a hand on his chest. "You ... you guys think *I'm* Doctor Mind?"

"Yes," said the first Black Pawn. He gestured at his mouth. "Were you not listening to me when I laid out our plan to hold you hostage in exchange for a handsome sum of money from the Chess King?"

Brave Storm shook his head rapidly. "No, no. I mean, I heard you, but I'm not actually Doctor Mind. You've got the wrong guy. I'm his brother." He abruptly pointed at me. "*He's* Doctor Mind, not me."

"Gee, thanks," I said in a sardonic voice. "Pointing the crazy terrorists at *me* instead. With a big brother like you, who needs enemies?"

Brave Storm rested a hand on Goggles' shoulder. "Sorry, bro, but I've got a kid to look after. Granted, you are in my will to become Goggles' guardian in the event of my death, but I'm kind of hoping to live long enough to at least see him graduate high school."

Goggles looked up at Brave Storm in alarm. "I hope you live a lot longer than that, Dad. I don't want you to die, even if that means I get to live with Uncle Roger, which ... hmm, wait a second. That would actually be cool now that I think about it."

FAKE CHESS

Did I ever tell you how wonderful my family was? Yeah, I was starting to rethink that assessment of them.

But before I could argue with my loving family about whether throwing me to the wolves was actually a good idea, the first Black Pawn shouted, "Liar! You do not fool us with your deception, Doctor Mind. We expected resistance, but watching you attempt to throw your older brother under the bus is dishonorable. Then again, Americans do not seem to understand the concept of *honor*, especially in chess."

I looked at the first Black Pawn in annoyance. "But he's right. *I'm* Doctor Mind, not him. We're brothers."

"We know that Doctor Mind has a brother," said the first Black Pawn, "but to be utterly frank, we think all you Americans look exactly the same."

The other Black pawns nodded in agreement with their leader and one of them even said, in a strangely deep voice, "I still cannot tell the difference between Barack Obama and Donald Trump."

Before I could get insulted by that, the first Black Pawn continued, saying, "We also know, based on our research, that Doctor Mind uses trickery and deception to fight criminals. Therefore, it is logical to assume that the real Doctor Mind would attempt to trick us into thinking his brother is the real Doctor Mind, even going so far as to coach his young nephew into pretending to be his son to deceive us and save his own sorry life."

I blinked. "You guys have a higher opinion of my deception skills than I do."

"On the contrary, liar, we are chess players," snapped a female Black Pawn, her voice very gravelly. "We know that Doctor Mind is a chess player. Chess is all about mind games, misdirection, and causing your opponent to question their own perceptions of reality. Indeed, true Grandmasters can even drive their opponents into bottomless insanity from which they will never recover for the rest of their days."

"She is correct," said the first Black Pawn with a solemn nod. He jerked his gun in Brave Storm's direction again. "That is why we know you are the *real* Doctor Mind. Come forward. Now."

Lumberjack suddenly raised a hand, like a boy in school, and said, "Hold it! If you Cheskian terrorists cannot tell us Americans apart, then it's obvious what we must do."

The first Black Pawn glared at Lumberjack. "Oh? And what would that be?"

Lumberjack stepped forward and said, without a hint of irony in his voice, "I am Doctor Mind."

Shining Armor also stepped forward just then, a determined look on his face, and said, "No, I am Doctor Mind."

It was Cavewoman's turn to stride forward, put her hands on her hips, and said, "No. Me Doctor Mind."

And then Holiday Man stepped forward, thrusting his chest out, and said, "Actually, we're *all* Doctor Mind. Every last one of us."

"Yeah," said Paranoyd, stepping in front of me. "Try to tell us apart now, jackass."

The first Black Pawn somehow managed to look entirely unimpressed while wearing a mask that completely covered his face.

I, on the other hand, was honestly touched by how my teammates all stepped up to defend me and my brother. Although we'd been working together for a few months now, I hadn't realized just how much they all cared about me. It reminded me of when I said we were all family on TV during our first live interview together as a team. It'd been a great big lie at the time, but now, I wondered if there was more truth to that statement than I originally believed.

"Very Spartacus," said the first Black Pawn. He raised his gun and fired it into the air, the bullet striking the glass ceiling overhead and sending bits of glass falling to the floor. "But I can think of one way to figure out which one is the real Doctor Mind: Process of elimination. We shoot every single one of you who claimed to be Doctor Mind and the last one standing is the real Doctor Mind. How does that sound?"

As one, all my teammates who were willing to put their lives on the line to save me not even a second ago magically teleported behind me and Brave Storm. Okay, they really just hid behind me like a bunch of scared puppies, but they moved so fast it might as well have been teleportation.

Did I mention how much my teammates really loved me and were willing to sacrifice themselves for me? Yeah, I was starting to rethink that, too.

The first Black Pawn lowered his gun, aiming it at Brave Storm again. "Enough of this American nonsense. Doctor Mind, come here. Now. Or we'll start shooting."

Brave Storm gulped, but I guess he must have decided there was no point in continuing to argue with a crazy guy with a gun because he gave Goggles a quick hug and an "I love you" before walking through the crowd of people toward the Black Pawns. I gave Brave Storm a brief, brotherly pat on the back as he passed, but that just masked how utterly powerless I felt watching him walk like a lamb toward the slaughter.

Once Brave Storm reached the Black Pawns, the first Black Pawn roughly grabbed him by the shoulder and jerked him back toward a couple of Black Pawns who stood behind him. The Black Pawns grabbed Brave Storm and immediately tied his arms together behind his back, two Black Pawns standing on either side of him holding the ropes which bound him. It pained me to see my older brother being treated like that, but again, I was basically powerless to save him.

"Wonderful," said the first Black Pawn. He looked at Brave Storm. "Thank you for coming forward willingly with only a minimum amount of fuss. It will make our departure that much easier."

"Just ... don't hurt my family, okay?" said Brave Storm, his voice quiet, his gaze never looking away from the first Black Pawn. "Take me, but if you lay even one finger on my family—"

"As I said, Doctor, now that we have you, we will not harm any other airplane passengers, family or otherwise," said the first Black Pawn. "You have my word."

Brave Storm nodded. He then looked at me and Goggles, a worried look in his eyes. I tried to communicate with my eyes that everything would be okay and that we'd find a way to save him, but I don't know how well I managed to communicate that.

Then the first Black Pawn turned to his companions and said, "All right, men! We have captured the target. Now it is time for us to leave before the police arrive."

Crap. Once the Black Pawns escaped, I would never find them. Even if I did, I might not be able to save Brave Storm unless I could pay the ransom or convince the Chess King to do so.

No. I *couldn't* let them get away, not that easily, anyway. Brave Storm was my brother and the father to my nephew. He didn't deserve this.

Thinking quickly, I glanced over my shoulder at Lumberjack and whispered, "Lumberjack, do you still have my bag with my Crown in it?"

Lumberjack held up a basketball bag for me. "This?"

I nodded, still without taking my attention off the Black Pawns. "Yeah. Open it quietly and hand me my Crown so I can use it to stop the Black Pawns from escaping."

Lumberjack nodded in return and started unzipping the basketball bag, which made a zipping sound that I thought was far too loud in this terminal.

But the Black Pawns did not seem to notice yet. The first Black Pawn was talking into a burner phone, perhaps coordinating their escape plan with their fellow terrorists on the outside, while the others trained their guns on either Brave Storm or the other passengers, though none pointed directly at me right now.

That was good. Now that they were focused more on escape than threatening the hostages, it meant I might be able to put on my Crown and use it before they realized it.

But perhaps that was also why they were surprised when, without any sort of warning at all, someone smashed through the glass ceiling overhead, sending an absolute shower of razor-sharp glass shards falling to the floor below. The person landed on the ground in a traditional three-point superhero landing, his appearance causing the other airplane passengers to gasp in surprise. Even I was startled by the guy's entrance and I knew a thing or two about making dramatic, unexpected entrances.

The Black Pawns, however, immediately trained their guns on the guy, but did not open fire immediately. Not that I blamed them, because the guy's appearance was rather striking, especially when he rose to his full height.

Standing in the center of the terminal, his long golden cape flowing behind him, was a superhero. I didn't know how else to describe him. He was clad from head to toe in full gold-and-brown spandex, his mouth hidden under a metal plate that curved around either side of his face. His head was covered with a golden mask, while his body had chess piece designs etched into it. In fact, his chest symbol was a horizontal view of a chessboard, complete with all of the pieces on the board arrayed correctly.

I had no idea who this guy was, and based on the puzzled expressions of my teammates and most of the other airplane passengers, neither did most of us.

But the little Cheskian girl excitedly pointed at the superhero and said, in a very cutesy voice, "Checkmate! It's Checkmate, Gaga!"

"Indeed it is, my granddaughter," said the grandmother, sounding as if she was on the verge of tears herself. "I never thought I'd live long enough to see him in person myself."

"Checkmate?" Goggles said to the grandmother, drawing her attention to him. "Who is Checkmate?"

As if in answer to my nephew's question, the superhero standing in the middle of the terminal suddenly slammed both of his fists together in front of his chest, his eyes glowing with righteous anger. He glared at the Black Pawns, who actually seemed to be trembling with fear at the sight of him.

"We are in the endgame now, Black Pawns," said the superhero in a surprisingly young-sounding Cheskian-accented voice. "Because now Checkmate, the superhero of Chess City and Cheskia's greatest champion, is here!"

CHAPTER FIVE

Okay, I know that superheroes are supposed to be weird and all, but Checkmate certainly took the cake. I mean, a chess-themed superhero named Checkmate? I didn't know whether to find that clever or stupid.

None of the Cheskians acted very surprised to see him, although the Black Pawns looked very alarm and worried.

All, that is, except for the first Black Pawn, who did not tremble or look even remotely afraid of Checkmate. He simply met Checkmate's gaze without flinching, although I guess that was pretty easy to do when you were armed with a machine gun and the other guy wasn't.

"Checkmate," said the first Black Pawn. He swung his gun at Checkmate. "Die."

The first Black Pawn squeezed the trigger on his gun and unleashed a barrage of bullets at Checkmate.

But Checkmate pulled his cape in front of him and deflected the bullets easily. The bullets struck the walls, floor, and ceiling, but did not hit Checkmate or us. Guess his cape must have been bulletproof or something.

The first Black Pawn must have realized how pointless shooting Checkmate was, though, because he stopped shooting and, looking over his shoulder at his fellow terrorists, barked, "Get the hostage out of here! I will keep the hero pinned."

LUCAS FLINT

"Not so fast, Black Pawn!" Checkmate said.

He swept his cape aside and, drawing a pistol from his side, took aim and fired several bullets at the Black Pawns. His bullets struck the heads of the two Black Pawns holding my brother hostage, striking their helmets with sickening *cracks* and making the Black Pawns collapse onto the floor. Brave Storm winced, but then looked around once it became clear he was unharmed, puzzlement on his face.

Checkmate, however, rushed forward, his long legs allowing him to cover the distance quickly. But then the first Black Pawn fired his machine gun at him again, forcing Checkmate to cover himself with his bulletproof cape. This time, one of the bullets ricocheted off of Checkmate's cape and nearly struck one of the remaining Black Pawns in the foot, forcing that Black Pawn to stagger away.

While the Black Pawns continued to shoot at Checkmate, I realized that Checkmate was the perfect distraction. I turned around and, grabbing my basketball bag from a shocked Lumberjack, unzipped it and looked inside. My Mind-Bender Crown sat, unharmed and shiny, within the bag, the gem on the forehead practically sparkling under the lights above. I quickly put my Mind-Bender Crown on my head and felt the familiar warmth as it activated.

Grinning, I turned to face my teammates and whispered, "Okay, guys. Since Checkmate has the Black Pawns distracted, this is our chance to strike. I'll save Brave Storm while you guys evacuate the passengers to the nearest exist over there."

I pointed toward the exit on the eastern side of the room, which appeared unprotected.

"But what if the Black Pawns notice and try shoot us?" asked Paranoyd, his face pale. He winced at a particularly loud burst of gunfire nearby.

I waved a hand dismissively. "Don't worry about the Black Pawns. Between me and Checkmate, they'll be a bit distracted."

FAKE CHESS

"All right, Uncle," said Goggles, nodding, a determined expression on his face. "Good luck."

I nodded back in return and then stood up. As I slowly made my way toward the battle, I heard my teammates going around and whispering to the other passengers to follow them. Fortunately, the other passengers must have listened because I saw them creeping along behind or beside my teammates, doing their best not to draw the attention of the Black Pawns.

Not that there was any need to even pretend to be silent or stealthy, though. Aside from the loudness of the Black Pawns' guns, there was also the tiny detail of Checkmate himself, who had dropped his bulletproof cape in favor of doing crazy gymnastics to avoid the gunshots. Seriously, the guy put Olympic gymnasts to shame with his rolls, cartwheels, jumps, flips, and all kinds of other crazy moves he did. I didn't know if this guy had any superpowers of his own or if he was just well-trained, but either way, none of the Black Pawns seemed to notice me creeping up on them.

To be fair, neither did Brave Storm. Although the Black Pawns who had been holding his ropes were down, he was very much still tied up. He had dropped to the floor himself, however, to avoid getting caught in the middle of the gunfire, which was probably the smartest thing he could have done in his condition. Heck, even I was crawling along the smooth, cold tiled floor now, keeping my head as low as I could as I approached my brother.

"Hey, Bryan," I said once I got within hearing range of Brave Storm, rising to my feet. "Bryan, it's me, Roger."

Brave Storm glanced at me and his face broke into a happy, relieved smile. "Bro! Good to see you."

"Same," I said. I jerked my head backward. "We're getting you and everyone else out of here while Checkmate distracts the cosplayers."

Brave Storm nodded before looking down at the ropes around his body. "Good idea, but I won't get far tied up like this."

I grabbed the rough-hewn ropes and tugged on them experimentally before shaking my head. "You're right. They're on too tightly. Let me try to remove them with my telekinesis."

Putting the tips of my fingers against my crown, I focused and felt the Crown on my head grow hotter before it activated. I focused on unraveling the ropes around Brave Storm's body, but it was tricky because the Black Pawns had tied him up pretty tightly. Even so, my telekinetic 'fingers' were far more dexterous than my physical fingers, and a second or two later, the ropes fell harmlessly off Brave Storm's body.

"Thanks!" said Brave Storm as we both scrambled to our feet. He shot me a grin. "Times like these make you wish we weren't related sometimes, eh?"

"Yeah," I said. I pointed toward the exit, where I saw Goggles, Lumberjack, and the others herding the other airplane passengers. "Go join the others outside. I'll be right behind you."

"You sure?" said Brave Storm. He glanced at his fists. "If you need backup—"

"I'm fine," I insisted. "You don't have your upgraded armor or even your ax. I'm the only Faker with my equipment. It will be safer for both of us if you leave."

Brave Storm pursed his lips but nodded. "All right. Stay safe."

With that, Brave Storm turned and ran toward the others. I watched him go for a moment, feeling relief knowing that he was safe.

But I also knew that the fight with the Black Pawns was far from over, so I turned around ... and found myself staring down the hot, slightly smoking barrel of the first Black Pawn's machine gun.

The barrel of the machine gun was so close to my face that I could practically taste the gunpowder, heat, and smoke coming off of it. The stench made me feel ill to my stomach, but I didn't dare move, because the other end of the gun, including the trigger, was in the hand of a very pissed-off-looking Black Pawn.

FAKE CHESS

Despite his featureless mask, I got the feeling he was shooting a death glare at me.

"So you were the real Doctor Mind after all," said the first Black Pawn. He glanced at my helmet. "The Crown on your head proves it."

I gulped. "Yeah. Maybe next time, believe someone when they say who they are."

Black Pawn shrugged. "Anyone can claim to be anyone. Isn't that right ... Checkmate?"

Against my better judgment, I glanced in Checkmate's general direction.

Checkmate stood a few feet away, among the fallen forms of the first Black Pawn's allies, who all lay in various states of injury around him. Checkmate himself looked almost entirely unharmed, though he was panting slightly, perhaps a bit exhausted from the physical effort of fighting them. Oddly, I noticed bits and pieces of chess pieces around his feet, too, though where those came from, I had no idea.

Yet Checkmate hardly looked ready for a nap. If anything, he looked even more pumped up, his eyes glaring at the first Black Pawn, his gun pointed squarely at the first Black Pawn's head.

"Let the Doctor go, Black Pawn," Checkmate said, "or you will not live long enough to regret your decision."

The first Black Pawn laughed. "You know you cannot pull your trigger faster than me. One bullet is all I need to end this man's life permanently."

"And lose a valuable hostage who you could ransom for money?" Checkmate questioned. "Don't make me laugh. I know how you Black Pawn types operate. You claim to fight for the people but only care about money and power, else why take hostages in exchange for cash?"

"Revolutions require funding as much as any other type of business, Checkmate," said the first Black Pawn. "Not that you would understand, however, given your silver spoon."

Checkmate stiffened. "I don't know what you are talking about."

The first Black Pawn chuckled. "Everyone knows who your father is, boy. Or did you think your 'secret identity' is very secret? I may be the son of a humble Cheskian chess shepherd, but even I am no fool. Although I am afraid I cannot say the same for you."

Okay, I was even more confused now. Who was Checkmate, really, and why were they acting like his real identity was such a big deal? Did he come from a well-to-do family or something?

Not that there was really time to ponder those questions, though. With a gun in my face like this, I really didn't have time to play around or think. I needed to find a way to escape this situation, preferably with my brain as bullet-free as possible.

The first Black Pawn had almost literally stalemated Checkmate. If Checkmate tried to shoot the Black Pawn, the Black Pawn would shoot me. Even if Checkmate killed the Black Pawn, I'd still die. On the other hand, if Checkmate allowed the Black Pawn to take me prisoner and escape, then that wouldn't be good, either. I didn't know much about Checkmate as a person, but he seemed to be a genuine superhero or trying to be, anyway, so he probably would feel awful if I died or got taken hostage.

It was a brilliant plan, really. It's something I might have come up with Brave Storm back when we were LARPing as superheroes and supervillains. Heck, I was almost certain we'd played out a similar scenario during one of our cons, only it had been me trying to stop Blood Storm from killing an innocent civilian. My solution back then, however, was not possible for Checkmate, mostly because it had involved using my telekinesis to shove a whole potted planet up Blood Storm's ... eh, I wasn't going to think about that or the hours of apologizing I needed to do to make Bryan feel better afterward.

But then I noticed something about the Black Pawn. Despite his bravado, his mocking of Checkmate, he was trembling. It was

FAKE CHESS

a very slight tremble, one I doubted even Checkmate noticed, but I did. It even extended to his gun hand and trigger finger, which briefly made me feel worried that the Black Pawn might pull the trigger and kill me accidentally because of his nerves.

But then I asked myself: If the Black Pawn was as in control of this situation as he appeared, then why was he so nervous?

The answer came to me almost immediately, causing me to relax.

After all, I now knew I was in no danger at all, nor was Checkmate.

The Black Pawn, however, was.

And that was why he was more freaked out at the moment than either of us.

The Black Pawn must have noticed how relaxed I looked, however, because he snapped, "Why do you look so at ease, Doctor? Do you not realize just by how thin a thread your worthless life is hanging?"

I looked down the barrel of the Black Pawn's gun at his faceplate. If he'd had eyes, I would have glared into them. As it was, all I did was stare into my own reflection in his featureless mask and say, "Actually, my life is just fine. Yours, however, isn't."

The Black Pawn grunted. "Oh? Tell me again, brilliant Doctor, who has a loaded machine gun being pointed directly in their face right now?"

Again without breaking eye contact with him, I said, "No one."

The Black Pawn briefly faltered, clearly taken aback by my answer. "No one? Are you blind as well as dumb, Doctor?"

I shook my head slowly. "No. I just know that your machine gun *isn't* loaded at all. That you actually wasted all of your bullets on Checkmate, which did you no good, seeing as Checkmate is still alive and unharmed and all your friends have been defeated."

LUCAS FLINT

The Black Pawn made a weird growling noise in his throat. "How do you know that my gun isn't loaded? I've indeed used up a lot of its ammunition trying to shoot Checkmate, but as I said before, I need only one bullet to kill you."

"Agreed," I said. "Which is why you won't be killing me today, because you don't have even one measly bullet. Pretty disappointing, isn't it?"

The Black Pawn shoved the warm barrel of his gun against my forehead suddenly. "Prove it, then. Stare down the barrel and tell me how many bullets are left in my gun."

Doing my best not to roll my eyes in irritation, I said, "I don't need to look down the barrel of your gun to prove that your gun is empty. If it was full of bullets, you wouldn't be trembling like an earthquake at the moment."

The Black Pawn glanced at his own body, which was, indeed, trembling even more than before. "I-I just have very jumpy nerves."

"No," I said. I pressed my forehead against the barrel of his gun even harder. "You don't. But if you want to prove how much of a delusional liar I am, then go ahead. Pull that trigger. Put a bullet in my brain. Doubt you'll last long afterward, but won't it feel good to put a bullet into the brain of an uppity American superhero who has no honor?"

The Black Pawn hesitated. His trigger finger trembled, his hand trembled, and *he* trembled. I, on the other hand, waited patiently to see what he would do next, knowing that I was right and the Black Pawn's gun was as empty as a box of Mike & Ike's after Goggles got through with them.

But one thing I didn't know was how much it hurt to get slapped in the face with a gun. Especially a big, heavy machine gun.

Because that was what the Black Pawn did. Rather than pull the trigger, he slammed his gun into the side of my face, sending me crashing to the floor, my senses dazed from the impact. The

FAKE CHESS

blow left me dazed for a moment, although I was still cognizant enough to see the Black Pawn hurl his empty weapon at Checkmate, who caught it with both hands to avoid getting hit by it, and then turn and run like hell toward the exit on the opposite side of the terminal.

And damn did that Black Pawn move fast when he wanted to. He ran so fast that he got halfway to the exit before either Checkmate or I could react. In fact, he was just about to go through it when someone new stepped through the revolving door and stopped in front of the exit, forcing the Black Pawn to screech to a halt on the tiled floor.

The newcomer was a rather shapely woman, also dressed like a pawn, although she was a White pawn rather than a Black one. Her face and head were obscured by a face-covering bulb-like mask/helmet, with the letter and number 'D2' painted on in bright red paint. She looked a lot like a certain other pawn cosplayer I'd run into before. Perhaps his sister?

"What the—?" said the Black Pawn in astonishment, taking a step back. "One of the Eight—?"

D2 nodded and said, in a voice that sounded awfully familiar for some reason, "Correct. Bye."

With that, D2 kicked the Black Pawn straight in the bishops. The Black Pawn whimpered like a puppy and collapsed onto the floor, twitching every now and then like he'd been electrocuted.

At almost the same time the Black Pawn fell, I suddenly heard police sirens somewhere in the distance, along with the screeching of tires on pavement. The Cheskian police must have arrived, although I did not see them.

My focus, instead, was on the woman apparently known as D2, who stood over the fallen Black Pawn with her arms folded in front of her rather generous chest. Even Checkmate was looking at her, though for some reason he was staring at her with annoyance.

LUCAS FLINT

D2, however, ignored him and looked over at me. Gesturing at the fallen Black Pawn before her, D2 said, "Welcome to Cheskia, Doctor Mind. More specifically, welcome to Chess City, otherwise known as the chess capital of the whole world. I hope you enjoy your stay and your participation in the International Superhero Chess Tournament."

CHAPTER SIX

To say that I was stunned (and maybe a little stressed out) by the Black Pawns' terrorist attack was an understatement, to say the least. When I received the invitation to come to Cheskia, I had expected to treat it more or less like an extended foreign vacation. And in my, admittedly limited, experience, most foreign vacations did not involve getting almost kidnapped by cosplaying terrorists at the airport the very second you step off the plane.

Truly, Cheskia had some strange customs.

But I did not get to voice these complaints to D2, mostly because shortly after her arrival, two dozen armed Chess City police officers, who all wore White pawn-like armor over their bodies as well, burst into the airport and immediately took charge. They instantly arrested the fallen Black Pawns, who, surprisingly, were still alive. Even the ones that Checkmate had shot in the face had survived, which was when I learned that Checkmate didn't shoot bullets from his gun, but dense, miniature metal pawns that were a bit less deadly but apparently no less painful than actual bullets.

The Chess City police briefly interrogated me, but once it became clear I had nothing to do with the Black Pawn terrorist attack, they let me go. Or rather, when I name-dropped the Chess King while explaining what brought me to Cheskia, they not only let me go but asked me if I needed some fresh coffee and a donut to relax after a long, stressful day. It seemed to me that the police did not want to cross the Chess King's path, even accidentally, although that did not stop me from accepting the coffee and donut they offered to me because I never say no to free food and I *was* hungry after such a long flight.

The police also nearly arrested my friends, in particular Cavewoman, who they for some reason mistook as an escaped gorilla. That took more time than I would have liked to convince them that my teammates actually helped. Fortunately, the other airplane passengers were willing to testify to my teammates' helpfulness, so the police let them go. Granted, I did have to convince Cavewoman not to smash in the skulls of the officers who called her a gorilla, but I felt we got off pretty easy, all things considered.

The police also took the other passengers from us. An ambulance arrived at roughly the same time as the police and treated all of the travelers. Most of them had escaped the attack with no injuries at all. The only exception was the Cheskian businessman who'd been shot. They'd been forced to take him to the nearest hospital, but I overheard the ambulance workers talking among themselves and they did not sound very concerned about the businessman's survival. Which meant that either he wasn't as injured as he appeared or Cheskian medical professionals had much less sympathy for people who got shot than their American counterparts.

As for Checkmate, he left not too long after talking with the police and giving them his version of events. I was under the impression that the police distrusted Checkmate even more than me, which seemed odd, given how Checkmate was apparently the superhero of Cheskia. Of course, I hadn't even known that Cheskia had a superhero until I was on my flight, so maybe Checkmate was not as popular as he seemed in the airport.

Before he left, Checkmate made a cryptic comment to me about how he looked forward to seeing me 'soon.' I tried to ask

FAKE CHESS

him if he was also going to participate in the chess tournament, but he refused to answer. Which seemed weird to me, but then again, everyone in Cheskia seemed weird to me so far.

And that brought us to the mysterious woman who called herself D2. After the police took over the Black Pawn situation, D2 introduced herself as our contact with the Chess King. She'd apparently been waiting in our shuttle just outside the airport when the terrorist attack happened. The Chess King himself had sent her to pick us up and take us to our hotel. Along with the Black Pawn's comment about her being one of the 'Eight,' that all but confirmed to me that D2 was likely related to E2 in some way, although I didn't ask her directly, mostly because I suspected I wouldn't get a direct answer from her.

That, and we were all *dead* tired after a twelve-hour flight and then having to deal with a terrorist attack on top of that. That is probably why my teammates and I simply loaded up into the shuttle that D2 had arranged for us without argument. Although we might have all been superheroes who were in pretty good physical condition, that did not mean we were invincible or had no limits, and I felt like we had nearly hit ours today.

"My apologies for the rough start to your stay, Doctor," said D2 suddenly while we were on the shuttle. "Normally, most guests do not get attacked by terrorists when they arrive in Cheskia."

Snapping out of my thoughts, I looked to my left. D2 sat in the bus seat on the other side of the aisle, her hands resting on her knees, which were draped over one another.

That was when I noticed that, unlike E2, D2's robes looked a bit more like a dress than robes. She wasn't quite as thin as E2, although it was hard to tell because her costume was not exactly form-fitting. She also wore shoes that were tipped with the heads of the queen piece from chess. A cinnamon-y smell wafted off her body, a positively heavenly scent.

Rolling my shoulders, I said, "It's fine, D2. That is your

name, right?"

"It is what I am called, yes," said D2 vaguely. "You may refer to me that way, if you wish."

I raised an eyebrow, but before I could figure out what she meant by that, Goggles, who sat in the seat next to me, leaned around me and shot D2 a happy smile. "Thanks for saving us! Between you and Checkmate, those Black Pawn dudes didn't stand a chance."

D2 shrugged modestly. "It was nothing, honestly. I should have reacted sooner. I really only stepped in at the end. Had I gotten there sooner, perhaps we could have ended it much more quickly with less bloodshed."

Cavewoman, who sat in the row behind D2, suddenly leaned over the top of her seat and said, "No modesty. Be strong woman. Men can't do anything without us. Women strong."

D2 looked up at Cavewoman, probably wearing a perplexed expression on her face underneath the mask. "Um, I do not see what the differences between the sexes have to do with saving innocent lives."

"What Cavewoman is trying to say is that we're grateful for your help," said Brave Storm, who sat in the row behind me, next to Shining Armor. Brave Storm had a blanket draped over his shoulders, even though it wasn't that cold and we were no longer talking with the ambulance workers, who had given him the blanket. "Even if you just came in at the end, you made sure that none of those terrorists escaped."

"Who *were* those guys, anyway?" asked Paranoyd, who had unfortunately been forced to sit next to Cavewoman on the bus. "Those 'Black Pawn' guys or whatever they called themselves. I've never even heard of them."

D2 sighed and rubbed the back of her neck. "That is because, outside of Cheskia, they are not very well-known. They're a terrorist group that seeks to overthrow the Chess King and replace him with the Black King, who is the leader and founder of their

FAKE CHESS

group."

"Black," said Shining Armor, "as in the black chess pieces, right?"

D2 nodded. She gestured at herself. "Yes. As you can see, those of us who consider ourselves servants of the Chess King typically wear white."

"Do the Black Pawns regularly try to take foreigners hostage like that?" I asked.

"No," said D2 with a shake of her head. "Normally, their activities are limited to money laundering and occasionally attacking government buildings or bombing businesses. They also try to incite riots every now and then, but those are usually put down quickly. Honestly, they're more of a minor annoyance than a major threat. I wouldn't worry about them while you're here. You will have nothing but the best security at the castle, so the Black Pawns won't be giving you much trouble during your stay."

They certainly did not seem like a 'minor annoyance' to the guy who'd gotten shot, or to Brave Storm, who I could tell was still pretty shaken up over the whole nearly getting kidnapped deal. Even so, D2 sounded confident in the castle's security, so maybe she was right.

"All right, then," I said, resting my chin in my hand. "But what about Checkmate, the superhero who helped? I'd always heard that Cheskia is one of the few countries in the world that doesn't have superheroes."

Despite wearing an expressionless mask, I sensed I'd asked D2 a rather sensitive question. It was her body language. She became stiffer, her shoulders in particular tensing. That just made me more suspicious and told me I was on the right track.

"Checkmate's relationship with the Cheskian government is ... complicated, to say the least," said D2 in the delicate, professional tone of a spokesperson who had experience choosing the best words to describe a negative situation in the least negative way. "He was not supposed to be there today."

Goggles gulped. "Is Checkmate a vigilante or something? I hope not, because he seemed really cool."

"No, he is a legal superhero," said D2. "It's just that he and the Chess King have something of a strained relationship, to put it lightly. The people of Cheskia love Checkmate, but the government ... well, he's not part of the Four Arms and doesn't usually work with them, so that's where the conflict comes from."

I nodded in understanding, although in truth, I knew she was lying or at least omitting certain parts of the truth. One of the advantages of having my background in lying and bullshitting is that my lie detector is pretty darn reliable, but even more reliable is my ability to detect when people are leaving *out* certain information that they do not want other people to know about.

And D2—likely on orders from someone higher up the food chain than her—was definitely omitting some rather important information regarding Checkmate and his relationship to the Chess King.

I suppose I could have asked her directly about it, but again, I noticed she was good at choosing her words carefully. Most likely, she'd run circles around me verbally until we either got to our hotel or I got tired of playing with her. It was an annoying thought to think, but for now I'd have to wait until another time to get more information. Maybe I'd even get a chance to see Checkmate himself and ask him in person, although I had no idea when I'd get to do that.

Goggles must have been thinking along the same lines as me because he said, "Will Checkmate at least be entering the tournament?"

D2 nodded. "Yes, he will, although I do not know if he will play against your uncle or not. We shall see how the brackets are set up."

"The tournament is starting tomorrow?" asked Lumberjack, who sat in the row behind Cavewoman and Paranoyd, next to

FAKE CHESS

Holiday Man, who was still clutching his stuffed bunny. "That seems a bit early. I was hoping we'd get a few days to rest, relax, and chop down some trees."

"You may do what you wish while you are visiting Cheskia," said D2. She gestured at me. "But Doctor Mind will have to play, seeing as he is the only participant on your team in the tournament."

"Fair enough," I said. I leaned a little closer toward D2. "So what, exactly, is the prize for winning the tournament, if you don't mind me asking? None of the emails or letters I've received from y'all have said what it is, other than claiming it's something that 'everyone' will want."

D2 leaned back in her seat, steepling her fingers together, clearly amused by my question. "That is also something you will find out tomorrow. It is supposed to be a secret, but I can say this: It is not a prize you will win at any other chess tournament in the world. It is wholly unique to Cheskia."

I scratched my chin. "Wholly unique to Cheskia, eh? Let me guess, I'll get another free vacation here or something?"

I got the impression that D2 was smiling at me mysteriously underneath her mask. "You will see."

I frowned deeper. More mysteries on top of even more mysteries, but this was a subject that I didn't care about as much as the others. D2 was right. I'd just have to wait until tomorrow to find out.

Instead, I asked, "Back in the airport, the Black Pawn called you one of the 'Eight,' but didn't get to finish his sentence before you took him out. As well, back in America, I played a high-stakes chess game with a man who looked a lot like you, but he called himself E2. What did the Black Pawn mean when he said that?"

"That?" said D2. She put a hand on her chest. "I am one of the Eight Pawns of the Chess King. The Black Pawn likely recognized me, even though he is clearly a no-name nobody who

I have never met before in my life. We are somewhat infamous among the Black Pawns because of our undying loyalty to the Chess King."

"Eight Pawns?" said Goggles. "But aren't all citizens of Cheskia called pawns? That's what our flight attendant said to us back on the plane."

D2 put her hands together like a teacher that was trying to explain a complicated concept to young children. "Capital 'P' Pawns. While all citizens are pawns, only eight of us at any one time are ever known as the Eight Pawns. We are handpicked by the Chess King himself from various chess tournaments all over the country to serve him faithfully. We receive special training, new code names, and direct assignments from the Chess King himself once we are chosen. It is considered the highest honor that a pawn can achieve in this country and, because there are only eight available spots, it's very competitive."

"So you guys are basically like Cheskia's Special Forces, then?" Holiday Man piped up suddenly.

Turning in her seat to look at Holiday Man, D2 said, "More like the CIA. The Eight Pawns are considered the elite of the elite. We do jobs for the Chess King all over Cheskia and even the world. Indeed, we are regularly sent to chess tournaments in other countries to scope out the talent there, as well as act as ambassadors for Cheskia to foreign countries."

"You mean like E2?" I said. "He looked just like you, only he called himself E2."

"So you played against E2, then," said D2 with a nod. "Interesting, but not surprising. I thought I heard E2 bragging about playing against you. He isn't very good."

My eyes widened. "Isn't very good? But I thought you said that you Eight are the elite of the elite."

"By Eight standards," said D2 without hesitation. "E2 is the weakest among us, which I always thought was problematic given how he is the King's Pawn. If you had played again A2, or even

FAKE CHESS

worse, F2, you definitely would not be here today."

I tried not to show it, but D2's words stunned me. When I'd played against E2, I had had to use every trick in the book, and even then the guy damn near beat me. If what D2 said was true, though, then E2 was actually the weakest of the Eight. I hoped I wouldn't have to play against any of them anytime soon.

"Wow," said Goggles. "Why are you guys all named with letters and numbers?"

"Because each of us represents a different square on the board when viewed from White's point of view," D2 explained. "E2, for example, is named after the e2 square, I am named after the d2 square, so on and so forth. It's a simple theme naming scheme that has existed for centuries, a proud tradition, with each member being the successor to generations of Pawns. It's quite the honor to be handpicked by His Majesty for such a role."

"Uh-huh," I said. "Are any of you guys going to be in the tournament or—?"

D2 shook her head. "No. I'm afraid only superheroes are allowed to participate in this tournament. We Eight Pawns have other roles to play, but rest assured that you will still see us often during the tournament, even if not as your direct competitors."

"What about the Chess King?" asked Shining Armor. "When will we see him?"

D2 giggled, a sound that was strikingly familiar to me, although again I could not place where I'd heard it before. "Good question. The answer to that is just outside your window, as we have now arrived at your lodgings."

Curious, I looked out the bus window to my right as the rest of my teammates looked out their windows at our surroundings. I'd been so engrossed in our conversation with D2 that I had not paid attention to Chess City itself as it passed by our windows. My jaw dropped at the sight before us.

A huge stone castle towered over our comparatively tiny bus. Multiple towers rose from within stone walls that were at least ten-feet-tall, if not taller. The walls were patrolled by white-armored soldiers who looked a bit like pawns, armed with swords, guns, and other weapons. Large flags depicting the Cheskian coat of arms blew in the wind atop the towers, while a large moat surrounded the castle's walls.

"Wow," said Goggles, who was staring out the window with me. "That looks like something straight out of the Middle Ages!"

"Castle Rook was indeed founded in the 1500s, not long after the Middle Ages," D2 agreed. "It is also the home of the Chess Royal Family themselves."

"That's cool and all, but why did we stop here?" said Paranoyd in confusion. "Is this some kind of historical tour of the city or something?"

D2 shook her head once more. "No, no. You misunderstand. Your lodgings are *in* Castle Rook."

I looked at D2 in disbelief. "You mean that we're staying inside a castle rather than a hotel?"

"And not just any castle," D2 added. She gestured at the Castle. "It is the personal home of the Cheskian Royal Family, as I just said. You will stay here for the duration of the tournament. You will sleep, eat, drink, and rest here. Think of it as a very high-scale resort."

"Amazing," said Brave Storm, his jaw dropping slightly as he looked at the Castle. "When y'all told us all of our travel expenses would be covered, I didn't think you meant *literally*."

"You are all honored guests of the Chess King," said D2, a hint of amusement in her voice. "So of course you will be given proper accommodations during your stay. And speaking of the Chess King, as his honored guests, His Majesty will attend dinner with you in the Dining Chamber tonight after you are all unpacked and settled in."

"We're going to be having dinner with the Chess King himself?" said Goggles in awe. "That's amazing!"

"I am glad you seem to feel so honored," said D2. "The Chess

FAKE CHESS

King rarely deigns to dine with his guests unless they happen to be heads of state or ambassadors."

I scratched my head in confusion. "Why does he want to have dinner with us?"

D2 shrugged. "I do not know. The ways of His Majesty are often not clear to me. I would suggest that you wear your best clothes and show him the proper respect he deserves. That way, your stay will be more ... pleasant, to put it nicely."

I didn't like the way D2 emphasized the word 'pleasant,' nor was I particularly enthused about having to spend a whole week locked up in the same castle as the guy who'd ordered one of his minions to try to kill me and my friends during a game of chess.

But we were definitely in for it now, I thought as I looked up at the massive castle again. There was no going back now. We just had to go forward and do our best ... even if, as I suspected, our best wouldn't be enough.

CHAPTER SEVEN

Gotta admit, despite my reluctance to trust the Chess King or his minions, I *was* impressed by both the castle and his servants.

When my teammates and I stepped out of the bus with our bags in hand, half a dozen white-robed servants came forward and took our luggage for us. They insisted on carrying our luggage for us all the way up to our rooms, which I didn't mind. Although my luggage was pretty sparse and easy to carry, I still didn't enjoy having to lug it around everywhere. I did feel sorry for the servants when they had to take up Cavewoman's stuff, however. She had brought six or seven suitcases full of who-knows-what, six or seven *heavy* suitcases. The poor servants did their best to carry everything, but it was clear they lacked E2's weird inhuman super strength.

D2 took it upon herself to show us to our rooms on the third floor of the main tower. We passed through floor after chess-themed floor, hallways lined with statues of bishops, knights, rooks, kings, queens, and more, all in different styles and from different time periods. D2 informed us that each Chess King would have their own set of chess statues designed to add to the 'Hall of Chess,' as it was called, but only toward the end of their reigns or lives. The current Chess King had yet to commission his own set of chess statues, but seeing as he was still in charge and

FAKE CHESS

likely not going to die anytime soon, that was not surprising.

What was surprising, however, were the individual rooms that each member of the team got. Apparently, Castle Rook was big enough and had so many towers that the Chess King could afford to give each member of my team their own room. The only exception was Goggles, who shared a room with Brave Storm, although given their relationship, that made perfect sense.

And I have to say, the rooms were nicer than even some of the old four-star hotel rooms my brothers and I would get to stay in whenever we went with our dad on a business trip when we were kids. Lush shag carpeting covered the floors, while large queen-sized mattresses dominated the bedrooms, each bed being a four-poster bed with its own curtains to allow for maximum privacy at night. Every room had its own full-sized kitchen—not kitchenette—and bathroom.

The bathrooms were even better, with mirrors so reflective and clear that it was like looking into an alternate universe, with shiny faucets, bathtubs, and even curtains. Even the toilets were lined with what appeared to be gold. It was nuts. The rooms smelled heavenly, vanilla mixed with strawberry. And they were set at the perfect temperatures, too, neither too hot nor too cold.

The only real downside was that the rooms, like pretty much everything else in Castle Rook, had an almost obnoxiously on-point chess theme. The shag carpeting had the same black-and-white chessboard design that everywhere else did, the curtains for the windows, shower, and four-poster beds were covered with chess pieces, and the tiles on the kitchen counter were deliberately chessboard-like. The handles of the silverware were even shaped like different chess pieces, and that included the salt and pepper shakers, which were shaped like king and queen pieces respectively.

"These are your rooms," said D2, standing in the doorway of my room. She'd already shown everyone else to their rooms and was now showing me to mine, which was the last room. She held up a golden key shaped a bit like a king and held it out to me. "And this is your room key. I suggest that you do not lose it, as these keys are rather expensive to make."

Taking the golden key, which was heavier than it looked, I said, "When's dinner?"

"It will be tonight at seven," said D2. She glanced at the chess-themed clock behind me. "So you and your teammates have a few hours to unpack and settle in. If you need anything, simply ring the bell by your door and one of His Majesty's servants will answer right away."

I nodded. "Will we need to wear anything formal or—?"

D2 giggled. "The Chess King simply requests that you come dressed in your normal superhero costumes. That will be formal enough, I think."

I wondered how superhero costumes—especially the ones that my team and I wore—could possibly be considered 'formal,' but D2 had a light tone to her voice, so maybe she was joking. I just watched her walk off down the hallway for a moment before closing the door to my room and rubbing my forehead.

Dinner with the Chess King ... I guess it made sense, what with us being his personal guests and all. I wondered if it would just be me and my team or if any of the other tournament participants would also be there. If so, then this could be a chance for me to scope out the competition and see what kind of level I was dealing with here.

On the other hand, I was still very skeptical of the Chess King's motives. I knew there had to be more going on here than *just* a friendly tournament. Exactly what, of course, was still a mystery, but perhaps dinner with the Chess King tonight would answer a few of those questions. I hoped so, anyway.

"Good thing we don't have to wear suits," said Lumberjack's voice behind me all of a sudden. "Because I didn't pack any clothes aside from my costume."

Startled, I whirled around to see Lumberjack sitting in the

FAKE CHESS

recliner by the fireplace in my room, but he wasn't alone. Paranoyd and Shining Armor sat on the couch opposite him, the two looking quite relaxed, while Brave Storm and Goggles were bouncing up and down on my bed. Cavewoman, ironically enough, was in the kitchen, although it looked like she was just getting a glass of water. Only Holiday Man appeared to be missing, though I had no doubt he was somewhere nearby as well.

"What the—?" I said, looking at my teammates in surprise. "How did you guys get in here? I thought you were all in your rooms."

Goggles, still bouncing on my bed, pointed at a door on the other side of the room that I hadn't even noticed before. "We found out that each room is connected by a door! We sneaked in while you were talking to D2."

"Yeah," said Brave Storm, his voice slightly breathless, likely from all of the bouncing he was doing. "Surprised you didn't hear us enter. Lumberjack dropped his ax like three times."

"Four," said Lumberjack, petting the head of his ax with one hand like it was a fragile little animal. "Fortunately, my baby is very sturdy and the carpeting is very soft."

Shining Armor, who had his hands folded behind his head, looked at Lumberjack in surprise. "Hey, that's what my dad said my mom said when she dropped me on my head when I was a baby. What a weird coincidence."

Sighing, I said, "Okay, but where is Holiday—"

The door that connected my room to the others suddenly swung open and a literal clown rolled into the room on roller skates before hitting the carpet and tripping over himself. He fell face-first onto the floor, his big red nose making a honking noise upon impact, before pushing himself up on his hands and shaking his big, multi-colored afro.

"Who let the clown in?" I said, staring at the clown on the floor in confusion. "Does Cheskia even *have* clowns?"

The clown looked up at me with a grin, revealing the badly-applied makeup face of Holiday Man. "I'm not a *clown*, Doctor! It's me, Holiday Man. Or as I'm referring to myself this month, April Fool's Day Man! And what better costume for April Fools than that of a clown? Aren't I amusing?"

Holiday Man squeezed his fake red nose, which honked like an angry goose when he did. Jumping to his feet, Holiday Man nearly lost his balance and fell over again before grabbing the frame of the doorway for support. "Heh heh! I knew wearing roller skates was a bad idea. At least you guys got a good laugh out of it, right?"

I just stared at Holiday Man in disbelief. "Your gimmick is getting kind of old, you know that?"

"April Fool's never gets old!" Holiday Man declared. "I've got all sorts of fun practical jokes to play on you guys. Trust me, we're going to have a FUN time together!"

I sighed again and rubbed my forehead. I'd forgotten about Holiday Man's gimmick where he changed his superhero identity every month to align with whatever the major holiday of that month was. At least it was better than March, where Holiday Man became the ugliest crossdresser in the world in what I assumed was an unintentionally offensive way to celebrate International Woman's Day. Cavewoman certainly looked a lot less offended at the sight of Holiday Man's new costume than she had at the sight of last month's costume, but even she looked at a loss for words at his weird appearance.

Everyone, that is, except for Shining Armor, who held up a hand and said, "Clowns are fun! Can you make balloon animals for us? I want an elephant."

"We're not making balloon animals," I said shortly. I put my hands on my hips. "D2 says we're having dinner with the Chess King tonight. She recommended we rest and prepare ourselves for the meal, so I want you guys to promise me you'll be on your best behavior."

FAKE CHESS

"Hope the food is good," Paranoyd said, rubbing his stomach. "I'm starving after that stupidly-long airplane flight. Snacks and coffee do not make for a filling meal."

"Cavewoman agree," said Cavewoman, sipping her cup of water. "If food no good, Cavewoman lecture Chess King on patriarchal foundations of monarchy and ask why no make Chess Queen supreme ruler of Cheskia."

I glowered at everyone. "I get it, I don't particularly trust the Chess King myself, either, but since we're his guests, we have to be on our best behavior, even if the food isn't good and even if he isn't interested in hearing our theories about the foundations of monarchy."

Goggles, who had stopped bouncing on the bed with Brave Storm, rubbed his arms. "I've never been to a formal dinner with a king before. What should I wear?"

"Just our costumes, according to D2," I said. "Apparently, the Chess King doesn't mind … that."

I gestured at Holiday Man, who was now struggling to blow a balloon. He kept blowing air into it, but his lungs must not have been very strong because each breath barely inflated it. He eventually gave up and, throwing the flat balloon over his shoulder, said, "Good to hear! I'll do my best to make the Chess King laugh with my unique and hilarious sense of humor. I wonder what sort of pranks he'll like best? Maybe a whoopie cushion? Or maybe a good old pie to the face. That's always a crowd-pleaser."

"We're not hitting the leader of a foreign country in the face with a pie," I said. "Especially if it's a pie served at dinner tonight and especially *this* leader."

Holiday Man folded his arms in front of his chest and pouted. "Fine. I'll try not to be uproariously funny and entertaining, which is hard considering how I'm April Fool's Man and all."

Brave Storm, on the other hand, tilted his head to the side and said, "What do you mean by *this* leader, Roger? You make it sound like you're not terribly enthused about seeing the Chess King."

I looked at Brave Storm. "Remember E2? Although I doubt the Chess King will kill us here, I still don't think we should let our guard down around him."

"Why did you accept his offer to come to Cheskia at all if you don't trust him?" said Shining Armor with a frown. "We didn't *have* to come, after all."

I scratched the back of my neck. "Because I want to get to the bottom of this mystery. Why is the Chess King so interested in me? Why did he send E2 after me like that? I don't like leaving mysteries unsolved and this is a mystery I can't ignore."

"Plus, one should never say no to a free vacation, lad," said Lumberjack wisely. "It is, after all, a good way to chop down trees in foreign countries." He suddenly stood up and stretched. "On a totally unrelated subject, I think I will go for a walk around the castle grounds to, er, stretch my ax. Yes, that's exactly what I'll do. My ax needs a lot of stretching after so much flying."

I gave Lumberjack a deadpan look. "You're not planning to chop down any trees you see while on your 'walk,' are you?"

Lumberjack folded his hands behind his back innocently. "Why in the world would I ever do that, Doctor? I am but an innocent flower that happens to hold a grudge against all trees for the crimes they committed against my family. And like a flower, once I am fully bloomed, I will destroy all my enemies and avenge the deaths of my parents."

"Do flowers do that?" asked Goggles in amazement. "I thought they just looked pretty."

I raised my hands. "Fine. You guys do what you want, but I want everyone to be in my room by seven. I imagine the Chess King will send someone to pick us up, so I want us all to be ready by then, okay?"

Everyone nodded, although given their slightly-distracted expressions, I did not feel exactly confident that they shared my

FAKE CHESS

definition of 'best behavior.'

But I supposed we'd deal with that when we crossed that bridge.

For now, I needed to focus on getting ready for my dinner with the potentially insane Chess King of Cheskia ... and hope that we weren't about to walk into a trap.

CHAPTER EIGHT

F ORTUNATELY, WHEN seven rolled around, everyone gathered in my room just like I asked, clad in their costumes and everything. I did not ask any of them what they'd been up to in the intervening hours, but given how, a few hours later, I overheard a couple of castle servants complaining about what looked like a failed chopping attempt on one of the trees in the courtyard, I had an idea.

Anyway, I didn't really have time to think about it because D2 herself showed up not too long after. She guided us through the rather massive, complicated hallways of Castle Rook until we finally reached the Dining Hall.

The Dining Hall was easily the largest room in the castle I'd seen so far. Massive arches supported a ceiling that depicted a chess game in progress, with a white hand reaching for the White pieces and a black hand reaching for the Black pieces. Burning torches on the walls in between the tall windows that offered an excellent view of the outside provided much of the lighting, along with a crystalline chandelier. Banners depicting what I assumed was the Cheskian Royal Family coat of arms—a simple, four-box design featuring the King and Queen in one box, the Bishops in another, the Knights in the third, and the Rooks in the fourth—hung from the ceiling or partially obscured the windows.

FAKE CHESS

But what most stood out to me was the heavenly smell of delicious food, which sat along a stupidly long dining room table that went from one end of the room to the other. I smelled ham, mashed potatoes, steak, corn, and all sorts of other food. It was enough to make my mouth water instantly, although I did my best not to drool.

Lumberjack, however, seemed to have less self-control than I did, because he was practically drooling all over his beard at the delicious food. "The food reminds me of Canada. Especially the sausage, which reminds me of the sausage that my father used to make from the animals we'd raise ourselves."

"I am pleased you seem to like the smell of the food," said D2, who stood beside me, her arms folded behind her back. "The Cheskian Royal Family has been served by the Royal Chefs for generations. My father is the current Royal Chef and he is, not to be biased, one of the best chefs in the world."

I looked at D2 in surprise. "You're the daughter of the Royal Chef? I didn't realize you had a connection with the Royal Family aside from working for them."

D2 nodded. "Oh, yes. Although it was not easy for me to become one of the Eight, even with the advantages brought from living among royalty for all my life." She rubbed her stomach. "But even if I had not become one of the Eight, I would have still eaten better than even some of the nobles in the Chess King's court. One of the advantages of being the daughter of the Royal Chef."

I nodded in return and gazed out over the Dining Hall again, noting how empty it was. "Where is the Chess King, if you don't mind me asking? I figured he would be here already, but all I see is a bunch of other superheroes."

That was true. Perhaps I should have mentioned this before, but the Dining Hall was full of other superheroes. You could tell because they were all dressed as freakishly as us, although freakish according to whatever country they happened to be from.

61

Most were already seated at tables scattered around the Dining Hall, tiny king- and queen-shaped salt and pepper bottles next to their plates. A cacophony of different languages filled the air, ranging from Japanese to Portuguese to Russian and everything in between. Even heard some Swahili in there, of all things.

"Are those our competitors?" asked Goggles, standing on my other side, his gaze sweeping the room. "Wow. I didn't realize there were so many."

"Twenty-four superheroes representing twelve different countries," said D2. She patted me on the shoulder. "That's two superhero chess players per country. And you, Doctor Mind, are representing America."

I frowned. "Me? Seriously? But who is my second?"

"Howdy there, partner!" a loud Southern voice suddenly blared. "Nice to meet ya!"

Startled, I looked in front of me and found myself face-to-face with an obnoxiously fat, white-suited old man in a ten gallon white hat. He leaned on a black cane for support, a grin peeking out from his rather impressive mustache. He smelled vaguely of hay and sweat, causing my nose to wrinkle slightly.

"Hello there, Mr. South," said D2 politely. "I see that you've already found the fried chicken."

The old man—apparently named Mr. South—took a chunk out of the chicken leg in his hand, chewed quickly, and swallowed. "Yup! Good stuff. Not as good as what we've got in Georgia, but good enough for this old boy. The sweet tea ain't too bad neither."

"Doctor Mind, this is Mr. South," said D2, gesturing at the guy in front of me. "He's the other American superhero chess player representing your country, though he came on a separate flight."

Looking at Mr. South again, I said, "Oh, nice to meet you, Mr. South. Are you a Heroes United member?"

"Yup!" said Mr. South again, licking the chicken grease off

his lips. "I'm the superhero of Atlanta, Georgia, which also is where HU is headquartered. And I've definitely heard about you, Doctor."

I gulped. "You have?"

"Yup," said Mr. South in what I was starting to assume was some kind of vocal tick. He waved his chicken leg around. "But don't you worry nothin', young man. Whatever your past might be in America, here in Cheskia, we're gonna show all these foreigners why America is number one."

"Mr. South is currently the highest-ranked superhero chess player in the United States," said D2, her polite, even tone a sharp contrast to Mr. South's bombastic speech patterns. "That is why he was invited."

"Darn right I am," said Mr. South. "Tell ya what, I sure was pleased to receive that invitation from old Laskar, but not surprised. He's certainly getting on in his years, so I was expecting something like this to come along soon."

"What do you mean?" I said in confusion. "Is there something wrong with the Chess King?"

Mr. South gave D2 a disbelieving look and pointed at me with his chicken leg. "Miss, didn't ya tell Doctor Mind here what's going on?"

D2 shook her head. "I didn't. I assumed he had figured it out already."

"Figure *what* out already?" I said in annoyance. "I'm right here, you know."

"I can see that, boy," said Mr. South. He chuckled suddenly. "Ah, never mind. I'm sure you'll find out soon. Rumor says the announcement's tonight, but if y'all want, there's room at my table to eat with me and my crew."

Mr. South jerked a thumb over his shoulder at a table nearby, where a couple of teenagers—a boy and a girl wearing skintight black-and-white spandex costumes—sat ravenously eating their meals. The two teenagers bore a strong resemblance to each other and even to Mr. South, making me think they must be his children as well as his sidekicks.

Before I could decline his offer, however, D2 stepped forward and said, "Apologies, Mr. South, but Doctor Mind and the Fakers are having dinner with the Chess King himself tonight. Thank you for the generous offer, however."

A surprised look appeared on Mr. South's elderly features. "Eh? With old Laskar himself? Fascinatin'. That must mean ... ha! As clever as ever, the old man is."

"Mind sharing what you find so amusing, sir?" I said.

Mr. South waved his chicken leg again. "Naw. If you can't figure it out, spelling it out for ya would just be a waste of time. Pearls before swine and all that. Anyway, nice meeting ya. See y'all later."

Mr. South turned and walked over back to his table, where he plopped down onto his chair hard enough to make it shudder and groan under his weight. But the chair held and Mr. South started gorging himself on more fried chicken, eating even more and faster than his sidekicks were. It was kind of a disgusting sight, honestly.

I raised an eyebrow at D2. "Mr. South made it sound like he knows the Chess King."

D2 nodded, seemingly unfazed by Mr. South's pig-like appetite. "Indeed. I do not know their entire history together, but I believe they met once at an international chess tournament in London when they were both young. That is partially why His Majesty invited Mr. South to the tournament, although do not be fooled. I've studied some of Mr. South's games myself and he is an excellent player, though still not quite as good as His Majesty, of course."

Hmm. I hadn't realized that some of the players might have already met the Chess King before. I wondered how many of the other players had known Chess King before the tournament and which ones hadn't. I definitely fit in the latter category, although I

FAKE CHESS

now wondered if I was the *only* one who did.

D2 clapped her hands together suddenly. "In any case, let me get you all seated before His Majesty arrives. Come with me."

D2 moved rapidly toward the big table in the middle of the room and my teammates and I followed. I wanted to ask D2 more about what Mr. South meant by his cryptic comments about the Chess King, but D2 didn't stay still long enough for me to ask her anything. She just sat us all down at our respective seats on either side of the table with the practiced ease of someone who had done this sort of thing her whole life.

And just in time, too, because just as I took my seat, the big doors on the other end of the room swung open and all chatter in the Dining Hall ceased as every eye turned toward the now-open doors. A cold breeze blew in from outside, which I could feel even from here, making me shiver slightly and causing the candles on the table in front of us to shudder, though they did not go out.

"Why did the doors open?" asked Goggles, who sat to my right. He suddenly clutched my cape in fear. "Ghosts?"

"No," said D2, who stood behind us, her arms folded behind her. Her gaze was fixed on the open doors. "His Majesty."

As soon as D2 said that, a single Pawn appeared in the doorway, looking rather small in the massive open doorway. He appeared to be one of the Eight, like D2, and with an uncomfortable jolt, I recognized him as E2, who I hadn't seen since our 'game' in Freedom City last month. From a distance, the deceptively-skinny pawn cosplayer with 'E2' painted on his mask looked pretty much the same as ever, although I noticed he wore a rather thick fur coat, perhaps because of how cold the night was.

"All rise for the arrival of His Majesty King Magnus Laskar II, the Chess King of Cheskia, and his court!" E2 announced, his voice booming in the cavernous Dining Hall.

Everyone stood up from their table, including us. Admittedly,

I did have to grab Goggles and make him stand up with us, but fortunately, everyone on the team was standing by the time the Chess King himself appeared.

This was the first time I'd seen the Chess King in person, and I have to say, he looked more impressive in person than in the pictures I'd seen on the Internet. Tall and thin, the Chess King nonetheless walked with power and authority and confidence. He was draped in white robes that made him look like a literal king piece, but whereas the Eight Pawns' get-ups made them look kind of silly, the Chess King actually pulled it off.

By his side, her arm wrapped around his, was who I assumed to be the Chess Queen. She was a bit shorter than her husband and had darker skin, making me think she had to be of Indian descent (and I mean India Indian, not Native American Indian). She was also dressed like a literal queen piece, complete with big crown that looked almost too big for her head. Despite that, she walked with exactly the same sense of authority as the Chess King, if not more so. For some reason, I sensed that she might be more of a threat than her husband, although given how old both of them were, I doubted they would be that tough in a fight.

"That's him?" said Brave Storm, who stood next to Goggles. "Huh. I was expecting someone a little tall—"

"Shhh!" D2 hissed at Brave Storm suddenly. "Show some respect. The King's ears are everywhere."

D2's comment prompted my brother to look around suddenly, as if expecting to see the Chess King's literal ears everywhere. I, of course, understood what she meant, which is why I kept my mouth shut. I didn't want to get on the Chess King's bad side before I even got a chance to meet the guy. I liked to think I had a bit more sense than that, even if I still wasn't entirely sure about his motives for inviting me here in the first place.

And then a third person came in behind them. He was clearly a much younger man than the Chess King, wearing clothing that looked similar to the Chess King's get-up, but not quite as flashy.

FAKE CHESS

He didn't look like any chess piece I'd seen, though the two men who followed him—the ones who resembled walking castles—most definitely were the Rooks I'd heard about. I ignored them, however, to focus on the young man, whose youthful features made him look like a younger version of the Chess King. He looked strangely familiar, too, as if I'd just seen him somewhere, though I couldn't place where. The young man kept a respectful distance from the Chess King and even D2 seemed to tense at his appearance for some reason.

That was when I felt a burning gaze land on my face. I looked at the Chess King and saw that he was staring directly at me. His intense black eyes made me feel like he was not only reading my mind, but knew exactly who I was and how my mind worked. He only looked at me for maybe a second before turning his gaze to the rest of the competitors, although I felt like he was still looking at me without looking at me. It was a weird feeling and I didn't like it.

E2, who stood by the doors, stepped forward as the doors closed seemingly by themselves and, gesturing at the Chess King, said, "Competitors, may I introduce to you King Magnus Laskar II, the Chess King of Cheskia, and his wife, Queen Judit Laskar, the Chess Queen of Cheskia! Tonight is the traditional pre-game dinner, a Cheskian tradition where big, lavish meals are provided to the participants of a big chess tournament the night before. Tonight, you will eat and drink and be merry, while the Chess King and Queen will enjoy their meal amid the celebrations."

The participants started to clap, which I also did, although I didn't know why. Then again, based on the slightly puzzled expressions from the other participants, it was pretty clear that no one else really knew anything about Cheskian traditions and customs, either.

But both the Chess King and Queen looked pleased with the reception, so I assumed we were doing something right.

That is, until Goggles—the poor kid—suddenly pointed at the

young man behind the Chess King and Queen and said, "Hey! I have a question!"

All eyes in the Dining Hall turned as one to look at Goggles. My neck suddenly got a lot hotter, especially when I saw what appeared to be an annoyed scowl appear across the Chess King's expression.

Goggles, on the other hand, did not look perturbed by being the unwanted center of attention. He just kept pointing at the young man, who looked as astonished as everyone else by Goggles' interruption.

"Goggles," I whispered, gentling resting a hand on his shoulder. "Come on, man. This isn't school. This is a formal event that clearly has a lot of history and tradition behind—"

"What is your question, young man?" asked the shockingly deep, booming, Cheskian-accented voice of the Chess King.

Startled, Goggles and I looked up to see the Chess King looking directly at us again. Only this time, he was looking at both me and Goggles, rather than me alone, though that did little to alleviate the sheer pressure I felt coming from his intense gaze.

Goggles wavered slightly, perhaps feeling the same pressure that I did, but the kid showed some admirable strength when he said, "The guy behind you wasn't introduced. Who is he?"

Goggles' question prompted everyone to turn their attention from the Chess King to the young man behind him. The young man straightened up suddenly and raised his chin, although it was clearly a failed effort to look regal. I almost felt sorry for the guy.

I felt especially sorry for the guy when the Chess King whirled around and slammed the tip of his scepter into the young man's face.

The golden scepter crashed into the young man's face with the force of a meteor and it was all anyone could do to watch as the young man collapsed onto the floor of the Dining Hall like a falling building. A painful groan emitted from the young man as he clutched his face, while utter silence fell over everyone else in

FAKE CHESS

the room.

The Chess King, however, turned away from the injured young man, returning his harsh gaze back to Goggles. "That, my young American friend, is my son, Gary Laskar, the Chess Prince of Cheskia. And a massive disappointment to any father with decent chess skills."

CHAPTER NINE

I WAS USUALLY pretty good at figuring out if someone was being sarcastic or ironic. After all, I liked to think of myself as practiced in the art of snark, honed especially over the last two months dealing with the, er, 'eccentricities' of my teammates.

But even I was stumped by the Chess King's description of Gary as his 'favorite' son who was also a 'massive disappointment.' No matter how hard my brain worked, I just couldn't wrap my mind around how those two concepts could possibly coexist. Then again, my mind was still processing the fact that the Chess King had just assaulted his son in front of everyone and acted like it was just the sort of thing you do. Made me feel grateful that my late dad had never treated any of us that way growing up.

Except he should have done that to Fernando. Who would deserve it. Honestly.

Anyway, looking around, I realized I wasn't the only one who was questioning the Chess King's odd move. The other participants were exchanging looks with each other at their tables. Even jolly old Mr. South looked a bit unnerved by the Chess King's random act of violence, though there was a hint of resignation in his eyes, too, as if he wasn't that surprised. Given how Mr. South and the Chess King knew each other already, maybe he'd been like this since he was younger.

FAKE CHESS

That would be an awesome legal defense in court. 'Your Honor, my client has always been prone to violently beating his children for disappointing him. It isn't something he started doing when they became adults. Therefore, he's not guilty, Your Honor. Case closed.'

In fact, it was another sidekick—a young-looking Japanese teenaged girl dressed like a butterfly, of all things—who asked, in shaky, but clear English, "Is he okay—?"

"*Gary* is just fine," said E2 with a malicious chuckle. "The Chess King simply displayed his displeasure in the traditional way that a Cheskian father shows his disapproval of his idiot son's failure."

"By hitting them in the face with a scepter?" said a man in a monkey costume who looked kind of Brazilian, skepticism covering his face.

"You are a foreigner who simply does not understand the customs of our ancient people," said E2 smugly. "Again, show some respect."

"That is enough, E2," said the Chess King. He leaned on his staff. "I tire of standing here beating my disappointment of a son. Everyone, you may sit down and resume your meals while my wife and I sit down to have ours."

"You heard His Majesty," E2 snapped at everyone. He pointed at our chairs and said, in a tone that most people usually reserved for commanding dogs, "Sit!"

Everyone, including me and my team, immediately sat back down in our seats, though not without shooting E2 some rather ugly glares. Couldn't blame them. E2's friendly, humble personality was something that most people did not find very appealing (and that didn't even get into his attempted murder of my teammates).

While everyone resumed their meals, the Chess King and Queen walked over to us, escorted by their Rooks and E2. Gary, who apparently wasn't respected enough to be referred to by his actual royal title, followed behind them, but at a safe distance. The exact distance, in fact, that one would need to walk to stay outside of the reach of the Chess King's scepter. I wondered how often the Chess King hit Gary that he had apparently figured out how far he'd need to stand to avoid getting beaten by his dear father.

The Chess King took the empty spot at the head of our table, which just so happened to be the spot nearest me. The Chess Queen sat directly opposite me on the other side of the table while Gary took an empty seat on her left. Gary did not make eye contact with me or any of my other teammates, instead choosing to focus on the large steak in front of him, which he started to cut into and eat as if he hadn't eaten all day.

D2, meanwhile, drifted over to the other side of the table behind the Chess Queen, while E2 took up a position behind and to the right of the Chess King. That gave E2 a clear look at me, which I suspected was intentional, based on the way he looked at me.

"Ah, Doctor Mind," said E2 in a more professional tone than what he'd used to address poor Gary. "It feels like it's been an age since we last saw each other."

Smiling, I said, "Yeah, it has been a while since I kicked your ass in chess and stopped you from murdering my teammates. I hope you've gotten better at chess, at least."

Although E2's mask—which he must have repaired at some point since it was no longer broken from our last encounter—hid his face quite well, his tense body language told me everything I needed to know. I heard a soft snort across from me and looked at Gary, but he kept his face firmly focused on his food, even though it was abundantly clear that he was listening to every word we said.

"You should show more respect to the King's Pawn, Doctor," said E2, barely able to hide the seething anger in his voice. "For I was handpicked by the Chess King himself to serve as one of the

FAKE CHESS

Eight, so—"

"A decision I am starting to regret now," said the Chess King dryly. He sipped the wineglass before him and glanced at me. "Seeing as you defeated E2 in chess, perhaps you would like to be my new King's Pawn, Doctor. How does that sound?"

Taken aback, I said, "Um, er, that's generous of you, Your Majesty, but I'm afraid I'll have to decline. I like playing chess, but not quite enough to want to move to Cheskia and play it with you forever."

The Chess King nodded as if he'd expected me to say that. "Disappointing, but understandable. I suppose I'll have to look elsewhere for a suitable replacement for Bobby."

"Bobby?" I said. "Who's that?"

"That's my real name," said E2 in a tight voice. "Robert Bauer, but I'm sure it was just a slip of His Majesty's tongue, since we Pawns are always referred to be our code names."

The Chess King shrugged. "It is true that my tongue is becoming harder to control in my old age. Indeed, many things have become difficult for me as I've aged, although I hope my chess skills, at least, have not degraded to Bobby's level."

E2 jerked back at the Chess King's last jab, almost as if the Chess King had smashed his scepter into his face. It took all of my willpower not to smirk, although I needn't have bothered because a quick smirk crossed the Chess King's face before his usual bored expression returned.

"Anyway, I must apologize for the lack of proper introductions," said the Chess King. He held out a hand toward me. "You heard E2 introduce me before, but it is still a pleasure to meet you, Doctor Mind."

I took the Chess King's hand and shook it. "Same here, Your Majesty, although you don't need to refer to me by my superhero name. Mr. Manuel will work just fine."

The Chess King's grip on my hand tightened considerably, causing me to look at him in surprise. An intense, focused expression appeared on his elderly face and he said, in a strangely intense voice, "But this is a superhero tournament. I *like* calling superheroes by their superhero names."

I gulped. "Er, um, okay. If that makes you feel—I mean, you can do whatever you want, Your Majesty. You're the boss."

The Chess King's iron grip did not lessen for at least a second or two, but then he abruptly let go of my hand and sat back, a calmer expression crossing his face. "Yes. And you may refer to me as the Chess King, rather than by my real name."

I nodded politely. "Yes, sir. Of course."

The Chess King nodded in return and started digging into his own steak, swiftly cutting through it with his fork and knife. He popped a portion of the steak into his mouth and chewed and swallowed before starting on his other food, seemingly oblivious to my presence.

"Please do not mind my husband too much," said the Chess Queen across from me. She had a soft Indian accent and spoke far more softly than the Chess King. She reached over and patted him on the shoulder. "I keep telling Magnus to watch his blood pressure but he insists on getting so worked up about everything."

"It is not my fault I was born with a fire in my stomach," said the Chess King through a mouthful of mashed potato. He swallowed the potatoes and, glaring down the table, said, "Unlike my idiot son, who was born with ice cream in his stomach and rubber on his feet."

Gary winced slightly at the Chess King's remark, but he still didn't look up. He did mutter under his breath, "But which tree did the apple fall from, Father?"

"Gary has ice cream in his stomach?" said Goggles beside me, blinking at the Chess Prince.

"It's a Cheskian expression," D2 explained patiently. "It's ... well, perhaps this isn't the time to explain it, but it is not a *kind* thing one parent says about one's children, to put it one way. Same with the rubber feet comment."

FAKE CHESS

I noticed D2 glanced at the Chess King when she said that. Probably she didn't want to offend or annoy the Chess King by explaining the Cheskian idiom, which was fine by me. I already felt like I was eating dinner with a hungry tiger anyway. No need to make him even more unpredictable than he already was.

Sipping my wineglass quickly, I looked at the Chess King again and said, "So, um, Chess King, thank you for inviting us to your tournament and paying for our travel expenses. It was very generous of you."

"It is of no issue, Doctor," said the Chess King, waving his greasy fork at me. " 'One should always pay for top chess players.' That is what my father used to tell me, at least before he died."

"Oh," I said. "I'm sorry to hear that. When—?"

"He died when I was six," said the Chess King. "Perished after playing six hundred consecutive games of chess in a seventy-two-hour period. Like a true man."

I blinked. "Ah. Well. I see why your father was also called the Chess King, then."

The Chess King looked at me with that same intense expression suddenly, holding his fork, which had a bit of asparagus skewered on the end, in midair between his mouth and his plate. "My father was not the Chess King."

"He wasn't?" I said. "Was your mother royalty, then?"

The Chess King shook his head. He lowered the asparagus onto the plate. "She was a seamstress. Who did not die playing chess, but taught me almost as much as my father did about the game."

"Oh," I said, feeling more confused than anything now. "So how did you become the—?"

"That reminds me," said the Chess King suddenly. He dropped his fork and knife onto the plate and looked at the Chess Queen. "I was going to make an important announcement before someone pointed out my idiot son to me."

LUCAS FLINT

"An important announcement?" I said. "About what?"

The Chess King, however, did not seem to notice my question. He merely rose from his seat and held out a hand toward E2, who handed the Chess King a microphone that seemed to have come from nowhere. That was when I noticed the speakers hanging in the corners of the ceiling of the Dining Hall overhead, speakers which I had not even noticed until now.

But they sure became obvious when the Chess King spoke into the microphone and said, his voice blaring from the speakers, "Tournament competitors! I have an important announcement to make regarding the tournament and wish for all to hear it."

Again, every eye in the Dining Hall turned to look at the Chess King, although even if he hadn't ordered everyone to look at him, I felt like most people would have. The speakers hanging from the ceiling were loud enough to be pretty much impossible to ignore unless you were deaf, and even a deaf person might find it hard to ignore the sheer force of the sound waves that emitted from the speakers.

With every eye in the Dining Hall now on the Chess King, he began speaking, saying, "Welcome, tournament competitors, to the first-ever International Superhero Chess Tournament, hosted by yours truly! I am so pleased to see some of the best superhero chess players in the world gathered together here tonight to participate in this most ambitious tournament. A few of you I even recognize from past chess tournaments, both held here in Cheskia and in other countries, although there are many new faces as well."

The Chess King was probably referring to Mr. South, although I noticed the heroes at the Japanese table snort and mutter something to each other in Japanese.

Me personally, I was thinking that 'best superhero chess players' was a rather niche category of chess players. As a matter of fact, I wasn't even sure there were any chess-specific publications or groups dedicated to us. It made me wonder why

FAKE CHESS

the Chess King decided to hold a superhero-specific tournament, rather than one open to everyone. Cheskia was certainly no stranger to hosting World Championships.

His gray eyes scanning the Dining Hall, the Chess King said, "Yes, I fully expect this to be a tournament to remember. With representatives from some of the best chess-playing countries in the world, the talent in this room is almost hard to believe. But believe it I do, for I have reviewed the scores and rankings of each person in here and know exactly what sort of chess styles you prefer."

For some reason, I felt like the Chess King glanced at me when he said that, although it might have just been my eyes playing tricks on me.

"But you all know that already, I'm sure," said the Chess King. "I am well aware that I have not actually revealed the grand prize for winning the tournament. That was a deliberate effort on my part. I only hinted at the riches which await the eventual champion, but did not say what they were outright because I only wanted true chess players to accept my invite. Many players refused my offer because I would not say what the grand prize is, which is fine. I do not need such shortsighted, greedy people here. I need only those who have a genuine love for the game and a genuine desire to win no matter what."

Or a genuine desire to figure out why the heck you had one of your minions try to murder my friends, I thought, but did not say aloud.

"Since the tournament is starting tomorrow, however, I've decided that now is the best time to reveal the grand prize," the Chess King continued. "It is greater than money, greater than an all-expenses-paid vacation, greater, even, than the most prized titles and awards."

The Chess King's eyes swept across the Dining Hall and, again, for a moment I felt like they had landed on me, although they didn't linger for very long at all before the Chess King fixed his gaze on everyone again.

Pointing at the crown on his head, the Chess King said, "The champion of the International Superhero Chess Tournament will get to play a match against me. And if they defeat me, then I will abdicate the Chess Throne and the champion of the tournament will be declared the new Chess King of Cheskia, complete with all of the power and prestige that that title suggests."

CHAPTER TEN

To say that the Chess King's announcement landed like a bomb among the competitors was the understatement of the year. Everywhere I looked, shocked and stunned expressions appeared on the faces of the various superheroes from all over the world. Mr. South's female sidekick even outright fainted, forcing Mr. South and his male sidekick to grab her to make sure she didn't fall onto the floor.

Although Mr. South's female sidekick's reaction was, perhaps, the most extreme reaction, I understood her feelings quite well. Normal chess tournaments typically offered the winners things like prize money or stuff like that. They certainly never offered the winner leadership over an entire country.

But the Chess King's expression was not joking or sarcastic. He spoke with absolute conviction, as if delivering a dictate from God Himself. His challenging gaze even swept the Dining Hall again, as if daring anyone to stand up and declare their intention to defeat him.

The Chess Queen, too, looked very serious when her husband basically announced that anyone could try to take his job, and unsurprised. It made sense that she had already known this, but whether she was happy about it or not, I couldn't tell. She had a great poker face.

Gary, however, was a lot worse at hiding his displeasure. He balled his hands into tight fists, showing the whites of his knuckles against his skin. His expression was a weird mixture of resignation and grimace, like he couldn't decide if he should just accept things as they were or try to fight them. Granted, he also looked kind of constipated, but I liked to think he was just really bad at hiding his emotions unlike his parents.

Apparently, the Chess King saw no reason to elaborate on what he meant. He just handed the microphone back to E2, who also looked unsurprised by the Chess King's announcement, and sat back down in his chair. I glanced at D2, but she appeared as unsurprised as E2, so I assumed that she and E2 had already known about the grand prize for the tournament.

I could have asked the Chess King myself to explain his announcement, but to be frank, I was still processing his words. I just couldn't imagine myself leading a country, even a small one like Cheskia.

Fortunately, Goggles leaned across me toward the Chess King and asked, "Mr. Your Majesty, what did you mean that the winner would become Chess King? Does that mean just, like, getting to call yourself King of Chess or something?"

The Chess King paused when his spoonful of soup was halfway between his bowl and his mouth. He looked at Goggles with an amused grin. "It's not merely a *title* that the champion will receive, my boy. The champion will become the new Chess King of Cheskia in name, power, and right. In the same way that the winner of your presidential elections becomes the official President of the United States, the champion of the tournament will become the official Chess King of Cheskia and get to sit on my throne."

Snapped out of my shock by the Chess King's words, I, too, leaned forward and said, "With all due respect, Your Majesty, I'm not sure this is a great idea. None of us—that is, the competitors—are part of the Cheskian Royal Family or even

FAKE CHESS

Cheskian at all. Giving up the throne to someone who can beat you at chess is … strange, to put it one way."

The Chess King gave me a confused look. "What are you talking about, Doctor? This is the way Cheskia has always been run. The player who defeats the current Chess King then becomes the leader of the country."

I blinked. "That's how your government seriously works?"

"Yes," said D2, causing me and Goggles to turn our attention to her. She had not moved from her position behind the Chess Queen, who was quietly eating her steak. "The Kingdom of Cheskia is a chessocracy. That means that it is a government by and for chess players."

I blinked again and looked at the Chess King. "So you mean even *you* had to be really good at chess to become the Chess King?"

The Chess King nodded. " 'Have,' not 'had,' because as the Chess King, I am always in danger of losing my title to some new upstart. Quite a challenging job, I assure you."

"What His Majesty means is that leadership is not decided upon in a single election every four years, the way the American government works," D2 explained. "Leadership is instead decided by whoever is capable of beating the Chess King in a chess match. Any adult over the age of 18 can challenge the current Chess King to a chess match at any time. If the challenger wins, that challenger automatically gains the title of Chess King and all power in the Cheskian government switches over to him."

"My," I said. "That is a … unique way of running a government."

By 'unique,' of course, I meant 'stupid.' But I certainly wasn't going to say that to the Chess King's face, at least not directly. Let it never be said that Doctor Mind is not a prudent man.

"It is the way that Cheskia has always been run, right from its founding," said D2. "And it isn't a one-and-done deal, either, as you Americans like to put it. The Chess King must constantly protect his throne from all challengers, so the Chess King has a powerful incentive to keep honing his skills. For if he were to lower his guard for even a second, he would lose a game and his title and be thrown bodily out onto the streets by his former servants."

The Chess King nodded with a cheery smile on his face. "It's true. When I came into power fifty years ago, I *did* throw my opponent out onto the streets, where he was chased by the Royal Hounds, which no longer served him. It was quite amusing."

I grimaced. "I see. But, um, most of us competitors aren't even Cheskian citizens."

"Yes," said Gary for the first time, suddenly looking up from his own soup bowl at me. "Tradition says that only Cheskian citizens may challenge the Chess King to a duel for the leadership of the nation."

"Tradition also says that the children of the Chess King should not be running around in spandex playing as superheroes," the Chess King said without missing a beat, "rather than focusing on their royal duties and mastering their chess skills."

That seemed like an oddly specific jab at Gary, which must have worked because Gary looked down into his soup bowl again. He began shoveling spoonfuls of potato soup into his mouth, probably to avoid having to respond to his father.

Okay. There was clearly some weird drama going on in the Cheskian Royal Family that I was not aware of and which I wasn't sure I *wanted* to know about.

"If Uncle wins, does that mean he will get your wife, too?" said Goggles in horror, looking at the Chess Queen.

The Chess Queen chuckled. "Flattering, but no. Should Doctor Mind, or any of the other competitors for that matter, defeat my husband and take his title, I will have to find a suitable replacement for myself. The title of Chess Queen always transfers to the strongest female player in the country, so I would need to

FAKE CHESS

find a female player who can defeat me in chess."

Honestly, I would have breathed a sigh of relief for that alone if I wasn't too busy trying to avoid needlessly offending or insulting the Cheskian Royal Family. Although the Chess Queen wasn't exactly ugly as far as older women went, I just couldn't imagine being with her. Unlike certain guys I knew, I wasn't into older women. Just not my style.

"And you will not adopt my son, either," said the Chess King. He picked up a samosa and took a bite out of it. "Lucky for you, my idiot son will only be my problem. But if you are as unlucky as me, you might get an idiot son of your own someday."

I didn't know how Gary was constantly taking that kind of abuse from his dad without snapping. Based on how tightly he gripped his fork, however, it looked to me like Gary was at the breaking point.

"Right," I said. I cleared my throat. "But why are you offering the position of Chess King as the main reward for whoever wins the tournament, Your Majesty? Seems like a rather, er, generous gift."

The Chess King shot me a mysterious smile. "When I first came up with the idea for this tournament, I tried to think of what would be the most desirable prize that you superheroes would want. I considered offering a simple monetary reward and trophy like what most chess tournaments offer, but I couldn't stand the idea of simply copying what someone else has already done. It occurred to me, then, that I had one thing I could offer that literally no other chess tournament in the world could: The title of Chess King itself."

"That's it?" I said. "You just wanted to come up with a unique prize for people to win?"

The Chess King's mysterious smile grew even more mysterious. "And what is wrong with that? Unlike the leaders of other countries, I do not seek power for power's sake. I will reign on the throne only as long as my chess skills remain sharp.

Should they decline, it would only be right that I should lose my throne and be forced to abdicate."

"Indeed," said E2 suddenly. "That's why those Black Pawns are so despicable. They don't care about the traditions of our country. They seek to overthrow the Chess King by force, rather than by skill. Cowards, the lot of them."

Having recently had my own negative experience with the Black Pawns, I couldn't help but agree with E2's negative characterization of them. Granted, the Black Pawns were probably the sanest people in the country, seeing as they were trying to gain power the normal way rather than through playing chess. Then again, chess was significantly less violent than armed revolt, so maybe 'chessocracy' was a better political system than I thought.

"Yes," said the Chess King with a grimace. "Sometimes, I question whether I should have opened Cheskia's borders to the outside world. That is where ideas of revolution and force came from, for our chessocratic traditions have reigned in Cheskia since time immemorial. Indeed, legend has it that the very first Chess King established the 'Rule of Chess' during his reign to make sure that only the most competent player ever sat on the throne."

"Government and competence rarely go together in my experience," I said.

The Chess King shot me a smirk. "Because you choose leaders based on who says the nicest things or appeals to the broadest demographic. Democracy is essentially a glorified popularity contest, after all, whereas chessocracy is based on merit. Chess merit, granted, but merit nonetheless."

"Um, okay," I said. "I don't know if I would characterize our constitutional republic *that* way, but—"

"You are right," said the Chess King. "My apologies. We shouldn't discuss politics around the dinner table." He gestured at my barely-touched plate with his fork. "Please, finish enjoying

FAKE CHESS

your meal and we can discuss slightly less controversial topics, such as chess. Much more pleasant and infinitely less boring than politics."

I popped a samosa into my own mouth, chewing on the warm, flaky pastry, listening as the Chess King began to tell me stories about the games he'd played with some of the legends of chess.

I was only partially listening, however. I was mostly thinking about the Chess King's announcement and elaboration of the tournament's grand prize. His explanation cleared up a good deal of my confusion, but I still had a million questions.

For example, what were the Chess King's *real* motives in inviting us all to this tournament and offering us a shot at his crown? I wasn't convinced that it had anything to do with his desire to give us a unique prize. Giving people a chance to defeat you and take over your country wasn't the sort of opportunity you just handed out like candy, even in Cheskia.

No, I was convinced that the Chess King had very different motives for hosting the tournament, motives he was keeping to his chest.

And I was determined to get to the bottom of his motives, regardless of what they were.

CHAPTER ELEVEN

"ALL HAIL King Roger Manuel I, the Chess King of Cheskia! May His Chess-yness live forever!"

Lying on my bed in my room, I started and raised my head to see Brave Storm sitting on my room's couch next to Goggles. He'd removed his horned helmet, allowing me to see Brave Storm's face, which was identical to mine except older and slightly longer. He wore a big grin on his face, the same grin he wore whenever he was teasing me.

Folding my hands behind my head, I said, "That's enough, bro. I'm not actually the Chess King."

"Yet," Paranoyd added. He sat on a stool in the kitchen, a half-eaten chocolate candy bar in his hand. His eyes seemed to glow green. "Once you win this tournament, however, you *will* be. And you know what that will make us?"

"My friends who want to bum off me?" I said sarcastically.

"No!" said Paranoyd. He pointed his chocolate bar at me. "We'll be members of your inner court, which means we'll get all sorts of perks. That means I'll finally be able to quit my job at Denny's and be able to devote myself full-time to my Strange Mysteries YouTube channel!"

I looked at Paranoyd in confusion. "Wait, you mean you're still working for Denny's? I thought I was paying you enough that you could quit your job."

FAKE CHESS

Paranoyd returned the confused look. "You mean I could quit my job anytime I wanted? Huh. That didn't occur to me." He grinned. "I know the first thing *I'm* doing after we get home."

"Assuming we *do* go home," said Holiday Man, sitting on another stool in the kitchen on the other side of the island. He did not have a chocolate bar, although he did have a half-eaten chocolate bunny in his hands. "If Doctor Mind wins the tournament and becomes the new Chess King, then we might just stay here forever."

Cavewoman, who leaned against the wall next to the door of my room, shook her head. "Me no want stay here. Eastern Europe known for being sexist to women. Me move back to US, which also sexist to women, but that because this man's world where women have no power."

"Even though our president is a woman?" I said, raising my head to look at her skeptically.

Cavewoman waved a hand dismissively. "She Republican. She no count as real woman."

"I'm actually kind of excited about Doctor Mind becoming the new Chess King, personally," said Shining Armor. He sat on the floor in front of a puzzle of what looked like a medieval castle, which he had partially finished. He tapped his chest. "Then I'd get to be a *real* knight in shining armor to a *real* king. I would probably get to save real damsels in distress and pursue peace and justice wherever I go. I think it's great."

"Yes, but who cares about any of that?" said Lumberjack. He sat on the floor opposite Shining Armor, apparently helping him put the puzzle together. He picked up a piece and fit it in the upper right corner. "So long as the trees continue to exist, then it won't matter who sits on the throne. Unless Doctor Mind wishes to destroy all trees, that is."

"Even in the unlikely event that I win this tournament, we're not going to chop down all the trees in Cheskia," I said. "You'll just have to find something else to do."

Lumberjack pouted. "Fine. As your friend, I have to wish you good luck. But as a sworn enemy of the trees, I have to say I am disappointed."

I rubbed my forehead. "You guys are all missing the point. There's something weird going on here and I want to find out what."

"What do you mean, Uncle?" asked Goggles, tilting his head to the side. "Laskar is holding a chess tournament to find a suitable replacement for him as the Chess King. Doesn't seem very complicated to me."

"Yes, Goggles, but *why* is the Chess King looking for a replacement?" I said. "Why does he want to retire from being the Chess King? Why didn't he simply choose the best Cheskian players, rather than go to all of the trouble of inviting superhero chess players from all over the world? And why *superheroes*, specifically, especially since Laskar doesn't even seem to like us very much?"

"Those are all good questions," Holiday Man agreed. He popped the rest of his chocolate bunny into his mouth and started chewing it up. "But a more important question is where do they sell more chocolate bunnies in Cheskia. I brought this one with me from America, but if I'm going to have my fill of chocolate bunnies, then I will need to explore Chess City itself."

"Sounds like fun," said Goggles, clapping his hands together excitedly. "I'd like to explore the city with you. We really didn't get to see a whole lot of it on our way to the castle."

"Can we discuss our tourist plans later?" I said in despair. "Right now, this whole trip feels like one big puzzle that I haven't been able to make any sense of. I have all the pieces, but I don't know how they fit together."

Shining Armor glanced at the box for the puzzle that he and Lumberjack were putting together and frowned. "And you don't even have a box to act as reference."

FAKE CHESS

"We don't need boxes to figure out puzzles," Lumberjack insisted. He picked up another piece and slammed it, hard, into a part it clearly wasn't supposed to fit. "If necessary, we can force them all together and *make* them fit."

I grimaced. "I'm not sure we can solve all these mysteries that way."

Paranoyd suddenly looked at me again. "Solving mysteries, you say? Why didn't you put it that way the first time? I can definitely help you with that."

I looked at Paranoyd doubtfully. "You can?"

"Sure!" said Paranoyd. He jumped off the stool and tossed his empty chocolate bar wrapper into the nearby trash can. "In fact, I think I'll take a walk around this castle tonight and see what clues I can find. I'm a detective, after all, and I've solved loads of mysteries on my YouTube channel."

"You have?" I said. "Like what?"

"Like the case of the incongruity between hot dogs and hot dog buns," Paranoyd replied. "Why do hot dog packages always come with twelve hot dogs, while hot dog buns always come in packs of eight? I won't spoil the shocking answer, but if you want to watch it, just go to my YouTube channel and look for the video title 'MYSTERIES REVEALED: HOT DOGS AND BUNS.' It's my most popular video."

Goggles gasped and, pulling out his phone, started swiping across its surface quickly. "Really? I've always wondered about that myself."

"Yes," said Paranoyd grimly. "No spoilers, but the truth is *sickeningly* sinister and involves a grand conspiracy stretching back to Ancient Egypt, the pyramids, and the aliens who built them."

Goggles turned his attention to Paranoyd again. "What? Aliens built the pyramids? I thought humans did."

Paranoyd stroked his chin. "Again, no spoilers. Watch it for yourself."

Goggles nodded seriously and returned his attention to his phone. "I'll just subscribe to your channel so I can watch the video later."

"All right, but watch out," Paranoyd warned. "You can't put off the truth forever."

I was now starting to rethink Paranoyd's ability to get to the bottom of Laskar's true motives for hosting the tournament. On the other hand, I suppose Paranoyd couldn't possibly make it *worse*, although I had a strange feeling in the pit of my stomach that I was going to regret thinking that very soon.

Paranoyd looked at me again and gave me the thumbs up. "Anyway, no need to worry, boss man. I'll get to the bottom of this mystery even if it goes all the way to the top."

"You can try, I guess," I said unenthusiastically.

"I'm more interested in this Checkmate guy," said Brave Storm suddenly, causing Paranoyd and me to look at him. He was also looking at his phone, but it sounded like he was looking up more practical information than Goggles. "The chess-themed superhero who saved us from the Black Pawns back in the airport."

"Cavewoman forgot about him," said Cavewoman. She blushed. "Even though he kind of cute."

"What did you find out about him, bro?" I said, sitting up in bed to get a better view of Brave Storm.

Brave Storm shook his head. "Not much. He's barely known outside of Cheskia and even Cheskia's major newspaper, *The Cheskian Gazette*, doesn't have very many articles about him. Cheskian social media is plastered with pictures of him, though, so there seems to be a disconnect between the average Cheskian citizen's perception of him and how the Cheskian government views him."

"Interesting," I said, tapping my chin in thought. "That explains why D2 seemed so dismissive of him back in the airport and why the other passengers seemed to like him. I wonder where

FAKE CHESS

this disconnect came from."

Brave Storm's frown deepened. "Wait. I just found this article that says that Checkmate has been a 'prominent critic of the Chess King's handling of the Black Pawns.' It also says that a 2021 poll of the general population showed that Checkmate was more popular with the people than Laskar."

"So Laskar doesn't like Checkmate because he's not merely critical of his policies, but also more popular with the people?" I said. "Yeah, that sounds like government, all right. Good to know that some things don't change, even in foreign countries halfway across the world."

Brave Storm, his eyes still scanning his phone, said, "Yeah. That may be why Laskar hasn't done anything to him yet. Checkmate's apparently so beloved by the people that Laskar is afraid that major riots might break out if the government tries to do anything to him."

I tapped my chin again in thought. "Hmm, I wonder if Checkmate might possibly be able to explain some of the strange things we've seen since landing in this country. Does it say where Checkmate lives?"

Brave Storm quickly consulted his phone again and nodded. "Yeah. Checkmate's base is actually just a few blocks south of Castle Rook. It says it isn't open to the public, but you can apparently schedule meetings with him by contacting his agent."

"His agent?" I said. I shook my head. "Forget that. Checkmate knows who I am and why I'm in Cheskia. I'm sure we can get a meeting with him tomorrow before the tournament officially begins."

"Are you sure about that, Uncle?" said Goggles. "What makes you think that Checkmate will want to talk with you?"

"I don't know if Checkmate wants to talk to me," I said. "But it's worth a shot. It sounds like he is as skeptical of Laskar as I am. Since Checkmate has lived in Cheskia longer than me, he probably has a better understanding of Laskar's mind than I do."

"But what about my investigation?" asked Paranoyd with a pout. He gestured at his fedora. "I'm wearing my fedora and everything."

Folding my legs underneath me, I pointed at Paranoyd and said, "Okay, here's the plan. You can snoop around the castle grounds, see if you can find any clues that might help us figure out what's going on here. Maybe you can find some servants who might be willing to spill the beans or answer your questions. I, on the other hand, will head out tomorrow to meet with Checkmate and see if I can talk to him."

"A two-pronged approach," Paranoyd said thoughtfully. He grinned. "I like it."

"What about us?" asked Shining Armor, raising a hand like he was a child in school. "What are we gonna do?"

I looked at my other teammates. "Simple. You guys will come with me to Checkmate's base tomorrow. I have a feeling I'm going to need some support."

"Does that mean we can go explore the city a little bit?" asked Holiday Man eagerly.

I shrugged. "If you want to play tourist for a bit, that's fine by me. I probably won't need all of you with me, so if some of you guys just want to have fun, you can."

Holiday Man pumped his fist. "Awesome! Watch out, Chess City, because April Fool's Man is going to prank *all* of you!"

I grimaced. "Maybe don't have *too* much fun. Remember, no international incidents."

Holiday Man honked his gag nose. "Of course. I'd never cause an international incident, Doctor. Not unless it's funny, anyway."

I sighed and rubbed my forehead again. I was starting to regret bringing my teammates along on this trip, but on the other hand, if I'd left them in Freedom City, I wasn't sure there even *would* be a home for me to go back to.

FAKE CHESS

And anyway, I already know how to wrangle the eccentricities and oddities of my teammates.

It was Laskar's eccentricities—if you could call them that—that I didn't know how to deal with.

If I could deal with them, that is.

CHAPTER TWELVE

Have you ever walked down the street of a city in a foreign country and felt a bit out of place?

That's nothing compared to how I felt as Goggles, Cavewoman, Lumberjack, and I walked down Central Street toward Checkmate's base.

That's because we stood out, almost literally. All of the Cheskian citizens we saw on the street were painfully white. By 'white,' I mean they wore all-white clothing and costumes that made them look a bit like pawns, although their pawn masks did at least open up at the face, letting us see their actual faces. Even their faces were pretty darn white. I mean, I knew we were in Eastern Europe and all, but the skin tone of the average person looked whiter than snow.

The cobblestone streets were also pure white. You would be forgiven for thinking that a snowstorm must have blown through recently, but my phone's weather app said the next Cheskian snowstorm wasn't supposed to happen until next week. The buildings were also made of the same white stone and even the streetlamps were shaped like bishops, though their lights were dim in the sun overhead.

Seeing as my friends and I were still in our colorful superhero costumes, we stood out like a sore thumb. It didn't help that most of the Cheskians gave us a wide berth or shot us suspicious looks.

FAKE CHESS

A young mother even pushed her stroller across the busy street to avoid walking by us, which I would have been offended by if not for the fact that I could kind of understand why she might be a little suspicious of Cavewoman and Lumberjack.

Lumberjack, on the other hand, did not seem to understand why anyone would treat him with suspicion. Walking beside me with his ax resting on his shoulder, Lumberjack said, "Is it me or are these Cheskians very unfriendly people? We've been walking for at least five minutes and we haven't even gotten one 'Hello' or 'How are you doing?' or even a 'Cool ax, bro. How many trees have you cut down with it?'"

"Cavewoman agree," said Cavewoman, ducking her head to avoid walking into an overhanging shop sign for what looked like a chess shop. "Men afraid of strong, independent woman who no need no man. Patriarchy."

"The women are also avoiding us, though," said Goggles, walking behind me and glancing up at Cavewoman. "I think that Cheskians in general just aren't very friendly people."

"You man," Cavewoman responded with a dismissive wave. "You no understand what woman be like in man's world."

Goggles then looked at me and raised an eyebrow. "Why did we bring Cavewoman and Lumberjack with us again, Uncle?"

I sighed. "Because they were the only two who volunteered to come with me. And I needed to leave Brave Storm with Shining Armor and Holiday Man because they need an adult to make sure they don't cause an international scandal."

Lumberjack patted me on the shoulder with one of his big, rough hands. "Do not worry, Doctor! I see no trees in the immediate vicinity, so I will not run off to chop them down. You can rest assured that I will be on my best behavior during our meeting with Checkmate."

"Me see plenty of men to smash," said Cavewoman, eying a couple of guys working at a borscht stand, who immediately hid behind it when she passed, "but me not smash. Me save that for later."

I licked my lips uncertainly but didn't respond. Instead, I just thought about what happened last night after I laid out my plan to everyone.

Paranoyd had left my room almost immediately afterward, claiming that he was starting the investigation right away. He said he'd have some clues for us in the morning, but when we had breakfast in the Dining Hall, Paranoyd was nowhere to be seen and none of us knew where he was. I asked D2, but she said she hadn't seen Paranoyd, either, although she promised to have the Castle servants report any Paranoyd sightings to her, which she would then pass onto us.

In any case, after breakfast, my team and I split up. Cavewoman, Lumberjack, Goggles, and I were going to Checkmate's base to visit him, while Brave Storm, Holiday Man, and Shining Armor were going out on the town to explore Chess City to see if they could find Paranoyd. It seemed unlikely to me that Paranoyd had left the castle last night, but I didn't know that for sure and that we did need to make sure he was okay. Paranoyd was not the sort of person who just wandered off for no reason. If something had happened to him, we needed to find out what.

I was hoping that our meeting with Checkmate would not take too long. I didn't want to miss registration, which meant I couldn't spend too much time outside of the castle or wander too far from the grounds.

But I was confident that we would talk with Checkmate and be back in the castle well before lunch. Checkmate struck me as a fairly taciturn person, so I doubted he would waste much time talking. I was more concerned about what my teammates might say than what Checkmate might say. Despite telling Lumberjack and Cavewoman that I would do all the talking, I wouldn't put it past either of them to say something stupid that would get me and Goggles in trouble with Checkmate.

So why did I allow them to come with me at all? Mostly

FAKE CHESS

because I was still skittish after the Black Pawn hostage situation in the airport. Although I had not seen or heard any news about the Black Pawns since yesterday, I was still worried that they might try to kidnap me again. It seemed unlikely that they would try to kidnap me in such a public setting, but you never knew. Cavewoman and Lumberjack were the strongest members of the team, physically-speaking, so if we got into a fight, their muscular bulk would be very helpful.

But then I glanced at Lumberjack eying a wooden bench suspiciously and Cavewoman throwing an ugly scowl at a random guy who almost bumped into her and I wondered if I'd made the right choice.

I had no more time to regret my choices, however, before we finally reached Checkmate's base. Like pretty much every other building in Cheskia that we'd seen so far, it was heavily chess-themed. Painted pure white, the doors were flanked by two life-sized rook pieces, which I was almost certain weren't secretly robots in disguise, although I couldn't be sure about that. The door handles were knights, while the windows were covered with blinds that made it impossible to see inside. Behind the building, I caught a glimpse of some sort of white vehicle that was parked behind it, although I couldn't tell exactly what it was.

"Is this the place?" said Goggles, looking up at the rather unremarkable white building. "I was expecting something fancier."

I glanced at my phone's map app. "My map app says this is indeed the place."

"Do you think Checkmate is home?" asked Lumberjack, scratching his long black beard. "Looks rather empty to me."

I shrugged. "Only one way to find out."

I walked up to the front door of the building and pressed the doorbell. As soon as I pressed the doorbell, I heard the sound of wind chimes coming from somewhere within the building, but again, no response from Checkmate.

"Must be sleeping," said Cavewoman with a snort. "Men always sleep. Women work all time. Hard life."

I rolled my eyes. "I know it's still kind of early in the morning, but I doubt Checkmate is actually sleeping. He might be busy with other things, but—"

I was interrupted by the front door opening suddenly and I found myself standing face to face with Checkmate himself.

Checkmate looked much the same as he did yesterday. His brown-and-gold costume made him stand out even more among the utter whiteness all around us, his dark eyes peering out from between his mouth guard and his helmet. He looked slightly startled to see us for a moment before saying, "Doctor Mind? What are you doing here?"

I gave Checkmate my best, most persuasive, and friendly smile. "Hi! My teammates and I just wanted to come by and properly thank you for saving us from the Black Pawns in the airport yesterday. In all the hubbub afterward, we really didn't get a chance to properly sit down and thank you ourselves."

Checkmate nodded. He looked a little nervous for some reason. "Thank you for your thoughtfulness, Doctor. I am just glad that I was able to prevent the Black Pawns from killing more innocent people. They get away with far too much in this country. It is time that someone stood up to them, in my opinion."

I blinked. "Er, I suppose …"

Checkmate smiled. "Sorry. I forgot that you are not Cheskian and therefore do not know or understand our political situation. That is fine. I do not understand your American politics, either. For example, I still do not know the difference between Barack Obama and Donald Trump."

I blinked again. "They are very different."

"Maybe," said Checkmate, "but they look the same to me."

Shaking my head, I said, "Never mind about that. We did not come here to talk politics."

"Hmm?" said Checkmate, tilting his head to the side. "What

FAKE CHESS

would you like to talk about, then?"

I looked up and down the street briefly but did not see too many other people around other than ourselves. "I wanted to find out more about Laskar's true motives for hosting the tournament. I was hoping that you might be able to give me better insight into Laskar's mind, seeing as you know him better than I do."

Checkmate's eyes hardened. "You wish to know what is going on in that old fool's mind, eh? Join the club."

"I take it you and the Chess King do not get along very well?" I said.

Checkmate's gaze hardened even more. "I am surprised you would ask that question, Doctor. You saw with your own eyes last night how well we get along."

"Last night?" I repeated. "The last time I saw you was at the Cheskian International Airport. I don't remember seeing you in the Dining Hall and I definitely don't remember seeing you interact with Laskar in any way."

Checkmate shook his head. "I was right there, even if you didn't know it was me."

Lumberjack suddenly gasped behind me. "Wait a second, are you saying that you are the Chess Queen in disguise?"

What did I say about expecting Lumberjack or Cavewoman to say something stupid?

Fortunately, Checkmate simply looked more confused than offended. "N-No. I am not the Chess Queen. Why would you even think—"

"Ignore my friends," I said. I rubbed my forehead. "We're just trying to figure out who you are. Last night was kind of a blur."

Checkmate, still looking slightly confused, nonetheless nodded. He reached up and undid the clasps on his helmet, saying, "Then let me show you my real face. Showing is often easier than telling."

Taking his helmet off, Checkmate looked at us and it was my turn to gasp.

LUCAS FLINT

Staring at us was the face of Gary Laskar, the Chess Prince himself.

CHAPTER THIRTEEN

GARY OR Checkmate or whatever he wanted us to call him invited us into his base for further discussion. As it turned out, his base looked like it might have been a renovated office building, complete with an empty receptionist's desk at the front and a small conference room where he herded us. He offered me and my teammates coffee, an offer I accepted, even though I'd just had coffee at breakfast. I was mostly still in shock from finding out that Gary and Checkmate were one and the same, although it helped that I was a bit of a coffee fiend. Not an addict, though. I could quit anytime I wanted.

Sitting down in one of the squeaky leather office chairs in the conference room, I looked across the wooden table at Gary, whose helmet rested on the table in front of him.

Gary himself sat with his shoulders slightly slumped, his arms folded in front of his chest, a look of resignation on his face.

"Wow," said Goggles, who sat beside me. He had a cup of orange juice rather than coffee, mostly because I didn't feel comfortable with letting Goggles drink coffee yet. "I had no idea that you were actually Checkmate, Your Highness."

Gary sighed and rolled his shoulders. "Please, Goggles, we're all superheroes here. No need to address me with my royal titles."

"Okay," said Lumberjack. He held out his ax toward Gary. "Want to go cut down every single tree in the country?"

Gary gave Lumberjack a puzzled look. "Why?"

"Ignore him," I said again. I steepled my fingers together, looking at Gary over the top of my steepled fingers. "I have to say this is rather unexpected. How come no one told us that you were Checkmate last night? Heck, why didn't *you* tell us that?"

Gary scowled and looked down at his helmet. "Because Father does not approve. That is why."

"Father?" I repeated. "You mean Laskar, right?"

"He is the only father I have, so yes," said Gary. He sighed. "Unfortunately."

Goggles and I exchanged puzzled looks before I looked at Gary again. "I take it that you and your father don't have the best relationship."

"That is putting it mildly," said Gary. He gave a short, bitter laugh. "We have not had the 'best' relationship since I decided to become a superhero. After that, Father started treating me much the same way he treats pond scum."

"Ouch," said Goggles. "Does Laskar dislike superheroes or something?"

Gary shook his head. "Not really. He does like superheroes. He just doesn't like *me* being a superhero."

"Ah," I said with a nod. "I think I see the problem now. You want to be a superhero, while your dad wants you to be something else."

"Precisely," said Gary with a single, tired nod. He smiled at me shyly. "Ever since I was a little boy, I've always wanted to be a superhero. And I've always wanted to be a superhero because, in part, of *your* influence, Doctor."

I blinked. "My influence? What do you mean?"

Gary clasped his hands together excitedly. "I am a big superhero fan, especially of American superheroes. I follow the careers of many superheroes, but I've been following yours more than any other these past three years. You really inspired me to not just like superheroes, but to become one myself."

FAKE CHESS

"Oh," I said as a sudden case of Impostor's Syndrome came over me. "That's nice to hear. I didn't realize I had fans in other countries."

"You most certainly do," Checkmate assured me. "I was especially impressed by your defeat of the supervillain Death Skull back in January. I watched the whole thing on the Internet, even when Death Skull called you a 'pseudo-hero' because he mistakenly believed you were a con artist who had no idea what he was doing."

I chuckled. Only slightly nervously. Just slightly enough that hopefully Checkmate would not notice. "Heh. Yeah, that was, um, something."

"It was an evil lie promoted by an evil person," Checkmate said. He winked at me. "But who is surprised when supervillains lie, eh? It's in their nature. I've certainly dealt with my fair share of lying, deceptive supervillains over the years."

"Cheskia has supervillains, too?" said Goggles. "How come we haven't heard of them?"

"Because Cheskia is a rather obscure country compared to America," Checkmate replied frankly. "There is a reason you haven't heard of the Grandmaster, the King's Elephant, Pawnkiller, and Purple Dinosaur, among others—"

"Purple Dinosaur?" I repeated. "Who is Purple Dinosaur?"

Checkmate gave me a funny look. "A very evil—almost depraved—supervillain who nearly destroyed the entire country last year. Many people died thanks to him. I myself was in the hospital for weeks after our final climactic fight."

"I see," I said. "Purple Dinosaur isn't exactly a chess-themed name, though."

Checkmate gave me an offended look this time. "So? With all due respect, Doctor, not *everything* in Cheskia is chess-themed. That is an inaccurate stereotype perpetuated by hack writers who do not do their research. Our country has many other non-chess-related things, such as … such as …" Checkmate struggled for a moment before shaking his head. "The point is, I also fight a lot of supervillains and I wouldn't be where I am if not for your inspiration, Doctor."

"Okay," I said. "Although I take it your dad isn't happy with your career choices."

Checkmate scowled. "He is not, but then again, he's never been happy with anything I've done. He's always treated me like I can never live up to his ridiculously high expectations. Why, then, shouldn't I do what *I* want to do, rather than what *he* wants me to do?"

"What does your dad want you to do, if you don't mind me asking?" I said.

"He wants me to become a professional chess player, like my siblings," said Checkmate sullenly. "But I do not want to be because I do not like chess as much as he does."

"Siblings?" Goggles piped up. "I didn't know you had siblings."

"I have many siblings," said Checkmate, "most of whom I barely know. Father has had many children with many women and to this day I still do not know who they all are."

I sipped my coffee in surprise. "Wait, are you saying that your dad is cheating on your mom?"

Checkmate sighed. "It's not that simple. Although the Chess King and Chess Queen jointly rule Cheskia together, they do not *have* to be married, as both positions are determined by the player's skill. It is common for a Chess King to have his own harem of women while the Chess Queen does her own thing. Indeed, it is rare, historically-speaking, for the Chess King and Chess Queen to actually love each other in the way that married couples are expected to. Usually, mutual respect for each other as skilled chess players is the best you can ask for, but even then, their relationship might not get that far."

"Sounds complicated," Lumberjack remarked.

"Me like it," said Cavewoman. She downed the rest of her

FAKE CHESS

coffee and slammed the empty cup on the table. "Marriage useless patriarchal institution which oppress women. Me like Chess Queen more now."

I bit my lower lip. "I don't know. It sounds like the Chess Royal Family is a bit ... what's the most politic way to put this —"

"Dysfunctional?" Checkmate offered. "Broken? Strained? Or possibly even nonexistent? Trust me, all of those words and more could easily describe my family. It's another reason I want nothing to do with them. Although ..."

"Although what?" said Goggles.

Checkmate shrugged. "I think Father does genuinely love Mother, though he's not very good at showing it."

I frowned. "Your family structure does sound a bit strange."

"It has to do with how the Cheskian government is set up," said Checkmate. "Because the Chess King and Queen are determined by merit rather than blood, it means that the people in those positions are constantly changing. That, naturally, makes it harder for solid relationships to form, not helped by our informal caste system, where the Chess King and Queen are expected to marry and procreate only with people of similar skill level. It leads to messed up families and even worse politics."

I grimaced. "That sounds messed up all around. Makes me feel a bit better about our own politics. Even though those are pretty messed up most of the time, too."

Checkmate shook his head. "It does not matter. You said you wanted to know why Father is hosting this tournament, yes?"

I nodded quickly. "Yeah, do you know why?"

"Because Father doesn't want me or any of my siblings to succeed him," Checkmate replied. "That's why."

Goggles frowned. "I don't get it. The Cheskian line of succession isn't determined by blood relation anyway, right? So why would your dad be afraid of you or one of your siblings succeeding him as Chess King someday?"

105

LUCAS FLINT

Checkmate took a bite out of a donut and swallowed. "Because, even though Cheskia does not have a line of succession based on blood, it is traditionally expected of the Chess King's children to challenge their father for the throne. Especially sons. That is why most Chess Kings have been related to the previous. It creates a sort of self-reinforcing feedback loop, where a Chess King comes to power based on his chess skill, which he then teaches to his children, who then use said knowledge to defeat their father and become the new Chess King, only for them to have children who *they* teach their chess skills to, and so on."

I nodded. "That explains how the Cheskian government has survived for this long. I would think that a 'chessocracy' would be very chaotic."

Checkmate sighed. "Don't be fooled. What I described is more or less how it works ... in theory. In action, there have been plenty of new Chess Kings who weren't related to the previous one at all who won the title fair and square. When that happens, it is traditional for the new Chess King to utterly impoverish the family of the original Chess King, if not outright eliminate them, to ensure that the previous Royal Family does not pose a threat to his rule."

Goggles grimaced. "Yeesh. I forgot how serious you guys take chess around here."

"Me think it make perfect sense," said Cavewoman with a nod. "If me in Chess King's shoes, me eliminate all threats to Cavewoman power ruthlessly. Except women because women got to stick together in a man's world."

Lumberjack looked at Cavewoman in surprise. "I didn't realize you had such a politically practical mind, Cavewoman. You always seemed like a dainty thing to me."

'Dainty' was the last word in the English dictionary that I would use to describe Cavewoman, a sentiment she seemed to agree with because she gave Lumberjack the harshest death glare I'd ever seen her give someone and snapped, "Me no dainty. Me

FAKE CHESS

big and strong. Big and strong as any man."

"Uh-huh," I said. I turned my attention back to Checkmate, ignoring Cavewoman and Lumberjack's argument. "So I take it you are upset about the tournament because you think your dad doesn't want you to be his successor?"

Checkmate folded his arms in front of his chest. "No. Truthfully, Doctor, I don't want to be the next Chess King. I want to be a superhero, as I feel that superheroes are often more effective at protecting innocent people than government. But Father sees me as his biggest mistake, I think, because I am not afraid to call him out and do not wish to follow in his footsteps. In fact—not trying to 'toot my own horn' here, as you Americans say—I probably am the best chess player out of all of my siblings."

I tilted my head to the side. "You are? Have you ever actually beaten your father or—?"

"No," said Checkmate. "But out of all of my siblings, I have gotten the closest. I've only ever beaten him in a handicap match, but the Cheskian Constitution specifically says that both the current Chess King and his challenger must play with a full board for it to be considered an official Challenger Match. Practice matches and handicap matches do not count."

I stroked my chin. "Interesting. Do you think that Laskar is holding this tournament anyway just to make sure you don't become his successor?"

Checkmate frowned. "That would be an odd way to go about doing it, seeing as I am also participating in the tournament."

"Good point," I said. "Although now I am worried we might play against each other at some point."

"Almost certainly," Checkmate agreed. "That will be fun, I think. I watched E2's footage of your chess game with him back in America and was impressed by your quick-thinking and your tactics. I cannot wait to test my skills against yours."

Without knowing how good Checkmate was, I couldn't say what my odds of defeating him were, but his statement reminded me of another question I had. "Right. Well, I've noticed that Laskar seems to have taken a special interest in me for some reason. Do you know why that is?"

Checkmate shrugged. "Sorry, but I don't. In fact, I rarely know or understand what goes through Father's mind. As I said, we aren't close."

I bit my lower lip in frustration, but nodded. I had expected an answer like that, but that didn't mean I liked it. It meant I was basically back right where I started, although I liked to think that I at least understood Cheskia itself a bit better now.

And hey, if I did well enough in the tournament, I might be able to ask Laskar myself.

"All right," I said. I finished what remained of my coffee and placed the cup back on the table. "Thanks for talking with us, Checkmate. It was informative, if nothing else."

Checkmate nodded again. "No problem, Doctor. As I've said, I've been a big fan of yours for years now, so I am always happy to talk with you about pretty much anything." He held out a hand toward me. "But make no mistake. If our paths cross in the tournament, I won't hold back and I expect the same from you."

I hesitated for a moment before taking Checkmate's hand and shaking it. "Of course."

You may have wondered why I hesitated before shaking Checkmate's hand. That's because I really wasn't used to the sort of sincere intensity that Checkmate showed. I was so used to being the only chess nerd in my family that I didn't really know how to react to meeting someone who understood exactly what I was going through.

But honestly, I liked it.

And thought that, whatever Laskar's real plans were, maybe at least I'd get to play a good chess match at some point.

CHAPTER FOURTEEN

"Waste of time," said Cavewoman when we stepped out of Checkmate's base. She stood with her club resting on her shoulder, her usual scowl smeared across her face. "Us no closer to finding out truth about Chess King than before. Only mansplained by sexist man."

Goggles gave Cavewoman a puzzled look. "How did Checkmate mansplain to you? He spoke politely to all of us."

Cavewoman snorted and tossed her head back. "Me no have to explain to entitled man. Everyone out to get Cavewoman. That why Cavewoman need smash stupid men in head with club."

"I'm glad you showed a minimum of self-restraint back there," I said, folding my arms in front of my chest, "but I'm not sure I'd say it was a total bust. Checkmate did confirm a few things for us, such as his strained relationship with his father. That clarifies a few things."

"Such as what?" said Lumberjack with a frown.

I held up a finger. "For one, it explains why Laskar and Gary behaved so passive-aggressively toward each other last night. And second, it explains why Laskar is holding the tournament. He clearly doesn't value or respect Gary or any of his other children, to the point where he thinks hosting a superhero tournament with participants from all over the country is a better way to determine the next king of Cheskia than letting his own children beat him."

"But he's still letting his son participate," Goggles pointed out. "Doesn't that imply that he's at least willing to give Checkmate a chance?"

"Possibly," I said, stroking my chin. "Or he holds such a low opinion of his son's chess skills that he thinks Checkmate will get knocked out of the tournament early on. Which might be possible, although it depends on how good Checkmate is."

Goggles shuddered. "If he's the son of the Chess King, then he *has* to be good, right? I just hope you don't have to play him at some point, Uncle."

"Why?" I said, looking at Goggles in confusion. "Don't you have faith in your uncle's chess skills?"

"I do, but Checkmate is probably really good," said Goggles. "Don't you want to win the tournament, Uncle? Because if you do, then you'll get a chance to become the next Chess King."

I scratched my chin in thought. "I suppose that would be nice, but ... I'm still not sure I want to win."

"Not sure if you want to win?" said Lumberjack. "Why did you come all the way to Cheskia in the first place, then?"

"Because I wanted to know what the Chess King is actually up to," I said. "Although Checkmate gave us a useful glimpse into his father's mind, there's still a lot we don't know. For example, why is the Chess King so interested in *me* in particular? I'm almost certain I'm not the best superhero chess player in the world, so he has to have another reason for taking an interest in me."

"Good point," said Goggles. He shrugged. "Guess you'll just have to win the tournament and ask Laskar yourself."

I sighed. "I sure hope not."

"What are you so disappointed about, anyway?" asked Lumberjack incredulously. "You're a chess nerd, aren't you, Doctor? Playing in a chess tournament sounds like your dream come true."

FAKE CHESS

I frowned. "It would be under any other circumstances, but this isn't an ordinary chess tournament. Plus, I have to admit I am a bit concerned about my ability to win. I am not very familiar with the chess skills of the other competitors, so I don't know for sure how I match up against them."

"Couldn't you look up their chess ratings online?" Goggles suggested. "There are websites that rank players, aren't there?"

"Yes, but I don't know the names of every player in the tournament aside from Mr. South," I said. "I already know his rating, which is comparable to mine. The others are unknown to me and I have no idea who they are. The only way I will know is by entering the tournament and taking them on."

Lumberjack nodded. "I see. Well, isn't registration for the tournament later today or am I confused?"

"No, you're right," I said, rubbing the back of my head. I looked toward Castle Rook, which towered over most of the other buildings in Chess City in the distance. "Still, given the dead-end we've run into, we might as well head back to the castle early to meet up with the others and—"

Something as solid as a baseball bat slammed into the back of my helmet. The abrupt blow knocked me flat off my feet, causing me to hit the pavement hard. My head spun from the impact and I was barely aware of Goggles at my side in the next instant, shaking me, saying, "Uncle, Uncle, are you all right? Can you hear me? Uncle?"

With my head feeling like a split watermelon, I nonetheless managed to look up at Goggles' concerned face, which swam in my vision like we were underwater. "Goggles? Goggles, is that you? My head ..."

"Uncle, it's going to be all right," Goggles said hurriedly. He half-rose to his feet. "Just ... just stay there, all right? I'm going to find someone to help."

I was about to ask Goggles why he seemed so worried about me when suddenly talking felt like an impossibly Herculean feat.

111

LUCAS FLINT

The darkness at the edges of my vision overwhelmed my reason and I found myself drifting off into endless shadows and sleep.

CHAPTER FIFTEEN

"Doctor," said a familiar, Cheskian-accented female voice from somewhere above me, "Doctor Mind, can you hear me? Doctor Mind?"

I wish the woman would stop speaking. Not because her voice was annoying—it was actually quite pleasant—but because my skull felt like it had been cracked in two and the sound waves of her voice were bouncing around inside.

Indeed, I would have gone straight back to sleep if another familiar male Canadian-accented voice did not say, "I suppose if he's dead, then we'll just have to bury him. But without his head. Otherwise, he might come back as a zombie."

My eyes shot open and I sat up, breathing hard and looking around at my surroundings.

I was lying on my bed in my room in Castle Rook. Goggles and Brave Storm stood off to the side of my bed, surprised and worried looks on their faces. Lumberjack, meanwhile, actually stood on the bed over me, his ax raised above his head, an equally surprised look peering through his thickly-bearded face.

"Uncle's alive!" said Goggles, clapping his hands excitedly. "Yay! We thought you were dead."

Brave Storm sighed in relief. "Honestly, you looked pretty bad, Roger. You were out cold for a while."

Rubbing the back of my head—which hurt and was how I realized I was no longer wearing my Mind-Bender Crown—I said, "Yeah. Who would have guessed that getting hit in the head with a baseball bat would freaking hurt?"

Then I looked up at Lumberjack and snapped, "And what do you think *you're* doing holding your ax like that?"

Lumberjack blinked. "Making sure you don't come back as a zombie, of course."

I really wished I was still wearing my Mind-Bender Crown right now, because then I would have sent Lumberjack flying across the room. As it was, I just glared at him and said, "Clearly, I am not dead, so I'm not in danger of becoming a zombie."

"Right now," said Lumberjack. "But what if, when you die, you *do* become a zombie? It's a risk we take every time we die."

"Zombies aren't real," I said.

Lumberjack wagged a finger at me. "If you have seen the horrors created by trees that I have seen, then you wouldn't be so quick to say that."

I sighed. "Just get your dirty boots off my bed. Now."

Lumberjack jumped onto the floor. Lowering his ax to his side, Lumberjack said, "At least the trees didn't get you, Doctor. Otherwise, we'd be in *real* trouble then."

Rubbing my head, I said, "What happened? How did I get here?"

"A Black Pawn ran up out of nowhere and hit you with a baseball bat," Lumberjack explained. "I know how random it sounds, but it's true."

Puzzled, I shook my head. "At least I'm back here where the Black Pawns can't get me, if nothing else."

"True, but you will be in deep trouble soon," said the familiar Cheskian-accented female voice that I'd heard while I was asleep. "Especially if you do not get down to the registration in time to register yourself for the tournament."

Startled, I looked to my right and saw D2 standing there. She

FAKE CHESS

stood with her arms folded in front of her chest, her face as hidden as always by her pawn-like mask. Although I might not have been able to see her face, I could tell she was probably frowning at me.

"Registration?" I repeated, feeling a bit like a parrot. "For what?"

"The chess tournament," said Brave Storm to me, causing me to look at him instead. "You know, the one we flew all the way out to Eastern Europe to compete in?"

I cursed myself and jumped out of bed. "Dang it! I almost forgot. How long have I been out and when does registration close?"

D2 glanced at her watch. "Three hours. Approximately fifteen minutes."

"Fifteen—?" I almost gagged. "Damn it. We're not going to make it in time."

"Yes, we will," said D2. She walked past me, moving rather quickly. "Follow me. I know of a shortcut to the Castle lobby, where the registration table is."

I followed D2 and heard Goggles follow behind me as well. I also heard Brave Storm and the other Fakers wishing me good luck, but I did not look back or respond as Goggles, D2, and I left my room and ran down the hallway in the direction of the lobby as fast as we could.

"Fifteen minutes ..." I shook my head as we passed some stone statues of chess pieces on either side of the hall. "How long was I out?"

"Five hours," Goggles said cheerfully. "We thought you were dead, but fortunately you were just unconscious."

"Five hours?" I repeated. "How hard did that person hit me?"

"Very, if you were out for five hours," said D2 to my left. She ran effortlessly despite the long dress which almost went down to her shoes. "When your friends brought you back in, I had the Minister look at you, but he said you would be fine."

115

I glanced at D2 as we ran, frowning. "And what were you doing in my room with us, anyway? I don't remember inviting you inside."

D2 shrugged. "His Majesty learned of your assault and ordered me to monitor your health and make sure you were safe. Remember, His Majesty assigned me to keep an eye on you while you are staying here in Chess City."

I frowned even deeper. "Laskar sure found out about that quickly."

"His Majesty knows everything that goes on in his city," D2 replied. "The Chess King has eyes and ears everywhere. That is why it is wise to watch what one says, especially in private."

"You mean in public."

"I mean what I say."

I didn't press the subject. D2 seemed to be implying that our rooms were bugged. Not that I found that surprising, given how paranoid Laskar was, but it did make me rethink just how safe it was for me and my teammates to discuss our investigations while in our rooms. It made me wonder how much Laskar already knew about our investigations and what he was planning to do about them.

In any case, that would be something to worry about later. My watch indicated we had less than ten minutes before registration closed, so I just sped up the pace until we reached the castle lobby.

I immediately spotted the registration table, where a couple of cute young women with blonde hair were sitting, chatting to one another in Cheskian. The women wore t-shirts with chess piece designs etched into them, while the registration table before them had a tablet with what appeared to be a list of the names of the other participants. To the left of the tablet, a pile of t-shirts and paper programs stood, perhaps meant to be souvenirs for the participants to take with them after registration.

But I didn't care about any of that nonsense. I just rushed over

FAKE CHESS

to the table and, skidding to a stop in front of the women, said, "H-Hello. Is this the registration table for the International Superhero Chess Tournament?"

One of the women—whose name tag identified her as Anna—smiled up at me. "Yes, it is! You got here just in time. Registration is closing in five minutes."

"Yes, I know," I said impatiently as Goggles and D2 stopped on either side of me. "How do I sign up?"

Anna gestured at the tablet. "Simply type your name into the box on the tablet. Once your name comes up, simply click it. Then you will need to verify your information, click the blue 'REGISTER' button, and you will be all set for tomorrow's first match."

I nodded. It sounded simple enough, which was good because I didn't need more complications on top of everything else I'd done already.

So I bent over and, tapping the empty text box on the screen, entered my superhero name and then hit submit.

A big, ugly red 'ERROR' message popped up as soon as I submitted, along with a paragraph of information written in what I assumed was Cheskian, although since I couldn't read Cheskian I had no idea what it was saying.

Even without me saying anything, Anna must have read my facial expression because she turned the tablet toward her and frowned in puzzlement. "That is odd. It says your name isn't in the system."

"Isn't in the system?" I repeated indignantly. "What do you mean my name isn't in the system? Only reason I'm here is because the Chess King specifically invited me."

"Did you try inputting your real name, rather than your superhero name?" the other girl, whose name was apparently Gretchen according to her tag, piped up. "Some of the participants have entered under their real name rather than their superhero name, which may be part of the problem."

117

LUCAS FLINT

Sighing in frustration, I nonetheless refreshed the page and typed in my real name, only to end up with the same error message. If anything, though, I thought the error message somehow looked even angrier than before, as if it was annoyed by the fact that I'd made it show me the same page twice.

"How strange," said Anna when I showed her the error message. "Did you perhaps misspell your own name?"

"I didn't misspell my own name," I said. "It's not like, I dunno, Cerepaka or something impossible to spell like that. Must be a glitch in the system."

Anna, who was tapping the tablet's screen like she was doing some troubleshooting, shook her head. "It can't be a glitch. It was working perfectly fine all day today. You are the first person to run into this sort of glitch."

Folding my arms in front of my chest, I said, "Do you maybe have a paper form I can sign instead? Or are we all digital around here?"

"Unfortunately, we do not have a paper form you can sign," said Anna with an apologetic sigh. "This is the first year we are trying to digitize the registration process for a tournament. Part of Prince Gary's attempts to modernize chess tournaments in Cheskia."

"Prince Gary?" I repeated. "You mean Checkmate? So *he's* the one I should be complaining to about this?"

"Anna, I do not know if I would worry about any so-called 'glitches,'" said Gretchen. She looked at me suspiciously. "What if the tablet is working just fine and this man isn't who he says he is?"

"Come on," I said in exasperation. I dug in my pocket and pulled out my passport, which I shoved into their faces. "See here? This is my passport. Has my real name on it and everything. Even has my superhero name if you need to verify it."

Gretchen eyed my passport skeptically. "It does look real, but how do we know if you are supposed to be in the tournament at

FAKE CHESS

all? Chess tournament registration fraud is a serious crime and—"

"Wait," I interrupted. "It's a *crime* to falsely register for a tournament you're not supposed to participate in?"

"Yes," said Gretchen in a serious voice. "A very serious crime. Those who commit chess tournament fraud may get anywhere from five to ten years in maximum-security prison, though the death sentence is also a possibility depending on how blatant your fraud is."

I blinked and looked at D2. "Please tell me she's joking."

"No, Gretchen is telling the truth," said D2. "Part of His Majesty's Anti-Chess Tournament Fraud Decree of 1989, which added extra penalties on top of the already existing chess tournament fraud laws that had existed. There was a terrible wave of chess fraudsters in the eighties that demanded swift and immediate action, which the Chess King did with support from the Chess Court."

Given how chess-obsessed this entire country was, I really shouldn't have been shocked to hear that, but somehow I still was. Honestly, I was mostly just worried about what might happen to me if I couldn't get registered. Would I be arrested for trying to do chess fraud or would I simply be barred from participating in the tournament? Not being allowed to participate in a tournament seemed unfair, but it was preferable to the death sentence.

Fortunately, D2 intervened for me, saying, "I can verify that Doctor Mind was personally invited to participate in the tournament. There is no chess fraud going on."

Anna shot Gretchen a triumphant smile. "See? It must be a glitch."

Gretchen sighed, almost in disappointment. "Fine, but that still does not explain where the glitch came from."

I waved a hand dismissively. "Technology can be very unreliable at times. I assume you probably have a way of manually registering people, right?"

"We do," said Anna as she continued to peck the tablet with her fingers, "and since D2 confirmed that you were indeed invited, I think …. Ah! Here we go."

Triumphant noises came from the tablet as Anna turned it around to face me. The words 'REGISTRATION COMPLETE!' appeared on the screen in bright neon colors that looked like something straight out of the nineties, while a digitized version of what I assumed was the Cheskian national anthem played happily in the background.

I sighed in relief. "Thanks. Does that mean I'm registered now?"

Anna nodded, a happy smile on her face. "Yes! You will be able to participate in tomorrow's match. You will receive an email in the morning with all the relevant information, such as the time and location of your first match, as well as the identity of your first opponent. Good luck!"

Rubbing the back of my head, I smiled back at her tiredly. I was glad we'd managed to get registered in time. I didn't know why they'd had to do it manually, but like I said, technology can be unreliable. Now I could focus on—

Something big and soft shoved me to the side, causing me to fall on the floor. Banging my head against the red carpeting of the lobby, my head spun briefly from the impact before I looked up to see who had knocked me over.

It was the world's fattest sumo wrestler.

CHAPTER SIXTEEN

Seriously, the guy was *huge*. He was probably as wide as me, D2, and Goggles put together, and a good deal taller than us, too. Mountains of flabby skin flowed down his body like molten lava, while his hair was done up in one of those cringy manbuns that younger guys think looks cool but only makes them look stupid. He smelled like cherry blossoms for some reason, too.

Even worse, the guy didn't even apologize to me. He just slammed his hands down on the registration table and said, in badly broken English, "We are here to register. This is registration table?"

Anna and Gretchen looked at each other in confusion before Anna said, "Yes. But there's only a minute left, so—"

"Please register me," said the guy. He slammed his fist down on the table. "Now."

Anna gulped. She pushed the tablet toward the sumo and said, in a slightly trembling tone, "Please put your name in here."

The sumo nodded, said, "Arigatō," and immediately began typing his name into the tablet. He resolutely ignored me and everyone else as he registered, which pissed me off because I was tired of getting knocked down.

Rising to my feet, I said, "Hey, Mr. Sumo."

The sumo glanced at me as if he hadn't even noticed I existed.

LUCAS FLINT

"My name is Sushimo. Mr. Sumo is different."

I blinked. "Sushimo—? Never heard of you, but that doesn't matter. You basically assaulted me."

Sushimo stared at me for a moment before turning his attention back to the tablet. "I am sorry. I did not see you standing there because of how tiny you are."

"Tiny?" I repeated. "I guess everything looks *tiny* to the freaking *moon*."

Sushimo paused and glared at me again. I really hadn't been exaggerating that much when I compared him to the moon, although now I was starting to think I should have thought through what I was going to say a bit more before I said it.

"You compare me to moon?" Sushimo said, almost growled. He turned to face me entirely, apparently having finished registering for the tournament. He towered over me, his mass very moon-like at the moment. "Big words coming from *small* man."

I did my best not to gulp. "It's not about size, but how you use it that matters. Didn't your girlfriend ever tell you that?"

A vein in Sushimo's head started throbbing and he raised a fist above his head. "For that comment alone, I crush your head like soda can."

"Father!" a young girl's voice suddenly called out. "Father, please, no!"

Startled, both Sushimo and I looked to the right to see a young Japanese girl—probably about Goggles' age—running toward us. She wore a bright pink spandex costume with wide butterfly wings and startlingly big eyes peering out through her helmet's goggles. Her long dark hair, done up in braids, flew behind her as she rushed to us.

"Butterfly?" said Sushimo, frowning. He suddenly said something to her in Japanese that I did not get, probably because I didn't speak a word of Japanese other than the word sushi, which I did not hear him say.

FAKE CHESS

The girl, apparently named Butterfly, skid to a halt before us and responded to Sushimo in rapid-fire, high-pitched Japanese that made even less sense to me than Sushimo's Japanese.

Sushimo, on the other hand, seemed to understand her just fine, because he pouted like a spoiled child before glaring at me and saying, "Next time," before stomping off toward the hallway and out of the lobby.

Blinking, I said, "What was that about?"

Butterfly bowed before me quickly. "Apologies, Doctor-san. My father, Sushimo, is not always an easy person to get along with. He is very proud and does not take kindly to insults."

"Your father—?" I said, looking at Butterfly. "Wait a second, is your dad a superhero? And are you his sidekick?"

Butterly bowed again, which seemed unnecessary to me. "Yes. We are Japanese superheroes from Tokyo."

"Japanese superheroes from Tokyo?" Goggles asked excitedly, suddenly appearing out of nowhere in front of Butterfly. "Are you and your dad members of the Kaiju Force?"

Butterly, startled by Goggles' sudden appearance, took a step back in alarm. "Ah, no. Actually, we're independent superheroes who are not currently associated with any superhero team in Japan. My father is not as famous as the Kaiju Force, although he has worked with them on occasion when dealing with threats to Japan that are too big for one hero to deal with."

I scratched my chin and glanced at Sushimo's repeating backside (much to my disgust). "Explains why I've never heard of him before. I assume he's a decent chess player?"

"One of Japan's best," Butterfly said proudly. "Father is a Grandmaster who, in his youth, was the Japanese chess champion. He even represented Japan in the Olympics one year and narrowly lost to the Ukrainian champion."

My eyes nearly fell out of their sockets when Butterfly said that. "Hold on. Sushimo is a *Grandmaster*?"

"Yes," said Butterfly. She frowned up at me. "I know that my

English is not that good, but I hope I am communicating clearly nonetheless."

"A-Actually, I think you speak English pretty good," said Goggles with a slight stutter. He cleared his throat abruptly. "Er, I mean, you speak English pretty well."

Butterfly giggled at Goggles' gaff and played with her braids. "Thank you. Although the English language is a huge obsession of mine, I am still pretty self-conscious about it, especially when speaking with native English speakers like you two."

"Don't be," Goggles said hastily. "I mean, you speak English better than most of my classmates, even gooder than me."

Butterfly giggled again. "Forgive me for my impudence, but I think you mean 'better,' not 'gooder,' which is not a word."

Goggles chuckled nervously and what little bits of his face that were not hidden by his mask were bright red. "Uh, yeah. See? You already sound like a real English speaker."

Butterfly giggled for the third time, but did not say anything in response.

Myself, I just watched the two interact and realized that Goggles was already crushing hard on this girl, despite having met her literally five seconds ago. I didn't see it myself, but then again, I wasn't a fourteen-year-old boy with raging fourteen-year-old boy hormones, either.

In any case, I drew Butterfly's attention back to me with a wave and said, "Sushimo is a Grandmaster? That's … impressive."

I almost said 'intimidating,' but I didn't want to sound like a coward in front of a teenage girl who wasn't even half my height. I was obviously not a Grandmaster myself, not even an International Master. If this was the kind of competition I was dealing with, then it sure looked like my Cheskian vacation was going to end sooner than I expected.

Butterfly beamed with pride. "It is. We are from a long line of Japanese chess players. In fact, my great-grandfather was once

FAKE CHESS

the best chess player in all of Asia and came pretty close to winning the World Championship, only to be beaten out by the Chess King before Laskar."

I was even more intimida—I mean, impressed. "So your family already has a history with Cheskia?"

Butterfly nodded. "Yes. It's why Father was so quick to accept the Chess King's invitation to the tournament. He sees it as a way for our family to regain our lost pride. He's not interested in the crown so much as he is in the potential to restore our family's original greatness in the chess world."

I scratched my chin again in thought. "No wonder he seems so ... so ..."

"High-strung?" Butterfly offered. She smiled sadly. "Yes, Father takes chess very seriously. So do I, but I try to have a sense of humor about it, at least."

"Yeah, you're really funny," said Goggles quickly. "Like, hilarious."

Butterfly blinked at Goggles. "Funny? Did I say a joke? I don't remember telling you a joke."

"No, no, that's not what I mean," said Goggles, waving his hands back and forth. "It's just—"

"Butterfly-chan!" Sushimo's loud voice rang out across the lobby.

Startled, we looked in the direction from which Sushimo's voice had come and saw his massive form standing in front of the hallway from which we'd emerged. Behind him, I could see about half a dozen of the other competitors and castle servants trying to get past his bulk, but he was so huge that it was downright impossible for anyone to go around him.

Not that Sushimo seemed to notice the people trying to get past his massive bulk, however. His dark eyes were fixed strictly on Butterfly, his meaty arms folded in front of his flabby chest, almost resting on top of his titanic, bulging belly.

What? He really *is* fat.

"Uh-oh," said Butterfly. She bowed at me. "Father is summoning me. I must go. But it is nice to meet you, Doctor-san, and you, too, Goggles-chan."

Goggles looked like Butterfly had kissed him on the lips when she said that, but he didn't say a word. He just watched her run off toward Sushimo like she was the only thing in the world.

I, too, watched her go, but for different reasons. I watched as Butterfly stopped in front of Sushimo and bow before him. The two Japanese superheroes traded some brief words in Japanese before Sushimo turned around and walked down the hallway, practically knocking down the long line of people who had been building up behind him. Butterfly followed him, though she gave Goggles and me one last friendly wave before disappearing down the hallway after her father.

"Huh," I said. "That was … interesting."

"Butterfly is pretty," said Goggles in wonder. "Maybe the prettiest girl I've ever seen. I couldn't even talk around her."

Oh, boy. My poor, naive little nephew hadn't just *fallen* for Butterfly. He'd crashed down to Earth on a flaming meteorite that exploded upon impact for her.

Putting a hand on Goggles' shoulder, I said, "Don't let her looks fool you, Goggles. Her dad isn't going to go easy on us just because you're crushing on her. If anything, that might make him hate us even more."

"Why?" asked Goggles in a genuinely puzzled voice, looking up at me in confusion. "It's not like I've even asked her out yet, but maybe I should. Think she'd say yes?"

Before I could give Goggles the honest but harsh answer to that question, D2 stepped forward and said, "I wouldn't worry about Sushimo if I were you. He hates His Majesty more than you or any of the other competitors. He might seem unfriendly and even hostile, but in the end, he only views you and the other competitors as a stepping stone toward his eventual confrontation with the Chess King."

FAKE CHESS

I looked at D2. "You sound like you know him."

"I've met him before at other tournaments," said D2. "Even played him once. He defeated me very easily."

I gulped. "Let's just hope I don't have to play him, then."

"You undoubtedly will at some point in the tournament," said D2, "assuming that neither you nor Sushimo get knocked out early."

Goggles' eyes sparkled from behind his, well, goggles. "Then that means I'll get a chance to see Butterfly again. Maybe even ask her out."

It was nice, I suppose, that Goggles had something to look forward to here. Me, I was starting to think that I was way, *way* out of my depth.

"Anyway, the match-ups will be announced tomorrow morning, with the first match starting sometime in the afternoon," D2 said. "By then, you'll find out who you will fight in the opening rounds."

"You wouldn't happen to know who I'm going up against, would you, D2?" I asked. "What with you being in the Chess King's inner circle and all that."

D2 shook her head. "Sadly, my current duties involve babysitting you and your teammates for the next week or so. The actual tournament match-ups, rules, ranking, and so on will be decided by the Minister."

I quirked an eyebrow, ignoring her comment about 'babysitting' us (which was actually not an inaccurate way of describing her role toward us). "The Minister? Who is that?"

"His Majesty's right-hand man and the man who runs most of the day-to-day functions of running a country," said D2. "Minister Ferz usually does behind-the-scenes work, which is why you haven't seen him around very often. I imagine he's doing some last-minute tournament preparations even as we speak."

"Is he the guy who came up with the tournament idea in the first place?" I asked.

D2 shook her head. "No. The tournament was His Majesty's original idea. The Minister merely helped him figure out the details to make it work. He's actually been very opposed to it ever since His Majesty first proposed it."

"He has?" I said. "Why?"

D2 shrugged. "I don't know. He seems to think that it's a useless waste of time, but since he's merely the Minister and not the King, he is obligated to follow His Majesty's will to the letter, no matter how much he might disagree with it."

I stroked my chin. That was interesting. I had assumed that everyone in the Cheskian government was as fanatically loyal to Laskar as E2 and D2 were, but perhaps they weren't as unified as they appeared. But that made sense. No government was ever fully united in anything, even traditional monarchies Cheskia (okay, technically 'chessocracy,' but whatever). And anyway, it didn't sound like the Minister was trying to do anything to interfere with the tournament, so it probably wasn't relevant.

On the other hand, maybe this Minister guy had more insight into Laskar's motives for inviting me to the tournament in the first place. If he was willing to disagree with Laskar, he might be willing to talk about him behind his back.

Unfortunately, I didn't get a chance to ask D2 to introduce me to the Minister, because she clapped her hands together and said, "Anyway, I think you two should head back to your rooms now that you are officially registered. While it is not too late, I recommend getting a good night's sleep tonight so you will be mentally prepared for the match tomorrow."

"What time, exactly, will the tournament start?" I asked.

D2 shrugged. "I don't know. Probably not before ten in the morning, but the tournament schedule will be up tonight. You should receive an email from the Cheskian government with the schedule for tomorrow's round, complete with the identity of

FAKE CHESS

your first opponent."

I nodded. I disliked not knowing the schedule, but supposed that D2 was probably telling the truth about not knowing. "All right. I'll keep an eye on my inbox for that, then."

D2 nodded. "Good luck, Doctor. It will be interesting to see how you fare against the others."

With that, D2 turned and left through a hallway on the opposite side of the lobby, leaving me and Goggles standing by ourselves in the lobby. Well, I suppose the registration girls were still seated at the registration table, but they were already putting away their computers and removing the tablecloth for the day.

Turning toward the way we'd come, I said, "Goggles, are you thinking what I'm thinking?"

Goggles looked up at me as we walked, a disgusted expression on his face. "If you're thinking what *I'm* thinking about Butterfly, then that's weird."

I sighed for a long, long time before answering. "I'm thinking about the tournament tomorrow, but more importantly, I'm thinking about the Minister."

"Why?" asked Goggles. "I mean, if you swing that way, Uncle, that's fine, but—"

"It's not about ..." I shook my head. "I'm thinking the Minister can help us figure out Laskar's real game here. And I want to know why the Minister apparently doesn't agree with the tournament."

"Could be that the Minister guy just thinks it's silly," said Goggles. "And I mean, it kind of is, if you think about. Superheroes playing chess? That's really silly."

I glared at Goggles. "There's nothing *silly* about chess, whether superheroes are playing it or someone else. Chess is serious business. No, I think the Minister has *other* reasons for opposing the tournament and it's up to us to find out why."

"If you say so, Uncle," said Goggles with a shrug.

LUCAS FLINT

I nodded and we both lapsed into silence as we made our way back to our rooms.

While Goggles was undoubtedly thinking about a certain cute Japanese teenage girl with whom he was smitten, I was busy thinking about what was really going on here. It seemed like there was more—a lot more—to this tournament than first met the eye.

CHAPTER SEVENTEEN

THE NEXT morning, I woke up bright and early to check my phone to see if the first round of the tournament had been emailed to me yet.

Unfortunately, no such email had arrived in my inbox, although I did discover an email from Mayor Addison back in Freedom City telling me about how he'd finally beaten Death Skull's high score in *Battle Emperor*. The postscript about a new supervillain blowing up the city bank seemed a bit more important to me, however.

Fortunately, I'd asked Rabbitman, one of the few fellow superheroes I was on friendly terms with, to look after Freedom City while I was away, so it sounded like Rabbitman was dealing with it.

With that out of the way, my teammates and I made our way to the Dining Hall to get some breakfast. I hoped also to see if any of the other competitors were awake and eating breakfast and, if so, whether they had heard any information about today's match-ups. I didn't know where D2 was, so I couldn't ask her.

The Dining Hall was packed with superheroes and sidekicks from all over the world. Breakfast was set up like a buffet, with a swiftly-moving line of chess players chatting among each other as they filled their plates with the food they wanted. The scent of eggs, sausage, pancakes, coffee, and more filled the air, making it hard for my stomach to *not* rumble at the smell of so much good food.

Goggles sniffed the air and rubbed his stomach. "Wow. That food smells and looks amazing."

"Agreed," said Lumberjack, who stood next to me. "The coffee reminds me of the lumberjack camp I once worked in. We'd get up early, make a nice big pot of coffee, and enjoy it all day long while working hard on murdering as many trees as possible."

"Coffee does sound good right about now," I said with a nod. "Wonder how dark it is."

"Cavewoman say she like coffee with lots of sugar and cream," said Cavewoman with a grunt. She stood on my left, her arms folded in front of her chest. "Me eat lot of bacon and eggs, too."

I noticed Goggles also glancing around the Dining Hall, and it wasn't a mystery as to who he was looking for. He was clearly searching for Butterfly, although a brief scan of the Dining Hall did not show either Butterfly or her father anywhere. Perhaps they'd already eaten before us? Or possibly were late.

In any case, I clapped my hands together and said, "All right, guys. Might as well get in line so we can get our food."

"Yay for food!" said Shining Armor with a smile as he and the other Fakers made their way to the end of the table, where they started scooping food onto their plates.

I tried to follow my teammates, only for someone to tap me on the shoulder, causing me to look around and find myself staring into the face of Mr. South.

Mr. South looked much the same as he did the first time I saw him. He had a huge, white ten-gallon hat that matched his fancy white suit quite well, black buttons resembling coal on snow. His suit strained against his bulging belly and his plate of food was piled high with chicken and waffles.

FAKE CHESS

"Howdy there, Doc!" said Mr. South in his normal bombastic, Southern-accented voice. "Haven't seen you since the orientation dinner. Heard y'all ran into Sushimo last night."

I frowned, leaning away from the big man slightly. "You did? I don't remember seeing you there."

"Chess players gossip more than my old gran and her pals did in my hometown in Georgia," Mr. South replied. "Hope Sushimo didn't intimidate ya too much. He likes to look tough, but trust me, he's softer than a cow's udder."

"An odd metaphor, but strangely appropriate," I said. I rubbed my stomach. "Speaking of food, I need to grab some breakfast. That Cheskian coffee over there is calling my name and those waffles look good, too."

Mr. South nodded, but then leaned in and said, in a voice too low for anyone else to hear, "Right, but I just wanted to make sure you knew that we're on the same side here. We're the American reps for this tournament, after all. Every other nation is gonna be gunning for us because America's the best and everyone is jealous of us."

I blinked and looked around the Dining Hall at the other competitors, but no one else seemed to be paying us any attention at the moment. "Really?"

"Yup," said Mr. South. "Guess you haven't noticed, but everyone saw you buddying up with Laskar at the orientation dinner. Everyone's already sayin' that Laskar's picked you to be his successor or that you were tryin' schmooze him to get some sort of advantage."

I looked at Mr. South in shock. "Why in the world would I ever try to, ugh, *schmooze* Laskar? I mean, I can be charming when I want to be, but I'm not interested in being *that* charming."

Mr. South shrugged his large shoulders. "I'm just tellin' you what I heard and what it looked like. Figured you weren't, but you gotta admit, it doesn't look too good to have Laskar treating you special like that. Good way to paint a target on your back is what I'm saying."

I shook my head. "Maybe we should try spreading a rumor that I don't want to be Chess King and I'm here for completely different reasons."

"Won't work," said Mr. South with a shake of his head, "but like I said, that's why we gotta stick together. I don't think anyone is gonna pull any hanky panky bullshit, but if people are thinkin' that cheatin' is on the table, then things could get dicey."

I looked at Mr. South with a skeptical expression. "What are they going to do, hire assassins to take me out or something?"

"Probably not," said Mr. South, "but son, I know or recognize most of these guys, and some of them are tough cookies. Take that guy over there."

Mr. South pointed at a table in the far right corner of the Dining Hall, where a surly-looking Russian man wearing a big winter hat sat with an even surlier-looking Russian woman. Aside from his big Russian winter hat, the man wore a costume that looked a bit like a nuclear reactor, although his massive arms were left exposed, and he ate his eggs with surprising delicacy. He was deep in conversation with the surly woman, who wore pink and white furs and looked like she would stab someone if they looked at her the wrong way.

"Who's that?" I whispered back to Mr. South.

"Ivanov 'Big Bear' Vladimir," said Mr. South. "Best superhero chess player in Russia. His dad was a high-ranking KGB agent and there're lots of rumors about Big Bear winning his games because his dad's old KGBuddies gave his opponents some not-so-nice visits. Ambitious and entitled, I wouldn't put much past him, especially with so much on the line."

I nodded. Big Bear's name did sound familiar to me now that Mr. South described him to me. I still wasn't convinced that he would try to hurt or sabotage me, but he did look rather suspicious.

FAKE CHESS

"And who's the lady arguing with him in Russian?" I asked. "She's kind of cute."

"And crazier than a rabies-infected raccoon nest," Mr. South added. "Everyone calls her Miss Winter. Not only is she dating Big Bear, but she's Russia's best female chess player, period. She's their second rep. Don't let her cute looks fool you. Bigger men than you have had their balls crushed by her in chess. Metaphorically, of course."

I grimaced. I'd already picked up on her being crazier than she looked, but the mental image that Mr. South's words painted in my head was definitely not a masterpiece. "Does she also have a history of sending secret government agents to harass her enemies or something?"

"Not from what I've read," said Mr. South, "but I'd keep an eye on her anyway. She's dangerous, that one is, although not as dangerous as *her*."

Mr. South dramatically pointed at a peacock sitting at a table on the far left side of the room, eating breakfast quietly with a couple of chimpanzees wearing loincloths.

I blinked. "They're letting animals play in the tournament?"

Mr. South cursed under his breath in frustration. "Damn it, son. Look closer. Those ain't no animals. They're predators."

I looked a little bit closer and saw that Mr. South was correct. The 'peacock' was actually a stunningly gorgeous Brazilian woman wearing a costume that made her look a lot like a peacock, complete with fancy headpiece and huge feathers fanning out behind her (making me wonder how she managed to sit on her chair without ruining them). Bright green eyes contrasted sharply with her clear brown skin, her full red lips laughing as she ate with the two men dressed like monkeys opposite her.

"That's Peacock and her sidekicks, the Monkey Boys," said Mr. South. "Brazil's top superhero chess player and their best chess player *period*."

"Peacock and the Monkey Boys?" I repeated incredulously. "Couldn't they come up with better names?"

"Don't let their names fool you," said Mr. South. "Peacock's got a genius-level intellect behind that pretty face of hers, while the Monkey Boys are sharp knives as well. Peacock is Brazil's rep while one of her sidekicks is Brazil's second rep. Think it's the tall one, but I'm not sure."

I nodded, although I found it hard to pay attention to Mr. South's words, partly because Peacock was so drop-dead gorgeous, partly because her costume was easily the most eye-catching and distracting costume in the room, and partly because I still couldn't get over the fact that a woman with a genius-level intellect had decided to become a peacock-themed superhero with monkey-themed sidekicks who called themselves the Monkey Boys.

And I thought that American superheroes were weird.

"And, of course, you already know Sushimo and Butterfly," said Mr. South, "although I take it you haven't met Sushimo's second, have you?"

I shook my head. "No, I haven't. Who is he?"

"Who is *she*," Mr. South corrected. "And the answer is No One."

I blinked again. "No one? You mean Japan has only *one* rep?"

"No," said Mr. South. "Her name is literally No One. I've never even seen her."

"Then how do you know she's here?" I said. "Or that she even exists?"

"Because No One is Japan's best female superhero player, that's why," said Mr. South. "Laskar would definitely invite her if given the opportunity. And her mysteriousness is part of her gimmick. She never shows up in person anywhere and only acts through computers and the like when playing chess. Some say she's really a ghost, but I think she's just good at playing up the mystery angle. Regardless, her career speaks for itself and I

FAKE CHESS

definitely wouldn't want to cross paths with her."

Again, I wasn't sure whether I believed Mr. South or not. I found it hard to believe that you could be an effective superhero or chess player without ever showing up in person, but then again, I didn't think guys who called themselves the *Monkey Boys* could be effective sidekicks, so what did I know?

"These are the big three groups we'll have to look out for in terms of playing dirty," said Mr. South. "Any one of them could knock us out of the tournament. And I mean legally, although some might decide to use some not-so-legal methods to get us out if they think they can't beat us."

"You mean we still don't know who we're going up against in the first round?" I asked in surprise.

"No," said Mr. South, shaking his head. "But I've heard rumors that the match-ups are coming in after breakfast this morning, so keep your eye out for that. Stay classy."

With that strangely ominous usage of 'stay classy,' Mr. South ambled back toward his table, where his sidekicks sat arguing with each other about something. Mr. South slammed his plate full of food in between the arguing sidekicks before sitting down himself between them, interrupting their argument and making them look at him in annoyance, although Mr. South did not seem to care. He just happily stuffed bacon and eggs into his mouth like he didn't have a care in the world.

Myself, I grabbed some coffee and made my way over to the table where my teammates all sat. I found it amazing that my teammates had managed to find a table with seven open chairs in the crowded Dining Hall, but as far as I could tell, we were the only team of our size here.

As soon as I sat down, Lumberjack, who was eating a huge plate of pancakes to my right, said, "What did Mr. South want to talk with you about, Doctor? It looked important."

I sniffed the air and, looking at Lumberjack, asked, "Is that maple syrup?"

"Yes!" said Lumberjack. He waved a thick chunk of pancakes on his fork in front of my face, nearly splattering the syrup all over my costume. "I found out that the buffet had a huge bottle of genuine Canadian maple syrup imported all the way from dear old Canada. It even tastes like Canada. Sweet, sugary, and not at all good for you."

Lumberjack then stuffed the syrup-covered pancakes in his mouth, munching on them with a happy expression on his face.

"Cavewoman no like maple syrup," said Cavewoman, her plate piled high with bacon. She popped several slices of bacon into her mouth. "Cavewoman like only meat."

"I dunno, Cavewoman," said Shining Armor as he took a bite out of his breakfast taco, "these breakfast tacos are pretty darn good, if not outright fabulous. Might have to go back for seconds."

"But Lumberjack did ask a good question, Uncle," said Goggles, who sat on my left and had a big bowl of porridge steaming in front of him. "Mr. South looked pretty serious."

"Yeah, he was, actually," I said as I sipped my coffee. "He was trying to warn me about the other competitors. Supposedly, they think that Laskar likes me better than everyone else, so they're all going to be gunning for me in the tournament."

"Seriously?" said Brave Storm, who sat directly across from me, his own plate piled with pancakes nearly as tall as Lumberjack's. "That sounds weird to me. It's just chess."

"And the leadership of an entire country as well," I said. "Remember the stakes are pretty high here. This isn't *just* chess, even if it's a chess tournament."

Brave Storm shrugged and stuffed some eggs into his mouth. "Maybe, but this all seems like a lot for just a chess tournament."

"Which is exactly what's been bothering me," I said in frustration. Then I looked around the table suddenly and said, "Wait, where is Paranoyd?"

FAKE CHESS

"Oh, he hasn't been back since he went to investigate Laskar, remember?" said Holiday Man, holding a half-eaten bagel in his hands. "I tried to text him but he hasn't responded."

That's right. I'd forgotten that Paranoyd had insisted on investigating Laskar on his own. I recalled Paranoyd saying something about heading into Chess City to follow a lead, but that had been a couple of days ago and apparently no one had heard from Paranoyd since.

And that wasn't a good thing. If Paranoyd was lost, then that meant we had to look for him. I didn't know Laskar very well, but he struck me as the sort of man who didn't like people prying into his privacy very much.

Before I could tell the others that, however, several loud *pings* echoed through the Dining Hall one after the other, occasionally in sync. The sudden noises startled everyone sitting around the table with me, but I realized that the pinging noises just came from our smartphones.

Pulling my phone out of my pocket, I glanced at the notification and started. "I just got a notification telling me that the match-ups for the first round are in."

"Well, what are we waiting for?" asked Goggles, leaning over to me excitedly. "Let's see who you're up against!"

I nodded and opened the email as all of my teammates crowded around me. I was also aware of the other competitors at their tables checking their phones to see who they'd been paired up with.

Scanning the email, I skipped the introductory paragraph that greeted all tournament competitors to the tournament and explained the rules and scrolled all the way to the bottom, where I found the complete match-ups for the first round, which was starting today at lunch.

It was difficult to spot my name at first because of how many names there were on the list, but I finally found my name at the very bottom, as well as the name of my opponent, and I suddenly

LUCAS FLINT

wished I hadn't:
   Doctor Mind VS Peacock

CHAPTER EIGHTEEN

"Peacock?" Goggles repeated in confusion. He looked at me. "Uncle, you aren't playing against a literal peacock in the tournament, are you?"

Shaking my head, I said, "Of course not. Peacock is another superhero and competitor in the tournament."

"And your first opponent in the tournament as well," Brave Storm observed. "Interesting."

"Where is she?" said Shining Armor, raising his head and looking around the Dining Hall. "Is she also here in the Dining Hall or—?"

I pointed toward the table in the corner where Peacock and the Monkey Boys sat. They were also hunched over Peacock's phone, chatting animatedly with one another. Peacock herself, however, was not actually talking with them. Her eyes were glued to the screen as if it was the most interesting thing in the world.

But I thought that, somehow, she was also looking at me.

"That's Peacock?" said Shining Armor. His eyes widened. "Wow. She's gorgeous."

"A true beauty," said Lumberjack in agreement.

"Yeah, she's pretty hot," said Brave Storm, scratching his chin.

"Not as pretty as Butterfly, but I can see the appeal," Goggles agreed solemnly.

"She's almost as pretty as my third wife," Holiday Man said. He rubbed the side of his cheek and grinned. "I wonder if she hits as hard, too."

I made a disgusted noise. "Are you guys serious?"

Cavewoman nodded. "Me agree. Stop objectifying Peacock with your male gaze, bigots."

"We're not objectifying her," Shining Armor said, folding his arms in front of his chest. "We're just appreciating her obvious natural beauty is all."

"While thinking about how she would look eating maple syrup," Lumberjack added. "Without any clothes on, that is."

"That's not the point," I said. I gestured at Peacock again. "She's my opponent. I thought you guys were supposed to be *my* cheerleaders, not hers."

"Don't worry, Uncle," said Goggles, patting me on the shoulder. "We'll cheer you on during your match against her. We probably won't be looking at you as much as her, but we'll still be your cheerleaders."

"Maybe," said Shining Armor, stroking his chin thoughtfully. "I mean, I know we're friends and all, but if Peacock ends up being the better player—"

I sighed in frustration. "With friends like these, who needs enemies?"

"No one does," said Lumberjack promptly. "Especially not the trees, who are the most ruthless enemies of all."

I sighed again. "Look, Peacock was one of the competitors who Mr. South pointed out to me. She's probably not as nice as she looks."

"I can work with not nice," said Holiday Man. "As long as I can stare at her, I should be fine."

"What I'm saying is that she might try to illegally knock me out of the tournament," I said in annoyance. "She might cheat, in other words."

Shining Armor looked at me in shock. "A woman of her

FAKE CHESS

beauty, stoop so low as to cheat? I could see Cavewoman do something like that, but Peacock?"

Cavewoman glared at Shining Armor. "What mean Cavewoman? Cavewoman pretty. Cavewoman prettier than every other woman in the world."

"Just because someone's beautiful, Shining, doesn't mean they're automatically good and righteous," I said. "She might use her good looks to try to get away with cheating."

Goggles frowned. "But until she actually *does* try to cheat, there's not much we can do about her, right?"

"Right," I said. I glanced at the schedule in my email again. "Interestingly, it looks like our match will be the very first match of the tournament. That means we have just a few hours to get ready."

"You're going first?" said Brave Storm. "When?"

"After lunch, according to the schedule," I said, showing my phone to Brave Storm. "See?"

"How are you going to prepare, Uncle?" asked Goggles. "Research Peacock's play style and tactics?"

"Probably," I said, lowering my phone, "so I'll finish up my coffee and go back to my room to—"

"Doctor Mind?" a female Brazilian voice said behind me.

Startled, I looked over my shoulder to see Peacock practically towering over my teammates to look down at me. My teammates must have been startled, too, because they all jumped to the side as Peacock peered down at us.

I hadn't realized it, but Peacock was a *tall* woman. And I don't just mean tall *for* a woman, but as in legitimately taller than most of the men in the room. Hell, she might have been the tallest person period, although it was hard to tell with everyone sitting down.

Regardless, she was close enough now that I could smell what I assumed was her perfume, which smelled like fresh rainwater in the jungle, wafting off her body. She also had a rather generously sized chest, which was about eye level with me, which made it difficult for me to focus on her face.

"Uh, yes, that's me," I said hesitantly. "And you are Peacock, correct?"

"That's right, brother," said a high-pitched male voice to Peacock's right. "And don't you forget it!"

Snapped out of my surprise, I looked down to see the Monkey Boys standing on either side of Peacock. Like their name implied, they were young-looking men who had an uncanny resemblance to monkeys. Their long, dark hair and even hairier bodies—very visible thanks to the loincloths they wore—only added to their appearance. They even had some sort of banana-scented cologne. At least, I couldn't explain why else they smelled like bananas.

"Apologies for not introducing my sidekicks," said Peacock, gesturing at the Monkey Boys. "These are Paulo and Carlos, twin brothers who have been my sidekicks since they were in high school. They are known as the Monkey Boys."

"I was aware of that, thanks," I said. I gestured at Goggles, who stood nearby, staring at Peacock with his mouth hanging open. "And this is *my* sidekick, Goggles. Goggles, say hi to the Monkey Boys."

Goggles shook his head like a wet dog and looked at the Monkey Boys and waved at them. "Hi! Are you guys actually part-monkey or do you just look like it?"

I cringed. Even I hadn't expected Goggles to ask a question like that.

"Just because we cosplay as monkeys does not mean we *are* monkeys," Paulo snapped. "Right, Carlos?"

"Right on, Ed," said Carlos, whose voice was somewhat deeper than Paulo's. "We are very offended by your offensive question, American."

Peacock, however, laughed and clapped her hands together. "Ha! What a silly question to ask, but also very funny. They do look part-monkey, don't they?"

FAKE CHESS

"But Miss Peacock," said Paulo in a whiny voice, "it was insensitive of him to ask—"

Peacock, however, ignored Paulo's whininess and winked at Goggles. "I take it you are going to ask if I am half-peacock? Because I can assure you, I am not, even though I wish I were sometimes."

I blinked. Neither Peacock nor her sidekicks seemed as vicious as Mr. South had made them out to be. Sure, they were weird, but you could say the same of me and my teammates.

Goggles scratched the back of his neck, clearly flustered by Peacock's attention. "Um—"

"So," I said, drawing Peacock's attention back to me, "I suppose you just came over to introduce yourself to me?"

Peacock nodded. "Of course. I prefer to get to meet my opponents at least once before I contend with them in the arena. Plus, I've been dying to meet you for a very long time since you defeated Death Skull two months ago."

"You knew about that?" I said in surprise.

"Who doesn't?" said Peacock with a wave of her hands. "It seems like everywhere I go, the superhero community cannot stop talking about Doctor Mind and his epic defeat of Death Skull. Even in Brazil, most superheroes think you're cool for it."

"They do?" I asked with a blank expression on my face. "That's ... nice."

Peacock nodded with a smile, although it looked a little forced to me. "It must be, but I wouldn't know. Personally, I'm not too bothered by the fact that an American superhero like you is currently more popular and famous in my home country than I am. It honestly doesn't bother me at all. Nonetheless, I felt compelled to meet you, if only so I can see if you meet the very high standards of your fans."

Translation: I am greener than the Jolly Green Giant and I would slit your throat if I could get away with it.

Okay, maybe I was exaggerating her attitude toward me a

little bit, but come on. She clearly saw me as some kind of threat to her popularity in Brazil. She hid it with some pretty passive-aggressive posturing, but I was smart enough to see through it and know that she was more jealous of me than she could say.

I'd probably look petty if I pointed that out, however, so I merely shrugged and said, "Well, it's nice to meet you. I've never been to Brazil myself, but I wouldn't mind going there someday."

Peacock's eyes glittered unnaturally. "Feel free to give me a call should you ever find yourself out that way. I'd be happy to provide you and your teammates with lodging."

I licked my lips uncertainly. "That's an awfully generous offer."

Peacock waved another hand. "Please. Everyone in Brazil knows the generosity of Peacock. Even my chess opponents know of it. But we must go. Come, Monkey Boys."

With that, Peacock turned and walked away back to her table, the Monkey Boys in tow, her fake tail feathers sashaying behind her.

"That was … weird," said Brave Storm. "Hot, but weird."

I looked at Brave Storm, deadpan. "Bryan, I know you've been single for a while, but I wouldn't try to flirt with the deranged lady who dresses like a peacock."

"Not any crazier than our costumes," Brave Storm said, tapping the horns on his head. "Besides, she didn't seem *deranged* to me. Just—"

"No," I said, shaking my head. "She was definitely pissed at me for being more popular than her in Brazil."

"Cavewoman agree," said Cavewoman. She tapped her forehead. "Me notice hostile feminine energy emanating from Peacock using me feminine powers of femininity. She definitely want murder Doctor Mind."

I gestured at Cavewoman. "See? Cavewoman agrees and she's a real woman."

"Is she, though?" said Goggles, looking at Cavewoman

FAKE CHESS

skeptically. "No offense, Cavewoman, but you've always seemed a little, uh, big for a woman."

Cavewoman furiously blinked away tears that were forming in the corners of her eyes. "Cavewoman no fat. Cavewoman strong. Cavewoman strongest of all."

With that, Cavewoman turned and ran away, loudly sobbing. She shoved a couple of Castle servants out of her path and disappeared into the hallway leading out of the Dining Hall. Her little outburst had drawn the attention of several other people in the Hall, although most of the other people were, thankfully, too busy studying the tournament schedules on their phones to notice.

"What was that about?" asked Goggles.

Brave Storm patted Goggles on the shoulder. "Son, women generally don't like getting called big, even if it's true. It's kind of insulting."

Goggles' mouth dropped open. "It is? Do you think I should apologize to Cavewoman? I hope she's not too angry with me."

"Probably a good idea," said Holiday Man with a nod. "You know how violent Cavewoman gets whenever someone insults her. I'd get on my knees and beg for her forgiveness if I were you."

Goggles nodded and ran off after Cavewoman, yelling, "Sorry, Cavewoman! I didn't mean to call you fat! Will you forgive me?"

As Goggles ran off, I just looked toward Peacock's table again, where she was now deep in conversation with the Monkey Boys. I couldn't hear what they were saying from here, but I could guess that they were planning how to take me out of the tournament.

And hopefully, they were talking about *legal* ways to take me out.

CHAPTER NINETEEN

THE NEXT several hours flew like a jet as I prepared for the first match. My preparations mostly involved sitting on my bed in my room searching the Internet on my phone for videos and analysis of Peacock's games.

Good news: Peacock was apparently a prolific chess streamer when she was not doing superhero stuff, so it was easy to find tons of videos of different chess games she'd played over the years. It was actually staggering how many videos showed up when I searched her name.

Bad news: They were all in Portuguese, a language I did not speak one word of, so I couldn't understand any of the commentary or words being spoken in the videos.

Fortunately, I didn't need to. The rules of chess are universal, after all, whether you're in America, Brazil, or Cheskia. As a result, I spent more time analyzing her actual chess moves than listening to the commentators, although it was hard to ignore them completely due to how loudly they cheered her on whenever she won or pulled off a particularly good move.

From that, I deduced that Peacock—who was an International Master—had a surprisingly aggressive playstyle, with a focus on ripping through the opponent's pawns and pieces and trying to check the king at every opportunity. It surprised me because Peacock didn't look that aggressive, but at the same time, it

FAKE CHESS

confirmed that she was indeed more bloodthirsty than she appeared.

In terms of weaknesses, I could not spot much, except that her aggressive tactics often meant she had weak if not nonexistent defense. Therefore, if her aggressive tactics did not work out the first time, it was often easy for her opponents to turn the tables on her and snatch a win with some effort.

But whether I would be able to do that, I couldn't say. I liked to think I was a good chess player, but I wasn't titled and had only played against a couple of International Masters before (including my father before his death). I'd never been able to beat even the weakest IM, but that was because I usually went in blind. This time, at least I had an idea of what I was going up against.

I did do *some* practice, however, mostly against online players on my favorite chess website. None of the matches lasted long, except for a match against someone whose username was ChessMeister1236. Fortunately, I managed to beat him two out of three times and even got a 'GG' from him, so that was nice.

My teammates were not of much help in devising chess tactics with me, but they did give me some alone time to study Peacock's videos on my own. Thus, when my phone beeped with a text message telling me to come to the 'Arena,' whatever that was, I felt like I was as ready as I was ever going to be.

So I gathered my teammates and we went to the Arena, which was located in the northern area of Castle Rook. Paranoyd was still missing, which made me anxious, but Shining Armor told me that he and Holiday Man were planning to look for Paranoyd during the first match, which calmed me somewhat.

Unfortunately, I could not bring any of my teammates with me into the Arena locker rooms. I didn't know why we needed locker rooms for a chess tournament, but the Arena apparently had them and only actual chess competitors were allowed inside. That's what D2, who showed up to show us to the Arena, told me were the rules, so we had no choice but to comply.

"Good luck, Uncle," said Goggles as we stood outside the locker rooms. He held up his hand for a high-five. "Show 'em who's boss!"

I high-fived Goggles in return as Brave Storm clasped me on the shoulder and said, "Good luck, bro. You can do it."

"And if you can't, you can at least say you tried," Shining Armor added in what he probably thought was a helpful comment, although it wasn't.

"Cavewoman will root for woman," Cavewoman said, folding her massive arms in front of her chest. "Always."

I looked at Cavewoman in bewilderment. "What? Why? I thought you were on my side."

"Women need to stick together," said Cavewoman as if that was a good excuse for betraying me.

"Don't worry, Doc," said Holiday Man, patting me on the back. "You've still got the rest of us. We'll be rooting for you even if you aren't as sexy as Peacock."

"So long as there are no trees in this tournament, I'll be happy," said Lumberjack. He suddenly gave me a big, crushing bear hug and said, "Good luck, Doctor! May all trees tremble at your might!"

Lumberjack then let me go before I could respond and walked away with my fellow teammates. D2 and I watched them go until they disappeared around the corner of the hall, likely heading to the public seating where spectators could watch.

"You certainly have some … unique friends," said D2.

I sighed and rubbed my forehead in exasperation. "If by 'unique' you mean 'crazy,' then yes, they are very unique."

D2 nodded. She then took a step back and said, in a far cheerier tone than before, "Then good luck! May the gods of chess guide you to victory and beyond."

With that, D2 turned on her heel and practically bounced away, leaving me feeling more confused than ever. Who were the

FAKE CHESS

'gods of chess' and how were they supposed to 'guide' me to victory? Nothing any of these people said made any goddamn sense and it wasn't because they were people from a different culture than me, either. They were just plain *weird*.

Shaking my head, I turned around and walked into the locker room, closing the door behind me on my way in. As locker rooms go, it was pretty small, but also very clean. Definitely cleaner than the boys' locker room back in my old high school, although given how my high school had been built on a radioactive dumpster fire, that wasn't exactly a high bar to meet.

Regardless, I sat down on the bench and glanced at my watch. The first match of the tournament would start in approximately five minutes, so I took advantage of this time to prepare myself mentally for what was coming next. Chess, after all, was more mental than physical, so mental preparations were even more important than physical ones.

But my brief attempts at meditation were ruined by my phone ringing loudly in my pocket. Annoyed, I fished my phone from my pocket and glanced at the screen, my annoyance quickly vanishing when I saw who was calling me.

It was Paranoyd's number, flashing on the screen before me in bright colors. The picture of Paranoyd's young face smiled up at me from my phone, so it was definitely him.

Weird. Paranoyd goes missing for a couple of days and then abruptly decides to call me literally five minutes before the start of the tournament?

Annoyed, I answered the call and said, "Paranoyd, where have you *been*? The tournament is literally starting in five minutes, so unless your explanation is gonna be shorter than a novel, I'm afraid we'll have to talk later."

No response. Just heavy, labored breathing.

I frowned. "Paranoyd? You there? This isn't some kind of practical joke, is it? Because I've got a match in five minutes and really don't have any time to play around with you right now."

Still no response.

"All right, then," I said, "if you aren't going to say anything, then I'm hanging up. We'll talk later. *After* I win the first round of the tournament."

"No," said a deep, Cheskian-accented voice that was definitely not Paranoyd's voice. "You won't."

I paused. "You're not Paranoyd."

"But I do know where he is."

I licked my lips nervously. "Who are you and what did you do with Paranoyd? And how did you get this number?"

"You should know who we are already," said the Cheskian with a chuckle. "We tried to get you at the airport, or have you already forgotten? I know Americans have very short attention spans, but that was only a couple of days ago."

I tensed. "The Black Pawns."

The Cheskian voice laughed. "Good job, Doctor. Seems you are not so dumb after all. Yes, that's us. More specifically, you're speaking with the Black King's Knight."

I frowned. "Wait, there's a Black King?"

"Who is irrelevant to this current discussion," said the Knight. "Anyway, some of our Pawns caught your detective friend snooping around in places he shouldn't. So naturally, I had my men capture him and hold him prisoner. That is how I got this number. We are using your friend's phone."

I bit my lower lip. I'd already figured as much, but it was good to have it confirmed, even if it didn't really help me figure out how to save Paranoyd. "What do you want?"

"Many things, Doctor," said the Black Knight. "For now, we simply want you to lose the first round against Peacock."

My eyes widened. "Are you working for or with Peacock in some capacity? Because if so—"

"Of course not," said the Black Knight in a disgusted tone of voice. "We'd never side with a foreigner like her. But we do know that Laskar doesn't want her to win. He wants you to win.

FAKE CHESS

If you win, then Laskar profits, so naturally, we think you should lose."

"In what ways does Laskar profit if I win? Is he betting on me?"

"Irrelevant. What matters is what will happen to your detective friend if you refuse to throw the match."

I froze even more. "What, exactly, *will* happen to Paranoyd if I don't throw the match?"

"Many things, Doctor," said the Black Knight. "And none of them good."

I pursed my lips. "How do I know you even have Paranoyd? Perhaps you just stole his phone and didn't actually kidnap him."

"Fair enough. Speak to him yourself if you doubt my words."

A second later, I heard Paranoyd's weak, barely-conscious voice say, "D-Doctor Mind? Is that you? Hello? Doctor, can you hear me? They've been making me watch boring chess videos all day. I think I might be going in—"

I heard a slap through the phone, followed by a pained groan from Paranoyd, and then the Black Knight's smooth voice again. "See? We have your friend. Alive, if not necessarily unharmed."

That had definitely been Paranoyd's high-pitched, nerdy voice. I'd recognize it anywhere. And, although I obviously couldn't see him, I could tell that he was in danger.

"Again, this can all be averted if you throw the match," said the Knight. "Deliberately lose, go home to America, and never, ever come back. We'll even give you your friend back, not quite unharmed, but close to it. What do you say?"

"I don't like it."

"Is that a no, then? Because if so, I'll tell your friend. It'll be the last thing he hears before he dies, knowing that you are responsible for his death."

The phone call ended before I even realized it. I tried dialing Paranoyd's number again, but it went straight to voice mail, so I hanged up.

Damn it. Out of all of the situations that Paranoyd could have gotten himself into, getting kidnapped by terrorists and being used to blackmail me into losing the tournament was easily the worst.

But I was more frustrated at myself for not doing more to find Paranoyd before the tournament started. Perhaps I couldn't have seen something like this coming, but I feel like I could have done more to help.

Before I could decide what to do, a loud, Cheskian-accented female voice blared over the locker room speakers, yelling, "Superhero Chess Tournament Competitors! The first match of the tournament is starting now. Please go to the Arena to participate or be disqualified immediately!"

Damn it times two. I was going to be late for the first match and I didn't know if the Black Knight would count that as throwing the match or not.

Either way, I didn't like being late, so I got up from my bench and hurried toward the Arena, hoping that my brilliant mind would come up with some sort of solution to this seemingly insurmountable problem.

But even as I ran, my mind kept drawing blanks.

CHAPTER TWENTY

It wasn't my fault that it took me at least two minutes to find the entrance to the Arena. The locker rooms were bigger than they looked and, despite connecting to the Arena, they didn't have a clearly marked door like you'd expect.

Fortunately, I was able to find the entrance because it was a big set of wooden double doors set at the end of the locker room. The doors had a queen and king painted on each side and they pushed open easily when I pressed against them and stepped out into the Arena itself. My jaw dropped when I saw the Arena for the first time.

The Arena was massive. It had to be two or three football fields long and easily three times as wide. Massive stadium walls rose up on every side, with a wide field of neatly-cut grass painted to look like a black-and-wide chessboard dominating the center.

Thousands of cheering Cheskians sat in the stands that ringed the stadium, screaming and shouting, waving flags and banners with various chess slogans on them. At least, I *assumed* they were chess slogans, because all of the messages were in Cheskian, a language I could read about as well as I speak (that is to say, not at all).

I had emerged onto a metal platform with a physical chess set before me. I saw a similar platform on the other side of the field, where Peacock was standing. She was blowing kisses to the audience, which seemed to have a big chunk of her fans, who practically swooned at her kisses and waves.

At least, I assumed she was. It was really hard to see Peacock due to how far apart we were. We certainly weren't close enough for us to play on the same chessboard, which made me wonder how we were supposed to play against each other. Just shout our moves really loudly at the top of our lungs at each other like some bad shonen anime?

Before I could ponder the logistics and practicality of long-distance chess, a loud voice boomed from the speakers overhead, saying, "Welcome, citizens and chess fans of Cheskia, to the first-ever International Superhero Chess Tournament!"

Startled, I looked up and saw what looked like a drone with four massive speakers hanging from it floating in the air overhead. A middle-aged Cheskian man, clad in a white business suit with a checkered tie, stood on the floating platform/drone, his bald head shining under the bright, warm lights overhead.

"This is your announcer speaking, Mikhael Checkna!" the announcer yelled. "You might know me from my Internet show, *Chess Is All That Matters*, the most popular chess-related Internet podcast in the world! I was hired by His Majesty King Laskar himself to announce and commentate on this tournament, a job I will treat with the seriousness and trust it deserves!"

Quite a few of the people in the audience screamed Mikhael's name, although I had no idea who he was. Granted, I wasn't a big podcast guy, so that was probably why I didn't recognize him, but I guess some of his fans were in the audience based on their reaction to his appearance.

Mikhael pointed at Peacock. "Without further ado, let me introduce the competitors in the first match! On this side of the arena, we have the beautiful and exotic Peacock. Hailing from the country of Brazil, Peacock is as skilled a chess player as she is jaw-droppingly gorgeous!"

FAKE CHESS

A huge roar of applause went up for Peacock, along with a round of Cheskian-accented voices chanting her name over and over again. In fact, as soon as Peacock was introduced, an entire segment of the audience pulled up a series of cardboard parts to form a gigantic drawn image of Peacock that could be seen quite clearly.

Peacock herself was smiling and waving at her fans. She looked humble and even taken aback by the obvious love that her fans had for her, although I could tell that she was practically reveling in the worship. Even from a distance, it was obvious how much she enjoyed all the adulation she was receiving from her fans.

"And Peacock's competitor is the famous—or infamous, depending on who you ask—Doctor Mind, from the United States of America!" Mikhael announced, pointing at me. "Some say that he is a brilliant up-and-coming superhero chess prodigy, but others say he's just a con artist whose greatest superpower is his ability to bullshit his way out of any situation. Regardless of your opinion, Doctor Mind is a chess force to be reckoned with in his own way and I have no doubt he'll put up a great fight against Peacock!"

I thought Mikhael's description of me was surprisingly fair, even if he did somehow describe me as both a prodigy and a con artist at the same time. Personally, I didn't think of myself as either and wondered where the hell he got that information from. Were people already talking about me behind my back? I was used to that in the superhero world, but I didn't realize I was already infamous enough among the chess community to be a target of rumor there.

In comparison to Peacock, my fan response was ... nonexistent, to put it politely. While people did look at me, it was clear they only did so because Mikhael pointed me out and not because they actually liked me. I even saw a few of Peacock's fans raise signboards above their heads that said such nice things like 'DOCTOR MIND IS LAME!' and 'DIE DOCTOR MIND DIE!'

Which seemed like things that you shouldn't be allowed to say in a chess tournament, but seeing as neither Mikhael nor anyone else associated with the tournament paid the slightest bit of attention to Peacock's overly-enthusiastic fans, I figured there was no point in complaining.

"Yeah!" a familiar young male voice called out in the utter silence of the stadium. "Go, Uncle! Show her who's boss!"

It took me a moment to locate Goggles, who was seated in a front seat at the bottom of a nearby set of seats. Brave Storm and the other Fakers also sat with Goggles, with Shining Armor holding a rather hastily-made signboard reading 'GOOD LUCK DOC,' while Cavewoman held up a sign which read 'GO WOMEN.'

I waved rather weakly at my team, who, as far as I could tell, were my only fans in the whole stadium. Joy.

"Anyway," Mikhael continued, obviously trying to move on from the awkward silence, "now that I have introduced all of the competitors, it is almost time to start the match! But first, an explanation of how this match will play out, as we will be using the latest state-of-the-art chess technology, developed by Cheskia's finest scientific and technological minds, to play this game."

Mikhael raised what looked like a detonator above his head and pressed the red button.

At once, gigantic, holographic versions of the White and Black chess pieces sprang into existence on the chessboard on the field between Peacock and me. The holographic chess pieces were about two or three stories high each, yet still not tall enough to block my view of Peacock and vice versa. At the same time, 3D images of the numbers and letters denoting each rank and row appeared in the appropriate spaces.

The smaller chessboard before me suddenly lit up as well,

FAKE CHESS

showing the current ranks and rows as well as a holographic representation of Peacock's side of the board. Twin holographic timers appeared in the air between us, with my timer closer to me and Peacock's closer to her.

"Behold, Cheskia's newest HoloChess technology!" Mikhael announced. "HoloChess 2.0 makes it easier for fans to follow along with their favorite games. The massive holographic chess pieces play exactly the same as normal-sized chess pieces. To move the holographic chess pieces, simply move the physical chess piece on the board before you and the HoloChess 2.0 system will follow the movement and move its holographic equivalent! Go ahead and test it out."

Frowning, I grabbed the Queen's Pawn in front of me and put it on d4.

As soon as I moved the Queen's Pawn onto d4, its holographic equivalent flickered and moved as smoothly across the giant chessboard as if I'd moved it myself. It came to a stop on the d4 square, and when I moved my d4 pawn back into place, the holographic giant followed.

"Simple yet elegant, yes?" said Mikhael. "This is the first time that HoloChess 2.0 technology has been used in an actual tournament and, thus, the first time that the world beyond Cheskia has seen it in action! But do not worry. His Majesty the Chess King has announced that he will be making this technology available for chess players and organizations outside of Cheskia to purchase next month! That way, everyone can play the Chess of the Future just like these lucky players!"

That comment drew lots of ooing and awwing from the crowd. I hadn't realized that the International Superhero Chess Tournament was being livestreamed before an international audience, but that made sense. I wondered how many people back in Oklahoma were watching and, if so, what they thought of this. Since it wouldn't be a very good use of taxpayer money, I imagined that Mayor Addison was already preordering it.

LUCAS FLINT

But I now knew why this tech looked so familiar to me. It was identical to the HoloChess tech that E2 and I used during our chess match back in Oklahoma, except bigger, more advanced, and fancier (and probably pricier, too). I wondered if E2 had been using a prototype or perhaps a previous, less advanced model of the HoloChess system.

Regardless, you are probably wondering why I am not asking why the government of any country would invest so much time and resources into creating a glorified holographic chessboard. Because you have to remember that Cheskia is itself a giant chessboard and all anyone seems to care about here is chess, so this really isn't that weird as far as chess goes.

"Now that I have explained the system, it is just about time for the tournament to start," Mikhael continued. "The rules are simple. Losers are kicked out of the tournament but may remain to watch the next matches, while the winners face the other semifinalists until only one is left. Eventually, the Tournament Champion will get the opportunity to play against the Chess King himself for the ultimate prize: The title of Chess King of Cheskia, with all of the power, wealth, and glory that that title carries with it."

I gulped. I still wasn't sure about all this, especially after that weird phone call I got from the Black Pawns threatening to kill Paranoyd if I didn't throw the match.

But it was too late to go back now.

At this point, I had to play … whether I wanted to or not.

CHAPTER TWENTY-ONE

PEACOCK RAISED her right hand into the air and declared, "As White, I shall make the first move! Are you ready to lose, Doctor?"

I bit my lower lip. "Actually, I want to save—"

A rotten tomato suddenly flew out of the crowd behind me and narrowly missed my head, falling onto the ground of the stadium far below. Looking over my shoulder, I snapped, "Who threw that?"

"One of my *adoring* fans, no doubt," said Peacock with a sigh, pressing the back of her hand against her forehead. "Back in Brazil, my fans are known for their uncontrolled passion for me, to the point where they have started several riots anytime I lose a chess match. Or even when I just come close to losing, sometimes."

I cracked my fingers. "Then tell your 'passionate' fans to stop throwing fruit at me."

Peacock shrugged. "Even I can't control their passion, for that is just how my people are."

I pointed at the audience. "But everyone other than my teammates are Cheskian, not Brazilian."

Peacock snorted. "My fans are my people, not my fellow countrymen, whom I share nothing more than an unfortunate genetic and geographic legacy with. But anyone who passionately loves me and my chess skills ... ah, *that* person is one of my people."

"We love you, Peacock!" some random Cheskian guy in the crowd shouted.

"I named my daughter after you, Peacock!" a Cheskian woman called out, holding up a baby that must have been her daughter. Poor girl.

Peacock blew more kisses toward the audience. "I love you as well, my fans!"

I groaned. So her 'people' were whoever mindlessly worshipped her like a goddess. What a humble woman.

I didn't have time for this nonsense. Somewhere in the city right now, Paranoyd was being tortured by the Black Knight's goons. And unless I threw the match, they would definitely kill him.

As much as I hated to admit it, I had to lose this match. Winning was fun and all, but not if it meant losing one of my friends. I didn't even particularly want to be the King of Cheskia, anyway.

At the same time, I also needed to let the other Fakers know that Paranoyd was in danger. Yet how could I convey that without letting the rest of the world—including, I was sure, the Black Knight's spies in the stadium—know that that was what I was trying to do?

Guess I would just figure it out as I went along, like I usually did.

So I looked at Peacock and snapped, "Enough peacocking!

FAKE CHESS

Are you going to play your first move or not?"

Peacock huffed and brushed back her long hair. "Fine! I do not like your tone, Doctor, but we are here to play. The faster I beat you, the closer I get to the throne, which is all I really want out of this tournament anyway."

Peacock grabbed f2 pawn and pushed it forward onto f3. At the same time, the massive hologram of the f2 pawn followed the movement of the real, much smaller one, coming to a rest on the holographic f3 square. Then she looked at me and said, "Your move, Doctor."

As soon as Peacock finished her move, her fans cheered like she'd already won the game.

But I ignored them to study the chessboard more closely and consider my next move.

I could try to force a Fool's Mate, but it was difficult to do using Black, and that was assuming Peacock would even fall for it. Even if she realized what I was doing, she might think it was a trick or something and play something differently. No doubt Peacock was playing to win, which was fine, but I didn't know how to force her to win without her realizing it.

And anyway, the competitive part of me hated the idea of losing to Peacock at all. I had no way of knowing if the Black Knight would keep his end of the deal and spare Paranoyd if I threw the match. He might just go ahead and kill Paranoyd anyway, so why not do my best and try to win?

So I grabbed the f7 pawn and moved it forward two spaces to f5, causing the hologram on my side of the board to follow my move exactly. It was a bit weird but also kind of cool to watch.

Peacock huffed again. "Is that all you are going to do, Doctor? What a simple move, but then, Americans are known for being simple."

I shot Peacock an annoyed look. "Lady, you just moved your pawn forward one square. Don't criticize *me* for being simple."

Peacock chuckled. "That is because you do not see what my real plan is. Anyway, my turn! I already know what I want to do, even before you made your move."

Peacock grabbed her g2 pawn and, with a completely unnecessary flourish, moved it forward two spaces onto the g4 square. Her fans in the crowd went wild when she did that, chanting her name over and over again as if she'd won the game already. Based on how much Peacock was smirking, she also seemed to think she'd won. "Your move again, Doctor. Perhaps it will even be your last."

I frowned. Why Peacock felt so superior to me, I didn't know. It was probably her fanboys stroking her ego, but I had to admit, I was a little nervous. Neither of us had lost any pieces yet, but I could tell Peacock was getting ready to go on the offense.

So I studied the board again … and then realized that Peacock *definitely* wasn't as good a chess player as she thought she was.

I looked up at Peacock in disbelief. "Did you just do that?"

Peacock, who was busy posing for photos from her fans, paused and looked at me in annoyance. "Do what?"

I gestured at the chessboard. "Move your g2 pawn to g4. That wasn't a blunder or anything?"

It was Peacock's turn to frown now. "Why would that be a blunder—Oh, God, no."

It was my turn to smirk now. "Oh, God, *yes*."

I grabbed my Queen and moved her all the way to h4, causing her to attack Peacock's King and get me—

"CHECKMATE!" Mikhael screamed. "Doctor Mind has

FAKE CHESS

checkmated Peacock! With a Fool's Mate, no less! That makes Doctor Mind the undisputed winner of the match!"

Ordinarily, I would have stayed to accept the congratulations from everyone and rub it in Peacock's shocked face.

Instead, however, I whipped out my phone and shot off a group text to the Fakers:

Paranoyd is in danger. He is being held prisoner by someone named the Black Knight who will kill him as soon as he finds out that I won the match.

My fellow Fakers pulled out their phones when they get my text, shocked looks on all of their faces. But they all also immediately rose to their feet and rushed out of the stadium with Lumberjack and Cavewoman leading the way, much to the confusion of the other people sitting in the stands around them. My phone *pings* with a message from Goggles, telling me that he's already tracked Paranoyd's phone to a warehouse in the city and that he would meet me in the locker rooms while the rest of the team would go to the warehouse to help Paranoyd.

Grinning, I turned and left the stadium myself, running as fast as I could, hoping against hope to save Paranoyd before the Black Knight got him.

CHAPTER TWENTY-TWO

I RAN THROUGH the streets of Chess City as fast as I could, with Goggles on my left and Brave Storm on my right. We passed tons of Cheskian citizens going on their way to and fro from work or running errands, with the Cheskians moving out of the way if they saw us coming.

Holding my phone up to my ear, I said, "Lumberjack, how does the situation at the warehouse look?"

"Not good, Doc," said Lumberjack in a grim voice. "We've managed to locate the building, but it's locked. Cavewoman is trying to bash the door open, but it's pretty thick."

I scowled. "What about Paranoyd? Do you know if he's okay?"

"No idea," said Lumberjack. "None of the lights in the warehouse are on and, like I said, we haven't gotten inside yet. But—"

A gunshot could suddenly be heard over the phone, followed by Lumberjack cursing in what sounded like French. "Oops! Looks like someone saw us. One of those Black Pa—no, wait. Two. No, three. Actually, there are a ton of those guys and they are pouring out of the warehouse like rabbits."

More gunfire exploded out of the phone, forcing me to briefly pull my phone away from my ear to avoid going deaf. "Stay safe! Brave Storm, Goggles, and I are on the way. Just don't get shot

FAKE CHESS

and try to make sure they don't get away. We're coming."

I ended the call, prompting Brave Storm running beside me to ask, in a slightly out-of-breath voice, "I thought I heard gunfire."

"You did," I said grimly. "Lumberjack and the others found the warehouse, but it sounds like the Black Pawns found them. We need to get there. Fast."

"But we're running as fast as we can," said Goggles, who sounded even more winded than Brave Storm. "We'll never make it there in time, not on foot."

I scowled. Goggles had a point. According to my phone's GPS, the warehouse was located about four blocks south of our current position. That was a fifteen or twenty-minute walk, depending on how fast we walked. Even then, that was assuming we didn't run into any problems or delays along the way, which was far from certain. By the time we got there, the fight would likely be over one way or another.

That was when I heard the roaring of an engine behind us and looked over my shoulder. My jaw dropped.

A monster of a vehicle was ripping down the streets of Cheskia toward us. It looked like one of those military humvees you see sometimes, except painted black-and-white like a chessboard, complete with king-piece hood ornament.

I grabbed Goggles and jumped off the street with Brave Storm, just barely avoiding the massive truck, which skidded to a stop next to us. My heart pounding and the smell of burnt rubber filling my nostrils, I looked up at the tinted windows in time to see the passenger window descend, revealing that the driver of the truck was none other than Checkmate.

"Checkmate?" I repeated in disbelief. "Where did you get that monster?"

"It's the Chessmobile," Checkmate explained. He thrust a thumb over his shoulder. "Now get in. You three look like you need a ride, as you Americans like to say."

Although I was still in shock over Checkmate's massive

truck, I didn't question his story. I just jumped into the passenger's seat beside Checkmate while Brave Storm and Goggles hopped into the back seats. Before any of us could buckle in our seat belts, however, Checkmate slammed his foot on the gas pedal and the truck went roaring down the street, forcing more Cheskians to jump out of its way to avoid getting run over. I tried to wave apologetically at them, but we were driving too fast for them to see me.

Besides, Checkmate didn't look very worried. He wore a look of absolute determination on his face, his eyes narrowed and focused as he drove the truck like a madman.

Even weirder, what sounded like Cheskian rap music blared out of the speakers of his truck, to which he banged his head in a steady rhythm that made it obvious he listened to this music regularly. I couldn't understand a word of the music, but I didn't like rap in general, so I doubted knowing the lyrics would have helped me like it better.

"Do you even know where you are going?" I asked Checkmate, raising my voice to be heard over the loud music.

I wasn't sure if Checkmate nodded or he was still just banging his head in time with the music. "Yes! Police scanner tells me about gunshots reported at the warehouse on Kasparov Avenue. As guns are banned in Cheskia, that can only be our destination."

I frowned. That was actually a surprisingly logical deduction on his part, so I just sat back and tried to hang on and silently mouth apologies to every Cheskian we ran off the streets.

Thus, a trip that should have taken ten, fifteen, twenty minutes on foot was reduced to less than five. We ripped around a particularly tight corner, almost knocking over a pawn-shaped fire hydrant, before I heard gunfire and the windshield of the truck cracked.

Checkmate abruptly slammed his foot on the brakes. The tires of the car screeched like banshees against the pavement, which would have definitely thrown me out of my seat if not for my

FAKE CHESS

seatbelt. Even then, my body strained against the seatbelt, causing me to lose my breath.

Checkmate, on the other hand, just bent over and pulled out his chess gun from under his seat. Loading it with bullets shaped like pawns, Checkmate snapped, "I'll draw their fire while you and your teammates get into the warehouse!"

Before I could offer my thoughts on that particular plan, Checkmate kicked open the driver's side door and dove out onto the street. A hail of bullets from the rooftops above followed, but Checkmate somehow avoided all of them. Rolling to his feet, Checkmate ran toward the shelter of a nearby alleyway while occasionally shooting his pawns at the Black Pawns situated on the rooftop of the building nearby.

"Wow," said Goggles in amazement. He looked at me with shining eyes. "Did you see that? Checkmate just jumped into that hail of bullets like it was a shower! He's so cool."

"Hopefully he doesn't decide to shower in them," I said, "otherwise that might be the last 'cool' thing he ever does."

Brave Storm unbuckled his seatbelt and leaned forward. "Regardless, Checkmate's plan is working. He's drawn most of the gunfire away from us."

Brave Storm was right. Through the cracked windshield, I saw a good portion of the Black Pawns now firing their guns on Checkmate, who was crouched behind an abandoned food truck called 'PIECES & PAWNS,' which I assumed must have sold ice cream or something based on the cartoony drawing of a child eating a white ice cream cone. The food truck must have been tougher than it looked because none of the Black Pawns' bullets were getting through.

As for my teammates, they were also scattered around the street, either hiding from the gunmen or else fighting the few Black Pawns that had decided to get up close and personal. Lumberjack, for example, was swinging his ax at a Pawn who wore what I assumed was medieval Cheskian plate mail, who blocked Lumberjack's blows with his shield before slashing at him with his sword. Holiday Man and Cavewoman were crouched behind an abandoned car, doing their best to avoid getting hit by the gunmen, while Shining Armor was caught in a sword duel with a Black Pawn who showed surprising dexterity with a sword. None of my teammates looked injured, but it was clear that the Black Pawns were keeping them pinned down or distracted.

Unfortunately, the Black Pawns clearly were not ready for a superhero like me.

"All right," I said. I glanced over my shoulder at Brave Storm and Goggles. "Bryan, distract the Black Pawns while Goggles and I break into the warehouse. Can you do that for me?"

Brave Storm frowned. "I don't know. While my armor *is* bulletproof, I don't know if it's *that* bulletproof."

"I know," I said, "but remember the enhancements we made to your armor before we left the States? Now would probably be a good time to use them."

Goggles gasped. "But Uncle, Dad hasn't even got a chance to test the enhancements yet. For all we know, they might even kill him."

I looked at Goggles in alarm. "I know they're still experimental, but I don't think they'll *kill* him if they don't work. I mean, would I ever give a member of my own family experimental technology if I thought it might have a high chance of killing them?"

Goggles shook his head rapidly. "Nope. I was mostly saying that just to be dramatic and cool. I think Dad will be fine."

Shaking my own head in disapproval, I said to Brave Storm, "So you want to give the new tech a try?"

Brave Storm nodded, albeit with great reluctance. "I ... suppose. But can I give it a new name? I don't like the one you gave it."

I smirked. "My tech, my rules. Besides, it's not the *worst*

FAKE CHESS

name in the world. It's better than some of the alternatives I came up with."

Brave Storm pursed his lips. "Fine. I'll use it."

"Great," I said. I took a deep breath and rested my hand on the handle of the passenger's door. "On the count of three, we'll all jump out together, okay?"

Brave Storm nodded, even as his armor started to make whirring sounds, with blue lights beginning to shine along his shoulders. Goggles gave me the thumbs up.

With another nod of my own, I said, "All right. One ... two ... three!"

I thrust open the passenger's door and leaped out into the street. At the same time, Brave Storm and Goggles followed me out of one of the truck's back doors and we rolled onto the street and on our feet, making a beeline for the warehouse.

As expected, that caused several of the Black Pawns—at least, of the ones who weren't distracted by Checkmate—to turn their guns on us. Before they could fire, however, Brave Storm launched himself in front of me and Goggles and yelled, at the top of his lungs, "Eat Cotton Candy, you stupid LARPers!"

Several compartments suddenly opened along Brave Storm's armor and about a dozen mini-missiles launched out of them toward the Black Pawns. The Black Pawns, not wanting to get blown into pieces, did their best to retreat, but some of the slower ones were not so lucky and took on the full blast of the missiles.

A huge explosion erupted from the edge of the warehouse's rooftop, sending chunks of debris flying everywhere while knocking several of the Black Pawns onto the streets below.

It was an amazing sight. Back in Freedom City, I'd decided that Brave Storm needed an upgrade to his armor. So I paid to get mini-missiles installed in his armor to give him a long-range option, which I nicknamed Cotton Candy because that was what I'd been eating at the time and I thought it would annoy my brother (which it did). This was our first time using Cotton Candy

171

in the field, so I was happy to see that it worked.

Unfortunately, some of the survivors just knelt against the edge and started firing at Brave Storm.

But I activated my Mind-Bender Crown and telekinetically caught their bullets and launched them right back at them. The Black Pawns were forced to retreat once again, this time to avoid their own bullets, although I did manage to nail a few of them, causing them to fall down on top of their allies who had fallen in the last assault.

"Thanks!" Brave Storm called out as Goggles and I ran, more missiles starting to poke out of his armor. "I'll keep 'em busy! You guys just save Paranoyd."

I didn't respond except with a quick thumbs up. Goggles and I reached the nearest entrance into the warehouse and, kicking the door open, we immediately rushed inside.

CHAPTER TWENTY-THREE

THE SECOND we stepped into the warehouse, more gunfire echoed throughout the building and Goggles and I immediately dropped behind a nearby crate. The sound of bullets striking the crate filled the air until they stopped.

"We saw you, Doctor!" a male Cheskian-accented voice called out. "Do not think that you can hide from us forever!"

I scowled. Damn it. I should have expected that there would be more Black Pawns in here waiting for us.

"Goggles," I said, "how many Pawns do you see?"

Goggles risked a look around the crate before a hail of bullets forced him to pull his head back. "Um, about six, but there might be more."

I groaned. "Six. We'll need to distract them if we're going to beat them."

"Do you want me to distract them?" asked Goggles, raising his hockey stick. "Because I'm pretty good at distracting people."

I shook my head. "No. Too dangerous. We need something else."

My eyes darted to the ceiling overhead, where I noticed a series of thick, heavy-looking metal chains hanging. I experimentally tugged on them with my telekinesis, just enough to determine that they were looser than they looked.

"Come on out, Doctor," said the Black Pawn again, his voice sounding way too close for comfort now. "Or we will *make* you come out."

I gritted my teeth and whispered to Goggles, "I'm going to do something crazy, so I want you to stay down until I tell you. Okay?"

Goggles pursed his lips, but nodded. He crouched lower to the floor and put his hands on his head. "I'm ready when you are, Uncle."

With a nod, I took another deep breath and abruptly stood up. Turning to face the Black Pawns, I telekinetically yanked the chains above and sent them flying toward the Black Pawns like snakes.

The Black Pawns tried to shoot the chains, but the bullets merely bounced harmlessly off of the metal chains. The chains slammed into the Black Pawns with the force of a runaway boulder, knocking them all down bowling pin style onto the floor.

Moving quickly, I swung my hands around and forced the chains to wrap around the Black Pawns, tying them all together with the same chains. In seconds, all six of the Black Pawns sat on the floor unarmed, chained together as tightly as I could manage, their heads lolling on their chests, clearly unconscious from the impact of the crash.

Lowering my hands, I said, "Okay, Goggles, it's safe to come out now."

Goggles peered over the top of the crate and his jaw fell open. "Wow. Go Uncle!"

I nodded and began walking forward. "Thanks. Now come on. Paranoyd should be around here somewhere."

We walked past the unconscious Black Pawns without another look. Perhaps it would have made sense for us to interrogate one of them about the location and status of Paranoyd, but we were rapidly running out of time and I didn't want to waste any of it trying to get these Black Pawn guys to tell me something they obviously didn't want to tell me. Besides, I figured Paranoyd shouldn't be too hard to find, given how small

FAKE CHESS

this warehouse was.

"Paranoyd!" I called out as we walked, doing my best to ignore the sounds of battle coming from outside. "Can you hear me, Paranoyd? Paranoyd?"

But I got no answer from the big warehouse full of crates and boxes, other than my own voice echoing off the walls.

That was concerning. Either Paranoyd had been gagged and therefore was unable to respond ... or else we really were too late.

"Paranoyd!" Goggles cried, cupping his hands around his mouth to make his voice louder. "You there, dude? It's us! Doctor Mind and Goggles!"

Again, no answer, which did nothing except increase the growing sense of anxiety in the pit of my stomach.

Until I heard movement overhead and looked up in time to see something falling down from the ceiling. The object stopped about halfway between the floor and the ceiling and hung there, slowly rotating on the spot.

At first, I thought it was an oversized sack of potatoes or possibly a bag of rocks, but as the bag turned toward us, I gasped when I saw who it was.

It was Paranoyd. He was trapped inside a body bag of some sort. His domino mask hung limply on his face, his nose clearly broken, his right eye blackened like someone had punched him. He was missing his trademark fedora and had some dried blood on the edge of his mouth. His eyes were closed and he didn't move much, if at all, in the cocoon/body bag.

"Is that Paranoyd?" asked Goggles in a voice full of horror. "He looks ... dead."

I took a step toward Paranoyd to check, but then Paranoyd's eyes shot open and he screamed, "He's behind you!"

Puzzled, I whirled around on the heel of my foot in time to see a black sword coming down toward me.

Without hesitation, I jumped backward, just barely avoiding the blade, which slammed into the concrete floor, sending tiny chunks of concrete flying. Goggles also jumped back with me and raised his hockey stick defensively, while I raised my hands toward my Mind-Bender Crown, ready to use my telekinesis, but then I was shocked and didn't do anything.

I don't know *why* I was shocked to see a horse-headed man in black medieval armor standing before me, his sword still embedded in the concrete floor. This was freaking Cheskia, after all.

It would be weird if something *wasn't* explicitly and blatantly chess-themed.

What *was* surprising was the electrical cable running from the base of the sword to what looked like a battery pack on the knight's back. It hummed with electrical energy, especially when the knight yanked his sword out of the floor and pointed it at me.

"Good reflexes, Doctor," said the knight in a familiar deep masculine voice. "You move almost as quickly as thought."

I scowled. "You must be the Black Knight, the one who told me to throw my match with Peacock."

The Black Knight nodded. "A pleasure to finally meet you face-to-face, Doctor. I've been following your adventures in Freedom City very closely since your defeat of Death Skull the Murderer. You are shorter than I expected."

I scowled even more. "My height is not the current topic of discussion, thanks."

The Black Knight shrugged. "True. But your snooping friend is."

The Black Knight gestured with his sword at the bound Paranoyd, who was staring at the Black Knight with pure fear in his eyes now. He even flinched when the Black Knight pointed, even though the Black Knight stood a good distance away from him right now.

"No," I said sarcastically, "I actually came here to play a long and drawn-out game of chess with you. Paranoyd being here is *totally* a coincidence."

FAKE CHESS

Goggles looked up at me with confusion. "It is? But I thought he was the whole reason we came here."

"Sarcasm is clearly not your sidekick's superpower, Doctor," said the Black Knight before I could more or less say the same thing to Goggles. He lowered his blade. "Perhaps he understands violence better."

The Black Knight's sword suddenly exploded with green energy and he launched forward, swinging his blade at us. Goggles and I separated to avoid the Black Knight, who landed where we'd been standing before and whipped his head to the left and the right as if trying to figure out who to go after next.

I made it easy for him by telekinetically throwing the biggest crate I could find at him. The huge crate flew through the air toward the Black Knight, who glanced up at it with the same kind of concern I might show to a bird flying overhead.

Without hesitation, Black Knight slashed his sword through the crate, causing the whole thing to simply *shatter* in midair. Where once was a massive crate that weighed at least five hundred pounds was now bits and pieces of wood that rained softly down on the Black Knight's armor, occasionally bursting into flame when they touched his sword.

"Impressed?" said the Black Knight upon noticing my stunned expression. He raised his sword, which still hummed with energy. "This is no ordinary sword. It is an electro-boosted shatterblade, a prototype weapon that the Cheskian army is planning to make standard issue among its soldiers. Mine, of course, was stolen, but it works just as well either way."

"Holy shit," I said. "You mean the Cheskian army is creating weapons that *aren't* blatantly chess-themed? I didn't know the Cheskian government was even capable of that level of restraint."

The Black Knight grunted. "Because you refused to throw the match, that means I have no choice but to kill you *and* Paranoyd."

I quirked an eyebrow and glanced at the frightened and immobilized Paranoyd. "Not that I am complaining, but why

177

didn't you kill Paranoyd already? I figured he would have been dead by the time I got here."

The Black Knight laughed. "Why, because we were never planning to kill the boy in the first place. We only kidnapped him because we saw him as a way to get to you, a plan which worked wonderfully. A shame I didn't think of it myself."

"I guess you must not be the shiniest piece on the board, then," I said. I cringed. "Damn it, am I making chess-related jokes now? Must be something in the water."

Although I couldn't see the Black Knight's face, I could tell I must have pissed him off based on his body language. He put both hands around the handle of his electro-whatever sword and said, "Your American humor won't save you from being shattered into a million pieces."

"Just why do you want to kill me so badly anyway?" I asked. "I've never done anything to you Black Pawns and yet you guys have tried to kill me at least two times since I got here. It's ridiculous."

"Because you stand in the way of our efforts to overthrow Laskar," said the Black Knight. "Though you do not know it, there's a power struggle going on in this country, one that has both blatant and subtle moves. And your very *presence* in this country is an insult to this country's *true* successor to the throne."

I raised an eyebrow. "The true successor? Do you mean Checkmate"

The Black Knight swore in Cheskian. "No. I and my fellow Black Pawns serve the Black King himself, who is the true successor to the Cheskian throne."

The Black Knight spoke of the Black King as if his name alone was sufficient explanation for every weird or stupid thing that had happened in this country since I got here. Unfortunately for him, that name literally meant nothing to me.

So I said, "Um, who exactly *is* the Black King, if you don't mind me asking? I've heard about him, but still don't know much

FAKE CHESS

about him."

The Black Knight tilted his head to the side. "I am not surprised. Only Cheskians know what is *really* going on here, and you are definitely not a Cheskian."

"Why?" I said. "What *is* the Black King's story?"

The Black Knight raised his sword. "I am not going to tell you because you are the enemy. And enemies must be crushed."

I nodded. "That's fine. I wasn't actually interested in finding out the answer to that question. I just wanted to buy some time."

The Black Knight tilted his head to the other side, this time clearly in confusion. "Buy some time for wha—"

Thwack!

Goggles slammed his hockey stick into the back of the Black Knight's head. The blow sent the Black Knight staggering forward, cursing loudly.

Then I stepped forward and focused on the Black Knight's electro-sword, which I grabbed with my telekinesis and yanked out of his hands. But I didn't just yank the sword out of his hands. I also took with it the battery pack, ripping it off of the Black Knight's armor in a rain of sparks and wiring.

Pulling the futuristic weapon over to my side, I said, "Sorry about that. I was just looking to even the playing field a little. That sword of yours was too … oppy? Is that what the kids say nowadays, Goggles?"

Goggles groaned. "Uncle, it's OP. As in 'overpowered.' Not oppy."

I shook my head. "Whatever. Point is, I got your sword, Knight. What are you going to do about it?"

The Black Knight had recovered from Goggles' blow, but looked weaker. The back of his armor sparked and snapped and he seemed to be struggling to stand. I guess having the battery ripped out of his back had probably hurt a lot more than I thought it would.

LUCAS FLINT

Yet the Black Knight did not whine or complain. He didn't even threaten me. He just held up one hand, where a button popped out, and said, "I'm not going to *do* anything about it, Doctor. Except blow you to pieces."

With that, the Black Knight pressed his thumb down on the button on his palm.

And the battery pack exploded next to me.

CHAPTER TWENTY-FOUR

I DON'T KNOW how I moved so fast, but I still didn't move fast enough.

My Mind-Bender Crown suddenly flared to life and I tried to form some kind of telekinetic barrier around my body, to soften the blow of the explosion and keep me from getting blown to itty bitty pieces.

It worked. Sort of.

Barely.

Not really.

Sweet Jesus.

The blast struck me like, well, a bomb. The impact sent me flying. I slammed into another crate hard enough to smash it open, causing dozens of individual chess pieces to fall all over me. The crash made my head spin and made my spine feel like it'd gotten snapped in half by a particularly angry luchador. It didn't help that my ears were ringing from the blast, which meant I couldn't hear a thing.

My costume hadn't fared too well. It had not been incinerated entirely, but there was now an ugly blackened spot on my chest that was too warm for my liking. Thanks to the fireproof, layered design of my costume, my skin didn't get burned, but it was still too hot and my chest felt like someone had dropped a very heavy bag of hot potatoes on it.

Even so, I forced myself to look up to see where the Black Knight was ... and felt my heart drop through my stomach.

Goggles was busily attacking the Black Knight, slamming him in the head over and over again with his hockey stick. The Black Knight, on the other hand, seemed more annoyed than anything with Goggles, raising his arms to block Goggles' stick.

That is, until Goggles started to tire from the attacks, slowing down enough for the Black Knight to grab his hockey stick and yank it out of his hands. Then the Black Knight kicked him in the gut, the blow sending Goggles rolling across the floor until he stopped at the foot of an old forklift.

"Goggles!" I said. I struggled to get to my feet. "Stop attacking my nephew, you monster. Kill me if you must, but leave Goggles alo—"

The Black Knight's fist smashed into the side of my face and knocked me flat on the ground. My head spinning from the impact, I nonetheless managed to look up in time to see the Black Knight standing over me, cracking his knuckles like he was getting ready for the beating of a lifetime.

"That was always the plan, Doctor," said the Black Knight without even a hint of mercy in his voice. "Although once I finish killing you, I may need to put your poor virgin of a nephew out of his misery as well."

"That virgin bit ... was uncalled for ..." Goggles called out weakly from the other side of the room, although I'm not sure the Black Knight heard him.

Regardless, I knew this situation was bad. Black Knight was clearly faster and stronger than me. My telekinesis was an advantage, but not a particularly big one when you considered how close he was.

But then my eyes fell on Paranoyd, who was still cocooned in his body bag that was suspended from the ceiling, and an idea occurred to me. It would probably make Paranoyd hate me, but it's not like I had any other choice.

FAKE CHESS

With a simple application of my telekinesis, I slowly but surely pulled Paranoyd's body bag backward. Paranoyd's eyes widened with surprise, but I did a weird thing with my fingers that I hoped he would interpret as my signal to him to keep quiet. Fortunately, he did, which was good because if he'd made any noise, the Black Knight would definitely have heard him.

Speaking of the Black Knight, he raised both of his hands over his head and knives thicker than steak knives popped out. "Whilst my Pawns are doing a good job keeping your teammates distracted, I know it's only a matter of time before they receive back up from the police. Therefore, I will end your life now."

I looked up at the Black Knight and spat. "Gotta catch me first!"

With that, I rolled past the Black Knight, got to my feet, and ran toward the other side of the warehouse like a mad man. I heard the Black Knight curse in Cheskian behind me, followed by the clanking of his armor and boots as he ran after me.

That was good. Keep chasing me, big guy. Just don't look up.

Once I judged I'd run enough, I 'accidentally' tripped over my cape and fell down onto the floor. I even screamed really loudly to make my accident look real. Unfortunately, I think I overdid it because when I fell, I really did bump my knees, forcing me to grab them and groan in pain.

That was when the Black Knight's shadow fell over me. I looked up to see the Black Knight standing above me again, his gleaming horse head helmet focused down on me.

And *not*, I noticed, on the ceiling.

"Is this what the infamous Doctor Mind of the United States of America has been reduced to?" said the Black Knight, scraping his knives against each other. "Running away and tripping over his own costume like some small child learning how to walk? If I were your father, I'd be ashamed to call you my son."

My temper spiked at the mention of my father, which is probably why I screamed, "You're not my dad!"

And that's probably also why I didn't just let *go* of Paranoyd's cocoon, thus letting gravity turn it into a 150-pound wrecking ball falling at speeds that would kill the average person. I pushed it with my mind so it would go fast enough to cause some *serious* damage.

Paranoyd screamed overhead, giving the Black Knight a moment to look up ...

And then get slammed by Paranoyd's entire body bag cocoon with the force of a wrecking ball.

The blow sent the Black Knight flying. He crashed into the wall on the other side of the room, his armor heavily dented and even cracked from the impact.

You'd think I was done, but I wasn't. I *would* have ended it there, but the Black Knight shouldn't have mentioned my dad. Not if he wanted to go to jail with all of his limbs intact.

Rising to my feet, I reached out with my telekinesis to grab the biggest, heaviest crates I could. It strained my telekinesis to the limit, but I didn't care. I wasn't going to hold them for much longer. I planned to give them to someone else.

The Black Knight was already getting back up. He groaned and ripped himself out of the wall, stumbling a bit as he struggled to remain standing.

I *probably* didn't need to throw hundreds of pounds of wood and chess equipment at the Black Knight.

It was *probably* overkill and might even outright *kill* him.

But goddamn, was it *satisfying* when the crates smashed into the Black Knight with a collective *boom*. The boxes exploded open, dropping hundreds of pounds of chess pieces and equipment everywhere. The boom was so deafening that even I cringed at it, not looking until the dust had settled.

Where the Black Knight had once stood, there was now just a huge pile of broken crates and chess pieces. One such chess piece, in fact, rolled off the pile, onto the floor, and at my feet, where it bumped into my boot and stopped.

FAKE CHESS

It was a black knight piece, and a fairly fancy-looking one at that.

Picking up the black knight piece with my hand, I glared at it. "Who's the disappointed father *now*, huh? HUH?"

"Uncle?" said Goggles' puzzled voice behind me. "Are you talking to a chess piece?"

Startled, I whirled around and hid the black knight piece behind my back. Goggles stood a few feet away from me, rubbing his stomach but otherwise in good shape despite the ass-kicking he'd received from the Black Knight.

"Of course not, dearest nephew," I said in my best fake voice. "I was merely taunting our, uh, vanquished enemy. Yes, that's it."

Paranoyd, who was now swinging back and forth slowly in his cocoon, said, in a deadpan voice, "No, man, you were *totally* talking to a chess piece. I saw."

I scowled. "Maybe you should go see your optometrist because I definitely wasn't talking to a—"

My rational and entirely honest defense of my actions was interrupted by the sound of movement behind us. I turned around to see that the sound was coming from the pile of wood and chess pieces that the Black Knight was buried under.

"What was that?" I said.

"What was what, Uncle?" asked Goggles as he stepped up next to me. "I didn't hear anything."

I frowned. "Odd. I thought I heard someone moving in the—"

A black armored hand burst out of the pile of destroyed crates and chess pieces without warning, followed by another, and then the hands slammed down on the pile and pushed. The horse-headed helmet of the Black Knight—now slightly crushed thanks to the pile of junk I'd dropped on top of it—rose from within the pile, followed by the rest of the Black Knight's body, until soon he stood tall on top of the heap, looking down at us with obvious anger.

Honestly, though, he didn't look particularly intimidating to me. His armor was scratched, crunched, and even broken entirely in several places. His breathing came hard and fast and, like I said, his horse head helmet was crunched, making him look a bit drunk.

Even so, I couldn't help but say, "What the hell? I thought you were dead."

The Black Knight chuckled, although it sounded very painful. "It will take ... a lot more ... a lot more than that ... to kill me ..."

Yep. Dude was definitely in no position to fight.

So I said, "Look, man, you obviously need some medical attention. If you give up now, Goggles and I could get you to the nearest hospital pretty quickly."

The Black Knight, however, shook his head. "No. I want nothing to do with a White-run hospital. I'd rather die than let those dirty Whites touch me with their dirty White hands."

"In another context, that would sound *really* racist," Paranoyd added.

"Still, you know you can't beat us," I said. "So why not just give up?"

The Black Knight's shoulder slumped. "I never said I was going to fight you. I just have one final message to deliver to you from the Black King."

I raised an eyebrow. "Oh, yeah? What is it?"

Without warning, the Black Knight pointed a finger sharply at me. "He ... is ... coming ... for ... you ..."

With that, the Black Knight suddenly tipped over forward and crashed onto the pile, sending plastic chess pieces and bits of wood flying everywhere, and leaving me, Paranoyd, and Goggles all feeling pretty awkward and confused.

CHAPTER TWENTY-FIVE

SHORTLY AFTER the Black Knight's abrupt collapse, the Chess City Police Department—recognizable thanks to the knight heads on their badges—burst into the warehouse, screaming in Cheskian while waving their guns around. It took way too long to convince them that the Black Knight was dead and that no, we *weren't* his collaborators, mostly because none of the police officers spoke a lick of English.

Fortunately, Checkmate and my teammates also arrived not long after, having finished taking care of the remaining Black Pawns, so Checkmate was able to speak in our defense. That was probably the only reason why the police let us go, because they looked like they *really* wanted to arrest them a couple of dumb American superheroes.

Paranoyd, as it turned out, was okay. We did take him to the nearest hospital, where the doctor—who thankfully *did* know some English—assured us that Paranoyd did not seem to be suffering from any injuries more serious than some nasty bruises and maybe a few cuts. He did, however, 'prescribe' Paranoyd a chess training regime so he could get his game on, although I don't think Paranoyd intended to follow it.

In any case, we went back to Castle Rook after that, heading straight for our rooms. And by 'our rooms,' of course, I meant *my* room, which for some reason had ended up being the main room where everyone gathered to discuss important events like this.

"That was crazy," said Brave Storm, reclining on my room's couch, with Goggles and Shining Armor sitting next to him. He rubbed the back of his head. "Those chess pieces *hurt*, man."

"Chess pieces?" I repeated, sitting on my bed, where I was looking up some information on the Internet. "What chess pieces?"

"That's what the Black Pawns' guns were shooting," said Holiday Man, who sat at the small kitchen table, eating from a bag of brightly-colored Cheskian candy that room service had left in my room at one point. "They *look* like bullets, but if you look closely enough, you see they are actually carved to resemble chess pieces."

I raised an eyebrow. "So Checkmate *isn't* the only guy with a gun that shoots chess bullets here in Cheskia. Why does that not surprise me?"

"Probably because that's all they sell in Cheskia," said Shining Armor, who was scrolling through his phone, his helmet sitting on his lap, while his messy brown hair stood up from his head. "I'm looking at Cheskia's biggest online gun store and they only sell bullets shaped like chess pieces. Pawns, bishops, knights, rooks, kings, queens ... you name it, they got it."

"I wonder if that's, like, a law or something that Laskar imposed on the land or if it's just the culture," said Goggles, scratching his chin in thought. "It's weird either way."

"For sure," I said. I looked over at Paranoyd. "So, Paranoyd, how are you feeling?"

Paranoyd sat in one of the recliners in my room. He had his hat and domino mask back on, but he still slumped in the recliner, his eyes barely keeping open. "Better. It will be a while before I'm fully back to normal, though. That was pretty traumatizing. I'll probably need therapy when we go back home."

"We'll see if insurance will cover it," I said, "but anyway, Paranoyd, can you tell us anything about the Black Pawns? Did you discover something important?"

Paranoyd shuddered. "There's not much to say. I was investigating near this coffee shop that had a really cute barista when I noticed a couple of guys dressed in black talking with each other. They were actually talking in English, which surprised me, and it sounded like they were talking about something serious."

"Serious?" I questioned. "What do you mean by that, exactly?"

Paranoyd rubbed his chin. "They talked about their 'next attack,' although they didn't say who or what they were planning to attack. It was enough to pique my curiosity, so I tried to discreetly follow them when they left. Unfortunately, I followed them into a dark alley, where their friends jumped and captured me."

"Did they torture you?" asked Goggles, putting his hands over his mouth in worry.

Paranoyd shook his head. "No. Not really. They just really harshly interrogated me about, well, everything relating to you, Doc. Wanted to know about your business, your family background, your chess skills … it was really intense. They didn't even ask me for my name. It was honestly kind of insulting."

"Well, I'm sure you didn't tell them anything important, right?" I said. "Probably told them to shove off."

Paranoyd bit his lower lip. "Um … actually, I squealed like a pig. Sorry."

I stared at Paranoyd in disbelief. "What? Why?"

Paranoyd held up his hands. "Hey, it was either that or let them beat me like a rag doll. And besides, it's not like I told them anything *really* important. For example, I didn't give them your bank account information or social security number."

I frowned. "Because I don't let you handle the business' finances. And *this* is why."

"See?" said Paranoyd in an obvious attempt to make me feel

better about this disastrous situation. "I didn't compromise nothin'. Our business is perfectly safe."

I scowled. "What exactly *did* you tell them about, then?"

Paranoyd scratched the side of his head. "Like I said, they mostly asked about your family background and chess skills. Especially your family background. I don't know why, though."

I rested my chin on my hand. "Why were they so interested in my family? I understand my chess skills, seeing as chess is the official religion of this country and all, but I don't know what relevance my lineage has."

"Yeah," Goggles piped up. He gestured at himself, me, and Brave Storm. "We're just a bunch of Hispanic dudes who are in the oil and entertainment business. Not that it's anything to be ashamed of, but it's not like we're related to Cheskian Royalty or anything like that."

Paranoyd shook his head again and rubbed his face. "I really don't know. As I said, it's as much a mystery to me as it is to you guys. They just seemed really, *really* interested in you. Especially the Black King."

That caught my attention. "You saw the Black King?"

"I didn't actually *see* him, no," said Paranoyd, shaking his head. "I spoke to him through a smartphone. He wasn't there in person. Heck, I'm not even sure that that was his voice I heard. It was distorted with some kind of voice modulator. Made him sound like a robot."

I stroked my chin, thinking about what the Black Knight told me. "Interesting. Did the Black King have anything interesting to say?"

Paranoyd screwed up his eyes like he was thinking very hard about that question. "Um ... no, he didn't."

"He said nothing?" I said. "That's boring."

Paranoyd shrugged. "Sorry. I'm just telling you the—"

The door to my room abruptly slammed open and D2 walked in, a hop in her step like she had some really good news to share

FAKE CHESS

with me.

"Hello, Doctor!" said D2 with a little wave. She glanced around the room at my teammates. "I am pleased to see that you and your teammates appear to be doing well after your clash with the Black Pawns earlier today. What could have been an awful tragedy was stopped thanks in no small part to the efforts of you and your team."

"Uh, you're welcome, D2," I said, a little taken aback by her oddly happy attitude. "It was nothing, really."

D2 came to a stop in the middle of the room and put her hands on her hips. "Nothing? Thanks to you and your teammates, over two dozen Black Pawns, plus a Black Knight, were captured. The Black Knight, in particular, is an excellent catch, because Black Knights are famous for escaping situations that Black Pawns cannot. No doubt he has some important intel on the Black King's current position that will help His Majesty checkmate him once and for all."

It was a wee bit disturbing, I'll admit, to hear D2 use literal chess terminology to describe the arrest of over two dozen armed and violent terrorists, but that was to be expected because Cheskia. "Oh. We were just trying to save our friend."

D2 clapped her hands together excitedly. "That makes it even better! What is nobler than putting one's life in danger to save the life of a friend? Especially from villains such as the Black Pawns? It is the true mark of a superhero."

"But Checkmate helped," said Goggles, who had turned around on the sofa to look at D2. "We didn't do it entirely on our own."

D2 waved a hand dismissively. "Yes, I am aware that Checkmate was present, but you eight are the real heroes of today. For that, His Majesty, the Chess King, would like to thank you all."

"Er, no problem," I said, rubbing the back of my neck. "Now is that all that you wanted to tell us or—?"

D2 shook her head. "Not at all. I have another message to deliver to you regarding the tournament straight from the Chess King himself."

Clearing her throat, D2 pulled out a folded letter from her pocket and, unfolding it, began reading, saying,

"*Dear Doctor Mind,*

Congratulations on winning the first round of the tournament. I watched your match against Peacock with great interest and was very impressed by your overall performance. In particular, I enjoyed the way you checkmated Peacock, getting her king when she least expected it. It was probably the most thrilling chess match I've watched in some time and helps me better understand how you were able to dominate E2 in your match against him back in the States.

"*Thus, I would like to invite you and the other winners of the first round of the tournament to a private dinner with me tonight. This invite is for you only, not your teammates, though you may bring your sidekick and a plus one if you wish (your sidekick can also bring a plus one).*

"*The dinner will be a celebratory dinner located in the Cheskian Royal Family Dining Room Chamber. Please be ready by 6:00 PM tonight to come. One of my Pawns will come by your room to escort you to the Dining Room Chamber. Please wear your best dinner clothing for the evening.*

"*Signed, His Majesty Magnus Laskar II.*"

"Roger gets a private dinner with the King?" said Brave Storm when D2 finished reading the letter. He grinned at me. "Lucky. I bet the food is amazing."

"But why doesn't he want us tagging along?" said Shining Armor, rubbing his stomach. "Did we do something to offend Laskar?"

D2 shook her head. "No. This is simply the traditional private winners' dinner that is held after the first round of a tournament held in Castle Rook. Because it is meant to be a private event,

FAKE CHESS

only a limited number of people are ever invited, including the winners."

"What kind of food will be served there, if you don't mind me asking?" asked Holiday Man with an amused grin on his face.

D2 tapped her chin. "It varies from year to year, but chicken is often a main dish, along with traditional Cheskian meals such as chessboard sandwiches and King and Queen noodles."

"So would you say it's a winner chicken dinner?" Holiday Man prompted.

I sighed, while D2 tilted her head to the side in confusion. "Um ... I suppose you would—"

"It's just a stupid American joke," I said to D2. "Don't worry about it."

"Ah," said D2 with a nod. "Yes, well, it will be a fun and fancy event for all, I am sure."

"I'm sure," I said. I scratched my chin. "But it did say I could take a plus one, right?"

"Who are you taking with you, though, Doc?" said Shining Armor. He glanced at Cavewoman. "Cavewoman?"

Cavewoman, who had been sitting at the kitchen counter with a big bowl of fruit in front of her, growled out, "Me no want to go on date with Doc. Cavewoman no need no man. Cavewoman her own plus one. Plus ones outdated patriarchal concepts that oppress women."

I shuddered. "Hell no. I'd never take Cavewoman on a date anywhere."

Cavewoman glared at me. "Why not? You think me ugly?"

I looked at Cavewoman in confusion. "What? I thought you just said that the concept of plus ones was oppressive or something like that."

Cavewoman rolled her eyes. "Stupid man no understand nothing. Not like me. Me get top grades in Women's Studies class in college. Me smart."

I just shook my head, while Goggles said, "Do you think

Penny would go with you if she was here, Uncle?"

"Probably," I said. "But she couldn't come with us because of that big journalists' conference that was going on in OKC at the same time as the tournament. I might just have to go it alone."

"Or ..." D2 hesitated. "You could take me."

Startled, I looked at D2 in surprise. "Wait, are you asking *me* out?"

D2 held up her hands quickly. "No, no, of course not. It is just ... people who come to the winners' dinner are usually expected to have a partner with them. It would be a huge faux pas if you came just by yourself. And you most certainly do not want to embarrass yourself in front of His Majesty. It would be a disaster."

I frowned. "Why do I even *care* about looking good to Laskar? No disrespect intended, but getting his respect wouldn't change my standing in the tournament one way or another, would it?"

D2 folded her hands behind her back. "Perhaps not, but you must understand the importance of proper dress and etiquette among the Cheskian Royal Family. If you do not come dressed your best, with a partner, then you will simply create unnecessary scandal."

Lumberjack looked at Doctor Mind with a serious expression. "You heard the woman, Doctor. If there's something that the Fakers *don't* do, it's cause unnecessary scandals. Right, folks?"

"Cavewoman no care," said Cavewoman with a shrug. "Me stay here and sleep."

I pursed my lips. I wished I could do that, too, but unfortunately it sounded like the 'invite' was more of an order, so I said, "Fine. You can be my plus one if you want. Not like I have anyone else to ask."

D2 stood up a little straighter when I said that and said, in an unusually happy tone, "Most excellent! I will inform His Majesty of your acceptance and will see you tonight at six."

FAKE CHESS

With that, D2 turned and left my room, practically skipping like a little girl. It was strange to see, especially since she was still dressed in her pawn cosplay.

As soon as D2 left, Brave Storm shot me a mischievous grin. "I think a certain lady rather admires you, little bro."

I looked at Brave Storm in confusion. "What do you mean? D2?"

"Yeah," said Brave Storm. He gestured at the door to my room. "Can't you see it? She obviously likes you quite a bit. I wouldn't be surprised if she made up the whole bit about needing a plus one just to make sure she got a date with you."

Goggles gasped. "Wow! Imagine if Uncle and D2 fell in love and got married. I'd have a Cheskian aunt, which I'm not sure if that's a good thing or bad thing, but—"

I held up a hand while rubbing my forehead in exasperation. "Hold on, now. Let's not get ahead of ourselves. We don't even know if she likes me or not, much less if we're getting married. One step at a time."

"You're right, Uncle," said Goggles. He suddenly perked up. "Do you think that Butterfly might be willing to come with me to tonight's dinner if I asked her?"

"Go ahead, kid," Shining Armor said, patting Goggles on the shoulder. "Doesn't hurt to ask."

Goggles smiled a big smile, but then frowned and wrapped his arms around his body. "What if she says no, though?"

"Can we get back to the fact that Laskar is obviously holding this party for completely different reasons than he said?" I said. "I know I'm not going to be the *only* match-winner there, but I'm still sure there's more going on. Especially now that we know more about the Black King."

"True," said Paranoyd, "but if you think about it, this could be a great opportunity for you to actually talk to Laskar. He might be willing to answer some of your questions. Worth a shot, anyway."

I frowned. Although I was a little annoyed at everyone getting distracted by D2's apparent crush on me, I had to admit that it was understandable. I hadn't had a conversation with Laskar since the dinner on the first night of the tournament, much less a private dinner. This might be the opportunity I needed to get to talk with the guy.

Or maybe I would just end up wasting my time around a bunch of other anticompetitive chess players who probably saw me as a threat to take out more than anything.

Guess there was only one way to find out.

CHAPTER TWENTY-SIX

AT SIX o'clock that night, I stepped out of the bathroom wearing my suit and gestured at it. "Well? What do you guys think?"

Brave Storm, who still sat on the couch reading a book, looked up at me and wrinkled his nose. "It looks a little ... old."

I frowned in annoyance, glancing down at the black suit which I'd packed along with my other clothes before leaving America. "It's Dad's wedding suit. Of course it's going to look *old.*"

"Why didn't you buy yourself a new suit for the event?" Lumberjack asked. He was busy sharpening his ax near the dining room table, using an old flint rock. "Something in flannel, perhaps."

"I'm not going to a lumberjack convention tonight," I said. "And besides, I didn't realize I'd need this suit at all. I only brought it along in the first place because the tournament invitation suggested on the back that formal wear is recommended for certain events."

"I think it looks good on you, Uncle," said Goggles, who sat on the couch next to Brave Storm, wearing a suit of his own. He patted his red tie. "It matches my suit, at least, even if it is older."

Brave Storm patted Goggles on the shoulder. "That's because I'm not cheap like your uncle and got you something nice and new before we left."

"Which you could only afford because you're working for *me* now," I pointed out. "I doubt your Pete's salary would have been able to cover that."

Brave Storm rolled his eyes. "Eh, well, if D2 is as head over heels in love with you as I think she is, she probably won't mind the old suit. Much."

It was my turn to roll my eyes, but then there was a knock at the door and Goggles jumped off the couch. "Must be our dates. I'll check!"

Goggles rushed over to the door and pulled it open, saying, "Hi, ladies! You're on … time …"

Puzzled, I said, "Goggles, are you okay?"

"I believe your nephew is just fine, Doctor," came D2's familiar voice, though it sounded a lot less muffled than it normally did. "He's just a bit starstruck, I think."

Goggles shook his head like a dog and then pulled the door open entirely. And then it was *my* turn for my jaw to drop.

A beautiful Cheskian woman with long, straight blonde hair stood in the doorway. She wore a fancy blue dress with chess pieces on it, while a necklace with *D2* hung just above her rather generous cleavage. Her split dress let me see one of her legs, which showed off her amazing thighs. Her lips seemed to sparkle under the light and her skin was so clear I could practically see through it. She even smelled amazing, like vanilla and strawberries.

"Wha … huh?" I said eloquently.

The Cheskian woman chuckled and brushed her long hair back. "What's the matter, Doctor? Do you not recognize me? I suppose that makes sense. You are more familiar with my work clothes than my formal wear."

I blinked, shook my head several times, and then looked at her again before shaking my head one last time. "D2 … is that you? But you look so familiar …"

FAKE CHESS

D2 waved a hand with an air of humble dismissiveness. "Eh, I am a very typical-looking Cheskian woman. You have probably seen a million women like me on the streets of Chess City. I'm nothing special."

I couldn't tell if D2 was being genuinely humble or if it was all some sort of act, but Holiday Man appeared out of nowhere suddenly and said to D2, "Hey there, hot stuff. Want this old clown to show you a good time?"

It was amazing how fast D2 slammed her fist into Holiday Man's head. Even more amazing was the dent it left in Holiday Man's skull, visible when he collapsed onto the floor, although I had to admit he deserved it.

"Apologies," said D2 in a colder voice than before. She flicked her eyes to me rather suggestively. "I prefer doctors to clowns."

I gulped. Okay, maybe Brave Storm had a point about D2 having a crush on me. Though the way she was looking at me with *those* eyes, I wasn't sure it was *just* a crush, if you catch my drift.

"Right," I said, shaking my head again to try to clear it. "Erm, if you are ready, then I guess we're just about ready. Only I'm not sure that Goggles' date is here yet—"

"You mean young Yumi?" said D2. She gestured at Goggles. "I believe Goggles here has found her already."

Puzzled, I looked at Goggles, which is when I noticed that he wasn't staring at D2, like I thought. Rather, his eyes were focused on the young woman who had been standing *behind* D2, although I wasn't sure how Goggles saw her first.

The young Japanese woman was rather small, with a cute round face, her hair done up with what looked like chopsticks in it. She wore a simple, rather modest pink dress, a shy smile on her red lips.

"Hello," said Butterfly, waving shyly at Goggles. "You look nice."

Goggles literally punched himself in the face (which seemed unnecessary to me) before saying, in a slightly breathless voice, "Uh, you, too."

The two of them just stared at each other awkwardly for a moment, bringing back fond memories of my own teenage years, when I, too, had suffered from teenage awkwardness with my dates. And by 'fond,' I mean I'd done my best to repress all of those memories in the deepest, darkest recesses of my brain for eternity.

D2 clapped her hands together. "It looks like everyone has their dates. The winner chicken dinner is starting soon, so we should be leaving."

Brave Storm waved goodbye from the couch at us. "Have fun, kids! But not *too* much fun!"

I groaned, although D2 just chuckled while both Goggles and Butterfly looked embarrassed. Brave Storm's embarrassing words were enough motive for me and Goggles to take D2 and Butterfly out of my room. We walked down the hallway together, presumably in the direction of the Dining Hall.

"So ..." I said, glancing at D2, who walked next to me. "Where exactly *is* the winner chicken dinner? The Dining Hall?"

D2 giggled. "No. This is a private dinner. As such, it is in a private room."

"Private room," I repeated as we walked. "And exactly what 'private room' are we talking about—"

Without warning, my next step missed the floor and I went tumbling straight down into a seemingly bottomless pit. I screamed until my butt landed on a slide and I went sliding all the way into absolute darkness, the wind roaring behind me. I heard Goggles and Butterfly screaming behind me, while D2 was laughing somewhere in the shadows nearby.

A few seconds later, a bright light appeared up ahead and then we swept into it and landed on what felt like a huge pillow. I rubbed my eyes as they adjusted to the light.

FAKE CHESS

"Ow," I said, rubbing my eyes. "What the hell was that—"

Screams of terrified young people behind me made me look over my shoulder in time to see Goggles and Butterfly launch out of the slide. They landed hard on the pillow behind me, both of them gasping for breath, their otherwise nice clothes looking a bit rumpled from the slide.

"You guys okay?" I asked.

Butterfly shook her head and made some kind of whining noise, while Goggles just stared at the ceiling and muttered over and over again, "The darkness ... so much shadow ... never-ending midnight ..."

A soft laugh beside me made me look to my left. D2 sat beside me, looking as fabulous as ever, despite presumably having gone down the same slide as us. Only her hair looked a little messier, and even then, it made her look more beautiful, not less.

"That was so fun!" said D2, clapping her hands together happily. She brushed hair out of her eyes and smiled at me. "Did you have fun, too, Doctor?"

I blinked and looked over my shoulder at the massive slide behind us. "What *was* that and where *are* we?"

"That? Was one of the many secret slides hidden throughout Castle Rook," said D2. "As for where we are, see for yourself."

Skeptical, I looked around and was startled by what I saw.

We had emerged into a large, fancy-looking dining room that, while not as big as the Dining Hall above, was nonetheless very fancy. A long dining room table covered in a tablecloth with a chessboard-like design on it ran the length of the room, around which half a dozen or so other people in fancy suits and nice dresses were seated. I spotted both Mr. South and Sushimo easily enough, the two of them seated with women who I assumed were their wives, chatting animatedly while eating their food. The others, I was less familiar with, save for one:

The Chess King himself.

Laskar sat at the center of the table, next to another elderly-looking Cheskian gentleman who I did not recognize. The other man wore a neat white fez on his head and wore robes that made him look a little bit like a Jedi, though he seemed to be wearing a necklace with chess pieces hanging off of it. An empty fireplace with a large flatscreen TV hanging over it stood behind Laskar's seat.

"This is the private room where the winner chicken dinner is taking place," said D2, gesturing at the table. "Unfortunately, it appears that we were a bit late, as it's already started, but His Majesty seems to have left a few spots open for us."

That was putting it mildly. Four empty chairs stood side by side opposite Laskar, with signs that clearly read 'RESERVED' hanging off of them. I most certainly hadn't reserved any seats for us and I doubted Goggles had, either, which meant that D2 probably did, or maybe Laskar himself.

Goggles sat up behind me and sniffed the air. "Yum! I smell chicken!"

Goggles and Butterfly both scrambled off of the bouncy pad and rushed over to the nearest open chairs. D2 and I had to move a bit more carefully ourselves due to how unstable the pad was, but soon we reached the floor and took our seats beside Goggles and Butterfly. The two teenagers were already ravenously eating the chicken, showing little restraint despite what I'd tried to remind Goggles about manners earlier. Typical teenage boy.

On the other hand, it was hard to blame him when I saw all of the delicious food on display before us. Fried chicken, roasted chicken, grilled chicken, salads, fruits, sauces, vegetables of every kind ... it was hard to know where to start.

"Hello, Doctor," said Laskar as I surveyed the food before us. "I am glad to see that you could make it. And you even brought a date."

Laskar nodded at D2 when he said that, prompting her to smile and say, "It is truly an honor to be allowed to dine with you,

FAKE CHESS

Your Majesty. I feel like the luckiest woman in Cheskia at the moment. Truly a blessing."

My BS meter was going off when D2 said that. She clearly was only saying that because Laskar expected her to. Not that I was surprised, given how loyal the Pawns were to Laskar, but it did lower my opinion of her a bit.

Still, I said, "Yes, thanks for the invitation. The food looks fabulous. I don't even know where to start."

"The fried chicken is the finest fried chicken you will ever find anywhere," the fez-wearing man seated next to Laskar suggested. His voice was slightly higher-pitched than Laskar's, though he looked a bit older. "I cannot recommend it enough."

I looked at the fried chicken, which did indeed look and smell absolutely delicious, making my stomach growl. "Hmmm ... that does look good, but being from Oklahoma, your fried food would have to be pretty good to beat ours."

Laskar chuckled. "I brought in some of Oklahoma's finest fried food cooks to prepare this chicken for tonight. So if it reminds you of home, that's because it is."

"He's right, Uncle," said Goggles through a mouthful of fried chicken. He waved a chicken leg at me. "Tastes just like Grandpappy's Fried Chicken Shack."

"Stop waving your food around like that," I said to Goggles. "It's rude."

"It is fine, Doctor," said Laskar as he sipped his wine. He nodded at Goggles. "Your nephew's antics have made me like him. Reminds me of when my own son, who is useless, was when he was your nephew's age."

I had a hard time imagining Checkmate being anything like Goggles when he was young, but I nodded nonetheless and took a leg of fried chicken onto my plate, along with some mashed potatoes and gravy. D2, I noticed, took merely a small salad and some pirogies, which she began to eat quietly.

"Anyway, I forgot to mention my other special guest for this evening, Doctor," said Laskar. He gestured at the fez-wearing man sitting next to him. "This is Minister Ferz, the Minister of Chess in Cheskia, and my right-hand man."

I paused, holding the chicken leg halfway between my mouth and the plate, and looked at the old man. "Wait a second. Your name is Ferz and you wear a fez?"

Ferz tapped the hat on his head. "Yes, I do. What is the problem with that? I like fezes."

"Nothing," I said quickly. I reached out a hand across the table to shake his. "Sorry about that. I have heard of you, but this is the first time I've gotten to meet you in person."

Ferz shook my hand with a rather strong grip. "Same to you. I also watched your match against Peacock with His Majesty. Even I did not see that checkmate coming."

I smiled sheepishly. I did not remember seeing Ferz anywhere in the audience, but I had been awfully concerned with escaping Peacock's trap that she'd set for me, so maybe I just missed him. "Honestly, it was luck more than anything. If Peacock had spent less time, well, peacocking in front of the audience instead of focusing on the chessboard, she might have actually beaten me."

"True," said Ferz, "but please, don't undersell yourself, Doctor. I can tell that you have great chess skills and instincts. Who taught you to play the game, if you don't mind me asking?"

That question made me pause for a moment. "My father taught me. Before he passed away."

"Oh," said Ferz. "I am sorry to hear that. Was he a great chess player?"

"He was decent," I said. "Never ranked too highly, but he did play a few tournaments and was definitely the best in our family. My grandfather, though, was definitely a grandmaster."

Ferz nodded. "How fascinating. It sounds like your whole family has a history of playing chess. Very Cheskian. I like it."

I frowned. That seemed like an odd thing to say to me.

"Very Cheskian indeed," said Laskar with another sip of his

FAKE CHESS

wine. "So Cheskian, in fact, that I wager he'd make an excellent king, certainly better than my useless son, anyway."

I frowned again. That seemed like an even odder thing to say to me.

Or rather, to Ferz, who merely rolled his eyes and said, "We shall see, shall we, Your Majesty? The tournament is still far from over."

"Indeed," said Laskar without missing a beat. "It will be interesting to see who wins. Don't you agree, Doctor?"

I nodded politely. Clearly, there was some kind of hidden conflict going on between Laskar and Ferz right now, though for the life of me, I didn't know what it was

Then I remembered what D2 had told me earlier about how Ferz had been against the tournament in the first place. It looked like what she said was true, then, at least if how they treated each other was any indication.

Clearing my throat, I said, "So, uh, Your Majesty, where is your wife the Queen? I thought she'd be here tonight."

Laskar sighed and looked into his wineglass. "My poor wife has to deal with chronic migraines. She had one such migraine tonight right before we headed out to this dinner, so I brought Ferz with me instead."

I pursed my lips. "Sorry to hear about your wife. My mother also dealt with chronic migraines for most of her life. Not a fun thing to have to deal with."

Laskar nodded. "Sickness, in general, is not fun, but it is unavoidable, I suppose. As is aging. Growing old. Graying hair."

Laskar gestured at his gray hair as he spoke. "Indeed, eventually you get so old that you can no longer do or enjoy some of the things you used to like and do. It can even affect your ability to lead those around you, thereby putting not merely yourself in danger, but others as well."

Interesting. Was that why Laskar had started the tournament? Because he was growing old and worried he would no longer be able to lead Cheskia as well as he once did?

That seemed like a distinct possibility to me, but at the same time, I felt like I was missing something. A piece of the puzzle that would help me find out what was really going on here.

Without warning, the doors on the other side of the room burst open and E2 stumbled inside, panting hard as he rested his hands on his knees. Everyone turned their attention to E2's sudden entrance, including D2, who even rose halfway out of her chair as if she was trying to decide whether to go to E2's aid or stay where she was.

Laskar, on the other hand, just glared at E2. "What is the meaning of this interruption, E2? You knew that the private winner chicken dinner was tonight and that I'd specifically given you and all of the other Pawns orders not to interrupt save for a terrible emergency."

Looking up at Laskar, E2 said, in a slightly breathless voice, "But sir, this *is* a terrible emergency. It is, in fact, the worst possible emergency, so terrible that you needed to be told about it in person rather than over the phone."

Even I was unnerved by how frantic E2 seemed. As much as I disliked and distrusted E2, I didn't think he was faking his panic.

Laskar's annoyed frown faded slightly, as if, he, too, could sense just how bad this situation had to be if E2 was acting this way. "What happened, E2?"

E2 looked up at Laskar. He seemed almost hesitant to answer.

"I said, what happened, E2?" Laskar said, his voice quieter, but also scarier.

E2 gulped and rubbed the back of his head. "It's your wife, Your Majesty. The Queen. She's ... she's dead."

CHAPTER TWENTY-SEVEN

A HEAVY SILENCE fell over the room like the world's largest, wettest blanket. It felt as if everyone had forgotten whatever else they'd been discussing in light of this disastrous news. Even I couldn't help but forget my own reasons for coming here to focus on E2's dramatic announcement.

Laskar, in particular, looked like a professional boxer had just punched him in the face. He swayed a bit where he was standing, causing a worried-looking D2 and Ferz to rise from their seats, perhaps to make sure that Laskar wouldn't fall over onto the table.

"What ... did you say, E2?" said Laskar. His voice was flatter, but no less heartbroken. "I believe I must have misheard you. You said that my wife is dead."

E2 gulped, which was his way of nonverbally saying *Please don't shoot the messenger*. "I did, sir. Her body was found in your room. With a knife in her chest."

Laskar clutched his own chest in response, as if he could feel the knife as well. "What ... when?"

"Just a few minutes ago, Your Majesty," said E2. "One of her maidservants went to check on her to see if she needed more medicine for her migraines and found her body in the condition I just described. I've already spread the message to all of the castle servants and guards to keep an eye out for anyone who looks even remotely suspicious."

Laskar rubbed his forehead. "I ... I don't understand. Who did this? And why?"

E2 shook his head. "Unfortunately, Your Majesty, we still don't quite know for sure. The Cheskian City police have been called and are sending their best detectives to work on the case."

Geez. However ambivalent I might have found Laskar, I had to admit I felt sorry for the old man. He might have been a chess-obsessed freak who ruled over a country of fellow chess-obsessed freaks, but he really seemed to love his wife and I couldn't imagine how awful it must be to lose a spouse like that.

"What about the security cameras?" Ferz asked. "Did the security cameras catch anything?"

Laskar glared at Ferz. "There are no security cameras in my private chambers, Ferz. There cannot possibly be any footage of the crime."

Ferz patted Laskar gently on the shoulder. "I know that, my lord, but there *are* security cameras in the hallway outside your room, yes? What are the odds that the murderer was caught sneaking into or out of your personal chambers? We may not get to see the actual crime itself, but it might give us a clue, at least."

Laskar frowned for a moment. Despite the obvious grief the man was experiencing, I could tell that the wheels in his chessmaster mind were already spinning like crazy.

Pointing at E2 again, Laskar said, "E2, play the security footage in the hallway outside of my room. Now."

"Now?" E2 repeated incredulously. "But Your Majesty, the police still haven't arrived and it would be rather premature if we —"

Laskar slammed his foot down on the table, rattling the food plates and even knocking down a few glasses of wine. "I said *now*, E2. Or else."

E2 wisely chose not to continue to argue the point. He pulled out his phone and tapped the screen several times before the TV

FAKE CHESS

hanging over the fireplace behind Laskar turned on. Laskar whirled around to face the TV, while everyone else looked up from their seats. I could tell that more than a few people were uncomfortable about this whole ordeal, but Laskar did not seem to notice or care. His eyes were fixed strictly on the TV above us, like it was the only thing in the world.

At first, the screen showed static snow, but a few more taps from E2 and then black-and-white security footage of a hallway in Castle Rook that I did not recognize appeared. Another few taps and the security footage sped up, showing what I assumed was the entirety of today up until the time of the murderer.

Not that we saw much. Mostly it was Laskar and his wife leaving their room or coming back, with the occasional appearance of one of their servants coming to clean up. A few government officials, such as Ferz, also stopped by, usually to chat with Laskar briefly before moving on.

All in all, the security footage did not seem terribly interesting until the footage reached 6:15 PM, approximately about the time that E2 found the Queen's corpse. Laskar held up a hand, obviously indicating to E2 to stop, which E2 did.

For the next five minutes or so, we simply watched the screen. It showed the empty hallway outside of Laskar's bedroom, which was so empty that I wouldn't have been surprised to see a tumbleweed cross it.

"I don't see anything," Goggles muttered. "Maybe they didn't get the murderer on camera?"

I was almost inclined to think that, too, until a figure in a dark cloak appeared in frame. The figure was tall and somewhat broad-shouldered, although his flow-length black cloak completely covered his body, while his hands were fitted with thick leather gloves. An equally dark hood covered his head, though with his back to the camera, it would have been impossible to see the man's face anyway.

The man stopped in front of the door to Laskar's bedroom. He looked up and down the hallway briefly, perhaps to make sure it was empty, before he began fiddling with the lock. It only took him a second or two to undo the lock, allowing him to open the door and slip inside.

"That must be him," said Laskar, his voice quiet and hoarse, but still very much audible. "The bastard."

I couldn't even begin to guess who the guy might have been. My best guess was that he was likely a Black Pawn spy. Given their terroristic tactics, that seemed like exactly the sort of thing they would do. Of course, the guy wasn't *dressed* like a Black Pawn, but maybe he was just one of the few people in this country who realized that cosplaying as your favorite chess piece 24/7 was kind of weird.

The next couple of minutes were some of the tensest in my entire visit to Cheskia. With every eye on the screen, we were waiting for when the assassin would come back out and show himself, perhaps even make it easier to see his face or identify him.

But for some reason, even though there couldn't have been a long time between the time the assassin went inside and when he exited, the footage never showed him leave.

"Where is he?" Goggles whispered. "Did he leave through one of the windows or something instead?"

"Possibly," D2 replied in a distracted voice. "His Majesty's room does have many windows, but I would think that one of the servants on the grounds would have noticed someone scaling the side of the castle."

Suddenly, E2 slapped himself on the forehead and said, "My deepest apologies, Your Majesty! I accidentally hit pause on the security footage. That's why it has been stuck on the same image of the door. Excuse me."

Everyone collectively groaned at E2's confession, while Laskar's eye twitched like he was about to jump off the table and

FAKE CHESS

murder E2 on the spot.

But then E2 pressed play again and the door to Laskar's room creak open again. The hooded assassin stepped out, his head down to prevent us from seeing his face. He briefly glanced up and down the hallway again before heading back the way he came, this time moving a little more quickly than before. No doubt he was afraid of getting caught and wanted to vamoose as quickly as possible before someone stumbled upon him.

"That's it?" said Butterfly, sounding disappointed. "But we didn't even get to see his face."

"What useless footage," Laskar spat. "Even if it did give us a suspect, that means nothing because we still have no clue who he is or why he killed Judit."

I nodded, but then Ferz raised a hand and said, "Actually, do you not have cameras on *both* ends of the hallway? If we just switch perspectives slightly, that should make it easier for us to see the face of the man."

Laskar looked down at Ferz in surprise, as if that thought had not occurred to him. "Ferz, you are a genius! E2, reverse the camera. Now."

E2 dutifully obeyed and then the footage on the screen changed. We were now looking at the door from the other end of the hallway. As before, we saw the hooded assassin step out, look up and down the hallway again, before heading in the same direction as in the previous footage.

Only this time, the assassin was walking *toward* the new camera, which he must have somehow been aware of because he continued to walk with his head slightly bowed, using his hood to obscure most of it.

But then the assassin accidentally stumbled on a part of the carpet. He almost fell, windmilling his arms comically for a moment, but managed to catch himself at the last minute and stand upright. The movement caused his hood to fall back for the briefest of seconds, but then he pulled his hood down his face and immediately resumed walking, as if he hadn't just embarrassed himself on camera.

"Rewind a couple of seconds and zoom in on the man's face," said Laskar, pointing at the screen. "Right when his hood falls down."

E2, again, obeyed, tapping his phone and rewinding the footage. He paused it at the exact moment that the assassin tripped and started windmilling, before playing it again, this time in super duper slow motion. That let us see in detail as the assassin tripped on the carpet and caught himself, the movement making his hood shift just enough to let us see his face.

E2 paused again and zoomed in, focusing specifically on the assassin's face.

And boy did I recognize the face. Honestly, I would have recognized it anywhere, even though I was sure that my eyes were lying to me like little bitches.

Because the assassin's face was an exact duplicate of my own, down to my nose hairs.

The dining room became as silent as a graveyard at midnight when everyone saw my face. Even I became very still, unable to believe my own eyes, but equally unable to deny what I was looking at.

"Uncle ..." said Goggles in a disbelieving voice. He looked around D2 at me with big eyes. "Is that you?"

Before I could answer, D2 suddenly grabbed the back of my head and slammed me facedown into my uneaten mashed potatoes. I then heard an all-too-familiar *click* as a couple of overly-tight, cold metal handcuffs were snapped over my wrists.

"Hey!" I said through a mouth of mashed potato. "D2, what the hell are you doing? You're treating me like some kind of criminal!"

I felt vibrations across the table and looked up to see Laskar standing over me, his eyes as cold and uncaring as a blizzard.

FAKE CHESS

"That is because you *are* a criminal, Doctor Mind," said Laskar. "For the murder of my wife, Judit Laskar, the Queen of Cheskia and the love of my life, you are under arrest."

CHAPTER TWENTY-EIGHT

Did I tell you that Castle Rook has dungeons? Because it has dungeons.

Really deep, really *dark* dungeons.

And like everything else in the entire country of Cheskia, the dungeons are also chess-themed. Black-and-white tiled floor, with bars colored alternately in black and white, and of course your usual chess-themed guards. These guys looked a bit like pawns, although, unlike the capital 'P' Pawns, these guys didn't have numbers and letters painted on their faces or anything like that. In fact, their pawn masks had face holes carved into them, letting me see their scowling, not particularly friendly-looking faces glaring at me.

Not that I could blame them. Like everyone else in Castle Rook—and, probably by now, the whole country of Cheskia—they thought I had murdered their queen in cold blood. Although none of them seemed to speak English, their tones made it clear that they were probably talking about how much they wanted to kill me for doing what I did to Queen Judit.

I, of course, would have defended myself, but again, the guards didn't speak English, and even if they did, they probably wouldn't listen to a word I said. Besides, it wasn't like they had the authority to let me go or fight for my innocence.

FAKE CHESS

And my cell wasn't very nice, either. Just a simple ten-by-ten room with narrow stone walls, a tiled floor, and a toilet and sink in one corner (neither of which, based on their smell and appearance, appeared to have been cleaned in ages) and my cot in the other. It also had a chess set built into one of the walls, too, although I didn't know why. Did they think that prisoners would get bored and needed some way to amuse themselves or something?

In any case, I couldn't escape on my own. D2 and E2—along with like a dozen guards—had escorted me straight from Laskar's private dining room to the dungeons. Which wasn't as far as you might think. In fact, I'm pretty sure that the private dining room and the dungeons are right next to each other, which seemed like an odd design choice to me, but I couldn't deny that it made it transporting falsely-accused foreigners innocent of wrongdoing to the dungeons very convenient.

Because we'd gone straight to the dungeons, I'd been unable to bring any of my things with me. So I didn't have my Mind-Bender Crown, which left me more or less powerless. They'd even confiscated my phone, probably worried that I might try to use it to plan an escape or something. They did let Goggles go, as they didn't think he was involved in the murder, but I wasn't sure if or when I'd ever get to see Goggles or any of the others ever again.

Honestly, I wasn't even sure how they got away with this. I was an American citizen, after all. While I always did my best to comply with the rules of whatever foreign country I happened to be visiting, I was pretty sure that I wasn't allowed to be arrested and held prisoner like this. I was no international law expert, but didn't diplomatic immunity apply to this case or something?

Not that it mattered. Without my phone, I couldn't call my lawyer and ask him for advice. All I could do was sit here in my nice suit that I'd gone to all the trouble of bringing with me from Oklahoma and wait for ... whatever was going to happen next.

My thoughts were interrupted by the sound of a door ominously opening and closing somewhere in the distance, followed by a series of footsteps coming our way. It sounded like a whole group of people were making their way toward my cell. I even heard some voices, but they were too far away and mixed together for me to make out what they were saying to each other or what they were saying at all.

But then the group finally appeared, allowing me to see the familiar faces of Goggles, Brave Storm, and Lumberjack, along with D2 and half a dozen armed guards. I noticed that none of my teammates were carrying their weapons. Even Lumberjack did not appear to have his trademark ax with him, which signified how serious this situation was.

"Uncle!" Goggles cried, running over to my cell door and wrapping his hands around the bars. "You're still alive! Thank God. I thought you were dead already."

"Already?" I repeated, rising to my feet and walking over to the bars. I looked at D2. "Has Laskar already decided to have me executed? Even though I haven't even gotten a fair trial yet?"

D2 folded her arms behind her back. She was back in her usual Pawn costume, which did a good job at hiding her face. "His Majesty is still investigating the Queen's murder and discussing his options with Minister Ferz. Until His Majesty announces a decision, you are to remain here in your cell."

I scowled. "So accused criminals in Cheskia don't get trials? Nice justice system you got there."

"You will get a trial soon enough," said D2. She gestured at the cell. "You are simply being kept here until a trial date has been set. It is to ensure that you will not attempt to flee the country before your trial begins."

"Flee the—?" I repeated. "You're talking about me like you've already decided I killed Queen Judit."

"I've made no decisions in the matter," D2 said quietly. "I do only what His Majesty orders me to do. Nothing more. Nothing

FAKE CHESS

less."

I scowled even more at D2. I'm not sure why she pissed me off so much. Perhaps because I'd been starting to feel attracted to her and this felt like a betrayal.

Lesson learned. Never let a woman's good looks trick you into thinking she's actually a decent person. You'd think I'd have learned that lesson by now, but I guess it's something a guy needs beaten into his head regularly.

"Can you give us a moment to talk with Doctor Mind?" Brave Storm asked D2. "Alone?"

D2 nodded. She stepped back, but did not leave entirely. "You may talk with him, but only while I and the guards are here. And we will be listening to every word you share with him."

It was clear that Brave Storm didn't like those conditions, but he also did not try to argue with them. Made sense, even if I didn't like them, either. I was, after all, an accused murderer of the Queen of Cheskia herself. They probably didn't want my teammates to try to plan some sort of escape attempt with me behind their backs.

But Brave Storm nodded. "Fair. How much time?"

D2 held up five fingers. "Five minutes. Go."

"Doctor, did you really murder Queen Judit?" asked Lumberjack immediately.

I looked at Lumberjack in disbelief. "Of course I did, Lumberjack."

Lumberjack's jaw fell open in complete disbelief. "What? I didn't know you had it in you to murder, Doctor."

"I was being *sarcastic*, Lumberjack," I said, not bothering to hide my annoyance. "I didn't kill Queen Judit. I wasn't anywhere near her room when she was found dead."

"But you were on the security footage, were you not?" asked Lumberjack. "We saw it on TV today."

"On TV—?" I repeated. I looked at Brave Storm. "Are they playing the security footage on TV now?"

Brave Storm nodded. "Yep. It was all over the news this evening. Couldn't understand a word the news anchors were saying, but it was pretty easy to put two and two together and figure out what was going on."

"You mean you didn't know I'd gotten arrested until you saw the news report?" I asked.

"Goggles actually told us before it became national news," Lumberjack explained, gesturing at Goggles, who still clung to the bars as if for dear life. "We didn't believe him at first until D2 backed up his statement with proof."

"I'm sorry, Uncle," said Goggles, leaning against the bars. "If I had my way, I'd bust you out of prison and we'd go back to Oklahoma and never, ever come back here ever again. I really hate Laskar right now. I wish I could take a gun and shoot—"

"That's enough, Goggles," I interrupted hastily, glancing at D2 and the guards, who were listening perhaps a little *too* closely to Goggles' rant. "I understand that you are *upset* and emotional, but you should still watch what you say. No need to get yourself in trouble, too."

Goggles pursed his lips, but nodded stiffly. "If you say so, Uncle. But I still want to save you."

I reached out through the bars and scuffed up Goggles' hair, as he was still in his nice suit and not wearing his normal helmet. "I know, kid, I know, but at the moment there's nothing anyone can do for me. We have to wait for my trial, whenever that will be."

Lumberjack stroked his beard in thought. "I've been giving this matter a great deal of thought, Doctor, as you know I am prone to do whenever we find ourselves in great trouble. And I do believe I know who *really* killed the Queen."

I shot Lumberjack a surprised look. "You do? Who did it?"

Lumberjack raised a finger toward the ceiling. "Why, it was the *trees*, of course."

FAKE CHESS

"The trees?" D2 repeated, who I'd briefly forgotten had been listening to our every word very carefully. She glanced at the guards with clear confusion. "I do not understand."

"Elementary, my dear Watson," said Lumberjack. He began pacing up and down in front of my cell. "You see, trees are very sneaky and evil. It is clear, based on the footage alone, that a tree impersonated Doctor Mind (who bears a striking resemblance to trees himself), murdered Queen Judit in her bed, and then slipped away sight unseen, likely to commit even more atrocities in the name of the trees. Were I given the opportunity to view the crime scene, I could likely find evidence to corroborate this theory of mine."

D2 and the guards just looked at a complete loss for words at Lumberjack's theory, which made sense. After all, they were not used to Lumberjack's, er, interesting viewpoint on trees, so naturally they wouldn't know what to make of his strange theory.

"But ..." D2 was clearly struggling to keep up with Lumberjack's line of thought. "Trees cannot murder people."

Lumberjack stopped and whirled around to point a single finger at D2. "But that is where you are wrong, my cosplaying friend! On average, trees kill over three thousand people each year in the United States alone, with that number rising ten times in Canada and far higher in other, more densely forested regions of the world. Trees, being the bloodthirsty monsters that they are, must always be treated with proper caution and suspicion."

"Even if a tree could somehow move and impersonate someone, *why* would they do that?" D2 asked. "What would a tree gain out of impersonating Doctor Mind and framing him for the murder of Queen Judit?"

"An excellent question," said Lumberjack. He stopped and paused, clearly giving the matter serious thought (and probably giving it more thought than his own belief system). "Because trees are evil and love to sow chaos and discord wherever they go, it's fair to assume that the trees in this case simply wish to spread misery and fear. They probably get off on ruining the lives of innocent people like our fair Doctor, so the only answer is to cut down every single tree in Cheskia and, eventually, the whole world. Leave not even one tiny sapling to grow. Eliminate them all with extreme prejudice."

I would have paid good money to see the absolutely bamboozled expressions on the faces of D2 and the other guards. Even with their masks hiding their faces, however, I could tell that they weren't sure whether to believe Lumberjack or not.

I knew, of course, that Lumberjack was 110% serious about the trees being behind Queen Judit's murder. Although I had to admit that it was amusing to see D2 and the guards look genuinely unsure how to respond or what to say.

So I said to Lumberjack, "Nice theory, but still isn't going to help me get free."

"True," said Lumberjack, "but I happily volunteer to be one of your character witnesses in your trial. I believe I could give an accurate description of your fairness and upright moral character to the judge."

I didn't trust Lumberjack to be a good character witness—or any other kind of witness—for me at my upcoming trial, but I also didn't want him to know that. "Uh, thanks. By the way, where is everyone else?"

Brave Storm jerked a thumb toward D2. "She said that only three guests can visit prisoners at any one time. Paranoyd, Cavewoman, Shining Armor, and Holiday Man are waiting for us to return with an update on how you're doing."

I nodded. Another thing that made sense. Probably D2 feared that I might get my friends to try to break me out of prison if she let them *all* visit me. By limiting visitors to no more than three, that meant that D2 and the guards would always outnumber us. I wondered if this was a general policy for all prisoners or if I was a special exception.

FAKE CHESS

Either way, I was still pretty pissed about this situation. Falsely accused of murder, thrown into jail, and now not even allowed to see most of my friends? Were they going to torture me next or something? I suddenly found myself wishing I'd researched Cheskia's laws on cruel and unusual punishments before we got here, but how was I supposed to know I'd be framed for the Queen's murder?

"What about the other tournament participants?" I said. I then looked at D2 pointedly. "And what about *my* place in the tournament? I can't play in the tournament from this jail cell."

D2 folded her arms behind her back. "The tournament is currently on pause until your trial is over."

I frowned. "On pause? You mean I *haven't* been banned yet?"

D2 did not answer that question, but I interpreted her answer as a 'no.'

That was odd. If I was going to trial for the murder of Queen Judit, then wouldn't they ban me from the tournament? Even if I was found innocent of all wrongdoing, my trial alone would create a huge delay in the tournament. It seemed to me that their two options were to either end the tournament entirely and send someone home or ban me from the tournament and continue on as normal. This whole pausing business was very suspicious, in other words.

"We don't know what's going on with the tournament," Brave Storm admitted. "For that matter, we don't know what the other participants think. As soon as Goggles told us what happened, we came straight here and didn't talk to anyone."

I nodded. "Makes sense. I suppose most of the participants are either in bed or eating dinner right now."

"Butterfly thinks you're innocent, too, Uncle," Goggles said. "She told me so. Said she didn't think you murdered Queen Judit. So you've got at least one supporter among the other competitors."

I smiled. "That's nice of her. What about Sushimo? What does he think?"

Goggles bit his lower lip and looked down at the floor. "Um, apparently according to Butterfly, Sushimo is currently celebrating your arrest with fine Japanese wine he brought with them for exactly this sort of occasion. Doesn't seem too disappointed."

I sighed. I still didn't know why Sushimo hated me so much, but I had bigger things to worry about at the moment. "Until we know if I'll ever see the light of day again, I guess Mr. South will have to take over for me as America's champion."

"You mean the fat, sweaty Southern guy in the tacky white suit?" said Brave Storm. He grimaced. "I feel like you'd be a better representation of America than him."

I shrugged. "It doesn't matter, seeing as I'm stuck in this cell for who-knows-how-long. So until I get out—"

A ringing noise suddenly echoed through the hallways of the dungeons, causing all eyes to fall on D2. She pulled out her phone, which was making the ringing noise, and, answering it, said, "Hello. This is D2. Who is—"

D2 stopped speaking. She was clearly listening quite intently to whoever had just called her, although without being able to see her face, I couldn't tell if she was hearing good news or bad news. The other guards watched D2 with alertness.

Finally, D2 nodded, said, "Understood, sir," and hung up. She then looked at the guards and barked, "Take the prisoner to the Courtroom!"

"The Courtroom?" I repeated in surprise. "Why?"

D2 turned her gaze to me, her featureless mask looking quite eerie in the dim light of the dungeons. "Because your trial is going to start in approximately ten minutes and we don't want to miss it."

CHAPTER TWENTY-NINE

TEN MINUTES seemed like awfully short notice to get ready for a trial. Good thing I was wearing my nice suit already, although given how I fully expected to receive the death penalty for my 'crimes,' what I wore really didn't matter that much.

And hey, I guess the Cheskian legal system was actually faster than the American legal system. Of course, that did not work in my favor, but I suppose one cannot have everything in life.

D2 and the guards escorted me through the dungeons and up into the Castle, where I was taken to an unmarked wooden door on the second floor that I'd likely passed multiple times in the past without even noticing. Brave Storm, Lumberjack, and Goggles, to my surprise, were allowed to tag along, although it did not sound like Lumberjack would get to be my character witness like he wanted, which was probably the best thing that happened to me so far today.

D2 went in first and then the guards practically shoved me inside. I stumbled over my feet, not helped by the fact that my wrists and ankles were chained together. In fact, I fell flat on my face onto the floor, my hands not doing much to break my fall thanks to the chains around my wrists.

"What are you doing on the floor?" came D2's sharp voice. "Get back up."

D2's hand grabbed the back of my suit and hauled me up to my feet. Blinking rapidly to take in my new surroundings, I was a bit surprised by what I saw.

I appeared to be a courtroom of some sort. At least, that's what I *assumed* it was. I had never been in a Cheskian courtroom before, so I didn't know if Laskar sitting on his throne, high above everyone else, was normal, or if the half a dozen or so mean-looking government dudes standing off to the side were also normal.

The government guys were all clearly based off of chess pieces. Rather than being mere Pawns, however, these guys wore white costumes patterned after knights, bishops, and rooks, respectively. That meant that Laskar almost had a whole chessboard of soldiers and officials to enforce his will, with the only missing 'pieces' being his wife (for obvious reasons) and the other Pawns aside from D2. Minister Ferz also stood by Laskar's side, his arms folded in front of his chest, his hands hidden inside the folds of his robes.

A single, uncomfortable-looking wooden chair sat in the middle of the room, which was where D2 pushed me. I staggered for a moment before sitting down roughly in the chair, whereupon two Knights stepped forward and tied my chains to the arms and legs of the chair.

Yep. The chair was *definitely* as uncomfortable as it looked. Of course, the heavy steel chains clamped tightly around my wrists and ankles didn't help matters, either, but the chair was so stiff-backed and hard on my bottom that it was torture all by itself to sit there.

I heard footsteps on the marble floor behind me and turned my head to see Goggles, Brave Storm, and Lumberjack enter the Courtroom. All three of them wore identical confused expressions on their faces as they took in the strange scene before them.

Laskar's eyes flicked toward D2. "Close the door. Now."

D2 nodded and disappeared from my sight before I could say

FAKE CHESS

a word. Then I heard the door close behind me, followed by an audible *click*, likely the sound of the door being locked.

That didn't bode well for me. Laskar had told her to *close* the door, not lock it.

But Laskar did not seem to notice. Instead, he simply nodded in approval before glaring down at me with the most hate-filled glare I'd ever seen. "Good. Now that the door is closed, we likely won't have any further interruptions. Or eavesdroppers who are trying to butt into something they have no business butting into."

I gulped. I didn't know if locked courtrooms were the norm for the Cheskian legal system or not, but I guess it didn't matter. Laskar just seemed to be doing his own thing and I doubted that either D2 or the other government officials would try to stop him.

Laskar glanced at one of the Rooks. "My Rook, what is the current status report of the investigation?"

The Rook, a short, squat man who nonetheless looked strong, cleared his throat before saying, in crystal clear English, "The Castle has been locked down and all servants are on high alert for the murderer, sir. As well, Chess City Police Department detectives are at the scene of the crime, searching for further evidence or clues to the murderer's identity."

I frowned. "Um ... excuse me for interrupting, but I thought you guys thought *I* was the murderer."

Laskar didn't even look at me. He simply nodded at the Rook before turning his attention to one of the Bishops. "My Bishop, have you consulted the gods about Judit's soul?"

The Bishop must have been a very old man, because when he spoke, his voice was as crackly as a pile of dead leaves. "The gods have been ever-so-silent, my King. Anna and I shall continue to consult with them."

"Gods?" I repeated. "What gods?"

"The gods of chess," D2 explained. "They are the deities which most of Cheskia worships. The Bishops are the leader of Cheskia's religion and have a direct connection with the gods, whom they regularly consult for guidance and aid."

Huh. I hadn't even realized that Cheskia had a religion at all, but Laskar turned his attention to one of the Knights and said, "What is the status of the Army at the moment, my Knight?"

"Sir!" said the Knight, saluting Laskar without hesitation. "Current Black Pawn activity is suspiciously quiet! Since the defeat of the Black Knight who kidnapped Doctor Mind's teammate, we have noticed no Black Pawn activity in the city or in its outlying suburbs. Command stations throughout the country have also reported an odd decrease in Black Pawn activity since the announcement of Queen Judit's murder to the world."

I blinked. "What do the Black Pawns have to do with anything? I thought this was supposed to be my trial."

Laskar finally looked at me, his gaze slightly less hateful than before. "The world does not revolve around you, Doctor, but if you think I have forgotten you, fear not. Because your judgment is about to come."

Laskar rose from his throne and marched down the steps toward me. He yanked a long, wicked-looking dagger out of nowhere and raised it above his head.

"Uncle!" Goggles cried. "No!"

I looked over my shoulder again to see Goggles, Brave Storm, and Lumberjack running toward me. But then D2 and the twin Knights appeared in between me and my friends, the Knights holding their sabers out toward my friends, while D2 wielded a gun. My friends skidded to a stop before D2 and the Knights, looking surprised and frustrated.

"Do not interfere with Cheskian justice, foreigners," said D2 in a deadly low voice. "Or be prepared to suffer with your leader."

"It's not worth it, guys," I said. I nodded at the door. "Go and tell the others. Try to get out of here. Save yourselves!"

"Wow, Roger," said Brave Storm, sounding genuinely surprised. "That's the most selfless thing I've heard you say in a

FAKE CHESS

long time."

I was about to snap at Brave Storm for wasting time when a shadow fell over me, causing me to jerk my head back to Laskar.

The Chess King now stood over me, knife in the air, a cold scowl on his old features. Even though I was a good deal more muscular than him, I couldn't deny that he looked absolutely terrifying at the moment. It was probably the knife and the fact that I was totally defenseless.

So naturally, I did the most heroic thing that I could do: I shut my eyes closed and started whimpering like a child.

Hey, you'd probably do the *exact same thing* under these circumstances, too, so don't judge.

"Whimper as much as you like, Doctor," came Laskar's voice that was colder than an iceberg. "It won't save you from your fate."

Although my eyes were closed, I thought I heard the swish of Laskar's knife as it came down toward me. I briefly debated whether to try to dodge or not, but I couldn't. Not with these chains on. I was basically trapped.

Any second now, Laskar's knife would land in my skull. And hopefully, my death would be instant or at least painless. I'd never died before but I didn't like pain, so I figured going out instantly would be preferable to suffering.

But I never felt the knife striking my skull.

At first, I assumed that maybe I had died instantly and painlessly after all. Granted, I thought I'd feel *something* when I died, but why would I? Again, I'd never died before, so there was no reason for me to assume that.

But I did hear the sound of metal slashing through metal and then felt the chains around my wrists and ankles loosen considerably. I experimentally tugged my wrists and ankles apart and then the chains fell off onto the floor with an audible *clunk*.

What the—?

I dared to open my eyes ... and saw that I was still alive.

Looking down at my hands and feet, I saw that my chains had indeed been cut off. They sat on the floor around me in a loose circle, looking like a bunch of metal snakes curled around each other. Yet as far as I could tell, I didn't have any injuries on my body at all. Not even a single nick. It was like Laskar's knife hadn't touched me at all, which was weird because I was pretty sure he was trying to kill me.

"Look at me, Doctor," came Laskar's voice, which was not nearly as cold as it had been before.

Startled, I looked up to see Laskar standing before me. He still held his fancy-looking stabbing knife, only now it was at his side, and completely bloodless. Not what you'd expect an executioner's weapon to look like.

I felt my forehead, which did not feel like it had a knife lodged into it. "Is this some kind of trick? A final deception on your part to make me lower my guard long enough for you to finish me off?"

Laskar looked at me like I was the biggest idiot in the world. "Why in the world would I ever do something as silly as that? If I wanted you dead, you wouldn't even be here."

I gulped and looked around the Courtroom nervously. "So ... am I getting a trial after all? I mean, not that I have a lawyer or anything, but I suppose that's better than getting put to death right away."

Laskar flipped the knife in his hand unnecessarily before putting it in the sheath by his side. Turning away, Laskar said, "That *was* your trial. And I have determined you are innocent of all wrongdoing."

I blinked. "Huh? What? I don't get it."

"Uncle is still alive!" Goggles cried out, almost startling me with how loud his voice was.

I turned in my chair to see that Goggles, Brave Storm, and Lumberjack had not moved from their previous positions, although D2 and the Knights had lowered their weapons. Both

FAKE CHESS

Goggles and Lumberjack were gushing tears from their eyes, while Brave Storm looked as if he had nearly had a heart attack himself.

"Indeed he is, young Goggles!" Lumberjack said. He pulled out a huge handkerchief from nowhere and blew his nose into it. "I didn't know what I was going to tell his wife and kids. How do you explain someone's husband or father getting executed by the leader of a chess-obsessed foreign country?"

Brave Storm looked at Lumberjack with a raised eyebrow. "Roger isn't married and doesn't have any kids."

Lumberjack blinked at Brave Storm. "He isn't? Then that would have been even sadder. No man should ever die a virgin."

"Virgin?" I repeated. "I'll have you know that I am *not* a—"

"Stop your bickering, children," said Laskar. "It is unbecoming of adults such as you, especially in this very serious situation."

Still annoyed with Lumberjack's inaccurate description of me, I looked back toward Laskar. The Chess King was sitting on his throne again, fingertips steepled together, while Minister Ferz stood by his side, furiously writing down notes. Ferz would glance up every now and then at me before returning to his work, whatever it is.

Rising from my chair, I said, "Sorry, *Your Majesty*. I think we're all just a little bit on edge after you faked out killing me."

A powerful hand grabbed my shoulder and spun me around to find myself facing one of the Knights, the male one specifically, who looked even more intimidating up close. I could see his brown eyes peering out from the holes in his helmet, glaring at me like I'd just insulted his mother.

"Watch your tone, American," the Knight said. "Do you not know that you are speaking to His Majesty King Magnus Laskar, the Chess King of Cheskia? Show some respect."

"It is fine, Sir Springer," said Laskar with a wave. "Doctor Mind is simply upset because he is unfamiliar with our unique legal customs. You may unhand him."

Sir Springer's grip tightened considerably. "But what if he tries to attack you, my lord?"

"He will not," said Laskar. His gaze met mine. "If he knows what is good for him."

I nodded. "I do know what is good for me. And getting brutally killed on the spot for attempting to kill the leader of a foreign country isn't exactly hygienic."

Laskar nodded, an approving look on his face. I meant every word I said, because I was still very much outnumbered here, and besides, it wasn't like Laskar had actually physically harmed me.

Sir Springer's iron grip felt locked on my shoulder, but then he finally let go and stepped away, although I could sense his unhappiness even without looking. Still, there was nothing Sir Springer could do to me unless Laskar ordered him and I doubted that Laskar was going to order my death now.

Brushing dust off my shoulder, I said, "So, what exactly *was* all of that, then? You said it was a trial, but it didn't look like any legal trial *I've* ever seen."

"Any *American* trial you've ever seen," Minister Ferz corrected me. "Cheskian legal trials are radically different from American legal trials, as is the Cheskian justice system from the American one."

"So it's common for someone to be accused of a crime they didn't commit, get thrown in jail, hauled off to a 'courtroom,' and then get fake attacked by the King of Cheskia himself in this country?" I said in disbelief. "That's actually worse than the American justice system. And that's saying something, because the American justice system is pretty messed up."

Laskar held up two fingers. "That is because Cheskia has *two* legal systems, Doctor. One which is for the ordinary people of the country and is much closer to the American legal system than this one, although with a lot more chess involved. And a second one that the Chess King has traditionally been put in charge of, more

FAKE CHESS

of a ceremonial tradition than a true legal system."

I blinked. "I don't get it."

"Five centuries ago, when Cheskia was first founded, the country was in turmoil," said Ferz, as if reciting a historical lesson. "Dozens of smaller ethnic groups struggled against each other in long, ongoing bloody chess feuds, often with hundreds of people dying in one chess match. That is, until the first Chess King arose and began to enforce order and stability onto the population through 'fake law.'"

"Fake law?" I repeated. "What does that mean?"

"In short, the Chess King takes a suspected criminal into his quarters and does exactly what I just did to you," said Laskar. He leaned back in his throne, looking quite relaxed. "I go at you with a knife, with the appearance of wanting to murder you in cold blood. I then see your immediate reaction to your incoming death and use that as a way to determine your innocence or guilt."

I blinked again. "That doesn't seem like a very reliable way to determine a person's innocence."

Laskar chuckled. "On the contrary, Doctor, inevitable death *is* the only reliable way to determine a person's innocence. Our true selves show themselves when we find ourselves faced with endless nonexistence. Death acts like a hose on a mud-covered car. It sprays us in the face with the force of ten thousand pounds of water, under which not even the muddiest car could hope to remain dirty forever."

That analogy made no sense to me at all, but I decided to use more diplomatic words and said, "So ... my reaction proved that I'm innocent?"

Laskar nodded. "Indeed, although I never thought you were guilty in the first place. Had you reacted with defiance or anger, I might have killed you, but since you closed your eyes and acted like a whimpering little baby—something that no hardened assassin would do—I decided that you were innocent."

That made even less sense than the analogy about the muddy

car. "If you didn't think I was guilty in the first place, then why all this theater? And why the *hell* have you let Cheskian news organizations publicize the 'fact' that I killed Queen Judit?"

Laskar held up two fingers again. "Two reasons. One, I needed to be absolutely sure that you did not, in fact, murder my beloved Judit. And second, because I needed to make sure that the *real* killers did not know that I was onto them."

I bit my lower lip. "I'm probably going to regret asking this, but who do you think are the 'real' killers, then?"

Laskar's eyes narrowed and his gaze seemed to lose its focus. "The Black Pawns, of course."

CHAPTER THIRTY

"THE BLACK Pawns?" I repeated. "You mean those terrorists who kidnapped Paranoyd and have been nothing but a pain in the butt ever since we got here?"

"There are no others," Laskar said. He glanced at Ferz. "Update on Black Pawn movements?"

"Still very inactive, sir," said Ferz, whose eyes were now glued to a tablet with a chessboard case. "Just as you predicted."

"*Exactly* as I predicted, you mean," said Laskar with a nod. He glared off into space again. "Those bastards. I should have exterminated that lot ages ago when I had the chance."

Feeling lost, I said, "How, er, do you know that the Black Pawns are behind your wife's assassination? Not that I disagree in the slightest, of course, but I am curious to know your reasoning nonetheless."

Laskar turned his glare from the air to me. Only his 'glare' was less 'I want to murder you' and more 'Stop wasting my time with stupid questions.'

"Because *only* the Black King would come up with a plan as devious as this," said Laskar. He steepled his fingers together again. "It's obvious what they were trying to do, and perhaps it would have worked under other circumstances. Unfortunately, they underestimated my brilliant chess mind and have fallen into *my* trap."

I blinked. I was doing that a lot, and not just because it was a natural thing for a person to do. "Well, it's not quite that obvious to me."

Laskar looked at me again like he thought I was slow. "Because you do not have my brilliant chess brain. That is why."

"Then could you explain it to me, please?" I said. Sir Springer gave me a disapproving look, causing me to hastily add, "Uh, Your Majesty?"

Laskar tapped the tips of his fingers together thoughtfully for a moment before saying, "You see, the Black King and his Pawns have been trying to overthrow me for years. They have tried many devious and cunning plans, but none of them have worked so far. That, I believe, is why this is their newest and deadliest plan yet."

I said nothing, as Laskar seemed to be on a roll, and I was afraid he might stop explaining things if I interrupted him too many times.

"Who else would benefit from the murder of my wife?" Laskar continued. "The Black Pawns, that's who. And do you know why?"

I frowned. "To try to create political instability from the death of one of Cheskia's rulers ...?"

"Wrong," said Laskar with a shake of his head. "That is a side effect, at best. No, Judit's murder was a distraction from their other, far more devious plan."

I tried to wrap my mind around that and failed because I lacked a 'brilliant chess mind' like Laskar. "Your wife's murder was a *distraction*? Who murders a queen as a *distraction*?"

"The Black Pawns," said Laskar, balling his hands into fists. "That's who. There's no low they won't sink to in their fruitless efforts to overthrow me. It is ... tiring."

When Laskar said that last word, his shoulders slumped and he suddenly looked a lot older than he was. I felt like I got a glimpse at the real Laskar for a moment, rather than the enigmatic

FAKE CHESS

and intimidating Chess King.

But then the Chess King returned in the next moment and said, "But I am not tired enough to see through their schemes. They clearly framed you, Doctor Mind, to make me focus on you and forget about the tournament."

I frowned and scratched my chin. "So they framed me as the murderer of Judit to distract you from … what? And how do you know I didn't murder Judit, either? Just a question."

"Because you were having dinner with His Majesty when the murder happened," said Ferz dryly. "And it is known that you do not have the power to clone or multiply yourself, so the logical explanation is that you were framed."

"By the Black Pawns, as I said," said Laskar. "If I had to guess, I'd say that one of the Black Bishops most likely wore a mask designed to resemble your face, sneaked into the Castle, and deliberately let his 'face' be seen so that I would think you were the murderer. It was a clever ruse, too, because I got so angry I almost stopped thinking clearly. Almost."

Honestly, I just felt more confused than anything. Although I was happy that Laskar did not think I was a murderer, I did have a few questions.

"So why let the media slander my name if you knew I was innocent from the start?" I said.

"So that the Black Pawns would think that their plan worked," said Laskar. He tapped the side of his head. "Think for once with that brain of yours. The answers to all of your questions are up here."

"It was a ploy on His Majesty's part," Ferz explained in a less condescending tone than Laskar's. "We wanted to trick the Black Pawns into thinking that they had managed to successfully frame you. The reason I've been studying Black Pawn movements and activity in the area is because we believe that they will start pulling back if they believe their plan has worked. It is how we verify His Majesty's theory about the Black Pawns being behind the assassination."

I nodded. That actually made a lot of sense, although it helped that Ferz was a better explainer than Laskar, who seemed to assume that everyone should be able to read his mind and follow his thoughts without explanation. It made me glad that Laskar wasn't *my* king, otherwise I think he'd be really hard to tolerate.

It also made Laskar, I admit, look smarter than I thought. Despite his apparent insanity, it was clear that Laskar actually was thinking several steps ahead. It was a glimpse of his terrifying chess prowess applied to politics rather than chess and made me wonder if I really wanted to face him in the tournament.

"Assuming that Laskar's theory is true, what then?" I said. "Why would the Black Pawns *need* to distract you? Are they trying to get into somewhere or steal something from you?"

"Yes to both," said Laskar. He stroked his chin. "Although it can be hard to predict their moves exactly, I think it is very likely that they are after the Futureboard."

"The Futureboard?" I said. "What's that?"

Laskar gave me a hard look. "Something you do not need to know about, as it has nothing to do with you."

Ferz, however, glanced up from his notebook at Laskar. "Your Majesty, I think that the good Doctor here deserves to know about the Futureboard. For better or for worse, he—and to a lesser extent, his friends—is now firmly involved in this conflict. We cannot keep him and his friends in the dark forever."

I was surprised when Ferz spoke up in my defense. I didn't realize that Ferz seemed to like me, although it may have had more to do with the fact that he was just a more reasonable man than Laskar in general.

And I was even more surprised when Laskar sighed and said, "Fine. With the Black Pawns, and by extension, the Black King, escalating their efforts, it is only a matter of time before they do something *truly* insane."

"Killing the queen *isn't* insane?" I said.

FAKE CHESS

Laskar shot me a harsh look. "No. It is simply chess."

I blinked. "You do realize you're talking about your *wife* here, right?"

"Judit would understand," said Laskar, "for she, too, understood that life is chess and chess is life."

Okay. Maybe Laskar was crazier than I thought.

Then Laskar gestured at one of his Bishops and snapped, "Get me the Holy Books. I need to show the Doctor the Futureboard."

The Bishop in question bowed. He left the room through a side door I hadn't even noticed and then returned not a moment later carrying a thick, ancient book that looked heavier than the average medical school textbook. He also carried a wooden podium with a wide base, which he put in the middle of the room, along with the book. The podium shuddered and swayed slightly under the weight but held nonetheless.

Curious, I walked up to the book, which allowed me to smell the old paper smell that most old books had. Written upon the cover of the book was a title I could not read, mostly because it was in Cheskian.

"What's this?" I asked the Bishop sarcastically. "The Chess Bible?"

The Bishop stared at me in shock. "How did you hear about the Chess Bible? It is one of Cheskia's greatest secrets!"

"It was just a—" I shook my head, deciding that sarcasm was clearly not a cultural import here. "Never mind. So. Chess Bible. I take it that it's the holy book of your religion?"

The Bishop nodded. He ran a finger lovingly and gently down the spine. "Oh, yes. This book was written ages ago, even before Cheskia was founded. Within these pages are a description of our religion's practices, gods, beliefs, and history. It was said that the chess gods themselves wrote it through the hands of some of the world's greatest chess masters throughout history. It also doubles as our country's foundational rulebook and constitution, the underlying basis of all of our laws."

I nodded in response, but frowned when a question popped into my head. "Forgive me, but I don't think I caught the name of your religion."

The Bishop gave me a simple look. "Chess."

"Ah," I said with another nod. "Chess."

"Enough of this dilly-dallying fluff," Laskar snapped. "Show him the Futureboard."

The Bishop immediately grabbed the cover of the book and pulled it open. With a loud *thud*, the Chess Bible stood open somewhere in the middle, which was actually a full-page spread of what appeared to be an ordinary chessboard. A caption was written under the illustration, but because that, too, was in Cheskian, I couldn't read it. I could certainly smell the dust and age on the book itself, though, which made my nose twitch.

"What am I looking at here?" I said, glancing at the Bishop. "A chessboard?"

"Not just any chessboard, Doctor," said Laskar with a grunt. "But the Futureboard. The chessboard that predicts the future."

I looked up at Laskar again, who wore a serious expression on his face. "The Futureboard does what now?"

Laskar sighed in annoyance and spun a finger around his ears. "It predicts the future. Are you deaf or just stupid?"

"I'm neither, sir," I said. I ran a hand through my hair. "I just don't understand how a normal chessboard is supposed to predict the future."

The Bishop rested a finger on the illustration of the Futureboard. "The Futureboard isn't a normal chessboard. It is a supernatural, even divine, object given to us by the chess gods at the dawn of time. It is said that the Futureboard resets every time a new King comes into power and that it is a reflection of the current power struggle in the Kingdom."

"So it doesn't predict the future in general?" I said. "Just the current political climate in Cheskia?"

Laskar sat up straight. "Do not make it sound so trite, Doctor.

FAKE CHESS

The Futureboard has ended many a Chess King's reign before it even had a chance to start. On the flip side, it has elevated other Chess Kings to heights they could never even dream of, giving them power the likes of which they could never achieve on their own."

"In essence, each piece on the Futureboard represents a different person in real life," the Bishop continued. He pointed at the king. "The king, for example, represents the current Chess King, in this case, Magnus Laskar II. Before King Laskar took the throne, his father, King Magnus Laskar I, was the Chess King. This bishop represents me, this knight represents Sir Springer, and so on. And the queen, of course, represents Queen Judit."

I nodded. "Makes sense so far. But what do the black pieces represent?"

The Bishop went silent for a moment. He had to have been expecting that question, so I didn't know why he seemed so surprised that I would ask that. "They represent the Black Pawns, including their king, the Black King."

The Bishop's finger went down to the illustration of the Black king piece, which looked no different from an ordinary Black king but somehow felt more intimidating to me. Maybe it was the lighting.

"So the Black Pawns aren't some kind of new terrorist group, then?" I said. "Have they always existed?"

"Yes," said Laskar grimly. "For as long as the White Pawns have existed, so have our counterparts, the Black Pawns. That includes the Black King, who is my brother, Emmanuel."

I started and looked up at Laskar in surprise. "How old *are* you?"

"No older than any man my age," said Laskar with a wave of his hand. "I am referring to our titles and roles. Every generation has its White King and its Black King. I am this generation's White King and my brother is this generation's Black King."

"I didn't even know you had a brother," I said. "How long

have you been fighting?"

"Since we were young men," said Laskar bitterly. "We started off as mere chess rivals, but that spawned into a much greater rivalry, for power beyond tournament money or worldwide recognition. That is because we were *destined* to clash with each other from the time we were born."

"Are you sure about that?" I asked. "You make it sound like it's inevitable."

"It was and is," Laskar said. He rested his chin in his hand. "To many foreigners, the Cheskian form of government makes no sense. How can a country have any stability in a chessocracy, where power is determined by who is the better chess player rather than hereditary lines or democratic voting? But that is because you people do not understand that Cheskia is not merely a country that loves chess above all. Cheskia *is* chess."

I thought back to the chessboard layout of the country itself, as well as the Black Knight's statement about the Black King 'deserving' to rule. It still didn't make sense to me, but I think I was slowly starting to figure out what was going on. "How long has Cheskia been this way?"

"Since the day it was founded over five-hundred years ago," Laskar said. He scowled. "Our forefathers were the original White and Black Kings, who then passed the titles down to their children, and so on until my brother and I inherited them."

"Right," I said. "So how does the International Superhero Chess Tournament play into this again? The ultimate prize, after all, is that whoever wins gets your throne. That doesn't sound like it fits the cycle you're describing to me."

Laskar smiled, which was the first time I'd seen him smile since Judit's murder. And I wasn't a big fan of the expression, to put it politely. "That is the *point*, Doctor."

"It is?" I said in confusion.

Laskar nodded. He glanced at the glass ceiling overhead, which—like everything else in this castle—had a chessboard

FAKE CHESS

design scratched into it. "Yes. With this tournament, I seek to end the endless cycle of White versus Black that has defined this country since its inception. By allowing myself to be defeated by a foreigner—that is, one who is neither White nor Black—I will finally put a stop to the cycle of White versus Black. And then, perhaps I can finally do what I've always wanted to do."

I frowned. "Which is—?"

"None of your business," Laskar replied. He pointed his scepter at me. "The point is that I cannot allow the Black King to defeat me and take over the country. Emmanuel lost his sanity long ago and is no longer fit to rule. Yet if he were to defeat me, then I'd have to abdicate the throne, and watch as a dark shadow falls over the land."

"But it would be *traditional*," Ferz muttered. "And we cannot go against *tradition*."

"We can when it is irrational and dangerous, Minister," said Laskar, shooting Ferz a rather ugly glare. "That is, unless you'd like to take me on in chess instead and become the White King?"

Ferz said nothing to that, but I didn't care even if he did. I was finally starting to understand why Ferz had been rumored to oppose the tournament, as well as why Laskar was running it in the first place.

Ferz, it was clear, was a firm believer in the White/Black system, while Laskar opposed it. Neither one had the power to save or destroy it on their own, but Laskar had actually managed to figure out a way to game it. I wasn't entirely sure that the plan would work, but given how successful Laskar had been thus far, I couldn't say it would fail, either.

Then Laskar pointed his scepter at me. "And that is also why I invited you personally, Doctor. I saw in you the potential for the next White King of Cheskia, someone who would be able to rise above the stale traditions of my country and end the cycle of violence and instability. It is my hope that you will be able to win the tournament and then defeat me and prove yourself worthy of the title of Chess King."

I blinked. "All because I beat one of your Pawns in chess?"

"Yes," said Laskar with utmost seriousness. "And that is why you must remain in the tournament and why the Black King has been sending his minions after you and your friends since the day you set foot in this country. Emmanuel knows that you are close to becoming the Chess King and wishes to kill you before you can do it."

I scratched my chin. "Wow. That is … that is a lot to take in. All of it."

"I know," said Laskar with a nod, "but I hope that you understand what the stakes are now. For Cheskia. For myself. And for you."

CHAPTER THIRTY-ONE

AFTER THAT, Laskar sent me, Goggles, Brave Storm, and Lumberjack away. He said that he would send out an official notice to the news stations and the other tournament participants clearing me of any wrongdoing or connection to the murder of Queen Judit and that I was also cleared to continue participating in the tournament. I noticed that Laskar did not mention whether the other Cheskians would believe him or not, although since only Laskar could decide who could and could not participate, I suppose it didn't matter.

I was escorted back to my room by D2, although none of the guards followed us. She said nothing along the way, which was fine, because I didn't expect her to have anything to say.

But my teammates—at least, those who weren't present for my 'trial'—sure did.

"Let me get this straight," said Paranoyd after I finished telling him and the others about what Laskar had told me. He was sitting on the floor of my room with a half-finished puzzle before him. "The whole country is literally a giant chessboard, there's a chessboard that can predict the future, there's some sort of metaphysical battle between the White and Black 'pieces,' and Laskar is holding this tournament as a way to override the whole cycle?"

Reclining against the fluffy pillows of my bed, I said, "You got it ... I think."

Holiday Man, who was sitting on one of the barstools at the dining table, looked up from his sandwich at me, a frown on his face. "What do you mean, 'I think'? You were there when Laskar explained it to you, weren't you?"

"I was, but it got kind of convoluted toward the end and I'm not sure I understand it fully," I said. "For example, I still don't know what Laskar wants to do after he's no longer Chess King. For that matter, I still don't know what he expects will happen to his brother if the winner of the tournament defeats him in a chess match."

"It is quite confusing indeed!" came Lumberjack's voice from the bathroom. I heard the sink turn off and Lumberjack walked out, patting his beard dry with a towel. "It would have been simpler to place blame for Queen Judit's murder on the trees, who I think are *still* involved somehow in some way."

I sighed heavily. "Simpler, maybe, but inaccurate."

"It is kind of weird, but good, too," Shining Armor said. He was sitting on the recliner, an open water bottle in his hands. "I mean, look on the bright side. At least you're not going to jail or getting executed for a crime you didn't commit, you know?"

"Cavewoman no like these Black Pawns," said Cavewoman with a scowl. She was also sitting at the dining table, where she was polishing her club. "They murder innocent woman and think they get away with it. Sexism. No justice for women."

"I'm sure that Laskar will get justice for Judit soon," said Brave Storm, who sat on the couch with Goggles, his helmet sitting in his lap. "He seemed really pissed off whenever anyone mentioned her."

"Cavewoman should be put in charge of solving murder," Cavewoman insisted. "Me good at bonking bad men on heads."

"If Judit was a man, would you be so eager to avenge her death?" I asked.

Cavewoman shook her head so quickly it looked like it would

FAKE CHESS

fly off her shoulders. "No. Men privileged scum. No need murder solved. Women got to stick together."

I sighed and shook my head. "All things being equal, I suppose this *was* probably the best outcome of that 'trial' I could ask for. I even know why Laskar is holding the tournament at all."

"Right," said Paranoyd, giving me a wink. He placed another piece of the puzzle into the half-completed puzzle before him. "That's what you were trying to find out in the first place, right? So it wasn't entirely unproductive, even if it was also really stressful for you."

"That's putting it mildly," I said dryly, thinking about how terrified I'd been when Laskar had come at me with his knife. Even now, knowing that Laskar had never intended to actually hurt me, the memory made my pulse quicken and my anxiety go up a little. "The only question left is, what do we do next?"

"What do you mean?" asked Lumberjack as he tossed the towel into the bathroom. "Don't you have another match tomorrow?"

"I do," I said. I'd checked my phone to see the updated schedule for tomorrow and noticed that my next match was scheduled for later that afternoon, although it didn't say who my competitor was for some reason. "But I'm still not sure if *I* want to continue competing or not."

"Why not?" asked Brave Storm. "Seems like a better gig than being the superhero of some small city in Oklahoma. The Chess King is pretty clearly loaded, if you go by the size and elegance of the Castle."

"I know," I said. "It is pretty tempting to have access to all of that money and power, but it also seems like a lot of work. I mean, it's tough enough leading a small team of superheroes. Imagine how much more difficult it would be to lead an entire *country* of people, even one as small as Cheskia."

Cavewoman shot me her usual death glare. "You call

Cavewoman tough to lead? Cavewoman no tough. Cavewoman likable and easy to get along with. Everyone agree that."

"Actually, not everyone agrees with you on that," said Holiday Man. "For example, *I* don't—"

Cavewoman smashed her club down on Holiday Man's head, the blow knocking Holiday Man onto the floor, where he lay with a dazed look on his face.

"Cavewoman likable and easy to get along with," Cavewoman repeated, this time more intimidatingly. "Everyone agree that."

I sighed, thinking about how most of our team's medical costs went toward healing Holiday Man whenever he got bonked on the head by Cavewoman. "The point is, it feels very overwhelming to me. I like fame and money as much as anyone, but ruling a country just isn't my style."

"So why not quit, then?" said Brave Storm. He glanced at his watch. "I don't know what flights are available at this time of night, but surely it shouldn't be *that* difficult to get a flight back to the US right now."

"That's the thing," I said. "I'm not sure I am *allowed* to leave. Laskar made it pretty clear that he wanted me to participate in the tournament, and that there would be consequences if I didn't."

"That sounds kind of illegal, boss," said Shining Armor. "You're not a Cheskian citizen. Technically, you don't *have* to obey him, right?"

"One would think," I said, "but Laskar has shown that he doesn't really care about things like individual liberty too much. I feel a bit like a pawn in a greater chess game than I can conceive."

Goggles gulped and looked at me with worry. "But if we leave now, then I'll never get to see Butterfly again. And I kind of like her."

"The Internet is a thing, you know," I reminded Goggles. "If you want to keep in touch with your girlfriend, you can just call

FAKE CHESS

her or email her or text her or whatever you kids do nowadays."

Goggles' shoulder slumped. "I know, but that's not the same as being with her in person."

Shining Armor shot Goggles a sympathetic smile. "I understand, Goggles. When I was your age, I went to a Christian summer camp where I met this cute girl. We fell in love and swore that we'd stay together forever and ever. It was the most magical weekend of my life."

Goggles sniffled. "Did you stay together?"

Shining Armor shook his head. "Nope. After camp, we tried to send each other letters, but then we both lost interest and moved on. I haven't even seen Marcia in years and last I heard she died in a car crash, so I'll probably never see her again. But it's the thought that counts."

Goggles just sank his face into his hands, which made me feel bad for him, but that didn't convince me to change my mind.

Although Laskar's explanation of the true purpose of the tournament had been very helpful in making sense of some of the stranger things I'd seen here, it also convinced me that I *shouldn't* be here. I mean, this place wasn't even my country. I should be back in America being the superhero for the citizens of Freedom City, not playing chess against superheroes from other countries for a shot at becoming king of a country that wasn't even my own.

Granted, those Black Pawn guys were obviously dangerous and the Black King guy sounded even worse, but that still didn't make it *my* problem, necessarily. Why did it have to be *me* who won the tournament and not one of the other competitors? Mr. South would probably make a decent Chess King if he just lost some weight.

But like I said, I didn't think I was even *allowed* to leave at this point. Laskar seemed convinced that I was the key to his plan to defeat the Black King and end the seemingly endless cycle of conflict between the Whites and the Blacks, but he didn't ask *me* if that's what I wanted and I was getting tired of getting used like a pawn myself.

But maybe I was looking at this wrong. Maybe, instead of trying to escape, I could just throw the match voluntarily. Deliberately play as badly as possible against whoever my next opponent was. It would probably piss off Laskar, but as far as I knew, there weren't any rules against throwing a match deliberately.

It was a risky plan, but at the same time, I didn't see any other way out of this. If I didn't throw the match, then I might win, and if I won I might play against Laskar, and if I played against Laskar, I might win and then become the new Chess King of Cheskia and I really didn't want that.

I was considering telling my teammates about my plan when my phone pinged suddenly. Pulling my phone out of my pocket, I saw that I'd gotten an email from the International Superhero Chess Tournament Committee with the headline 'LEADERBOARD OF CHESS PLAYERS FOR TOMORROW'S GAME.'

"What's that?" asked Lumberjack, leaning down next to me.

Jerking my head away from Lumberjack's face, I said, "An email from the International Superhero Chess Tournament Committee that runs the tournament. Looks like it's got the name of the guy I am going to play against tomorrow."

"You mean you don't know yet?" said Shining Armor, frowning at me from his recliner. "That seems weird to me."

"I think the Queen's assassination disrupted the tournament's schedule," I replied as I tapped the email subject line and started reading. "Regardless, I can now see exactly who … I am playing … against …"

The email was short and to the point. It listed my name, along with the name of my opponent in tomorrow's game, plus the time of the game and when we should be at the lockers to prep.

But I couldn't believe what I was reading. No matter how

FAKE CHESS

many times my eyes scanned the words, I could not believe that I was going up against Checkmate, the son of Magnus Laskar II, the Chess King of Cheskia, tomorrow at noon in the Semifinals.

CHAPTER THIRTY-TWO

I HAD TROUBLE sleeping the night before my next match. Out of all of the competitors who I could have possibly played against, why did it have to be *Checkmate*?

Unlike the other competitors, I actually kind of like Checkmate. And no, it wasn't just because he was my biggest fan, either. It was because he was a decent guy and a real superhero, more so than me.

Well, okay, the adoration and idolization I did like a little bit. Maybe a lot.

But that wasn't the point. The point was that I knew Checkmate had been looking forward to playing against me. If I didn't play to my absolute best, Checkmate would know. He had studied all my prior chess games and knew exactly how good I was. If I threw my match against him, then Checkmate would not only become disappointed, but might even lose all respect for me, too.

Which was probably Laskar's goal. To give me a competitor who I couldn't simply treat like he was just another random person. And even better, it would increase the odds of Checkmate getting knocked out of the running for the position of Chess King and therefore help to keep Checkmate as far from the throne as possible. I knew how much Laskar despised his own son and that was exactly the sort of thing I'd expect from him if his goal was

FAKE CHESS

to make sure that Checkmate did not win.

I still couldn't decide if Laskar was crazy or brilliant. He was probably a little bit of both.

I spent a better part of the night debating that question (and others) with myself, so when I got up in the morning, I was exhausted. It didn't help that for some reason my stupid body woke me up at six, rather than seven-thirty, which was my preferred time to wake up.

I could have gone back to sleep, but I decided that that was impossible at this point. I remembered that the Castle started serving breakfast at six, so I decided to get dressed and go to breakfast. I'd have to go by myself—the rest of my teammates were still asleep—but I didn't care. I didn't often get a lot of alone time anyway, so this might actually be good for me.

As expected, when I got to the Dining Hall for breakfast, it was practically deserted. Aside from some of the Castle servants putting the finishing touches on the buffet, there was no one else in the Hall.

So I got a big steaming mug of Cheskian coffee, along with a donut and bacon and eggs, and turned around to find myself face-to-face with Checkmate.

Checkmate was in his full costume, complete with shoulder pads that had mini replicas of king chess pieces on them. Although his mask hid his face, I could tell that he was rather tired himself.

"Checkmate?" I said, sipping my coffee, which was fresh and warm. "What are you doing here?"

Checkmate raised one finger. "Coffee first. Then we talk."

I didn't know what Checkmate meant or why he seemed so unusually serious, but I understood needing coffee.

So I stepped aside to let him get some coffee. Once Checkmate had his own mug, he directed us toward the table in the far northeast corner of the Dining Hall, well away from the Castle servants, I noted.

As soon as we sat down, Checkmate rested his coffee mug on the table and said, in the utmost serious voice, "I think we should contest our match-up."

Startled, I almost dropped my chocolate-covered donut, which I'd been about to dip into my coffee. "Not that I disagree, but why?"

"Because it is clearly a set-up," said Checkmate. He'd removed his helmet, which sat on the table next to him, allowing him to sip his own coffee cup. "My father wants to pit us against each other to knock me out of the tournament."

I blinked. "What a coincidence. I was thinking the exact same thing earlier. It's like we're twins or something."

Checkmate shook his head. "No. We are both great chess players and all chess players think along the same track. The only difference is elevation, but we are both close enough to my father to see his schemes."

I was frankly flattered that Checkmate put me even close to Laskar in terms of our mindset, as I thought that Laskar was as far above me, in terms of chess, as God was from an ant. "Uh-huh. What are you going to do about it?"

"What are *we* going to do about it, you mean," Checkmate corrected. "Because the only way we can stop my father's schemes is if we work together."

I nodded. I couldn't help but notice how intensely Checkmate spoke. He reminded me a lot of his father right now, especially when I was talking to Laskar last night. I could definitely see the family resemblance between them, though I had a feeling that Checkmate would not appreciate that comparison right now.

So I sipped my own coffee again and said, "Okay, but aren't you the least bit concerned about your mother's murder? I'd think that would upset you."

Checkmate gripped the tablecloth tightly with one hand. "Trust me, Doctor, there is nothing more I'd like to do right now than to go out onto the streets of Cheskia, locate the bastard who killed her, and beat him over the head with the thickest, most solid wooden chessboard I could find. For hours."

I gulped. "Glad you don't think I'm the murderer, then."

"I heard from Father that you were impersonated," Checkmate said, glancing at his coffee cup. "Which I had already put together. Being such a fan of your work, I just couldn't see you murdering innocent people for no reason."

I frowned. "If you and your father both saw through the Black King's schemes, then he must not be very intelligent."

Checkmate grimaced. "Do not underestimate my uncle. He and my father have identical IQs and chess ratings. Truthfully, I believe that the only reason why Uncle Emmanuel is not the current Chess King is because my father has refused to play against him."

I raised an eyebrow. "You think that your father is just *refusing* to play against your uncle because he thinks he won't win?"

Checkmate shrugged. "It is just my personal theory based on what I know about my father and Uncle Emmanual. I've studied their chess games from their youth and they were almost evenly matched, with Uncle Emmanual coming out ahead ever-so-slightly. They often drew, though never stalemated."

"Interesting," I said. "That does put what your father told me last night in a new light."

Checkmate looked at me. "What did my father tell you?"

I summarized everything that had happened the night before, starting with Queen Judit's murder all the way to the moment Laskar let me and my friends go. Checkmate was a surprisingly attentive listener, his gray eyes fixed on me the entire time, never interrupting me even once.

"The Futureboard ..." Checkmate said when I finished the story. "I have always known about it myself, but didn't realize that my uncle is after it."

"Or so your dad thinks," I said. "Given how the Black Pawns

apparently still do not *have* the Futureboard, I'm skeptical that they really want it."

"Agreed," said Checkmate with a nod. "The Futureboard would be useless for my uncle's goals. It wouldn't help him become the next Chess King, so I don't see why he would bother with it. Father must have just told you that to distract you from their real reasons for killing Mother."

I rested my chin in my hand. "Any idea *what* those real reasons might be?"

Checkmate looked into his coffee again. "I do not know. But I hope they are good reasons. While I know that my uncle and my mother did not always get along, I never imagined that he would kill her. But perhaps I should have."

I frowned. "Why?"

Checkmate looked up at me again. "In the conflict between the White and Black Kings, the Queen is very much a valid target. In fact, more queens have been assassinated in our country's history than kings."

My eyes narrowed. "Why?"

Checkmate began making circles on the wooden table between us with his index finger. "Because, just as the queen is the most powerful piece in actual chess, so the queen is the most powerful member of the King's Army. Take her out and the King is much weaker than normal, even if he still has the rest of his Army."

That sort of made sense. 'Sort of' because Checkmate was correct about the powerful nature of the queen in chess. But it seemed weird and messed-up to apply that same dynamic to real life.

Of course, as I'd come to learn over the last few days I'd been in Cheskia, 'weird' and 'messed-up' were the most fitting adjectives for the country and its people.

"Exactly what made your mother so powerful, if you don't mind me asking?" I said. "She just seemed like a normal lady to

FAKE CHESS

me. Did she have superpowers?"

"None that I am aware of, unless you count incredible natural chess talent as a superpower," Checkmate replied. He tapped the side of his head. "No, her real power came from up here. She was probably the smartest person in all of Cheskia. More than anyone else, Mother has been a thorn in my uncle's side thanks to her unique tactical skills. By taking her out, my uncle has effectively eliminated the most dangerous piece on the board, both literally and metaphorically."

I nodded. I was starting to understand the Queen's role in the Cheskian government, but then a thought occurred to me. "Both the Whites and Blacks have identical pieces on each side, yes?"

"Yes, that's correct. Just like a real chessboard."

"Then does that mean there's a Black Queen to go along with Judit's White Queen?" I asked. "And if so, who is she?"

Checkmate nodded. "Oh. The Black Queen. Yes, she's dead."

It was kind of eerie how matter-of-factly Checkmate said that. "Dead? Since when?"

Checkmate held up five fingers. "Since five years ago when my Mother killed her in a chess match. It is the main reason why the Blacks have been on the defense. Without their Queen, the Black Pawns had to resort to terroristic activities to achieve their goals."

My mind reeled at this revelation. "Your mom killed your aunt? In a *chess* match?"

Checkmate nodded again. "Yes, but in her defense, my aunt tried to kill *her* first because Mother was close to winning. It was entirely in self-defense. Plus, I never really liked her, anyway. She always seemed like a shrew."

I bit my lower lip as I considered the implications of this revelation.

On one hand, it shouldn't have been entirely surprising to hear that the Black King had a queen of his own. But on the other hand, it now put Judit's own assassination into greater context. It was now obvious that the Black King had had Judit killed to weaken, if not cripple, Laskar's own Army. Given how the death of the Black Queen five years ago had clearly weakened the Black Pawns, it seemed like the Black King was simply giving Laskar a taste of his own medicine.

Or possibly it was just revenge for his wife's death. Either way, it was now obvious to me that the conflict between the Black King and Laskar was intensifying if both sides had lost their Queens. Laskar appeared to have more pieces than his brother, but I knew that chess was not a game where the number of pieces mattered.

What mattered was how well you played them.

"Isn't it possible that your uncle just wants to play chess against your father for a chance at the throne?" I asked. "That is, after all, how leadership is decided in this country, right?"

Checkmate sipped his coffee. "Possibly. But I feel like my uncle has lost his mind. The terrorist attacks, the constant attempts on you and your friends' lives, and now the assassination of my own mother ... this is unprecedented in the history of relations between the Whites and Blacks."

"If your uncle is *that* crazy, then maybe your father is right to want to keep him from the throne," I said. I took a bite out of my chocolate donut, briefly savoring the sweet chocolate-y goodness in my mouth. "Otherwise, who knows what will happen?"

Checkmate sighed. "Maybe, but right now neither you nor I will face my uncle. We will, however, have to play against each other in today's match."

I nodded. "I know. But maybe I can just resign as soon as the match starts. That way, you can 'win' and then move onto the Finals, where you can eventually get to fight your old man, and maybe even win."

Checkmate practically slammed his fist on the table, almost spilling his coffee all over his pants. "Resign as soon as the match starts? Doctor Mind, what kind of honorable chess player would

FAKE CHESS

ever even *think* of doing that?"

I winced. I'd expected Checkmate to have this sort of reaction, but that did not mean I had to like it. "Er, well, won't it help? Because I don't want to be in this tournament anymore, but you do. Therefore, it would be to both of our advantages if I did that."

Checkmate shook his head so hard that I was worried it might go flying off his neck. "I could never accept a resignation from you. Not unless I truly backed you into a corner in a fair and even chess game, and even then, I'd rather checkmate you than force you to do that."

I stared at Checkmate in bewilderment. "But why? We've already established that you want to be the next Chess King more than anything. This seems like a simple way to—"

"It has nothing to do with what *I* want," said Checkmate. He pressed his fist against his chest. "It is about what the people of Cheskia will think of me."

Pausing before I sipped my coffee again, I said, "What do you mean?"

Checkmate looked me in the eyes, which made me feel a bit uncomfortable, though I didn't look away. "Doctor, you must understand that, although Cheskia is by no means a democracy, winning the approval of the people is still important if one wishes to become the next Chess King. No government can survive without some degree of approval of the people. Even the harshest dictatorships exist because the people are too scared or disorganized to fight back."

Understanding started to filter through my mind like boiling water through a coffee filter. "I think I see what you're getting at. Because this is a public tournament, you want to perform in such a way that the citizens of Cheskia see you as a worthy competitor for the Chess King title, yes?"

Checkmate nodded heavily. "Correct, Doctor. If there is one thing that the people of Cheskia hate, it is those who win through luck rather than effort. If I am going to prove to the Cheskian people that I am fit to be their king, they will not respect me even if I defeat my father. That's why I need your assurance that you will play to the best of your ability."

It was my turn to purse my lips and look all worried, because in truth, I was *really* worried.

Yes, Checkmate was likely right about the Cheskians wanting a true chess master as their king. It certainly lined up with how obsessed this whole country was with the game. I could see how belief that he just lucked out or didn't *really* earn his title could harm Checkmate's rule in the long term.

On the other hand, I still wasn't convinced that this was our best course of action. Because, although I was certain that Checkmate was the superior chess player between the two of us, there was always a chance, however slight, that I could defeat Checkmate and go on to face Laskar in the Finals.

That would also continue to paint a target on my back for the Black Pawns. For whatever reason, the Black King had taken a special interest in me and my team and probably wasn't going to let me go unmolested.

But then an idea occurred to me, a plan to get both of us what we wanted. The plan formed almost instantaneously in my plan, aside from a few details that needed to be hammered out. It was kind of a crazy plan, but at the same time, it was actually quite workable.

So I said to Checkmate, "Checkmate, while I appreciate your passion for chess, I don't know if I'll be able to play as well as you'd like me."

Checkmate's eyes practically exploded from his skull in anger. "If you are going to resign anyway—"

"I won't," I promised quickly. "But neither will I let this game get in the way of what *I* want: To stop the Black King."

Checkmate frowned. "Then what do you suggest we do?"

I smiled. "I've got a plan, but it has to remain between just

FAKE CHESS

you and me. I won't even tell my teammates about it."

Checkmate looked at me in surprise. "It's that secret? I mean, I feel honored that you'd share a top-secret plan with me instead of your team, but are you sure?"

I took another bite out of my chocolate donut. "Checkmate, I've never been surer about anything in my life. And if it doesn't work out, then we'll figure out our next move after that. Are you in or not?"

Checkmate held his fist up across the table before me. "I am always in, Doctor."

Fist-bumping was kind of cringe, but I went ahead and bumped his fist anyway just to make him feel better. Taking yet another bite from my donut—what? It was really good—I said, "All right. Listen closely, because our next match is this afternoon, so we don't have a lot of time to put it into action …"

CHAPTER THIRTY-THREE

Hours later, I was suddenly feeling a lot less sure about my big plan than when I'd been telling Checkmate about it.

Probably because I'd had plenty of time to think about it. In my mind, I could envision several scenarios where things went upside down and sideways in a variety of creative (and perhaps unlikely) ways. For example, my mind kept coming back to this image of Laskar descending onto the chess field, declaring that he was actually an alien from another planet here to conquer Earth, and then transforming into Godzilla and killing everyone.

Now, does that seem at all likely to happen? Of course not, but that didn't stop my mind from going there and going there and going there again.

The far more likely thing to happen was that I might accidentally beat Checkmate. And even that wasn't terribly likely, because like I said, Checkmate was definitely the better player between the two of us.

It was probably all the free time I had that made me think this way. I tried to fill it by watching videos of Checkmate's previous games, talking to Goggles and my teammates, and reading some business books on my phone, but none of that was enough to completely distract me from what we were about to do.

Perhaps I was worried that Laskar might anticipate our plan and find a way to counter it. That seemed like a silly concern, given how Checkmate had already assured me that Laskar wouldn't see it coming, but that did not make me any less nervous. I had already seen how Laskar had deduced the Black Pawns' role in the assassination of his wife from scant evidence. I could easily see him deducing our plan with even less.

But I was going to find out one way or another, because when I got a text message on my phone from the Committee telling me to go to the locker rooms and get ready, I knew that it was go-time. I said goodbye to my teammates—who all promised to cheer me on, except Cavewoman, naturally, who said she wouldn't cheer on anyone now that there were no women in the tournament anymore—and went to the locker rooms.

The last time I went to the locker rooms, I was the only person there. So you can imagine my surprise when I got to the locker rooms ten minutes before the start of the match, closed the door, made sure it was really closed (sometimes it's not), walked over to my preferred locker, and sat down on one of the benches, only to hear a familiar female voice in my right ear say, "Hello, Doctor."

I almost jumped out of my costume. Standing up and whirling around, I found myself face to face with D2.

D2 was back in her normal Pawn costume, which meant that I could no longer see her beautiful face. Despite that, however, I could tell that she was upset about something based on how stiffly she stood. With her arms folded behind her back, she reminded me of how my eighth-grade science teacher looked whenever she was confronting me when I was late for class (and boy was I late a lot).

"D2?" I said. I smiled at her awkwardly. "What are you doing here? I thought that the locker rooms were for competitors only."

D2 stepped over the bench, thus getting slightly closer to me, although still keeping a good distance. "I've just been waiting for you to show up."

I blinked. "Why? Am I going to get arrested again? Or did

Laskar give you another mysterious message to give to me?"

D2 shook her head. She stepped forward again. "This has nothing to do with Laskar. I am here of my own free will for personal reasons."

Internally, I breathed a sigh of relief. I'd been worried that D2 had somehow found out about my plan with Checkmate, but it sounded like she was here for completely different reasons.

Externally, I raised an eyebrow. "Personal reasons? What do you mean?"

D2 rubbed her arm. "I don't really know how to put this into words. It's difficult especially for me, because I am not very talkative, unlike E2, who can't shut up."

"What do you mean?" I said. "I'm sure you can tell me … whatever it is you want to tell me. If it's a secret, I promise not to tell anyone."

D2 chuckled. "That's sweet of you, Doctor, but what I want to tell you isn't exactly a secret. Or maybe it *should* be, as I do not know what His Majesty would think if I were to tell him."

D2 took another step toward me. We were now less than six feet apart. Subconsciously, I took another step back, even though I wasn't sure why. D2 didn't *seem* like a threat, but then again, I still didn't know why she was here. "It can't be *that* serious, can it? Are you going to tell me the nuclear launch codes for Cheskia or tell me to kill Laskar? Does Cheskia even *have* nukes?"

D2 took another step toward me and I took another step back. "It … has nothing to do with national security or anything like that. It's just that Laskar does not like it when his Pawns start to develop bonds with others. Bonds which could interfere with their mission."

D2 stepped toward me again and I, once again, stepped back. Only this time, I bumped into one of the lockers, meaning I had nowhere else to go.

That wasn't a problem for D2, however. She just walked up to me until there was less than half a foot between us and put her

FAKE CHESS

soft, small hands on my chest.

And I had to admit, I kind of like it, even if it was a little bit weird.

"Bonds?" I said. "What kind of bonds are you talking about? It's not like we're best friends or anything like that. We're barely even acquaintances."

To my surprise, D2 seemed to be struggling with her words. "I know, but ... wouldn't you *like* to be that?"

I blinked. "Acquaintances?"

D2 sighed. "So handsome, but also so stupid. With a brain like that, it's surprising you made it this far in the tournament."

"Handsome—?" Suddenly, I understood what D2 was getting at. "Oh. Um, wow. That's nice of you to say, but really, I'm not sure—"

"Not sure of what, Doctor?" asked D2 in a low, almost seductive voice that I couldn't deny was pretty darn hot. She ran a finger down my chest. "Of our feelings for each other?"

Whoa. I really didn't see this coming. "It's not that. It's just that this seems so sudden."

"I know," said D2. She looked down at her chest briefly. "I couldn't believe it myself, either. I've never been a believer in love at first sight ... that is, until I saw *you*."

Then she looked up at me. "And those feelings just became stronger and stronger with every passing day. Soon, I found myself thinking about you even when we weren't together. I didn't realize just how much I wanted you until you were invited to the chicken winner dinner, at which point I realized I can't live without you. I do not *want* to live without you."

D2 spoke so passionately that it took me by surprise. She pressed her body against me and, even though I didn't think her Pawn costume was all that sexy, I did remember how much of a bombshell she'd looked in her fancy dress the night before.

Which is to say that I kind of liked it. Not sure that I liked her, though, at least not that much.

Putting my hands on her shoulders, I said, "Slow down. We barely know each other. I think that talking about love at first sight and all that is a little too premature, wouldn't you say?"

"Is it, Doctor?" asked D2. She clutched the front of my costume with both hands, bringing our faces a little closer together. "I saw the way you were looking at me last night. When you opened the door and saw me in my nice dress. I could practically *feel* your eyes eating me up. And I *liked* it."

D2 said that last sentence with such intense desire that I couldn't help but quiver a little. I didn't know how she did it, but D2 was really good at seducing me in a Pawn costume. I hoped I wasn't developing a kink, because that would be weird.

"W-Well," I stammered, "I mean, you *did* look nice last night, even when you were arresting me for the murder of Queen Judit. Hard not to notice *those* curves."

D2 giggled, a sound that was also really seductive. "Why else do you think I wore that dress, Doctor? Did you really think that I wasn't planning to end dinner last night with a nice heaping plate of man meat afterward for dessert?"

My eyes widened. "Y-You were? But my teammates—"

"I would have kicked them out of your room," D2 replied. She brought her face within inches of mine. "Or just taken you somewhere else. I know of plenty of private places in the castle, after all. No one would have found us. For hours."

The way she said *For hours* ... whew, it was starting to get hot in here. I was even starting to forget about my chess match with Checkmate, which no longer seemed as important as it did a few minutes ago.

"And you've felt this way about me since we met in the Dining Hall?" I asked with a slight stutter.

D2 shook her head. "Before that, even."

D2 took off her mask. Her long, blonde hair flowed down onto her shoulders, allowing me to see her beautiful, inviting features that I had noticed the night before. A scent like

FAKE CHESS

strawberries and vermilion wafted off her hair, which was positively heavenly.

"Back on the airplane in which you landed in Cheskia," said D2, her voice no longer muffled by her mask, but still very sexy, "do you remember the flight attendant who you spoke with? What her name was?"

It took me a moment to start thinking again and an even longer moment to remember who she was talking about, but when I did, I started. "Olga? Is that ... you can't be her, can you?"

D2 nodded. She ran a hand along the side of my face, which sent all sorts of tingles along my skin. "Yes. That was me. His Majesty had put me on that flight precisely to make sure you made it here safely to Cheskia. Had Checkmate not saved you and your brother from the Black Pawns, I would have instead."

"So you were a spy, then?" I said. "I thought you were Olga's sister or something."

"At first," said D2. Then she rested her hand on my cheek. "But then it became so much more. I started to fall in love with you and your rugged, handsome looks. And the way you defeated Peacock a couple of days ago ... oh, that was positively *delicious*."

Now that D2 was no longer wearing her mask, I could actually see the lust in her eyes. They burned like a fire and I could tell that she *really* wanted me, that she wanted me so much that it shocked me she was already all over me like a monkey on a banana.

It was both arousing and a little scary at the same time. I'd often dreamed of a hot foreign woman trying to get into my pants, but I'd never imagined it would be in a situation like this.

Feeling her hand on my cheek, I said, "Uh ... um ... er ..."

D2 smiled at me seductively. "What's the matter, Doctor? You seem to be at a loss for words."

I gulped, which felt rather dry. "W-Well, it's like I said, this is just so sudden and we barely know each other, but—"

"But it's also so, so, *so* right," D2 whispered.

She then leaned in and kissed me right on the lips. An electrical current seemed to zap through her lips onto mine. An explosion of pleasure rocked my form, causing me to involuntarily grab D2 and hold her against my body.

I still didn't know if I loved her or not, but I did know that I *liked* this and didn't want it to end. I got so focused on kissing D2 and holding her against me that I forgot about literally everything else. In the back of my mind, a voice was trying to remind me that I had something important regarding chess to do, but I ignored it because of the much more immediate (and far sexier) distraction directly in front of me.

That is, until I felt a hot, searing *pain* explode along my left spleen. The pain made me break the kiss with D2 and look down at the source of the pain.

A knife was lodged into my stomach. Red blood leaked out from the knife, down my pants, and onto the floor.

But the knife wasn't just floating of its own accord, like some kind of evil knife that liked to go around stabbing people.

No, it was in D2's hand.

CHAPTER THIRTY-FOUR

Gasping for air, I looked up into D2's eyes, hoping for some sort of explanation for her actions.

But when I gazed into her eyes, I didn't see the love or even lust that had burned in them before.

No. All I saw was hate and cold amusement.

"D2 …" I said, my voice weakened with pain. "Why … I thought you loved me …"

D2 smirked. "You Americans really *are* stupid."

With that, D2 yanked the knife out of my stomach and kicked me right where her knife had been.

I did not know how D2 did it, but somehow she managed to hit me in exactly the right spot to make me wish I was dead.

I collapsed onto the floor and clutched my stomach, trying to staunch the bleeding. Not that I was having much luck. Hot blood coated my hands and made me feel even sicker than I already was.

Then D2's shadow fell over me and I looked up at her. Although D2 was not the tallest woman around, she looked positively gigantic from my current vantage point on the floor. She held the knife in her hand, its pawn-shaped handle flashing under the light when she flipped it with practiced ease.

"So pathetic," said D2. "This is the man who Laskar wants as his successor? This isn't even funny. It's just sad."

I grimaced. "Laskar? You mean ... you're not actually working for him?"

D2 tilted her head to the side. "Oh, I most certainly do. But my allegiance has changed. It has been different for a while. I work for his brother now, the Black King, as a double agent, as you Americans would say."

My eyes widened. "But you're a Pawn. I thought ... thought that meant you had undying loyalty toward him."

D2 chuckled. "Don't take the chess motif so literally, Doctor. As I said, I *was* once loyal to Laskar, but after learning about his plans to abolish our chessocratic system, I knew I could not support him any longer. He is a threat to our system, and I must eliminate him."

I bit my lower lip, doing my best not to let the pain overwhelm me, although that was five hundred times easier said than done. "O-Okay, but why me ...?"

"Because you are Laskar's favorite," D2 replied, "although it's hard to see why, given how weak and pathetic you are. Perhaps Laskar is getting senile in his old age."

I took a deep breath to steady myself. "The tournament ... my match with Checkmate ..."

D2 smirked even more. "Do not worry about that, Doctor. Worry, instead, about yourself."

With that, D2 kicked me in the stomach again. The blow made my head spin and my heart practically stop. It was all I could do not to scream in pain, even though I wanted to. But I was just in too much pain to do even that much. Nor could I focus long enough to use my Mind-Bender Crown or reach my phone, which left me more or less powerless.

"My long-term mission was *always* to get close to you," said D2, "close enough that I could off you as soon as the opportunity presented itself to me. I originally intended to do it the night of the chicken winner dinner, but when Queen Judit was killed, that interrupted my plans."

FAKE CHESS

I blinked. "But Q-Queen Judit was killed by your people, wasn't she? The Black Pawns ..."

"That's what Laskar thinks," said D2, "but he doesn't know that even the Black King did not see that coming, nor did he order any assassinations."

I gasped. "Then who—?"

"I do not know," said D2. She raised her knife. "Nor do I care. Now that Queen Judit is out of the picture, that makes the Black Pawns' plan to interrupt the tournament that much easier."

"You're planning to interrupt the tournament?" I said with another gasp. "W-Why? When?"

D2's smirk grew even crueler. "Within the next five minutes. Hence why you need to be out of the way. We do not need you interrupting our plans again."

I grimaced. That didn't make a whole lot of sense to me, seeing as I didn't see how my presence or absence actually mattered. Castle Rook had all sorts of other defenses, after all, which D2 had to know—

I paused, briefly forgetting about the pain emanating from my wound as reality sunk in.

D2 must have noticed, because she said, "Ah, so you aren't so stupid after all. Yes, I used my position as one of Laskar's Pawns to disable all of Castle Rook's security systems. Without, of course, anyone noticing. And by the time anyone does, it will be too late."

Damn it. I reached for my phone in my pocket, but D2 kicked my hand, causing me to pull it back.

"No, no, no, Doctor," said D2, waving a disapproving finger at me. "Remember what I said: My orders were to *kill* you, and I fully intend to make sure I get the job done."

With that, D2 brought her knife down toward my face.

But then the door to the locker room slammed open and a gunshot rang out. D2 jerked and staggered away from me, dodging several more gunshots that followed. The bullets ricocheted off the lockers, causing me to cringe and curl into a ball to avoid getting shot, although fortunately, none of them hit me. One of them *did* strike the floor less than an inch from my face, however, which made me pee my pants a little, but otherwise I was all right.

D2, however, wasn't. She was cursing up a storm in Cheskian, making me glad I couldn't understand Cheskian for once. She clutched her bloody shoulder while glancing toward the door and holding her knife before her, which I thought was impressive because I didn't think I'd be aware of anything if I'd been shot.

"Yeehaw!" came an obnoxiously loud male Southern-accented voice from the doorway. "Got 'em!"

Mr. South stepped into the locker room, toting two large pistols in his hands and a huge grin on his face. Behind him, his sidekicks—the boy and the girl—were also holding pistols and pointing them into the room.

"M-Mr. South?" I said in disbelief. "I t-thought you got knocked out of the tournament."

Mr. South blew the smoke off the tips of his gun barrels. "Sure did, but that don't mean I had to go back to America. Sure glad I stayed, though, because it looks like you were in a bit of a pickle, Doc."

"Pickle?" I repeated. "I got stabbed in the—"

A wave of pain washed over me and made me wince and groan. No one ever tells you how *bad* knife wounds hurt, but they do, and I didn't know if I hated them or D2 more right now.

Mr. South raised an eyebrow. "Weird way to say 'Thanks a bunch, Mr. South!', but I'll take it."

Before I could answer that, D2 hurled what looked like several pawns at Mr. South. Mr. South and his sidekicks shot the pawns out of the air (without caring about their bullets ricocheting off the walls, of course), but each pawn exploded into a white cloud of smoke that filled the room quickly and obscured

FAKE CHESS

our vision. I heard Mr. South and his sidekicks coughing and stumbling about inside the locker room, most likely blinded by the smoke. I even heard a couple of gunshots go off, but fortunately none of them hit me.

But I did hear several loud footsteps somewhere nearby, followed by a door swinging open and being slammed closed, and then Mr. South shouted, "Vac, blow us out!"

I did not know who 'Vac' was, but I did hear what sounded like a huge vacuum start up. The vacuum roared even louder in the confined space of the locker room, causing me to cringe, but surprisingly, the smoke all started getting sucked toward the other side of the room. I watched in amazement as the smoke zipped away from me toward whatever was making that god-awful vacuum noise.

The huge smoke cloud swirled inside the open mouth of Mr. South's male sidekick, who stood with his mouth hanging open. Once the last of the smoke disappeared into his mouth, the boy closed his mouth shut tightly, causing the vacuum noise to stop just as abruptly.

"Good job, Vac!" said Mr. South, slapping the boy on the back. "That's gotta be a new record for ya!"

The boy, who coughed up wisps of smoke when Mr. South slapped his back, said, in a slightly hoarse voice while rubbing his throat, "Sure is, but I also ain't *never* inhaling that much smoke again. Makes my lungs feel like they're on fire."

I blinked. "Vac?"

"That's his name," said Mr. South proudly. "Technically, his full superhero name is Vacuum, but we always call him Vac for short. Like Zack. He can suck up anything like a vacuum and then turn it into energy for his body."

Vac burped, causing more smoke to escape his lips, and rubbed his belly. "Yeah, but it usually takes a while for it to digest, so I can't use it right away."

That had to be one of the weirdest superpowers I'd ever heard of, but a fresh wave of pain washed over me like a particularly angry ocean wave and I doubled over again. Damn it. How much blood had I lost so far and how much more could I lose before I died?

"Oh, no!" said the girl in a high-pitched Southern accent. She darted across the room toward me and knelt beside me. "You look awful, Mr. Doctor. What happened?"

"D2 stabbed me," I gasped, looking up at the female sidekick's sympathetic eyes. "Really, *really* hard."

"Ouch," said Mr. South, he and Vac standing behind the girl, although I hadn't noticed them walk up. "Looks nasty."

I was going to say that it felt even worse, but then more stabbing pain shot through me and all I could do was grunt in reply.

The girl patted the side of my face like I was a small child. "Don't you worry, Mr. Doctor. We'll get you fixed in a jiffy. Daddy?"

At first, I didn't know who she was talking to until Mr. South stepped beside her and said, in a sickeningly sweet voice, "Yes, Princess?"

'Princess' looked up at Mr. South with a surprisingly serious expression. "I'm going to need your power to save Mr. Doctor's life. Are you ready?"

Mr. South slapped his huge, rippling belly. "Always ready to save a friend!"

"Hey, uh, girl?" I said, although even saying that much was a struggle due to my injuries.

The girl looked at me. "It's Princess. *Doctor* Princess."

I blinked. "Okay, *Doctor* Princess. What exactly are you going to—"

"Okay, Princess!" Mr. South said, his voice even louder than before. "I'm ready when you are!"

Doctor Princess—god I can't believe I said that—smiled at Mr. South before looking at me again and saying, in the sweetest,

FAKE CHESS

kindest, yet bluntest voice of all time, "This is going to hurt. A lot."

Doctor Princess put one hand on Mr. South's belly and one hand on mine. Her touch made my wound burn even worse than it already did, but for some reason I couldn't move. She wasn't even wearing any surgical gloves when she touched my wound. Some doctor. Maybe she was a better princess.

But all thought about the merits of being both a doctor and a princess were driven from my mind when her hands glowed. What felt like white-hot electricity shot up through my stomach and made me scream even louder than before.

And no, I *didn't* scream like a little girl. I'm Doctor Mind, *not* Doctor Princess. She was the one screaming. Probably. Maybe. There was a chance.

In any case, the pain—which felt like a hundred electrified needles plunged into my wound at exactly the same moment—didn't last very long. A hellish couple of seconds later, the pain disappeared, leaving me feeling exhausted and sweaty.

Doctor Princess' face swam in my point of view, a worried frown barely visible on her young features. "How do you feel, Mr. Doctor? Can you hear me?"

Dazed, I said, "Uh … I feel like I took a bath in electrified water."

Doctor Princess' frown turned upside-down almost instantly. "Yay! It sounds like you're going to be okay. What a relief."

"Yeah," said Mr. South, who stood outside of my view, but I could still hear him just fine, "but I didn't doubt you for one instant, sugar pie. You and your brother did great."

I blinked several times and looked at Mr. South, but then did a double-take to make sure I was looking at him correctly.

Mr. South looked radically different. Instead of being extremely overweight and hefty, he was muscular and well-built. His clothing hung far more loosely off his massive frame, but even with his loose clothes, I could tell that he was utterly jacked.

His skin was smoother and younger-looking as well, making him look as if he'd lost twenty or thirty years.

I blinked again. "Mr. South? Why do you look so ... young?"

Mr. South lifted the rim of his hat with his thumb. "Ask Doctor Princess! She can explain it ten times better than me."

"It's my power," Doctor Princess explained, causing me to turn my attention to her. She raised her hands. "I can take body fat from another person and turn it into healing energy, with which I can heal even the worst injuries, unless they're life-threatening. So I took Daddy's extra fat and used it to heal you."

"Healed?" I repeated. I immediately began touching my stomach. "I'm not healed. My stomach is ... still ... bleeding ..."

I did not feel any blood on my stomach, causing me to look down and see that my stomach was no longer cut open or even bloody. It looked as smooth as a baby's bottom and even felt like it, too.

"See?" said Doctor Princess. She pressed a hand against her own stomach. "I even fixed some damage that was done to your internal organs. You might feel a bit tired later, but you should be fine now."

I could hardly believe my eyes and hands, yet I also couldn't deny Doctor Princess' explanation. "Wow ... I mean, thank you. Seriously, I don't know how I can repay you."

"No need," Doctor Princess replied. "From one doctor to another, you're welcome."

I didn't know if Doctor Princess was *actually* a medical doctor—which seemed unlikely to me, given how young she looked—or if that was just her superhero name, but I just nodded and said, "Thanks anyway. But how did you guys even know I was in trouble?"

"Checkmate asked us to keep an eye on you," Mr. South replied. "Said he was worried that the Black Pawns might come after you again, but he didn't want you to know that you were being watched. So my sidekicks and I have just been stealthily

FAKE CHESS

following you for the past day or so without you noticing."

"You got lucky," Vac told me, his voice still quite hoarse. "When you went into the lockers, we thought you were going to be in the arena. But before we left, we heard stabbing sounds in here and came as fast as we could."

I shook my head in disbelief. Not that I thought they were lying or anything, but it did amaze me that Checkmate had hired Mr. South and his sidekicks to keep an eye on me without me even knowing.

Which was a very Laskar move, now that I think about it.

Checkmate was a lot more like his old man than either of them would admit.

"Well, thanks again," I said as I rose to my feet, leaning on the lockers for support, "but we don't have time to chat. We need to get to the arena ASAP."

Mr. South exchanged puzzled looks with his sidekicks. "Why? Are you afraid of missing your match with Checkmate?"

I shook my head. "Not exactly. D2 told me that the Black Pawns are going to attack the arena unless we—"

A loud *boom* from somewhere outside the locker rooms suddenly interrupted me, making the walls, floor, and ceiling of the rooms shake. It was followed by a series of terrified screams and gunfire that was even scarier than the explosion.

"What in Sam Hill's name was that?" Mr. South said, whipping his head around in alarm.

I grimaced. "The attack has already begun. Let's go!"

CHAPTER THIRTY-FIVE

EMERGING FROM the locker rooms into the arena of Castle Rook, I couldn't help but pause and take in the scene of utter chaos playing out before us.

Hundreds of Black Pawns were dropping down from black helicopters overhead into the arena or crawling over the walls into the seats. Frightened Cheskian citizens were running around screaming, either heading toward the nearest exits or trying to fight their way past the Black Pawns. Already, I could see several bodies among the stands or on the field, mostly of innocent Cheskian citizens, although a few Black Pawns stood out like sore thumbs as well.

I also spotted all of my teammates on the field or in the stands, trading blows with Black Pawns or protecting the Cheskian citizens. I even saw some of the other tournament competitors, such as Peacock and Sushimo, fighting like animals against the Black Pawns. Sushimo, in particular, was using his massive fat to block and deflect bullets back into their owners, which seemed impossible to me, but whatever.

"What the—?" said Mr. South, coming to a stop beside me, a look of disbelief on his thinner-than-usual features. "Where did all these Pawns come from?"

Mikhael Checkna, the announcer for the tournament, was flying overhead on his floating platform, frantically looking

FAKE CHESS

around the arena while still somehow continuing to have a running commentary on the whole situation as it unfolded.

"Unbelievable!" Mikhael cried into his microphone, his voice amplified by the huge speakers hanging overhead. "Hundreds of Black Pawns have invaded the arena and are attacking innocent people! Viewers and listeners, I cannot explain in any way how this happened under His Majesty's nose or where His Majesty even is, but I pray to the chess gods that the foreign superheroes below will—"

A stray bullet or something must have hit Mikhael's platform because one of the engines groaned and suddenly exploded. Fire whooshed out of the blown engine like water through a dam and the platform fell to the ground below, with Mikhael screaming his head off as he plummeted through the sky.

Acting instinctively, I put my fingertips against my forehead and activated my Mind-Bender Crown. I caught Mikhael—although not his platform—halfway to the ground and brought him telepathically over to my side of the arena.

Plopping Mikhael at my feet, I said, "Mikhael, what happened?"

Mikhael, his face paler than snow and his normally pristine black hair now messy, looked up at me with big eyes. "Doctor Mind? You're alive!"

I frowned. "Thanks for noticing."

Mikhael pointed at the speakers. "Before the match started, the Black King hijacked the speakers and told the whole arena that you were dead. He also had Checkmate blown up. See?"

Mikhael pointed across the arena field, which was when I finally looked at the HoloChess station where Checkmate would have stood.

It was nothing more than a gnarled, smoking mess of twisted blackened metal. It looked like it must have been an impressive explosion, too, because a good chunk of the seating near it had been destroyed by the blast as well.

"Good golly miss molly!" said Mr. South. "If Checkmate was standing there when the explosion happened, then that means ..."

Mikhael nodded, frowning sadly. "Yes. I tried to warn him, but he was too slow. He appears to have been totally vaporized in the explosion because we have not been able to find his body, although I suppose we haven't really had time to look for it."

This was bad. D2 had not mentioned anything about Checkmate getting blown up or killed. Even if Checkmate somehow did survive the explosion, I doubted he was in any condition to help us.

"And where's Laskar?" I asked, moving on to the next most important person on my priority list.

"His Majesty?" said Mikhael. He looked around, frowning. "I do not know. Last I saw, he was sitting in the Royal Viewing Box, but after the attack started, he vanished."

I followed Mikhael's gaze and saw that he was right. Laskar was nowhere to be seen in the box he normally sat in when overlooking the tournament.

"Did he run away?" Mr. South said in a sour voice, a scowl on his face. "Some leader *he* is."

"Not sure," said Mikhael. He looked up at Doctor Mind with hopeful eyes. "But you will be able to save us, yes?"

I bit my lower lip and glanced at the battle raging below. "I ... I think so. At least, I think I can distract the Black Pawns long enough for the citizens to escape. I'm not sure that my team and I can actually *beat* all these guys."

"Even that much would be helpful," said Mikhael. He clasped his hands together like he was praying to God. "Please, Doctor. No one else can save us."

I bit my lip even harder. Damn it. I hadn't come to Cheskia to put down a terroristic revolution, but at the same time, I couldn't abandon everyone, either.

And anyway, at this point, the Black King had made things pretty personal.

FAKE CHESS

The only question, of course, was how to best go about dealing with the Black Pawns. The entire battlefield below was a huge mess at the moment, with superheroes, Black Pawns, and citizens hopelessly mixed together. It would take an act of God to separate them all or make things even slightly organized.

I needed to distract the Black Pawns somehow, get them to turn their attention on me and my friends. But how could I do that? There were hundreds of Black Pawns and I was just one guy. Even if I got most of them looking my way, that wouldn't stop the others from continuing to harass the fleeing and scared civilians.

If only I had some way to speak to all of the Black Pawns at once, then I could—

Damn it, Doctor! You're a genius.

I knelt down in front of Mikhael and held out my hand. "Mikhael, give me your microphone. Hurry. It's important."

Although Mikhael looked as likely to give me his microphone as a mother was to give up her firstborn child, he nonetheless handed me the mic and said, "All right. Do what you need to do, Doctor.'"

Nodding in thanks, I stood up and, stepping forward until I was right at the edge of my chess table, I raised the microphone up to my lips and shouted, "Hey! Black Pawns! Look at who your assassin failed to kill!"

My voice boomed from the massive speakers with such deafening power that even I cringed slightly at the impact of the sound.

But by golly, did it work. Black Pawns all over the arena turned to look at me. In fact, my mere presence seemed to have paused the entire battle, as even my teammates and allies turned to look up at me with surprise.

"Uncle's alive!" Goggles yelled in a tearful voice. "He's back from the dead! Like Jesus!"

I grimaced briefly before saying into the microphone, "Er, not like Jesus. Like, at all. Because I wasn't dead in the first place."

"Then like Harry Potter!" Lumberjack yelled.

I sighed heavily. "No, Lumberjack, not like Harry Potter."

"What about like Aslan?" asked Shining Armor. He frowned. "Wait, is that the same as Jesus or—"

"The point is," I said, interrupting Shining Armor, "I'm still alive and I know you Black Pawns wanted a piece of me. What are you going to do about it?"

Sometimes, I wished my mind was faster than my mouth, because then I might be able to stop myself from saying things that would get more guns pointed at my face than I had ever seen in my life before.

"Watch out, Doc!" Lumberjack cried. "They might shoot you!"

And sometimes, I wished my 'friends' wouldn't bluntly state the obvious.

I didn't have time for a pity party, however, before hundreds of bullets came flying my way.

But I also didn't hesitate.

Putting my fingers back on my forehead, I focused my telekinesis on the bullets coming my way.

Now, I wasn't going to bother trying to catch each and every bullet individually. That was too fine of a control for even someone of my prowess. I could have disarmed the Black Pawns if I'd wanted to (probably; I'd never tried to disarm so many people at one time before), but bullets were smaller, faster, and much, much harder to catch.

Therefore, instead of my usual go-to of forming several mental 'hands' to catch the bullets, I decided to break out a new way of thinking about my telekinesis: As a solid, bulletproof wall made entirely from my thought and willpower.

The wall, of course, was completely invisible. It was the same move I'd tried to use to protect me, Goggles, and Paranoyd from the Black Knight's explosion earlier, only this time I tried to

FAKE CHESS

make it actually work.

Because it *had* to if I wasn't going to die a horrible, bloody death.

The bullets slammed into my telekinetic wall as one and I felt the impact more in my mind than physically. It felt like someone had dropped a thick math textbook on my mind and then threw an anvil on top for good measure. I staggered slightly from the blow, taking a step back, but never taking my fingers off my forehead.

Yet the wall held. It cracked. It shuddered. It felt like it *wanted* to break.

But it held.

It held.

Every eye in the arena was back on me again. The Black Pawns had even stopped shooting, lowering their guns to stare at me with surprise that I could see even with their masks covering their faces. So did my own teammates and the other superheroes and Cheskian citizens in the arena.

Hell, even *I* was surprised it worked. Or I would have been, if I'd had the time and energy to be surprised, which I didn't. I needed to keep the barrier up long enough to make sure that the bullets didn't get through.

And fortunately, they didn't. The bullets bounced harmlessly off the wall toward the ground below, making clinking noises as they landed on top of each other. In seconds, the only evidence of the Black Pawns' massive assault was the pile of spent bullets sitting on the ground below my station, where they could not hurt anyone.

I smirked and, holding the microphone up to my mouth, shouted, "HA! Take that, Black Pawns! Your guns aren't so useful now, are they?"

Of course, I shouldn't have tested fate like that, but I was too overjoyed and drunk with victory to care. That, and my mind might have gotten a little broken from the sheer mental toll that forming and maintaining the barrier did to me, but regardless, I was jubilant.

Until I noticed a Black Knight—probably the second Black Knight, different from the one I'd defeated—standing on the opposite side of the stadium among the ruins of Checkmate's station. His black armor helped him blend in quite well with the twisted, blackened smoking remains of the station, and I probably wouldn't have even noticed him at all if he hadn't been moving.

It's a good thing I did, though, because that man clearly had a rocket launcher and he was clearly taking aim at me.

The Black Knight pulled the trigger on his rocket launcher and a missile launched out. The missile flew too fast for my eyes to follow, so I tried to strengthen the shield in the hopes that it might be enough to stop it.

Naturally, it wasn't.

The missile slammed into my mental barrier and exploded. The barrier shattered and the explosion slammed into me, Mikhael, Mr. South, and his sidekicks.

We were all sent flying into the air ... and then falling down toward the ground below.

CHAPTER THIRTY-SIX

LET ME tell you something: Getting blown up by a missile is *not* my idea of a good time. It is probably not anyone's idea of a good time, but it is especially not mine.

Describing the sensation was damn near impossible. Think of a really big ocean wave crashing down on you, only for the wave to be made of fire and smoke and instead of drowning you it sent you flying into the air.

Okay, that probably wasn't a very clear analogy.

But it's hard to come up with a clear analogy when you are tumbling through the air, head over heels, unable to control your trajectory, barely even able to tell the difference between up and down. For that matter, the impact of the blast left me feeling dizzier and more incoherent than normal, obliterating my ability to think clearly.

One thought did repeat in my brain over and over again, though:

I wish I'd kept my stupid mouth shut.

As it was, people were screaming around me and perhaps I was screaming, too. I couldn't see where anything or anyone was. I thought one of the screams sounded a bit like Mikhael, but like I said, I was too disoriented to figure that out.

But then I suddenly felt myself start to descend. Looking down, I could see the arena ground below, which told me that we were at least headed down.

Unfortunately, I did not know how to keep us from smashing into the ground. Maybe the ground was softer than it looked and we'd just bounce like jello.

Or, most likely, we'd become a bunch of smashed pumpkins.

As it turned out, however, I was wrong on both counts: I didn't catch us, nor did we smash like pumpkins against the ground. Presumably, that was because we hadn't actually fallen far enough for us to suffer in that way.

But it still hurt like hell to slam into the ground and even bounce a couple of times. Fortunately, my helmet absorbed most of the damage, otherwise I was sure that my head really *would* have looked like a smashed pumpkin. I still felt very dizzy, however, and barely able to pay attention to my surroundings.

Shaking my head, I raised my head to look around at my surroundings nonetheless.

We'd fallen near the pile of bullets that I'd deflected with my barrier. In fact, Mikhael had actually fallen on the pile itself, his forehead bleeding and his nice suit all rumpled up, but otherwise he appeared unharmed, although I wasn't sure he was conscious. Mr. South had apparently grabbed both Doctor Princess and Vacuum before the blast, because he held both of them in his arms, having clearly protected them from both the blast and the fall. While Doctor Princess and Vacuum looked mostly unharmed, Mr. South appeared to be barely more conscious than Mikhael, his hat having flown off during the fall, blood running down the side of his face.

All in all, I thought we came out of getting blasted to bits by a rocket launcher surprisingly well. Maybe my telekinetic wall really did protect us from the worst of it.

Then I heard a loud cringing sound that made me freeze on the spot and look up.

My chess station looked better off than Checkmate's station, but just barely. It had clearly taken the worst of the blast itself, which must have hit it hard enough to make it creak. It appeared to be just barely hanging onto the side of the stadium, threatening to fall off and crush all of us.

In fact, as I watched, that threat became a reality when it detached and fell. A few hundred pounds of metal hurtled toward us like a meteorite through space and I just couldn't focus long enough to displace it.

But I didn't have to, apparently, because Cavewoman flew out of nowhere and caught the falling station on the back of her shoulders. Cavewoman grunted under the weight of the station, almost collapsing underneath it, but managed to remain standing regardless.

"Cavewoman?" I said, staring up at Cavewoman in shock (and doing my best not to look under her loincloth, where she did not appear to believe in underwear). "You saved us!"

Cavewoman grunted. "Me not save *you*, Doctor. Me save *her*."

Cavewoman nodded at the frightened-looking Doctor Princess, who sat with her arms around Vacuum, the sibling sidekicks trembling. Mr. South was sitting upright now, also staring in shock at Cavewoman's miraculous save, while Mikhael groaned and rubbed his forehead, propping himself up on his elbow.

I sighed. I should have figured that Cavewoman would only intervene to save another woman. Still, I couldn't complain too much. Whether she'd intended to or not, she'd saved my life.

Then Cavewoman grunted again and threw the huge station off to the side. Coincidentally, about a dozen armed Black Pawns had been rushing toward us at that exact moment, and they all got crushed rather anti-climatically under the massive chunk of metal. It was actually kind of funny to see them get smushed like that, although a little disturbing when I realized I didn't know if they were dead or just knocked out.

"There," said Cavewoman, standing upright and turning away

from me. She winked at Doctor Princess. "You welcome, sister."

Doctor Princess blinked. "Sister?"

"Never mind that," I said. I rose to my feet, although slowly because, even though I was sure I didn't have any broken bones, my body felt sore all over. "We need to stop the Black Pawns before—"

"Doctor!" Lumberjack cried out. "Watch out! The rocket launcher!"

Startled, I looked back toward the other side of the arena in time to see the second Black Knight taking aim with his rocket launcher again. Even from a distance, I could see the Black Knight about to pull the trigger and shoot yet another missile at me.

But then Checkmate burst out from behind the Black Knight and body-slammed him. The Black Knight staggered forward, but managed to whirl around to aim his rocket launcher at Checkmate, who grabbed the weapon and, yanking it out of the Black Knight's grasp, slammed the Black Knight in the face with it.

The blow sent the Black Knight falling backward toward the ground below, his arms and legs flailing, before he landed on several Black Pawns with a *thud* and did not get back up.

"Checkmate is also still alive!" Shining Armor cried. "Yay!"

The Cheskian citizens turned to look at Checkmate and immediately started up a chant of his name. The Black Pawns, on the other hand, shifted their focus from me to Checkmate, clearly surprised that even he was still alive.

From a distance, it was tough to tell, but Checkmate did look like he'd been in an explosion. His gold-and-brown armor was slightly blackened from the blast and one of the pawns on his shoulders had been blown off entirely, but other than he looked pretty good for someone who had supposedly been killed in a rigged explosion.

Rocket launcher in hand, Checkmate said, raising his voice to

FAKE CHESS

be heard, "Citizens of Cheskia! It is I, Checkmate, your hero! And I am here to protect you all from the evil machinations of the Black King and his Pawns!"

Another round of applause went up from the people, along with a renewed chant of Checkmate's name, this time in Cheskian. It was an amazing sound to hear, honestly, almost enough to make me tear up. I could now see just why Checkmate was so popular among the people of Cheskia.

But then another voice, this one even louder than Checkmate's, cracked the air like thunder, echoing loudly across the stadium and making everyone wince:

"Brave words coming from such an inexperienced young man. I wonder if you will sound so confident after I am done with you."

At first, it was hard to tell where the voice was coming from. It seemed to be coming from everywhere at once, but that was because it came from the speakers hovering in the center of the arena. In fact, now that I looked, I thought I saw someone—a dark shape—standing on top of the hovering speakers and looking down at everyone with kingly regality.

"Who is that?" asked Goggles, pointing at the figure overhead. "Another Black Pawn?"

Checkmate's eyes widened behind his own mask's goggles. "That is no mere Black Pawn. That is my uncle."

The dark figure jumped down from the speakers and landed on the ground in the middle of the arena. Four other figures jumped down with him, landing around him, forming a loose square that acted as a sort of makeshift barrier. Then all five figures rose to their full height.

The four figures that had formed the square around the central figure were like two sets of twins. One of the sets resembled rooks, while the other set resembled bishops. I could only conclude, then, that those were the Black Rooks and the Black Bishops.

Which meant that the figure in the center could only be the Black King himself.

Tall and gangly, the Black King was clad in a black costume, complete with black crown and flowing black cape. He carried a scepter in his hand with a pitch-black gem of some sort built into the top, while his brown eyes gleamed from beneath his crown.

Most shocking of all, however, was his face, which was an almost exact replica of Laskar's face, except narrower and thinner. In fact, the Black King gave the impression of not being as well-fed as his brother, although if he was able to jump down from the hovering speakers (easily a twenty- or thirty-foot drop) without harming himself, I think it was safe to assume that he was tougher than he looked.

The triumphant chanting of Checkmate's name had died down by now. Fear spread over the faces of every Cheskian citizen in the stadium, while the Black Pawns were clearly relieved to see their king finally arrive. All eyes were on the Black King, who was grinning like a child on his birthday.

"Uncle," said Checkmate, lowering his rocket launcher to glare down at the Black King. "I am surprised that you decided to finally show yourself after spending years hiding behind others."

The Black King chuckled. "Nephew, you of all people must know that in chess, even the king must occasionally move. Having lost so many of my pieces already, I determined that it was time I made my move and ended this charade of a chess game that we call a chessocracy."

"Through violence?" Checkmate demanded. "Uncle, that is not the Cheskian way. Our chessocracy only works when both sides are willing to play a game of chess to determine the winner. Otherwise, chaos will reign and the whole country will fall into ruin!"

The Black King chuckled again. "Yes, I am all too aware of that, my nephew. That is why I am ordering all of my Pawns to put their guns away and stand down, effectively immediately."

FAKE CHESS

As one, the Black Pawns lowered their guns to their sides, although a few even dropped their weapons entirely. The frightened Cheskian citizens who had been held at gunpoint by some of the Black Pawns immediately ran away, while my teammates and the other tournament competitors looked on in surprise as the Black Pawns they had been fighting lowered their weapons and turned their backs on them.

"What the—?" said Checkmate, looking around the arena in surprise as Black Pawn after Black Pawn put away or discarded their weapons entirely. "I don't understand. I thought this was a terrorist attack. Why are you giving up so easily?"

The Black King shook his head. "Dearest nephew, I am not giving up at all. I agree with you that the only way for me to become the next Chess King is to defeat my brother, Magnus, in a game of chess. And that is why I am, here and now, challenging my brother to a game of chess. Just the two of us, with the prize being the title and authority of Chess King of Cheskia!"

Stunned silence filled the arena at this proclamation. Nearly everyone, including the Black Pawns, looked shocked at the Black King's announcement.

Me, though, I was as surprised as anyone else, but I was more skeptical than anything. After everything the Black King had done—not just to me, but to everyone else—did he really believe that anyone would take him at his word about wanting a 'simple' chess game with Laskar?

Checkmate, being the smart guy he clearly was, must have had the same idea as me, because he said, "That's ridiculous! If you'd wanted a simple chess game with Father, you should have asked. Instead, you chose to stage the worst terrorist attack on Cheskia in fifty years, terrify your fellow citizens, and nearly kill many people—myself and Doctor Mind included—all in a failed attempt to take the throne by force! You are only doing this because you thought that Father would be here, even though he clearly isn't. Your lies do not fool me."

289

"Actually, Gary, I *am* here," said Laskar's familiar voice that came from the other side of the arena.

Everyone looked in the direction from which Laskar's voice came and saw Laskar himself walking across the field toward the Black King. He was accompanied by his Knights, Bishops, and Rooks, along with all of his Pawns (save for D2, who was conspicuously absent).

Laskar strode forward with the confidence of the king that he was. Despite being the oldest and shortest person in his little group, Laskar didn't need to wear his crown and royal clothing to look like the king that he was.

"What a twist!" Mikhael's voice boomed over the speakers that had not been destroyed in the fighting. "The Chess King of Cheskia, Magnus Laskar II himself, has returned! In fact, you might even say this is the return of the king!"

I groaned at Mikhael's silly reference, but my groans were drowned out by the screaming and cheering from the Cheskian citizens who had not been able to escape the arena. They had gone from chanting Checkmate's name over and over again to chanting Laskar's name, and they sounded even more excited about Laskar than Checkmate.

The Black King, by contrast, simply turned to face his younger brother, gripping his scepter tightly. "So you deign to show yourself after all, brother. What a lucky day for me."

Laskar and his court stopped several feet away from the Black King and his court, with Laskar showing not even one hint of fear in the face of his taller brother. "You will not consider yourself so lucky once I utterly demolish you in a game of chess."

"So the skilled Chess King himself has finally decided to stop running and hiding and face me like a real chess master?" asked the Black King slyly. He glanced around. "A shame so many people had to die to make this happen, but I suppose I shouldn't have expected anything different from my coward of a brother."

"Just because I refuse to participate in a system which makes

FAKE CHESS

no sense does not mean I am a coward," said Laskar. "Even if I were, at least I am not a murderer. The same, unfortunately, cannot be said for yourself."

One of the Black Rooks suddenly stepped forward and growled, almost like a dog, "Silence yourself, Laskar! You know nothing about the Black King. He is wise and just while you are —"

The Black King suddenly conked the Black Rook on the head, causing the Black Rook to shrink back and rub the top of his head sheepishly.

"Do not speak for me, my Rook," said the Black King without even looking at the unruly Rook. "Magnus is my brother, and now, my chess opponent. I, and I alone, shall address his comments. You are to remain silent, like a child that is to be seen and not heard."

The Black Rook did not respond, but even I could tell that the Black King had spanked him pretty hard. Not that I could blame him. Although I was pretty confident that I was healthier, stronger, and in better shape than the Black King, I also felt very intimidated by his mere presence.

Laskar, of course, was not. He gazed upon the Black King with little more than simple indifference. "I appreciate you wanting to talk to me man to man. It has been so long since we last spoke to each other like this that I thought you'd forgotten how to speak to an equal."

The Black King held up five fingers from his left hand. "Fifty years, brother. It has been fifty years since we last spoke face to face. Since the day you not only took the throne and established your rule, but stole the love of my life right out from under my nose."

I raised an eyebrow and glanced at Checkmate. Checkmate, however, was not looking at me. He was watching the discussion between his father and uncle with rapt interest.

As it turned out, however, I didn't need to ask Checkmate what his uncle meant, because Laskar said, "Judit never loved you, brother. Not really. She was always mine."

The Black King gripped his scepter so tightly that it almost looked like he was trying to break it. "Bishops! The board."

The two Black Bishops immediately slid past the Black King, moving more like ghosts than humans. They were carried a large card table and a chess set between them, which they set up in the middle of the field so fast that it looked like magic. Then the silent Bishops retreated back to their normal places behind the Black King as silently as spirits.

The Black King marched forward and sat down on a metal chair which the Black Bishops had set up for him, sitting on the Black side of the board (obviously). Laskar, meanwhile, had one of his Bishops unfold a metal chair for himself, a white one in contrast to the Black King's black one, and naturally took control of the White side of the board.

Laskar held out a hand toward the Black King. "Are you ready, brother?"

The Black King took Laskar's hand and shook it. "Always, brother."

Letting go of the Black King's hand, Laskar said, "Then let us duel for Cheskia itself."

CHAPTER THIRTY-SEVEN

I NEVER THOUGHT of chess as 'epic.' Sure, it was a game I always enjoyed playing because it was one of the few activities that my father and I bonded over when I was younger, but I had enough perspective to realize that chess was just a simple board game. It was only two people sitting across from each other pushing around little wooden or metal pieces onto marked squares on a board.

True, chess required great skill and mental fortitude, but in the end, it just didn't have the dramatic excitement of a physical sport like football or baseball or even soccer (and yes, chess is *totally* a real sport).

But I'd also never seen two of the strongest chess players in Cheskia—if not in the entire world—play a game with stakes higher than any prize money that you could win at a normal chess tournament.

How could I describe the intensity and speed at which Laskar and the Black King played? Despite their old age, the two men's hands moved across the board as fast as lightning. They moved so fast I couldn't even keep up. It was like watching a sped-up video in real life, only even more disorienting. Mikhael, bless his heart, attempted to keep a running commentary for everyone, but the movements of the Black King and Laskar were so fast that by the time he even began to guess at what they were doing, they were ten moves ahead of him. Eventually, Mikhael gave up, joining the rest of us mere mortals in watching the unfolding conflict before our eyes.

Pieces were captured and defended. Squares were controlled, only to be taken back just as quickly. No piece stayed on the same square for longer than a turn or two, if that. Several brilliant chess combos and strategies were implemented, the sort of strategies that would have ended in a decisive checkmate long ago if not for the fact that the target of the checkmate had already calculated the perfect defense twenty moves before the strategy was even conceived.

Children cried. Women fainted. Men watched stoically. The heavens themselves seemed to pause in pregnant awareness of the climactic battle playing out beneath its wide expanse. I wondered if God himself was watching the chess game from heaven, sitting on the edge of his throne with bated breath.

No. 'Game' was too simple a term to describe the epic conflict playing out before us. It was more like a battle between the gods. Each clash brought harrowing defeat that much closer to both, leaving the fate of the Earth itself in doubt.

In short, it was the most epic game of chess I'd ever seen in my life and I loved it.

But then, without warning, a scream of utter pain exploded across the arena, filling the air with a cry of agony. It was the sort of sound one would associate with having gotten shot with a gun or perhaps stabbed with a knife.

The noise had come from Laskar. The Chess King's hands had stopped moving, hovering in the air, his eyes glued to the chessboard set before him. Pure horror was set on his face as he took in the sight before him.

The Black King had also stopped moving, but he did not look horrified like his brother. Rather, the Black King wore an expression of pure triumph on his wicked old features, and the answer was obvious:

FAKE CHESS

The Black King had checkmated Laskar.

It was amazing. The board was bare of all pieces save for the White King, the Black King, and a single Black Pawn. The Black King had managed to pull off a king/pawn mate, although it took my mind several seconds to realize that, as my mind was still trying to catch up with the speed and ferocity of the chess battle that had unfolded before us.

Cheskian citizens and Black Pawns alike began whispering among each other, muttering in the Cheskian language. Silent tears fell down the cheeks of Laskar's loyalists, while triumph grins crossed the lips of the Black Pawns.

Yet it took until Mikhael made the announcement for anyone to truly react:

"I cannot believe it, but His Majesty Magnus Laskar II has lost to his brother, Emmanuel 'the Black King' Laskar. That means that Emmanuel Laskar is the new Chess King of Cheskia!"

A positively deafening roar of victory exploded from the Black Pawns. They started up their own chant, which even I understood was the Black Pawns praising their leader. The Black King's court joined in the chant, raising their voices until their collective chants reached a crescendo, and continuing despite that.

The Black King, however, did not celebrate his own victory. He merely smirked at Laskar and held out a hand toward him. "Good game, brother. I will be taking that crown now."

Laskar snapped out of his shock and looked at the Black King. He took his crown off his head—without even one word of protest—and handed it to the Black King, who took it and quickly replaced his crown with Laskar's crown.

"How many years have I coveted this crown," said the Black King, touching the crown on his head. "For fifty years, I have dreamed of this moment, the moment when I would defeat my brother in chess and take what was rightfully mine. It is only sad that I did not manage to get Judit as well."

Laskar said nothing to that. His gaze was averted, looking at the chessboard, as if unable to believe his own eyes.

Honestly, I felt kind of bad for Laskar. Yeah, he was kind of a jerk, but the guy *was* a legitimately good chess player. I'd seen him do things with chess pieces that I didn't know was humanly possible. And he was definitely not as crazy as his younger brother, who I could see being a real tyrant if left unchecked.

I clearly wasn't the only one who was far from thrilled about this transfer of power. The Cheskian citizens themselves, as I already pointed out, were sad. My teammates looked shocked, and even Checkmate appeared to be in utter disbelief over what had happened. Perhaps Checkmate had never seen his father lose a chess game before.

The Black King, obviously wanting to rub it in, leaned across the table toward Laskar and said, "What do you have to say to that, brother? Or do you have anything to say at all?"

Laskar nodded and said, in a quiet little voice that I strained to hear, "Yes, I do have something to say."

The Black King frowned. "What is it? Go on. Say it loud enough for *everyone* to hear."

Laskar raised his head, with a big, happy smile on his face. "Thank you."

The Black King frowned even more. " 'Thank you'? For what?"

Laskar jumped to his feet with the vigor of a younger man. He ripped off his cape and tossed it onto the ground before tossing his scepter carelessly over his shoulder, nearly hitting E2, who had to duck to avoid getting nailed in the head by the heavy-looking scepter.

The Black King's jaw hung open in shock as he stared up at his older brother. Hell, he wasn't the only person who could hardly believe what they were seeing. Damn near everyone—from Laskar's loyalists to the Black Pawns and everyone in between—stared at Laskar with confusion and fear. That included

FAKE CHESS

me, too.

"Woohoo!" Laskar cried out, dancing a little jig. "I'm free! Thank the chess gods, I am free at last!"

"Free?" the Black King repeated, perplexed. "Free from what?"

Laskar stopped dancing long enough to smile at the Black King. "Why, free from the chains of being the Chess King of Cheskia, of course! And it's all thanks to you, my brother."

With that, Laskar grabbed one of his Pawns—A2, according to her helmet—and started dancing with her. A2 herself was apparently in too much shock to resist Laskar's dance moves, as she danced with him, albeit awkwardly and clumsily. Not that Laskar was much better, but he certainly appeared to be having a better time than she was.

I looked around at my teammates. Goggles was smiling and clapping his hands like this was some kind of great performance, while the rest of my teammates were shooting me questioning expressions. I shot them a *I have no idea what the hell is going on here, either,* expression, although I didn't know if I was adequately conveying how confused I was to everyone.

The Black King finally stood up and pointed accusingly at Laskar. "Why are you so happy that you are not Chess King anymore? I thought you would have been angry, offended even. I expected you to scream at me and call me names."

Laskar stopped dancing with A2 and, leaving the hapless Pawn to fall over on her behind, rushed over to the Black King and swung an arm over his shoulder. "Young brother, why should I be unhappy or call you names when you gave me what I have so desperately desired for all of these years? You have given me a gift that is greater than any other. Today may be the happiest day of my life, right behind the day that I married poor Judit."

I noticed that Laskar did not mention his son's birth, which Checkmate also seemed to catch based on how annoyed he looked.

"But ... but ..." the Black King sputtered. "I-I thought you *wanted* to be Chess King."

Laskar laughed. He patted the Black King on the back hard before leaping away from him, jumping on the board with surprising dexterity and doing another little jig. The table shuddered but somehow held his weight.

"At one point, dear brother, I *did* want to be the Chess King," Laskar said, looking down at the shocked-looking Black King. "When our father was in charge, oh how I *dreamed* of wearing his crown and sitting on his throne. To have the power of the Chess King was to become a chess god, to achieve status and money and power the likes of which most people will never see!"

Then Laskar's shoulders slumped and he sighed. "But then, life went on. I grew older. And the riches, power, and prestige of the title lost most of its allure to me. I began to see my duties as chains and the country itself as a ball. I lost interest in ruling, lost interest in the politics, even lost interest in our very chessocratic government.

"I asked myself questions, such as what I really wanted to do with my life and what did I *really* want to be known for. It all came to a head five years ago, however, when I decided that I was done with being the Chess King, but I could not simply give up the title or resign. Instead, I concocted a scheme to find a suitable replacement for me while ensuring that I could continue to live *my* life and do what *I* want. Otherwise, I faced another ten, twenty, thirty years of being attached to the throne of the Chess King like I had been born in it."

"A plan?" the Black King repeated. He gestured at the arena. "Do you mean you planned all of this?"

Laskar laughed again. He hopped off of the card table like a bunny and, standing on one foot, grinned. "No! Well, not all the details. Many things changed between the time I made the plan and today. People died, other people turned out to be more or less cooperative than I thought, and more than once the entire scheme

FAKE CHESS

was in danger of falling apart completely. It was very much like playing high-level chess, only with infinitely higher stakes."

"So ... were you always intending to lose to me?" asked the Black King in a puzzled (and slightly disappointed) voice.

Laskar shook his head. "No! In truth, brother, you were one of those variables I mentioned that I did not accurately foresee. Which is ironic, given how we grew up together, so one would think that that would mean that I would have seen this coming. No, the real person I always intended to succeed me was not you. It was, in fact, Doctor Mind."

Every eye in the arena suddenly turned toward me, making me the center of attention. Which I did not mind normally, but under the circumstances I found it disconcerting, to say the least.

I wasn't sure why I was so surprised. After all, I'd already more or less figured out that Laskar was interested in me as his successor. I suppose I just didn't expect Laskar to come out and say it the way that he did. Figured he might be a bit more circumspect.

"Him?" said the Black King, staring at me in disbelief. "You were chosen to be his successor this entire time?" He suddenly laughed. "Then I was right! Right to send my Pawns after him to kill him. I knew from the start what you were doing, brother, and I derailed your plans completely. How does that make you feel?"

It was Laskar's turn to laugh now. "Oh, dear younger brother. You didn't hinder my plans in the slightest. After all, *you* aren't actually the Chess King."

"What?" the Black King practically screamed. He grabbed Laskar's clothes and pulled him up to his face. "What are you babbling about now, Magnus? I defeated you in a game of chess fair and square. By the most ancient and respected traditions and laws in our land, that means that I—and I *alone*—am the Chess King of Cheskia. You even admitted as much yourself."

Laskar continued to chuckle in the Black King's face. "I only said that to rile you up, brother. In truth, I lost a chess game long before our match five minutes ago. Indeed, technically speaking, I haven't been the Chess King for a few days. That honor belongs to Doctor Mind."

All eyes turned toward me again, including the Black King, who let go of Laskar's chest and turned to face me with a positively murderous glare in his eyes.

"Laskar, are you crazy?" I said to Laskar. "I've never played chess against you before. Even if I did, there's no way I could have won. You're a thousand times stronger than I ever will be."

Laskar wagged his finger at me like I was a naughty child he was correcting. "You might never have played against Magnus Laskar II, Chess King of Cheskia, but surely you can recall playing an online chess game against a certain ChessMeister1236 recently?"

My jaw fell open so far that my jaw felt like it was trying to unhinge itself. "Wait ... *you* are ChessMeister1236?"

"Who is ChessMeister1236?" asked Mr. South in a puzzled voice.

I rubbed the back of my neck. "In preparation for my match against Peacock, I was playing some online chess games against people from around the world. One of them was a guy whose username was ChessMeister1236. He put up a pretty good fight, but I managed to defeat him nonetheless. I didn't think much of it at the time, aside from noticing that ChessMeister1236 was from Cheskia."

Laskar grinned like a madman. "And ChessMeister1236 is me! That's my hidden online identity that I use whenever I want to test myself. I made it for the express purpose of playing against —and losing to—you, Doctor."

"Impossible!" the Black King roared. "If Doctor Mind had somehow defeated you, we would know. And even if he did defeat you beforehand, what is the whole purpose of the tournament, if indeed the victor is already decided?"

FAKE CHESS

Honestly, I had the same question, so I listened closely when Laskar clasped his hands together and said, "The tournament served two purposes. The first was that it let me lure you out of hiding, younger brother, so I could more easily capture you. The second was that I wanted to test Doctor Mind and pit him against some of the best superhero chess players in the world. That way, I would know for certain that I was wise in picking the right successor."

"Doctor Mind's victory was illegitimate," said the Black King swiftly. "Any honest reading of the ancient laws would show that Doctor Mind—"

"Is indeed the rightful Chess King of Cheskia," said another voice that seemed to come from nowhere.

Minister Ferz, the man who had spoken, walked out from the nearest arena entrance. In his hands was a massive, ancient-looking book that made the Bible look young, while in his other was some kind of chessboard that appeared to be set up as an in-progress game of some sort.

"There you are, Ferz," said Laskar to Minister Ferz as he approached. "I was wondering what was taking you so long."

Minister Ferz bowed. "Apologies, Magnus. It took me a while to locate the Book of Ancient Laws, plus I got distracted by all of the books."

"And what's up with the chessboard?" I asked, looking at the strange chessboard that Minister Ferz held.

Minister Ferz glanced at the chessboard. "This? This is no mere chessboard, Doctor. This is the Futureboard. And it predicted your victory against Laskar years before it happened."

CHAPTER THIRTY-EIGHT

"IT DID?" I said with a confused frown. "But I thought the Futureboard only reflected reality, not predicted it."

As I said that, I looked at the Futureboard a bit more closely. It was a simple, but ancient, wooden chessboard with assorted wooden chess pieces set atop it. It looked very simple, almost insulting simplistic, but for some reason I sensed that it was more important than it looked at first glance.

"That is true," said Ferz. He nodded at the board. "But tell me what you see."

Puzzled, I looked a bit more closely at the Futureboard and noticed that Black had clearly checkmated White. "Looks like Black checkmated White."

"Correct," said Ferz with another nod. He gestured with the law book at Laskar and the Black King. "It shows that the Black King defeated Laskar in a game of chess, but the Futureboard has only ever displayed chess games between the White and Black Kings. It does not—cannot—show games between the Chess King and anyone he may end up playing against, such as you, Doctor."

"I ... what?" said the Black King. He waved a hand dismissively at the Futureboard. "Who cares about what the Futureboard says? It still does not justify my brother's illegal actions."

FAKE CHESS

"You're right," said Ferz. "The Futureboard alone does not justify anything that you or your brother may do. But do you know what does? This book."

Ferz lifted up the huge tome that he'd lugged in with him. "This is the Chess Bible, written ages ago by the founders of Cheskia. It contains a complete and comprehensive listing of the rules that govern our chessocratic society, including the all-important details regarding the line of succession for the throne. And what Laskar did was not only legal, but even anticipated, to some degree, by the founders."

The Black King sneered. "Anticipated? The founders couldn't have anticipated the Internet five-hundred years ago."

"That's obviously not what he meant," I said. I gestured at Ferz. "Clearly, Ferz means that the founders anticipated the current Chess King would find a loophole that would let him leave the throne in secret, right, Ferz?"

Ferz shook his head. "Wrong. The founders *did* anticipate the Internet. See?"

Ferz opened the huge book to some random page in the middle that was incomprehensible to me because I couldn't read Cheskian and said, perhaps quoting and translating the passage at the same time, " 'Five hundred years hence, when the world is connected by a series of tubes that shall form an interconnected network of machines, chess players will be able to play chess with anyone around the globe at any time of day or night.'"

I looked at the Black King and Laskar. "Does it really say that?"

Laskar nodded seriously. "Oh, yes. That is a spot-on translation. Minister Ferz is the foremost scholar and expert on the ancient Cheskian language. Our ancestors were extremely smart, which you have to be to be any good at chess."

I turned my attention then to the Black King, but he still looked gobsmacked by the revelation that he was still not the Chess King. An understandable reaction, although I thought it was even weirder that their ancestors had somehow predicted the Internet, computers, and online chess hundreds of years before the first telephone was even created. Shit is wild.

"Reading further, then," Ferz continued, running a finger down the lines of text, "we can see here, quite clearly, that a Chess King who loses against an opponent is no longer Chess King, even if the Chess King in question is hiding his identity. As Laskar was using an alias on the Internet when he played Doctor Mind, this, therefore, proves that Doctor Mind is now the official Chess King of Cheskia."

Even I couldn't argue with that. I mean, I wanted to, obviously, but it seemed to my (non-lawyerly) mind that Ferz's interpretation of the laws was likely the correct one.

As for the Black King, he simply looked defeated. His shoulders slumped and his head hung as he mumbled, over and over again, "I beat Magnus for nothing ... I beat Magnus for nothing ... I beat Magnus for nothing ..."

Laskar suddenly appeared next to me and slapped me on the shoulder. "Good job, Doctor! I know you will make a fine Chess King, finer than me, even. I trust you to lead the Cheskian people into a new era of peace, prosperity, and chess mastery."

Laskar's slap on my shoulder seemed to knock some sense into me. Shaking my head, I held up my hands and said, "Whoa! Wait a minute, here. Who says I even *want* to be Chess King in the first place?"

Laskar looked at me like I'd grown two heads. "Why *wouldn't* you want to be Chess King? Don't you want to lead your own country?"

I shook my head. "No. Not really. Honestly, I just want to go back home and be the superhero for my city again. Leading an entire country is too much even for me."

Laskar grabbed my shoulders and shook me suddenly, forcing me to look into his wide, manic eyes. "But I picked you because of your obvious leadership skills. How can you just say *no* after

FAKE CHESS

all of this? I chose you because you were an outsider, someone who could step in and shake up the status quo of our chessocratic nation and government in ways that even I can only dream of."

"I don't understand what you mean," I said, feeling a little intimidated by Laskar's insistent attitude. "Is there something wrong with Cheskia that only I can fix?"

Laskar let go of my shoulders and thrust his arms out wide. "Just look around you, man! Think about our ridiculous it is that our entire form of government is decided by whoever plays chess the best. The constant, never-ending civil war between the Whites and the Blacks. The ways in which this conflict has decimated our country and made it impossible for us to produce anything other than people who play chess really well. It is disgusting."

All Cheskians in the area, Laskar loyalists and Black Pawns alike, gasped in horror at Laskar's words.

Laskar, however, whirled around and pointed at everyone. "Do not gasp at me! You know I speak the truth. How many of our precious resources have gone toward upholding a system of government that does nothing except hold us down? What would Cheskia—indeed, the Cheskian people themselves—look like if we were to replace the current system with something better and superior? What kind of peace, stability, and prosperity could we ascend to if we only tried?"

"But isn't chess life?" asked Mikhael doubtfully.

"Chess, indeed, is one of life's most important gifts," Laskar conceded, "but it is not the *only* gift and we can only appreciate all of life's gifts if we *use* all of them and do not get distracted by any single one, including chess."

That brought another round of shocked gasps from the audience. Hell, even I was genuinely surprised by Laskar's response. I'd assumed that everyone in Cheskia was too obsessed with chess to even consider the possibility that there was anything more to life than the game.

Even more interesting, people did not look quite as angry as I would expect them to. Sure, some of them *definitely* looked angry, particularly the Black Pawns, but others wore more thoughtful or confused expressions on their faces, such as Mikhael, who appeared to be pondering Laskar's words as if they'd struck a chord in his mind.

The Black King, however, pulled out a gun and pointed it at Laskar. "This is an outrage! Why are we allowing this old doddering fool of an idiot to lecture us about our most precious values? For insulting the game of chess alone, you must be put to death!"

Before the Black King could pull the trigger on his gun, however, a loud *boom* echoed through the air, followed by Goggles screaming, "Missile!"

Everyone looked up in time to see a large rocket—identical to the one that had blown up my HoloChess station—hurtling through the air toward the Black King. The Black King himself had just enough time to look at the missile before it slammed into his face and exploded. Everyone had to look away to avoid getting blinded by the debris and smoke which followed the blast, my ears ringing from the closeness of the explosion.

Finally, however, the explosion faded, making it safe for us to look back at what happened.

The Black King was nowhere to be seen. There was just a blackened spot of dirt where he had once stood. Only his crown had survived, although it had been twisted and broken by the blast, leaving it nearly unrecognizable if not for the distinctive 'V' shape in the center, which had somehow survived the explosion.

"What happened?" said Lumberjack, lowering his hands from his eyes to look at the smoking spot that had once been the Black King. "Who shot that missile?"

"I did."

Checkmate suddenly jumped down from his HoloChess station and walked toward the center of the field where most of

FAKE CHESS

the action was. In his hands was the rocket launcher that he'd stolen from the other Black Knight, although given how carelessly he tossed it aside after landing, it was clear that the rocket launcher was likely empty.

"You blew up the Black King?" one of the Black Rooks growled. "Why?"

Checkmate glared at the Black Pawns. "Because my uncle was going to kill my father. You heard him. He was so upset at being fooled that he was going to kill his own brother instead of accepting his defeat like a true man."

"Liar," the Black Rook snapped. "His Majesty was upset that Laskar wanted to overthrow our system of governance and our traditions."

Checkmate, however, shook his head. "No. He may have *said* that, but in truth, my uncle was simply upset that his ego had been bruised. An egotistical man, he couldn't live with the fact that he'd beaten my father, only to end up getting outsmarted by him in the end. And he especially could not abide by the knowledge that a *foreigner* now sat on the throne that he believed rightfully belonged to him. Thus, I killed him in self-defense."

None of the Black Pawns responded to that. In fact, they all looked rather ashamed of themselves now, as if they regretted serving the Black King now that Checkmate had so thoroughly deconstructed his motives. It was actually kind of impressive, even if it did seem a little overly dramatic.

Then Checkmate looked at me. "Doctor, I believe you owe me a chess match."

"What?" I said in surprise. "You mean right here, right now?"

Checkmate nodded seriously. He gestured at the table where Laskar and the Black King had played. "Of course. We were supposed to play against one another anyway, and I still wish to become the Chess King of Cheskia. And I presume that you, also, do not wish to be Chess King anymore."

I rubbed the back of my neck nervously. "Er, I mean, yeah, I don't, but this seems kind of sudden. Don't you think we should clean up things first—?"

"There is no limit for how long a new Chess King must wait before he can be challenged by someone else," Ferz noted. "If you do play and lose against Checkmate, the only notable thing will be that you will have the shortest reign of any Chess King in history. It would be unforgettable, at least."

I bit my lower lip, but decided that Checkmate had a point.

So I looked at Checkmate and said, "All right. White or Black?"

Checkmate, smiling, sat in his father's chair. "Your choice."

CHAPTER THIRTY-NINE

Honestly, despite wanting to get rid of the title of Chess King ASAP, I still played to the absolute best of my ability against Checkmate. I don't know why, other than I highly respected Checkmate as a superhero and as a chess player and wanted to give him the fight that he deserved.

But in the end, Checkmate defeated me and was crowned King Gary Laskar of Cheskia later that afternoon. They held his coronation ceremony right there in the arena, the whole shebang broadcast live on TV for everyone in Cheskia and the world to see.

Thus, the first-ever International Superhero Chess Tournament ended in a way that I don't think anyone, even Laskar, saw coming. But I couldn't say it was a bad ending. True, there was a lot of violence and complicated maneuvering, but I thought that Checkmate would make a fine Chess King of Cheskia, so I wasn't too worried about the country's future.

The Black Pawns basically surrendered after Checkmate got the crown. Apparently, they were all disgusted by the Black King's hypocrisy and willingness to throw out his own ideals for power, which I thought was rather principled of them. Checkmate even offered to pardon them if they would agree to serve him and all of them agreed. They basically just replaced their Black clothes with White clothing, so I didn't see that much of a difference, but I guess that was how they did things in Cheskia.

Anyway, there was a big celebratory dinner the next night before everyone left, where we got to say our final goodbyes to the other tournament competitors. I thanked Mr. South and his sidekicks once again for helping us, which Mr. South brushed off by telling me that I could call him for help anytime. Even Peacock and Sushimo came to tell me their goodbyes, especially Peacock, who seemed a little too interested in me now for some reason.

But the most tragic separation definitely had to be Goggles and Butterfly. Although I generally thought that teen romance was a waste of time that never lasted, even I was moved by how much the two of them obviously cared for one another. They exchanged phone numbers and social media handles so they could stay in contact with each other and promised to visit each other as soon as they could. How they intended to keep that promise, given how they were both teenagers who lived on opposite sides of the globe, I didn't know, but I did joke to Brave Storm that he'd better watch out because Goggles would be all grown up before we knew it (a comment which Brave Storm did not seem to find very amusing).

As for D2, I don't know what happened to her. I did tell Checkmate about her betrayal of Laskar and how she had run off, but beyond that, no idea where she was. Checkmate said he'd send his men to search the country for her and would keep me abreast of any progress they might make in apprehending her. He said that it was unlikely that D2 would keep coming after me now that the Black King was no more, as D2 had no personal reason for going after me anymore.

Even so, I found myself on edge in the airplane back to the US the morning after our big feast. I sat in a seat near the center row, with Brave Storm in the seat to my right and Goggles sitting in the window seat. But they were both asleep, as were the rest of my teammates seated in the rows around us. I wanted to nap, too,

FAKE CHESS

but I remembered how D2 had gone undercover as Olga the flight attendant and I kept worrying that she might try to gut me when I least expected it. Of course, none of the flight attendants I'd seen on the plane so far had looked even remotely like Olga, but that didn't help me relax.

Despite that, however, I did take a moment to go through my email on my phone and catch up on work. I could see that Mayor Addison had already sent me a million emails all by himself, most of them seeming to be about his recent 'epic pwnz' of the 'newbs' at Level-Up. I wondered if I was the closest thing Mayor Addison had to a friend.

My musings about the loneliness of Mayor Addison were interrupted when a hand landed on my shoulder. Startled, I looked up, expecting to see D2's unmasked face glaring down at me.

But to my surprise, I found myself looking up into the familiar face of Magnus Laskar II. He looked very different now that he was no longer in his fine royal clothing. He was dressed in a simple dark blue business suit and tan slacks, looking less like a former king and more like an ordinary businessman on a business trip. He even smelled like bad cologne rather than whatever nice cologne he'd worn as Chess King.

"Laskar?" I said, looking around briefly to make sure no one else was around. "What are you doing here?"

Laskar smiled. "What does it look like? I am also going to America. Just like you."

I stammered. "I-I mean, yeah, I can see that, but why? I thought you'd want to stay in Cheskia."

Laskar laughed and shook his head. "No way am I going to stay in Cheskia while my idiot son is in charge. I fully expect the entire country to collapse in on itself during his rule until someone competent and good at chess takes the crown away from him. I have little interest in being in the middle of all that, and since my idiot son isn't going to even consider asking for my advice, I figured America would be a safer bet for now. I did ask

Ferz to add my statue to the Hall of Chess before I left, however."

I blinked. "That is both oddly pragmatic *and* cynical."

Laskar chuckled. "I have been called worse during my reign as Chess King, but I'm just glad it is all over. You get sick of running a country after a while, which I am sure is something you understand."

"Not really," I said. "I was only Chess King for like five minutes."

Laskar slapped my shoulder. "Ha! I love your sense of humor, Doctor. Too bad you let idiot son beat you. That is the only part of my plan that *didn't* work, but in the end, I ultimately got what I wanted."

"But Cheskia is still a chessocracy," I pointed out. "I thought you hated that form of government."

Laskar waved at me dismissively. "Please. I only said that to make everyone angry at me and want me gone. In truth, I have little issue with chessocratic countries, of which Cheskia is the only one in the world. No, what I really wanted was freedom to travel the world and teach chess."

I blinked again. "You just want to teach chess?"

"Of course," said Laskar with a nod. He looked at me with utmost seriousness. "There is a serious lack of chess education in the world at large and no one is really doing anything to correct it. Therefore, I've devoted the rest of my life to traveling the globe, with the express purpose of teaching over two billion people chess by the end of my life, starting in America and then moving on from there."

My eyes widened considerably. "Two billion—? That's, uh, a lot of people."

"Indeed, but Judit would tell you that I've always had eyes bigger than my stomach," said Laskar. He sighed and looked away toward nothing in particular, as if looking at something—or someone—only he could see. "Judit would want me to do this."

I frowned. "I ... I'm sure she would, Laskar."

FAKE CHESS

Laskar nodded and then started. "Oh! And, of course, I also want to sell HoloChess technology to more countries. Traveling isn't cheap, as you know, Doctor, and I no longer have access to the Cheskian Royal Treasury, so I need to make a living somehow."

Somehow, that did not surprise me. "Yeah. And if you need any help with your business, let me know and I'll be happy to help."

Laskar nodded before slapping me on the shoulder again. "Thank you! Well, I must resume my quest to find the bathroom on this plane before I must return to my seat. It was a pleasure meeting you, Doctor, and I hope that you and your team continue to grow in your chess understanding and prowess! Perhaps next time we meet, we play a game, yes?"

I smiled. "Sure, Laskar. I think I'd like that."

Laskar smiled back before resuming his walk down the aisle toward the front of the plane. I watched him go for a moment before looking out the open window, past Goggles, who was snoozing as softly as a cat taking an afternoon nap.

Despite all the craziness that happened on this trip, I could honestly say I was glad we'd gone. I'd gotten to visit another country, meet some interesting people, and even become the leader of a foreign nation for like five and a half minutes.

But truthfully, I was even happier to know that we were on our way back home, back to America, and that hopefully, things would get back to normal as soon as the plane landed.

Because things couldn't *possibly* get crazier than what we experienced in Cheskia.

Right?

Other books by Lucas Flint

The Superhero's Son:

The Superhero's Test

The Superhero's Team

The Superhero's Summit

The Superhero's Powers

The Superhero's Origin

The Superhero's World

The Superhero's Vision

The Superhero's World

The Superhero's End

The Young Neos:

Brothers

Powers

Counterparts

Dimensions

Heroes

Minimum Wage Sidekick:

First Job

First Date

First Offer

First Magic

First Mentor

First War

The Supervillain's Kids:

Bait & Switch

Tag Team

Blood Gems

Prison Break

The Legacy Superhero:

A Superhero's Legacy

A Superhero's Death

A Superhero's Revenge

A Superhero's Assault

Dimension Heroes:

Crossover

Team Up

Amalgamation

Lightning Bolt:

The Superhero's Return

The Superhero's Glitch

The Superhero's Cure

The Superhero's Strike

The Superhero's Clone

Capes Online:

The Player Blackout

The Player Plague

The Player Revolt

The Player Hunter

The Player Glitch

The Player Flag

The Player Legion

Capes & Masks:

First Knight

First Storm

First Hero

First Movie

Tournament of Heroes:

Clash of the Heroes

Prophecy of the Heroes

Fate of the Heroes

Ashley Jason:

Ashley Jason and the Superhero Academy

Ashley Jason and the Lost Hero

Ashley Jason and the Dragon King

Ashley Jason and the Final Exam

VR Hero:

Reset

Trial

Frameup

Order

Future

Pseudo-Hero:

Fake Hero

Fake Comic

Available wherever books
 are sold!

About the Author

Lucas Flint writes superhero fiction. He is the author of The Superhero's Son, Minimum Wage Sidekick, The Legacy Superhero, and Capes Online, among others.

Find links to books, social media, updates on newest releases, and more by going to his website at www.lucasflint.com.

Milton Keynes UK
Ingram Content Group UK Ltd.
UKHW010720070823
426447UK00001B/183

9 798223 029663